Like a River Runs

BOOK THREE
of the Besser Trilogy

A novel within the Midnight Series

Dan Kovacs

THIS STORY IS ENTIRELY FALSE
(except for the parts that might be true)

prologue

GOOD ENOUGH

For once, it wasn't midnight.

Vincent sat back from the laptop on the kitchen counter. It was the only place he was ever able to concentrate on his writing.

He glanced briefly over the last letter before saving and exiting out of the document. It disappeared back into the folder, which was hidden amongst the chaos of the desktop.

It had taken him weeks to write the letters. Between the holidays and his scattered brain, he was easily distracted and ripped away from completing the simple task. Through his experiences over the past year, he recognized that writing down his thoughts was an easier way to communicate than face-to-face interaction. There was less of a chance that he'd muck up his point.

Regardless, it was done. *Better to have them done now while I still can*, he thought to himself.

Much like the books he'd written, Vincent doubted anyone would read the letters. An exercise in vanity to finally say all the things that always went unsaid.

He closed the laptop and examined the apartment. Largely the same but messier. He had an unwritten agreement between him and the mess that it needed to be addressed once a week. The clothes in the dryer had been there for . . . too many days; the dishes in the sink were stacked in a wobbly abstract art piece and became a larger tourist trap than Plymouth Rock; the bathroom was plagued with dried piss on the toilet seat and soap scum in the bathtub that was on the verge of starting up a revolution; items were scattered across the countertops, including the little yellow notepad which kept all the details about his life—just in case.

He contemplated knocking out half the chores tonight but determined there wasn't a burning need. The mess would be there in 2019 and assuming the inevitable hangover wasn't insurmountable, he would do it then.

Though music was playing, he heard the distant rumble overhead from a Boeing 737. It wasn't difficult to recognize the sound. After being in the apartment for a year and driving past the airport nearly every day, Vincent became intimately aware of the Southwest planes and their distinct noise. For a brief second, he wondered if it was going to crash into his complex, destroying his apartment and life in an instant. Thoughts of death sparked in his mind daily as he fought to push this one aside as quickly as it formed. Facing mortality was the new reality he only contemplated at the top of the parking garage as he stood on the edge. Sometimes he wondered if an accidental slip would be better than getting eaten alive by the disease.

Life had taken on a different meaning since the diagnosis and The Breakup and the night he told Dylan his pathetic story. Besides the thoughts of death and how they lurked in the crevices of every shadow, Vincent discovered that hook ups were his source of happiness. Grindr was the fountain of continuous men who provided all the necessary distractions. His impressions of what life would turn into were reduced to avoidable murmurs. Sure, he and Dylan were going through another fling phase, but Vincent knew it would dissipate once Dylan recognized he could not control Vincent's fate.

Life would also start moving rapidly. With Christmas over, he had no more excuses to hold back from telling his family. He intended to fly to Pennsylvania in January and get it over with. It was difficult to fathom how it would go and how things would change but continuing to run away from telling everyone was harmful. Vincent didn't need a repeat of his elongated coming out story.

He ripped himself from his steady stream of thoughts and glanced up at the clock. He had an hour to get ready. He set off to shit, shower, and shave, but not exactly in that order.

He stepped out of his room ahead of schedule in a button-down and jeans. The party was meant to be low-key, so Dylan assured him formal attire wasn't necessary.

Vincent pulled one of the pills from the bottle and swallowed it. He forgot there would be no hangover in the morning considering he couldn't drink anymore—at least it was strongly frowned upon and stressed by the doctors enough that he figured it was worth listening it. No matter. He didn't need alcohol to enjoy himself.

A random thought about Evan lodged itself into his brain. He let the thought linger and told himself he could text him if he really wanted to, but doubted he'd get a response back.

Vincent turned off the music, grabbed his glasses, and snagged the keys off the counter. He bumped into the fridge on his way to the door and knocked off the photo of the five of them (Lorenzo included) from the wedding back in September. It was the last happy day he recalled; it's not that life had been bad every day since, but Shit Creek seemed to be clogged more than usual.

Enough of that!

He put the photo back and finally made it to the door.

Something told him it would be a good night, but he had enough to be happy about already, all things considered. He just needed to keep fighting back against the shadows and invasive thoughts.

It was New Year's Eve, and he wouldn't be spending it alone.

And for now, that was good enough.

PART I

DEBITS & CREDITS

<u>one</u>

REPEAT

The alarm clock blared at 2 a.m.

It was a familiar sound, one she had been hearing for fifteen years. There used to be a time when the alarm was set for 3 a.m. and then nudged forward to 2:30 a.m., but as the years droned by with the same melodic tedium everyone strived to ignore, she found herself content with the current wake- up call. Content wasn't the right word but the only one that ever came to mind when considering the subject.

She threw back the covers, commenced the same routine, and completed it without exception.

Once downstairs, she let the dogs out. They trotted and stretched out in the yard, always slightly confused that they were up that early too. Ann summoned them back in and arranged their food on the kitchen counter for Leigh to give them during a normal morning hour.

Speaking of Leigh . . .

She and Lorenzo had recently returned from their honeymoon in Hawaii and she was as miserable as ever. Her attitude was completely soured due to still living at home. They received word during the trip that Lorenzo secured a contracting position at a company in New Jersey for the next year. He would start out by commuting from the house, while Leigh would go and scour apartments in northern Jersey on her days off.

Ann tried to reconcile where she went wrong, where she had slipped with Leigh. Sure, she was tough on her kids and loved them fiercely, but only with the best of intentions—

The sound of the metal bowl slipping from her hand and smacking against the table brought her back to the present. She muttered a curse as the dog food scattered in every direction. The rapid click of paws on the tiles meant the dogs were in a mad scramble to get whatever scraps fell onto the floor. She knew it would be a long day even though it hadn't started yet, which was the best summation of Ann's general outlook.

Jim appeared in the kitchen like an apparition in the night. He quietly moved to the fridge to grab his food and put it in the lunchbox like a toddler getting ready for school. His motions were robotic; the same routine for—*how old was Vin?*—twenty-five years.

After being married for several years longer than that, they learned how not every moment together needed to be filled with idle conversation. Comfortable silence was achieved long ago and continued with a strong passion that morning as they danced around each other, completing needless chores to kill time before their designated departure. Ann cleaned up the dog toys and wrote a note to Leigh stressing the importance of the needless chores she should do throughout the day; Jim poked at his phone with his pointer finger and answered emails for the job he was about to drive forty-five minutes to get to and spend the next twelve hours at.

As the clocks in the house all synchronized and approached 4 a.m., the car was started, and they left without much fanfare. The dogs stood transfixed at the garage door until they decided Jim and Ann weren't coming back inside.

Ann pushed the seat back and leaned into the sleep that clawed at her. The drive would be quick, and her nap would feel instantaneous, but it would be welcomed regardless.

The commute was a wind through College Hill, the outskirts of downtown Easton, a brief stint across a bridge painted an ugly shade of green, and a leisurely stroll through the shithole known as Philipsburg.

After holding their breath through the town, the Besser's hit the highway. The music was turned up and the cruise control set. Ann was snoring softly in the passenger seat. Jim passed deftly by each eighteen-wheeler that chugged along the highway. It went unspoken how dangerous it was for them to drive together to work. When the kids were younger, there was dread at the thought of an accident and how quickly they could lose their parents. Through the power of life insurance, a definitive value on their lives was established which proved to be a pretty sum of money if an unfortunate event happened. Thankfully though, no major incidents happened over the years besides several freak encounters including a rampant tire, a falling sign, and several declarations from the insurance company about acts of God. It was strange to Jim and Ann how there could be a separation of church and state and yet insurance companies could blame an incident on God. A different matter for a more boring day.

Ann woke up with a startle as the car tumbled into the unpaved parking lot.

Jim parked in his usual spot. A repeatable pattern was always human nature.

The next half hour consisted of the duo wandering around the building to turn on all the lights, kick starting the machines in the back office, and doing other miscellaneous prep work before the rest of the staff came in.

Jim finally sat down in his office as the clock inched toward 6 a.m. Ann's desk was less than five feet from his door so there was hardly a time when the two were far from each other.

Ann poked her head in the door and said, "I figured you would want to know—"

"Know what?" Jim asked before she could finish the thought.

"Vin and Evan broke up a week ago. He called to tell me about it the other day."

He took a second to digest the information as he continued to peck away at the keyboard.

"Jim?"

"I heard you," he replied. With one final click of the mouse, he leaned back in his chair and gave her his complete attention. "I always pictured him with someone . . . manlier? Like a football player?"

"Do you want me to tell him that?" she asked mockingly.

"No, but it would be nice for him to call me every once in a while," he confessed.

"Jim, the phone works both ways."

He scoffed at the comment and returned his attention to the computer.

Ann stepped from his office and returned to her desk. Her line of sight went all the way down to the other end of the store, where she could see some of the other employees starting to file in. Soon enough, her coworkers would be up in the kitchen department area, so she savored the last few minutes of peace.

Her mind drifted to Vincent. She was worried (not that she was ever *not* worried) about him and how he would move on from Evan. He was uncharacteristically coy about his life down in Dallas, which was entirely evident by the years of lying he did in regard to his sexuality, but more so than that, she didn't know who he spent his time with. Part of her struggled with the clingy mom persona and tried to rationalize how he was a mature, capable adult who had the mental ability to make friends and create a life of his own; on the other hand, Vincent was still the little boy that cried too much when he didn't get his way or who would lock himself away for hours reading a book or rotting his brain with video games. Did he have a group of friends in Dallas? Was he spending all of his time alone? She wasn't oblivious to him being on dating apps, considering he fessed up to meeting Evan on one. She had done enough digging to understand the implications of having a Grindr profile and the explicit nature of a "hook up," so naturally she worried. She was worried about his love life, his job, if he still liked living in Dallas, and all the other things she couldn't control.

She worried about Leigh and their fractured relationship.

She worried about Jim and how their age gap was finally noticeable.

She worried about her mom.

She worried about whether Vincent would be home for the holidays.

She worried about what to get the kids for Christmas.

She worried about continuing to wake up at the unholy hour she did and come to a job she absolutely hated. Would she be able to find something closer to home? Who would take care of the dogs during the day when Leigh wasn't living at home anymore?

The endless trail of thoughts consumed her on what seemed like an hourly basis. Her side of the family was stuffed with worriers and panicked individuals who all believed the worst was looming around the darkest corner.

Laura was the first to make it up to the kitchen department that morning. They exchanged pleasantries as Laura quickly dove into the details of her upcoming wedding. Ann listened intently as Laura was one of the saner people in the office—and one of the few females.

Bridgewater Lumber Company (or Bridgewater Home Center, as Jim was desperately trying to rebrand the business to) was dominated by men. More specifically, old, white men cropped up in every facet of the store. They worked the counter, selling merchandise to the contractors that came in. They operated the lumberyard out back and pulled together shipments to load onto the trucks. They were the salesmen who struggled to bring in new clientele and keep the existing ones satisfied.

It never bothered Ann that she was in the minority except for the one name who had the propensity to drive her to tears through immense frustration.

It was a name simple in its pronunciation, and, yet, managed to carry a wave of destruction that could take out city blocks.

Bob. Or how she liked to refer to him in private: Boob.

Boob was your typical workplace jerk. He was in a position of power, had been with the company for decades which meant he had job security, and everyone was aware of his behavior. Boob always had a stick wedged up his ass, which made each conversation as delightful as actually having a stick shoved up your ass. Countless times Ann had approached Boob with apprehension due to his unpredictable nature and many times she had walked away flustered due to his outbursts about the stupidity of the employees and how everything around the company was going to shit.

It was the type of negative attitude someone could get away with at a small business that lacked an HR department.

Ann had to be honest with herself though: Jim was not much different than Boob. Throughout her fifteen years at the company and being seated nearby Jim for a majority of it, she heard the yelling from his office as he berated employees. She always attributed his demeanor to him caring about the company, but after a while the mindset began to sound like an excuse and avoidance of the truth. If she was unhappy with Boob's behavior, why should Jim get a free pass? He was her husband and that seemed like a good enough reason as any.

The bottom-line for Ann was that Bridgewater Lumber Company wore her out. After so many years of the same people with the same poor behavior and the same commute, she had enough. She needed to escape. It seemed impossible for a woman in her fifties to go out and kick start a new career, but that is what she intended to do. Ann had been telling herself for months she would find a job closer to home. She was more than adept that clerical work and being an admin didn't bother her in the slightest. The money wasn't an issue either as a majority of her income was supplementary to Jim's. The issue was that she had these grand dreams of running away from the tedium of Bridgewater but had yet to make any moves. Weekends would be spent catching up on the television shows they watched or going out to do yardwork; she had yet to set aside any time to rebuild her resumé and begin applying to local places. She was idle. She wanted a change but didn't know how to start. Sound familiar?

The rest of the kitchen department staff arrived, looking so eager to trudge through another day.

Boob was always the last to show up and today was no exception.

He navigated up the three steps into the area and paused to catch his breath. Ann noticed his massive frame leaning against the railing as he struggled to regain his composure. His face was flush, but if the rumors were to be believed, that was from the years of heavy drinking.

Ann looked away sharply as he resumed his walk toward the semicircle of desks she and her coworkers sat at.

"Morning," Boob grumbled as he walked by. It was barely audible over the music from the speakers above. Christmas music was pumped out into the room even though it was only October.

"Cheerful as ever," Laura quipped.

Barely a minute passed before he sauntered out of the back office and over to Ann's desk.

"We lost the Milligan job?" he asked as if he hadn't just read the memo Ann put on his desk.

"Blackstone beat us on the price, and you said last week we couldn't go any lower."

"How the fuck do they even make any money when they go that low?" he spat out.

"Bob, we could have gone lower. You know that," Ann said.

"I never said we couldn't go lower."

She stared up at him with a dazed look. This game had been played enough times before to know that Boob had the world's shortest memory. Ann thought briefly about what to say next and instantly regretted it. "Laura was standing next to us when you said it."

Laura passed Ann a look of why-would-you-get-me-involved-in-this.

"That's not true," Boob stressed. "Laura barely has time to look up from her phone during the day, let alone actually get involved in a conversation that may bring us some money."

Laura blushed and busied herself on the computer.

Boob continued: "This company doesn't have a fucking chance if you people can't make a sale. I've been here for twenty years and have never seen it in such a depressing state. Ann, you're supposed to be the manager of this department, so get it together." He leaned in closer. The cologne wafted off him and smelled like a cheap bottle of vodka. The gold chain around his neck fell out from underneath his shirt; it swayed momentarily before coming to a halt. "We both know you would have been gone from this place a long time ago if it wasn't for Jimmy."

He receded back from the desk and carried his bulk to the office. The door closed with a mild thud.

"I'm sorry," Ann said.

"It's okay. In your defense, I was standing right there when he said it. Anyways, want to see pictures of my gown?"

Before answering, the phone was shoved in Ann's direction and she was greeted with the wedding dress. She glanced up to the top of the screen.

The clock showed 7:06 a.m.

Her day was finally starting.

○ ○ ○

Time passed at a rapidly decayed rate for Ann.

She had three appointments, two of which were with repeat customers.

One the nice thing about working in this part of Jersey was that the wealth was abundant, and for whatever reason, people truly enjoyed spending their money on lavish kitchens and bathrooms.

Much to her surprise, she spent the latter half of the day working on getting contracts written up from all three appointments.

She was halfway through the last one when she heard the scratching of keys across a desk and knew Jim was ready to go. He stepped out of his office and shut the door behind him.

"I'll be in the car," he said as he moved to the side door. It was their quick escape option from work and the sole reason Jim parked where he did.

"Okay," Ann said as she gathered her things.

She stood up and surveyed the surroundings. Two people sat to her left and two other people beside Laura. She wasn't particularly close with any of them and most of the conversations that passed between them was trying to figure out who should get which client and when they wanted to request days off. It didn't bother Ann too much. Work was never a means to make life-long friends; it served as the unfortunate avenue she needed to tread down in order to provide a good living for her kids. And to that end, she and Jim had done an amazing job in her humbled opinion.

Ann said goodbye to Laura and stepped out into the abyss.

Once in the car, she turned to Jim and said, "When are you going to fire Bob?"

"It's not that simple. Everyone knows he sucks, but he knows all the big contractors in the area and Cynthia is worried we would lose a lot of them if we let him go. It's not something we can do now. You know that."

Ann didn't respond. She stared out the window and watched the same scenery pass by as any other day. The leaves on the trees melted into a blend of colors, signaling a changing of the season. Soon, the days would get shorter and colder and darker.

Ten minutes into the drive, they came to a complete stop on the highway. Absolute gridlock.

Eventually, the radio cycled to its usual stint of commercials and then an update on the traffic. The disembodied voice spoke about a diaper truck that overturned on Route 78 and closed down all the lanes heading westbound.

Ann cradled her head in her hands and tried her best to stop the tears from breaking through. She was so fucking over this day. They had nowhere to turn off the highway, so they sat. The minutes turned into hours as the light of the day faded behind the trees.

The radio kept them company as they didn't talk much. The conversation would have delved into topics neither of them wanted to discuss: money, house renovations, retirement, and death.

Strangely, death was a topic that crossed her mind often. Her mother was in her mid-eighties; Jim was in his early sixties. She wasn't foolish. The nine year age gap between her and Jim finally seemed to weigh heavy. What would he do when he retired? *Would* he retire? What if his health declined? There was no way she could keep up with the house on her own. She'd have to sell it. But that's where the kids grew up. That's where Vincent took his first steps. That's where they had puppies skid across the kitchen floor. That's where . . .

She rehashed every flash of memory she could remember. The moments were insignificant—not remembered by anyone else but her. She'd given all the love she had to her family, but sometimes it didn't feel like enough. What would she leave behind? What was the point to all this?

Ann didn't have the answer and thankfully she didn't need one. The cars began to move, slowly like a train leaving the station, but soon they were cresting over Jugtown Mountain and bearing down on Phillipsburg.

The garage door closed softly behind them twenty-five minutes later.

They were home.

Chaos erupted as they walked into the house. Three dogs clawed over each other for the affection of the new arrivals. Toys were brought and deposited at their feet as if they were peace offerings. *At least I can look forward to this every night*, Ann thought to herself.

Her mood immediately soured—even more than it already was—when she noticed the dog bowls laying scattered across the kitchen, and the sous chefs worth of dishes on the stove and in the sink. Of all the things that really pissed her off, Leigh living like a slob sat firmly in the number two spot (wet socks being number one . . . for obvious reasons). On days where she didn't work, Leigh lounged around the house and did nothing of importance. Last time Ann checked, Leigh was on season forty-eight of *Grey's Anatomy*, so she wasn't exactly busy.

The idea of confronting Leigh would have led to personal satisfaction but would result in a shouting match where Leigh would profess her deep hatred of how her mom wanted things done a certain way and that she would get to cleaning up the dishes when she felt like it.

Leigh wasn't a monster; she just wasn't like her mother.

Ann unleashed a slew of curse words under her breath and Jim knew well enough to not inquire about it.

After the dishes were tucked nicely into the dishwasher and the dog bowls returned to the garage, Ann sat on the couch and stared into the television. Her reflection bounced back at her. Age tried to do its worst, but she navigated through it. Sure, the wrinkles were evident, and her weight was in constant flux, but she learned no one cared as much about her appearance as she did so any fear of judgement washed away. Truthfully though, that didn't mean she was entirely happy with the way she looked.

She leaned back into the couch. A cold nose poked her leg and she knew it was Rigby. Ann stretched out a hand and found the abundance of fur.

If she was lucky, she would get four hours of sleep tonight.

Just enough time to reset and do it all over again.

two

HOW MANY FRESH STARTS DO YOU GET BEFORE THEY TURN SOUR?

It took over six hours to drive out of Texas and what a boring time it was. A vast wasteland that would have made a flat earther feel validated in their delusional thinking.

For Evan Eaton though, it wasn't a completely unfamiliar one. He had ventured out to West Texas on several occasions during his brief stint in the recruiting role for his previous company. He was still proud of roping in several graduating students from Texas Tech to come work for his company—a place he disliked enough that he started looking for another job only six months into being there.

That was then.

With each passing minute, he was distancing himself further from Dallas, further from another failed attempt at getting it right. Denver would be different. It had to be.

"Don't do it," he warned himself.

Too late.

In popped Vincent. Thoughts of his oddly large head took up residence. The pain of the last week bubbled up and over the metaphorical surface. The awkwardness of the drive back from ACL, the nonsensical muttering between them when he dropped Vincent off and knew he wouldn't see him again before he left, the steady bouts of crying Evan endured as he packed up what little of his life the movers wouldn't be getting.

He looked over at the scars on his arm as a reminder. They were hardly noticeable to anyone, since Evan knew exactly where to do it so that no one could ever tell. Vincent certainly hadn't in the time they were together.

Evan continued his march to the Texas border and pulled into the only gas station for the next forty miles.

He stepped from the Jeep and stretched his legs. Izzie eyed him cautiously from the passenger seat.

He filled up the tank and went inside the convenience store to grab a few drinks.

At the register, the woman behind the counter said, "First customer of the day! I'm gun guess you ain't from 'round here. Where you heading to, sweetie?"

"Denver," he said weakly. Evan was never a fan of small talk. It never felt small to him; it was a monumental task to think of enough words to string together an answer. How was his day? Cold out there today, isn't it? What did you do this weekend? They were simple enough but sent him into a spiral. He was so transfixed on planning out every second of his day that he never made room for the inconsequential conversations individuals begged to have.

"I have a second cousin that lives up there with her family . . ."

"Oh, that's nice," he said as she finally swiped his first item across the scanner.

". . . They hate it," she quipped.

"Oh."

The lady methodically scanned the rest of his items and dropped them into a bag. After paying, she said one last thing to him, "My cousin is a damn yokel, so you are gun love it out there. Be safe, sweetie."

Evan smiled and told her to have a good rest of her day.

Back outside, Izzie had her nose pressed up against the window watching Evan move closer to the car. He shook his head briefly at her attachment issues and decided it would be a good time to let her out. She sniffed around the patch of grass near the gas pumps for a while before moving rapidly in a tight circle, indicating that she was closing in on finishing the task.

With Izzie back in the car and a full tank of gas, Evan surged toward New Mexico. He would pass through the upper right corner of the state, and not for very long, so the majority of the drive left would be through Colorado.

Two hours later, his phone rang.

"Hello?" he answered.

"Hi, honey."

It was his mom.

"How is the drive going? We have been thinking about you all day!" she continued.

Great, more small talk, he thought to himself. But everyone knows this is what mother's do, so he has grown accustomed to it with her.

"It's okay. Nothing really exciting about it so far. Based on what I've looked up though, I should be hitting the mountains at some point in Colorado and that'll be beautiful."

"So, I wanted to tell you something," she said, disregarding Evan's answer.

"Yeah?"

"I got married last weekend," she beamed.

"That's great!" he said, doing his best to feign happiness.

It wasn't an exciting story in the slightest. His mom had been married three other times and never got it to work. Evan liked her second husband as he was kind and not abusive, but Evan didn't understand as a kid that sometimes people just aren't meant to be together. Fast forward to a more present time, and his mom had met someone new. Evan met him once and saw how he doted over her every need. He also had a nice, cushy job that allowed his mom to quit hers. Evan didn't want to have shallow thoughts about his mom, but it really felt like she was in it for the money. In any case, over the few months they had known each other, it was obvious that they had an undeniable bond. Evan was at the point where he wanted his mom to be satisfied with life and finally figure her shit out.

This was not the answer though.

"I'm sorry I didn't tell you sooner. When you called and told me about the breakup, I didn't think it would be appropriate to drop that on you. And you were—*are*—stressed about the move."

"It's fine."

She dove into the details of why they chose to get married in the courthouse and how excited his kids were. Evan didn't listen to much of it.

At some point he cut in, "Mom, sorry but I got to go. The weather is getting bad over here and I need to concentrate."

"Oh . . . okay . . . yeah, I understand. Drive safe. Let me know when you get there! I love you so much. Please come home for Thanksgiving!"

"I will try. Love you too."

He disconnected the call and stared out the window at the cloudless sky. The mid-afternoon sun was moving toward the horizon. He was hoping to be in Denver by sundown.

Evan wanted to leave the conversation behind but couldn't. He just didn't get it. How could she possibly get married for a fourth time? And only after a few months of knowing each other? For fuck sake, he spent a year with Vincent and knew it would have taken years to fully understand how that enigma functioned.

Okay, okay. Let's think about something else, he tried to persuade himself. *I will have plenty of time to think about Vin later when I'm sitting alone in my apartment. Oh, I can't wait.*

The longest drive of Evan's life was the fifteen and a half hours from Kalamazoo to Dallas. The second longest drive of Evan's life was this one. The third longest drive of his life was after his mom divorced his dad.

They fled from the house and drove north, in search of another home. He was young, probably six, and didn't quite grasp how he wouldn't see his father ever again. He didn't like his father much considering the verbal abuse he spewed at Evan and his older siblings. There were some occasions where it got physical and Evan would hide in his room with his cat, Fluffy. He would grip his legs and pull them tight into his chest and count from one to a million in multiples of ten. At that young age, he didn't quite know all the numbers between one and a million, so he made them up as he went along. It kept his mind away from the present, from the disaster that was unfolding outside his room.

Over time, his dad tried to contact him. His siblings stressed how he sobered up and was a generally pleasant man to be around now, but he didn't care. He was never close with his siblings and didn't exactly trust their assessment, but at a much higher level, Evan didn't deal with cheaters or abusers. His father was his first foray into what it was like to be surrounded by an abusive individual; Kieran was the second.

Kieran was the person Evan envisioned spending the rest of his life with. Their relationship was abnormal from the start with Kieran being his high school teacher and all, but they quickly moved on from that. The first few years were great, and they learned how to appreciate the differences in each other. Kieran had dark thoughts that drove him to self-harm and a steady diet of pills to curb the schizophrenia. It was fine though because Evan loved him more than could possibly be described. They worked through it and Evan balanced Kieran and college and all the extracurricular activities he was involved in. And then they got the house. The excitement of taking the next step in their lives together quickly faded as the events within the house started to unfold. The culmination being the night Kieran chased Evan out of the house while being seemingly possessed. Evan knew the absurdity of the story and hardly ever told it, but he knew what happened that night and would never believe anything otherwise. The mental abuse he went through for months of feeling trapped in that place as Kieran was devolving into an animalistic state shook Evan to the core. On the other side of things, Evan always gave Kieran a convenient pass when he saw the suggestive texts he was sending other people. He finally had proof that their relationship wasn't what he once thought when he went by the house to pick up the last of his things and found a used condom in the bathroom. Evan had only moved out two days earlier. It seemed impossible that Kieran could move on so quickly from a six year relationship unless he already had some time ago.

For the beginning of his relationship with Vincent, he was worried there would be the monster lurking in the shadows. Vincent would turn out to be abusive or a cheater and absolutely ruin Evan's life, so he held back. He was hesitant for a long time and afraid of not getting it right again, and by the time Evan realized Vincent was neither of those things, it was too late. They had drifted apart, and it was evident how there was no chance at reconciliation.

And that's why the breakup hurt so much. Vincent was different. Vincent wasn't abusive. Vincent wasn't a cheater. But he wasn't very attentive and focused too much on fixing Evan. He also dealt with massive self-confidence issues that Evan was sure they could work through given enough time, but it didn't matter now. He could see the skyline of Denver in the distance. That would be home now. His time in Dallas would always be there, but he needed to focus on what was ahead.

The traffic was light in downtown Denver. He easily found the Skyhouse building. His new company asked him where he wanted to live as they helped with moving expenses, and after some research, Evan realized he wanted something familiar to live in, which is why he elected to move into another Skyhouse complex.

He went through the motions of parking, finding the leasing office, getting his keys, and being told where his apartment was.

Evan scooped up Izzie from the car and they both went up to find apartment 846.

Once off the elevator on the eighth floor, Evan wandered around briefly before realizing his place was sharing a wall with one of the elevators.

He took a deep breath to calm himself. He was oddly nervous that he was going to fuck this up. He was nervous that he would hate his apartment or his job or the city. He was nervous that he was never going to be settled and, instead, destined to a life of a vagabond, traveling from one place to another. He was tired of being nervous.

Evan turned the key and the lock disengaged.

This is it. This time will be different.

He opened the door and stepped inside.

three

SUNDAY FUNDAY

Back when the world was a tiny bit saner and before planes started flying into buildings, Sunday mornings used to be more eventful for the Besser clan. Leigh and Vincent would be shipped off to Sunday school to learn how to not be a piece of shit in the eyes of the Lord and Savior. Ann would usually pawn them off to someone else to take them over. Jim was likely working on one of his side jobs with their next-door neighbor, Ralph. They garnered quite the reputation and remodeled either a basement, bathroom, kitchen, or deck at everyone's house on the block. The craziness of the day would continue when Ann would pick up Vincent and his friends from Sunday school early to get them to their football game on time (of course, this only happened in the fall). Ann would wait outside and smoke one last cigarette before going inside the church to grab them. It was a nasty habit that she was very aware of, so no need to think differently of her, thank you very much. For those who may be concerned, she stopped smoking cold turkey fifteen years ago. Part of her wanted to be celebrated more for the achievement, but the other half rationalized that being celebrated on not continuing to do something that had a high likelihood of killing you was foolish.

In any case, time passed, as it normally did. Ann no longer had to stress about getting the kids to Sunday school or watch Jim slave away at one of his jobs or go and watch Vincent's football games. She missed seeing her kids excel at sports and the comradery built up amongst the team and parents.

She also missed those damn cigarettes but didn't crave them—there was a major difference. They certainly took the edge off.

Ann was half awake in bed. It was wasted effort to try and sleep in late when you woke up at 2 a.m. five days a week and had three dogs that lived on a similar timer. By 6:30 a.m., she heard the panting from the bedside as another dog went rogue and tried to squeeze between her and Jim.

She trudged downstairs, let the dogs out (which finally answers the very sought out question of *who* does it), and followed the same routine as any other day.

Several hours later, instead of lounging around the house all day, she took the dogs on a tour of the neighborhood. It took some minor nudging, but Jim reluctantly agreed to join as well.

The five of them embarked into the outside world.

The neighborhood looked largely the same for the past twenty years. The initial burst of houses brought in numerous people and different styles, but things seemed to level out. The same trees were planted; each house had a similar structure. It was a quiet, content slice of the American dream that didn't actually exist.

Ann, Jim, and the dogs moved across Wagon Wheel Drive and reminisced about the past, which is something old people did when life wasn't too exciting anymore. They talked about the time Jim was attacked by a legion of Japanese beetles. They talked about the time Leigh ran away from home but was actually hiding in a closet. They talked about how it would've been nice to have a third kid. They talked about how they made a good life for themselves and the joy they would find now is watching their kids be successful. They talked about all these things as they crested up the big hill on Ben Jon Road. There used to be a cornfield on the other side of that road, but it was stripped away and turned into an extension of the neighborhood, which is what happens when people get greedy and don't like looking at farmland anymore.

When they reached the top of the hill, all five were out of breath. Getting older meant your bones ached, and you couldn't climb hills anymore and that you'd die soon.

The sad part was how dying wasn't reserved for only old people. See, people died at all ages because that's how things worked. For example, Ann and Jim walked by the house of a former CIA agent who was shot and killed by another agent during a bank robbery ten years ago. He left behind a wife and two kids. There was no rationale for why he died that day.

Ann's phone buzzed around the time they completed the loop and found themselves outside the Besser Bungalow. She fished it from her pocket and felt her heart drop.

It was Walter, her mom's husband. He only called when there was a problem.

"Ann," he said when she picked up. "Your mom fell. She is in an ambulance right now being taken to St. Luke's."

The hospital was named after a fictional man who supposedly helped people, but no one could agree on the details.

"Is she okay?" A logical first question asked by Ann.

"I don't know."

"I'll pick you up and then we will go over," she said calmly. Ann was in a calm state because this wasn't the first time her mom had fallen. Apparently getting older also meant that you fall more.

Walter always called Ann whenever something happened because she was the only one who gave a shit. Ann has three other siblings who only made their obligatory appearances on holidays to see their own mother. In that regard, they were what the cool kids called "honey bunches of oafs."

Ann relayed the information to Jim. He grabbed the leashes and brought the dogs back into the house. Ann hopped in the car and drove to her mom's apartment.

As previously mentioned in another book, Doris (aka Ann's mom) lived in a rad apartment complex with a bunch of other old folks. The average age was ((27 * 3) / 9) * 9 - 3. Remember: parenthesis first.

As Ann pulled up to the entrance, Walter was already waiting and quickly made his way to the car.

"Hi, Walter," she said and leaned over to hug him.

Was it weird that her mom remarried after her dad died of leukemia? Maybe at first, but she came to realize her mom having someone to spend the rest of her life with was the most important thing.

"Hi, Ann," he responded. "She was in the bedroom and I heard a thud, so I rushed in there and found her on the floor."

"Was she conscious?"

"Yeah."

"Did anything seem broken?"

"No, but she said her shoulder hurt."

Life had this weird cycle where it started off that parents worried about their kids. The kids then got older and began to worry about the parents. This wasn't a new concept. It was human nature to care for the ones who raised you, but it was unfortunate to watch them deteriorate.

It didn't take long to find Doris. The lady at the desk pointed to the third room down the hall and the two of them went that way.

Inside, she was propped up in the bed with a look of contempt. She didn't like hospitals yet seemed to find herself in one far too often.

"What happened?" Ann asked. The get-right-to-the-point Jersey side of her took over.

"I fell," she answered weakly.

"I know that, but how did you fall? What were you doing?"

"The doctor already asked me all of this. I don't want to repeat it."

Ann's face flared briefly and then returned to a more static state. "Mom, you can't be so stubborn. You need to take the medicine the doctor gives you and use the walker around the apartment. It's pretty simple or we are going to keep finding ourselves here," she spoke as if her eighty-five-year-old mother had the intelligence of a toddler.

There was something unspoken between them. They would keep ending up at the hospital until the one trip that wouldn't have a pleasant outcome. The train was coming to the end of the tracks and Ann sometimes dipped into the hypotheticals about a time when her mom wouldn't be around. For her, it felt like life was becoming a series of jumbled thoughts about what if she lost her mom or husband or one of the kids or dogs.

Doris understood she was reaching the culmination of her life. She had talked with Ann about what was in her will and what she was going to leave specifically for her. In the moment, it didn't feel morbid; it felt like a business transaction. Doris was passing over a bill of goods for Ann to inspect and sign off on.

"I just hate being here," Doris said.

"It's going to be okay," Walter said reassuringly and placed his hand on top of hers. "Did the doctor say how long you'd have to be here? What about your shoulder?"

"Someone is coming by soon to take me to get an X-ray, but she didn't think that there was anything wrong with it. They want me to stay overnight just to make sure I don't have a concussion."

"Do you remember hitting your head?" Ann asked.

"Well, no. I don't remember much of anything."

Ann finally took a seat in the chair opposite the bed. Her mom looked frail in the moment, but generally speaking, she had been in good health for a majority of her life.

She loved her mom immensely and wondered sometimes about how she raised four kids. Ann was the youngest and learned enough from watching her siblings to understand what rules to break and which ones not to. Her parents were burnt out once Ann was a teenager and just happy to see all four of them healthy and moving out of the house.

Ann and Doris weren't particularly close when Ann was a kid. She grew up during a time where the degree of separation between child and parent was much more extreme. Doris never showed up to Ann's cheerleading events or inquired too much about boyfriends. It just wasn't in Doris' nature. Ann never held that against her. Things changed drastically though when Ann got married. She was young, barely twenty-two. Ann's dad took a sincere liking to Jim and the four of them took trips during the five years before Ann and Jim had Leigh. They traveled to Bar Harbor, Maine, down the coast to Florida, and to the Jersey Shore each summer. It was an idyllic life they had stepped into.

Of course, things changed when Ann's dad died.

Doris was alone at the house in the Poconos and it's lost to time now who first suggested it, but eventually Doris moved in. She lived with them until the point she married Walter. It was undeniable that an unbreakable bond formed between the kids and their grandmother during that time, which is the reason why they continued to be close with her into their adult life.

Ann loved her mom so much and the thought of losing h—

There was a soft knock on the door. It was Leigh.

"Wha—what are you doing here?" Doris said with a look of surprise.

"Mom texted me. I work one floor down, so I figured I would come up to see you."

Leigh looked exhausted and she wasn't exactly close to finishing her twelve-hour shift yet.

She walked over and gave Doris a hug. "What happened?"

Doris gave Leigh the recap she wouldn't give Ann. Leigh nodded and told her how she needed to be more careful and that if the doctor gave her medication, she needed to take all of it, regardless if she was feeling better. Ann was slightly bitter that Doris accepted this information from Leigh without complaint.

Leigh looked fleetingly at Ann. They had another fight the night before. Things were coming to a climax and Ann knew the next argument would be a blowout the whole neighborhood would hear. She didn't even remember what exactly they got into it about. That's how unimportant the whole thing had been, but Leigh is aggressively stubborn so she wouldn't be quick to forget.

Eventually, another nurse came by to take Doris to get the X-ray. She stressed how she'd be alright to spend the night alone, so Ann and Walter reluctantly agreed to leave.

An hour later, Ann stepped back into the house and was mauled by the dogs. She brushed them aside. She felt a headache rushing in and knew if she didn't take care of it now that it would bloom into a massive migraine. Ann wasn't sure if there was a difference in the words, but for her there was. A headache was something she could manage. It was what one might feel after a long night of drinking or when they hadn't eaten enough. She would pop a couple of pills, take it easy for an hour or so, and be on her way. A migraine was debilitating. She had these magic pills that were supposed to make them go away, but now they only dampened the pain. Her longest migraine lasted three days. She had barely moved off the couch and kept a corn bag pressed tightly to her skull the entire time. It was hard for her to describe the feeling. Maybe it was like the alien chest bursting scene, except this one was clawing at the inside of her skull and attempting to break loose. In any case, the headaches and migraines were her mortal enemy and she did battle with them far too often. She had visited enough doctors to gather there was nothing physically wrong with her, so the tiny white pills were prescribed, but we have already covered that they don't do much anymore.

Thankfully for Ann, the headache never escalated. She attributed it to the stress of the day. She would continue to worry about her mom and how Vincent was handling the breakup and what the fuck she was going to do with Leigh.

It all rattled around in her head for the rest of the day.

She didn't sleep much that night, which was common. Thoughts of what awaited her at work strangled the small amount of sleep she ever tried to get.

She would have given anything to go back to that simpler time when life was more chaotic but actually had meaning.

four

NEW KID ON THE CUBICLE BLOCK

The commute for Evan to his new job was laborious.

After gracefully exiting his eighth-floor apartment, he took three large steps to the elevator. Once downstairs, he trotted down a side hallway and out the door in the front lobby. He made a sharp left turn and walked for two point six blocks until he was greeted by a bland skyscraper. It hardly scraped the sky at the modest height of fortyish floors, but no one seemed to mind. The building was swallowed up by the others surrounding it, making it seem like the short, stubby kid out on the playground.

Evan moved inside and found the bank of elevators. His heart raced slightly as he took his place in line. Another new start. Another new opportunity for him to get it right. He spent his entire Sunday piecing together his apartment. It wasn't a difficult task since the movers organized his stuff with surprising accuracy. His cameras were neatly lined up on a shelf and his albums occupied another. Everything was orderly in his new apartment by early evening. Evan managed to have that tiny portion of his life figured out, but nothing else seemed to fall into place quite yet.

He stifled the urge to text Vincent. The gravitational pull of it was strong, but he fought valiantly against it. Evan wasn't one to rely on others and he didn't see the need to keep Vincent informed about his every move. It was a habit to break. They weren't together anymore, so Vincent had to be deprioritized.

His turn was finally up for the elevator and he took it to the twenty-sixth floor. The next half hour consisted of a mountain of paperwork he combed through. He was no stranger to a majority of it. As an HR representative, he had people sign similar looking paperwork a thousand times over.

After signing his life away multiple times, his new manager appeared. She was a middle-aged woman with a streak of feistiness and walked with an exaggerated hip swing. They exchanged pleasantries. Evan had talked with her enough on the phone to understand her time at work was spent to work, so he doubted they'd ever extend into conversations that didn't center around the business within the four walls.

At the end of an uneventful tour, Evan was deposited to his cubicle.

"Let me know if you need anything else," his boss said as she turned around and fled back to her office. Ten evenly paced steps later, Evan heard the door to the corner office close. It was the second to last time he ever saw her.

Evan stepped into the double-wide cubicle. His side was entirely empty besides the two monitors that were bouncing the company logo back and forth across the screen.

As for the other half of the cubicle, it looked like a fully functioning ecosystem. Bottles of lotion were askew across the desk. Two small Nerf guns sat near the edge, ready for use at any given moment. Tiny figurines from shows or movies he didn't know sat posed next to several coffee mugs with various motivational messages on them. Evan was expecting to find a cot and some pillows underneath. Intrigued by the randomness of it all, Evan leaned in closer and examined the photographs laid out on the walls. Smiling faces of friends and family dotted the empty space. It was impossible to tell who his new cube mate was from the photos. A sign that said **DON'T MESS WITH TEXAS** was mixed in the clutter. Back on the desk was a framed picture of a dog with the caption *I FOUND BIGFOOT* underneath. The dog looked about the size of Izzie and had a manic expression as if someone was holding a piece of food off camera.

"Get any closer and you'll be eating my pictures for breakfast," a voice behind him said.

He jumped slightly at the sound. "I—sorry. Just trying to get a feel for who I'm sharing the cube with."

Evan turned and faced the voice. It was a woman. He doubted she was much older than him. Her green eyes were piercing and hard to look away from.

"I can clear up that mystery for you." She stepped fully into the cubicle and extended a hand. "I'm Murphy but prefer Murph. If your name isn't Evan, then I've been lied to for the past week," she said.

"Nice to meet you Murph. I'm Evan, so your sources were right. You must be the other HR Coordinator?"

"Oh, indeed. I believe you have ranking authority seeing as I am just an Associate Coordinator. I told them many times I am capable of doing the job by myself, but they insisted on going out and finding a man with more experience. Typical. Now I feel threatened and will likely get extremely territorial," she said with a huge smile.

"I'll try to keep my distance," Evan said, not quite understanding the silliness in Murph's tone.

"As a peace offering, I brought you a cupcake I fully expect you to eat at"—she looked at the clock overhead—"9:23 a.m. exactly."

Evan probed for an excuse but couldn't think of a rebuttal before Murph dove into her backpack and removed a container that housed one fluffy cupcake.

"You really shouldn't have," Evan stressed.

"No fucking kidding. I had three of those bad girls last night and my boyfriend had four!"

Evan let out a snort of laughter at the unexpected burst of frustration. He knew they would be good friends because, let's be honest, characters are hardly ever introduced in novels if they don't serve some sort of purpose, and considering Evan had never seen a boob in his life, any romantic notion was squashed. That left two options: for them to either be friends or sworn enemies. Murph being the villain would be a waste of plot and character.

He accepted the cupcake and they both sat in their respective seats.

"So, I noticed the Texas sign. When did you live there?" Evan asked.

"The Big D. Born and raised. Well, saying I grew up in Dallas is relative since I lived outside the city most of my life, but it's easier to tell people that."

"I just moved from there myself. Small world."

"Wow! What are the odds! Sure, someone could probably easily find that out, but what would be the point, am I right?" she chewed on her rhetorical question for a moment before giving Evan a look. "Are you gonna eat that or what?"

"I . . . uh . . . it—okay fine," he conceded. Evan popped open the container and scooped out the cupcake. He examined it with growing interest and determined it was an ordinary dessert. He ate it in four bites as Murph watched on like a mother waiting for their child to finish all their vegetables at dinner.

"We should probably get some work done, huh?" she proposed.

"Yes, as if I had any idea what to do yet."

"That's what I'm here for!"

It turned out to be quite simple for Evan to pick up the basics. Working in HR meant you followed the same basic processes regardless of the company because there were standards to adhere to. What separated the advanced companies from the archaic ones was the level of automation involved. Luckily for Evan and Murph, they stumbled upon a company that had minimal manual processes, which made picking up the work exponentially easier.

Murph continued with the crash course for the remainder of the day. They were deep in conversation regarding how to process an employee after they left the company when a door slammed at the end of the hall.

"FUCK IT. FUCK ALL THIS SHIT!" the voice shouted. Several heads peeked over the cubicle walls to place where the disturbance was coming from.

The sounds of angered footsteps stomped down the pathway toward Evan and Murph's cube. Eventually, their boss was standing outside the cubicle, her face redder than a teenager with a canvas full of embarrassing pimples.

"Murph and Evan—both of you listen to me: I just quit. This place is an absolute nightmare. Management has no idea what they are doing. We are losing people in droves and they expect me to find replacements like they are tiny gnomes that grow out my ass. Run. Run far away.

"Murph, seeing how you now have the most tenure in the HR Department, I am putting you in charge."

Evan stared over at Murph. Her face was slack with no emotion as if someone placed her into standby mode.

With apparently nothing left to say, their former boss turned heel and headed for the elevators. She didn't even bother to pack up her belongings.

It took a while, but Murph eventually rebooted and turned to Evan. "Can we leave now and pretend this didn't happen?"

"I'd like that very much."

Internally, Evan was a fucking mess as they made their way out of the building. He dealt with an ever-expanding pile of dung at his old job, but never did he have a boss who walked into his office and pronounced in a grand gesture that they were quitting. He had done his research upon receiving the job offer at his new company and they seemed legit. Great reviews on various websites and the company itself was rapidly growing in the medical marijuana field, which showed no signs of being a fad. (Imagine explaining to someone back in the early 2000s that marijuana would be legal in a sizeable portion of states and some companies were so expansive that they needed an HR Department!) Now his first day ended in a blur as if he took too big a hit from a fat blunt. It wasn't what he expected, but that could be said for a majority of his life.

Evan and Murph now found themselves outside.

"Should I even bother to come back tomorrow?" he asked aloud.

She grabbed his shoulder and brought him to a halt. "Evan, yes you should. At least, I hope you do. It's not at all like she said."

"I will. I don't really have a choice," he said with a nervous laugh.

She nodded in solidarity. "I guess this is where we part ways. I have a short walk back to my apartment."

"So do I."

"Okay, I'll bite . . . where do you live?"

"Skyhouse."

"Get. The. Fuck. Out," she said, punching him on the arm in-between each word. "I live there too! This is all becoming so strange. Do you think it's fate? Were we both drawn to this city in the hopes of a new start only to find our hearts belong back in a place we have already been surrounded by people we left behind only because we thought there was something better ahead? I'm freaking out right now."

"I don't believe in fate," he said flatly.

"I was only kidding . . . sheesh. We gotta work on your dour demeanor. You are never going to find a boyfriend in this city."

Without realizing it, they had resumed their walk and were halfway back to the complex.

"Who said I was single? And how did you know I was gay?"

"Lucky guess. I have been working on my gaydar lately since I stumbled several times during my last couple of months in Dallas. I lived in Oak Lawn, mind you, so I became the minority as a straight woman."

"What a pity."

"Oh, hush. To answer your first question, I can tell you are single—actually, recently out a relationship—because you seem sad. You're too young to have picked up and moved without a reason."

"Maybe I hated my job enough to force me to leave."

"Sure, but I don't think that's the case. You ran from something."

"I'm sorry. Can we not talk about this now?" Evan asked defensively. Did he actually leave Dallas because of Vincent? No. No. There was absolutely no way. He had accepted the job offer before they had broken up. *But you knew well before then that it wasn't going to work out. Remember that letter you sent him in July?*

Murph ripped him from his thoughts. "What floor do you live on?" They were in the lobby.

"Eight."

"We are on seven," she said with a smile. "Want to come over for a drink tonight?" she asked, but it sounded like more of a demand.

Evan wanted to do nothing more than collapse onto his couch and watch *Hello, Dolly!* for the thousandth time, but he needed this. He needed a friend and the notion that he found one this quickly was incredulous.

"Yes. I can do that. Let's regroup in an hour?"

"I'll be waiting in anticipation. Apartment 711."

○ ○ ○

In an unsurprising non-twist, the seventh floor of the building looked no different from the eighth. It's almost as if the contractors, architects, and interior designers had no personality to add some flare. In any case, Evan knocked twice on the door.

There was no answer.

He knocked again and took a half step back. Finally, he heard footsteps and the seven locks disengage one by one.

The door flew open in a flurry and there was a scruffy looking man about Evan's age standing before him.

"Can I help you?" he said without a hint of happiness or frustration at the intrusion.

"Uh, I was meeting up with a friend, but you don't look anything like her."

"That's a relief. I've been mistaken for a woman too many times," he said evenly. With the bulging muscles and thick beard, Evan assumed the man was kidding. Understanding or appreciating sarcasm was not one of his top qualities.

"Do you happen to know a Murphy?"

"What's a Murphy?"

"My friend I'm supposed to meet."

"No, sorry."

"Okay, okay. I can't take it anymore!" a new voice said from behind Evan. He turned and saw Murph standing in the doorframe of the apartment across the hall. She was laughing uncontrollably. "That was so incredibly awkward to watch. Thank you for that. I needed to unwind after today. Sorry I told you the wrong apartment, Evan. I actually thought I lived there, but once I realized I didn't, I had no way to contact you." Looking past Evan, she continued: "Hello neighbor! I'm the mysterious friend that my compadre is looking for! Nice to meet you."

"Likewise," the man said. "So, can I go now?"

Evan turned back to him and nodded.

The door immediately closed, and the seven locks reengaged.

"I don't think we will be seeing much of him. Come on in, friend!" Murph said, waving him on.

Evan walked across the hall and moved into the apartment. It was a massive two-bedroom place with the occupants still being in a state of transition. Boxes were littered in several areas, pictures sat on the floor in their desired location, and the television was propped up on empty plastic bins. "Still trying to get everything organized, so apologies for the mess," Murph said, knowing what Evan was thinking about.

"No need to apologize. I'm straightening up as well," Evan said, rebalancing himself from the awkwardness he just encountered.

"First order of business. Let's exchange numbers so we never have to witness something like that again."

They swapped phones and punched in their contact information.

"Evan Eaton. Rolls off the tongue. I like it," Murph said after getting her phone back.

Evan looked down at his phone and saw the entered name as Murph Dawg with a heart emoji after it. "I don't get the pleasure of knowing your last name?" he asked.

"Well, I either tell you now and get the ridiculousness out of the way or you will just see it at work tomorrow, assuming you show up," she said with a half-smile. "Which would you prefer?"

Tired of the games, Evan said flatly, "Just tell me now."

"It's Law."

"Murphy Law," Evan said. "Oh, I could see that getting annoying."

Murph nodded solemnly. "From the way my mom tells it, my dad had the acute intelligence to give me the name. Obviously, I am not bitter about it anymore, especially since he is dead now," she said bluntly.

The statement caught Evan off-guard. "I'm sorry," he struggled to say.

"Anyways, the second order of business. Are you a fan of dogs?"

"Of course. I have one of my own."

"Future puppy date!" she said, clapping her hands together. "I didn't want to assume, so I put him in the bedroom. I'll let him out."

Murph moved down the hallway and to the closed door at the end. She opened it slowly and the dog nudged itself out and ran directly to Evan.

Evan knelt down to greet him and he yipped excitedly at the new guest.

"That's Sasquatch!" Murph informed him.

"Love the name." The dog was no more than ten pounds, but it seemed fitting regardless.

"It was my boyfriend's idea. He's got quite the imagination. I was hoping you'd meet him tonight, but he's staying late at work."

"What does he do?"

"He works for the Rockies in their front office. I'm not entirely sure how he got the job, but I imagine his intense passion for baseball helped."

"Is that what brought y'all to Dallas?"

"Correct. For a while I didn't want to go. You know that whole thing of leaving behind my family and yada yada. Of course, it didn't help that my dad was dying, but he was adamant I go. So here we are."

"What happened to your dad?"

"Cancer."

"Again, I'm really sorry."

"I know you are. Everyone seems to be. I don't mean that in a condescending way, but how could a complete stranger be sorry that my dad died? What if he was like a total asshole or never a part of my life?"

"I guess we are conditioned to pass condolences whether they're deserved or not."

"So insightful. Well, since you made me think of my dead father, now you have to tell me why you moved to Denver."

Evan sucked in a deep breath. "Moving is the only thing I know. I bounced around with my mom as a kid and never learned to settle anywhere. I thought Dallas would be different, but my job sucked, and I was in a deteriorating relationship that made me never really settle into the city."

"Relationships are always tough. I got lucky with Elliot. High school sweethearts and all that. Tell me about your ex," she demanded.

"Why?" Evan asked, somewhat confused.

"Because I want to know what your type is so I can be on the lookout."

"I will be taking some time for myself. No dates for me anytime soon," he said while shaking his head.

"You're boring. And I'm waiting for the description. Let's start simple: What was his name?"

"*Was*? We may be broken up, but he isn't dead," Evan said.

"Okay, okay. My bad. What *is* his name?"

"Vin."

There was the faintest moment of recognition on Murph's face. Evan didn't notice it. Sasquatch didn't notice it, but he was occupied with the toy octopus in the corner of the kitchen. We noticed it though.

Somewhere, someone was expecting Murph to instantly remember who Vincent was and their encounter on the parking garage rooftop, but Murph was constantly preoccupied with thoughts of her dad and the stress of moving and stepping back into a career. Their conversation was a drop in the bucket, a dot on the canvas.

Remember: Vincent was only a background actor in Murph's story. But maybe time will dislodge the memory.

Her moment of recognition disappeared, and she said, "I like that name. It sounds so suave."

"He was far from that, but I loved him regardless."

Murph raised her eyebrows at that. "So, love was on the table?"

Evan nodded.

"How romantic. Tell me more."

Even though he didn't particularly enjoy doing it, Evan gave an overly detailed history of him and Vincent. He explained how Vincent was a great listener but had absolutely no confidence in himself and burdened himself deeply with all the sins of his past, which Evan never believed were that significant in the first place. Listen: he didn't know everything, so it was obvious he would still think somewhat favorably of him.

Murph and Evan carried on their conversation for a while. It ended before Murph's boyfriend Elliot returned home, so Evan would have to meet him another day.

On his way out, he turned back to Murph and said, "Do you want to walk to work tomorrow? It would be best to face the mess together."

"Yes. That would be lovely."

"Meet you in the lobby at eight?"

"Sounds like a date. Get home safe," Murph said with one last smile and closed the door.

five

LAWN CHAIR CONVERSATIONS

Halloween was nothing more than a holiday overwrought with women that dressed up as whores and men that put on costumes of their favorite superhero to try and win the affection of the whores, but worse than that was how this egregious holiday cranked up the machine of consumerism and brainwashed all of the ignoramuses into opening their wallets for the Christmas season that was still two months away, but _even_ worse than that was the copious amounts of sugar-laced candy that was shoved down the throats of children who knew nothing more than stuffing their faces with the poison because everyone else was doing it, which generated the unbreakable hivemind tearing through modern society, but the worst thing of all was that Halloween was believed by many to have started out as a Christian holiday, which goes to show again how the church continues to stick their grubby, pedophile drenched hands in society and that everyone allows for this to happen!

At least, this is what the cashier at the grocery store told Ann in one unbelievably long breath as he swiped the bags of candy across the scanner. After finishing his diatribe, he paused his scanning momentarily to catch his breath. He placed his hands on the counter and sloped his face downward. His cheeks puffed in and out at a rapid pace like how someone would mimic while doing chest compressions.

Ann didn't have time for his shit and refused to acknowledge his rant. Her only contribution to their encounter was when he managed to ask through several breaths whether she would be using cash or card.

Considering Ann was old school, she elected for cash.

Back at home, she prepped for the trick-or-treaters by putting the candy into bowls. It was taxing work.

Normally, she would keep the front door closed and wait for the kids to ring it. After years of using this method, she discovered the outcome was less than ideal. There was a number of kids who ran away after ringing the doorbell and hearing the savage barks of two (now three!) friendly dogs. More than once had one of the dogs slipped under her leg and scampered out into the front yard while she held the door slightly ajar to hand out candy.

She elected to do something different this year.

Ann grabbed two lawn chairs from the garage and set them up at the top of the driveway. She walked back into the house and searched for Leigh. It felt like sabotage, but so be it. They had unfinished business.

Leigh was upstairs in Vincent's vacated room. She had been using it for storage since her belongings were endless. Clothes were piled high on his bed and half full boxes were littered across the space.

From an outsider's perspective it would look as if Leigh was getting ready for a move. That outsider would be correct.

As mentioned earlier, Lorenzo found out he secured a contracting position at a major pharmaceutical company in New Jersey. Not concerned about the ethical motivations of the company, he signed his name on the line and was getting ready to start there in another week. Leigh and Lorenzo were ferociously scrambling to find an apartment closer to his work. Given Leigh's flexibility as a nurse, she'd be able to start up at a new hospital without much trouble.

Given what we know about Ann, she had her doubts about the situation. She was beyond ready for Leigh to move out and properly start her life with Lorenzo, but they essentially had no idea what they were doing. Leigh didn't live in an apartment during college, so Ann seriously doubted she knew what to ask and look for during walkthroughs.

"Do you want to help me pass out Halloween candy?" Ann asked from the doorway.

"Not really. I have a lot of packing to do," Leigh responded without much hesitation.

"You two don't even have a place yet. What are you packing for?"

"We will find one soon and when we do, I want to move out of here as quickly as possible."

That stung, but Ann shook it off. She had grown used to Leigh's constant jabs. "Okay, but you'll still need to stay here on the nights you work. You wouldn't be able to drive that far after working twelve hours if you find a place near Lorenzo's work."

"I'm aware."

Ann shook her head as Leigh continued to sort out the leaning stack of clothes.

"By the way," Ann said, "that wasn't a question. Come down and help with the candy. I'll be outside in the driveway."

○ ○ ○

The first guest to trot up the driveway was Matty. This was the little cousin born right after Vincent moved to Dallas. Fast forward to a more present time and Matty was not the tiny doodad that he once was.

He was dressed up as . . . well, Ann had no idea. It looked like some awful mutation of a dog and muskrat.

"Hey Matty!" Ann said as he reached the top of the driveway.

"Hi! Can I have some candy?" he asked. After thinking momentarily, he added a *pleaseeeee!* to the end of his question.

"Of course. Take as much as you want, but don't tell your mom," Ann leaned in close to say. She waved down at his mom who was standing somewhat impatiently at the bottom of the driveway.

Ann continued: "Matty, what are you dressed up as?"

He kept digging through the candy to find the perfect pieces, but managed to say, "I don't know. I think I'm some awful mutation of a dog and muskrat."

"Oh."

"Did I take too much?" he looked up and asked.

Half of the bowl was gone.

"Not at all! Give me a hug. I'll see you soon, okay?"

"Okay," Matty said with a chuckle. He ran down the driveway and quickly disappeared into the darkness of the street.

Seeing no one else in the area, Ann got up and walked to the front door. The three dogs were watching her through the glass door with smudge marks staining various portions of the glass.

She went inside and refilled the bowl.

Upon returning to the lawn chairs, she found Leigh seated in one of them.

"How long have you been out here?" Ann asked, somewhat perplexed.

"The whole time," Leigh said nonchalantly.

"Oh."

A group of four kids trundled up the short incline. One was dressed as an astronaut, one was a ghoul of some ghoulish variety, and the last two were dressed as Romeo and Juliet. It was a bizarre combination.

"Trick or treat!" they shouted dutifully as they neared the lawn chairs.

Ann lifted up the bowl and each of them took a turn snatching up the candy.

This cycle repeated on a somewhat regular cadence for the next hour, but in the spare moments, Ann pressed Leigh.

"Where are you two looking for an apartment?"

"How are you two going to afford it?"

"Have you thought about all the furniture you need to buy?"

The questions were asked in an orderly fashion as if they were being read off a teleprompter by a seasoned newscaster.

Leigh grew visibly frustrated with each one and her answers continued to get shorter and snippier.

Eventually her anger broke through the surface.

"Would you just fucking stop?! We know what we're doing. I don't need you to keep micromanaging every moment of my life. You need to accept that we will never be close. We will never that perfect relationship you want. All you do is bug me with questions. Don't you realize I don't want to talk to you . . ."

Leigh continued on for a while. She talked about how Ann tries to buy her affection with gifts, but that it doesn't work. She talked about how Vincent was always the favorite and had it so easy growing up. She talked about all the topics she knew would terribly upset Ann because Leigh thrived at degrading someone to their lowest form.

At the end of her monologue (which was interrupted several times by eager trick-or-treaters), Leigh got up and went back into the house.

Ann was uncharacteristically quiet during the entire tirade. Vincent had suggested that she doesn't listen well, so it was something she decided to work on.

There was a lot she wanted to say. She wanted to talk about the time she and Jim helped Leigh buy a car since Vincent took the beat-up Sonata. She wanted to talk about the five-thousand-dollar loan they gave her and Lorenzo so they could afford their must-have honeymoon trip to Hawaii. She wanted to talk extensively about how Leigh had lived there rent free for years. Ann understood that bringing up any of those would lead to Leigh getting defensive because that was her technique when she felt cornered.

Above it all, Ann was sad. Sometimes people like to trump up sadness with flowery words to sound intelligent, but this was not the case. Ann was sad—the most basic and hurtful form of it. Moments flashed in her mind of when Leigh was a toddler, waving to the camera or laughing during dinner. What happened? How had she scorned her relationship with her only daughter so badly?

Is this what it felt like to lose a child?

No, of course not. Don't be ridiculous, she told herself. *There are people who have actually lost their child.*

Ann searched for an answer on what to do next. Metaphorically speaking, obviously. It's not like a map lazily dropped from the sky and conveniently on her lap where she unfolded it and gazed with wonder at the riddle and location.

The answer came to her without much fanfare. She determined that—

"Trick or treat!" a voice called out.

Ann looked up, expecting another kid adorning a half-ass costume, but instead it was her neighbor.

Colleen was the first person she met when the Besser family moved to Cornwallis Drive twenty-five years ago. Their family had transferred from Kansas City for a new position her husband was promoted into at the CIA. He had the unfortunate pleasure of making the terrible commute to Newark each day. Colleen and the family (with two kids older than Leigh and Vincent) quickly readjusted to life on the East Coast, considering Colleen and her husband grew up an hour away from Easton. Colleen and her husband were high school sweethearts and continued in that same manner until the day he was killed in accidental shooting by another CIA agent. This has been mentioned previously, but it's worth repeating to hammer in the notion that terrible things happen for no reason.

It had been over ten years since the shooting and the news vans lined up outside on the street for days, trying to get a sound bite from any acquaintance of his. It had been over ten years since all the family and friends that ever existed gathered together to celebrate the life of everyone's favorite person.

Colleen moved on and found love with another person, but Ann knew that there wasn't a day that passed where Colleen and her family desperately wished for him back.

Ann's current sadness crested to the top of the parabola upon seeing Colleen. Thoughts of her husband crept into frame and she was disappointed in herself for thinking that an argument with her daughter constituted as losing her.

Colleen experienced grief every single day. Ann didn't know loss. Sure, she lost her father many years earlier, but wasn't that always in the cards? It was a person's fate to witness the death of their parents. Death, taxes, and all that bullshit. Ann couldn't comprehend what that moment of loss would feel like. But even worse: what about the week after? The decade after? The lifetime spent wishing for a single moment more with them?

She choked back tears as Colleen slumped into the chair beside her. Colleen spoke of her Halloween visitors and how she was beyond ready for retirement. Her occasional laughter filled the nighttime air and it gave Ann hope.

One day, Ann would experience true loss, but she'd rebound and still be able to live a normal life. She would laugh with friends, spend money on useless objects, and travel to exotic places.

How much time would it take to reach that new normal?

There was no sense in her dwelling on the eventuality.

For now, she listened to Colleen talk and stared up at the stars above. They were particularly beautiful that night as if they were blooming flowers in the springtime.

six

FOLLOW IT

As it seemed to always happen, October morphed into November and the short commute to work for Evan and Murph became a sign of what was to come. The weather was beginning to dip into the frostier temperatures, but the real traumatic chill wouldn't be in effect for another few months.

Their routine was simple. Evan would wait patiently for Murph down in the lobby (as she was never on time, which she attributed to morning sickness—the act of getting out of bed in the morning for work) and then they would grab coffee from the same shop a block away. The office had free coffee, but as expected, it was atrocious. From there, they would mingle around the coffee shop until one of them made the slow crawl to the door.

After the madness of Evan's first day, work seemed to level out. It turned out Murph would not be in charge of the whole HR operation, which she was perfectly fine with. Evan took over temporary control given his previous experience. The company was small enough that they could survive without a true manager while they scoured LinkedIn to find someone qualified for the manager position.

Who cares about their work life though? It's just something dull to occupy their time.

With that in mind, let's jump ahead to the end of another uneventful workday.

Evan and Murph were ramping up a weekly tradition where they would grab dinner at a random restaurant. They discovered an app that served as a roulette wheel of potential options. Each time, they would trade off on who got to shake the phone and spin the wheel.

It was Evan's turn.

He selected five broad categories of restaurants and the distance they were willing to travel. He flicked his phone and the wheel kicked into gear. It landed on a Thai restaurant six blocks away.

"What do you think?" he said, handing the phone over to Murph.

"We cannot disobey the power of the wheel. Onward to"—she examined the name—"Oh, Thai, Thai." She thought for a moment. "Clever. I see what they did there."

Evan nodded in agreement.

"Okay, it looks like we need to walk up this way," he pointed directly in front of them.

A block up the road there was a flyer stapled to a wooden pole. Murph stepped closer and put her hand against it to stop the flyer from blowing in the wind.

"Look at this," she said excitedly to Evan.

He peeked over her shoulder and saw an arrow printed across the width of the paper.

It looked similar to this:

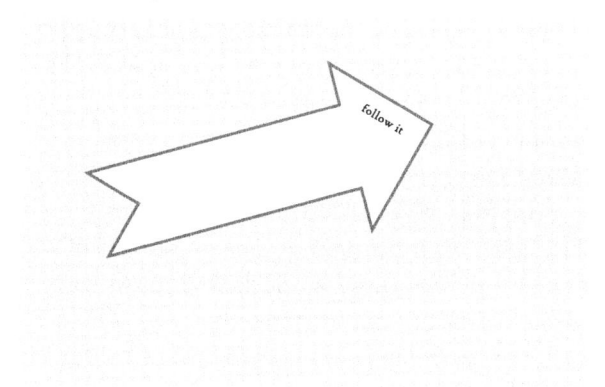

[arrow illustration with text "follow it"]

Evan pushed past Murph to look closer at the wording near the joint of the arrow. With his nose practically pressed against the flyer, he said, "Follow it. That's what the sign says."

"I couldn't have read that without you," Murph said with a tilted laugh and sarcasm that Evan wouldn't get. "Wait," a moment of clarity passed through her, "repeat that again."

Evan glanced back at her. His glasses slipped slightly down his nose and gave off the impression he was a judge who was about to deliver a harsh sentence. He towered over her, but not in a menacing way. Murph just happened to be a compact human.

"This flyer or paper or thing says *follow it*," he stated.

"Oh, wow," Murph said. She took a step back toward the street and collapsed her head into her hands as if they were waiting for communion.

"What's wrong?"

She picked her head up. "It's dumb. I'm being dumb. Dumb as a thumb."

"Murph, what's the problem?" Evan never excelled at riddles. He always preferred for people to just get to the point. Vincent spoke in flowery monologues that made his head spin. Whenever he was finished, Evan would need time to digest and attempt to formulate a response, which made Vincent grow restless because he always hated silence.

"That's the last thing my dad ever said to me. 'Follow it.' He was drugged up and barely coherent at the end, but there was this mumble that came out from him. I didn't hear him the first time, so I leaned in closer. He had similar green eyes to me, and they darted over in my direction. It was almost startling to witness the clarity that had been missing from him for weeks. Sometimes I wonder if he knew he was about to die. He mumbled the words again and I still couldn't hear him, so I squeezed his hand tighter and leaned in even closer." Murph moved away from the street and next to Evan. "I asked him to say it one more time. He did. The two words leaked out of him and his clarity collapsed back to what it was. His head lulled to the side and he was gone by midnight.

"I spent a lot of time thinking about those two words. They were cryptic. Follow what? What was *it*? I was frustrated by the whole thing. I felt like my dad owed me more than two fucking words. That was the anger of death and grief stalking me. After he died, I considered not moving to Denver with Elliot, at least not right away. I needed to make sure my family was going to be okay. I was the cornerstone that was left to make sure my brothers didn't turn into delinquents and my mom continued to function. But then those two words came crawling back in. At the viewing, at the funeral, at every moment I was thinking about the move or my family or my dad. I decided to embrace it. I decided to follow *it*. The first logical step was to go to Denver with Elliot, and obviously you know how that turned out. I finally recognized my family would be fine without me. I wasn't sure though if those words would ever have meaning again. What it a one-time thing? Was Denver the giant crescendo to my life that would help move everything into place? And now, they are right there! I feel silly for attributing the heaviness of my dad's death to words on a piece of paper, but it's a coincidence I can't ignore.

"With that being said," she took another step and poked Evan in the chest, "we have to see where this goes."

Murph wiped the tears from her face. It was a natural reflex.

"Do you see where the next one may be?" he asked, which was his way of agreeing to go on the quest.

"No, but it looks like the arrow is pointing up the block and to the other side of the street."

"Let's head that way then."

"But what if the arrow was flipped and we are heading in the wrong direction?"

"I'm willing to gamble that we are going the right way."

"But wait!" Murph called out. "What if it leads to some serial killer who wants to eat our toenails and play jump rope with our intestines?"

"I'd welcome it."

"Oh, look at you trying to be funny. It doesn't suite you," Murph said.

They crossed the street as Murph dipped into more theories about what the arrow may lead to. Evan assumed it would just lead to another flyer.

He was correct.

(In another plane of existence, they never found another flyer. They walked up and down city blocks with no luck whatsoever. They ended up going to Oh, Thai, Thai and sat in silence at the disappointment of the nothingness that happened. But given that plot is important, character building is vital, and everything hinged on discovering where it led, this book exists in the space where they did find another flyer and another one and another one and another . . .)

It didn't take long to find the second one. A block and a half up from where they were initially standing, they spotted the yellow flyer fluttering against the pole. The same arrow and wording except it was pointing up, which indicated that they needed to keep walking straight.

They continued to hunt down flyers for a half hour. They navigated through parts of downtown they hadn't seen before and complained about walking in circles several times even though they weren't.

They passed by Oh, Thai, Thai and looked at it longingly as both Murph and Evan desperately wanted to stop for food but felt too compelled to finish what they started.

The tenth flyer brought them to an alleyway. Several people meandered at the far end but didn't seem to be involved in the same quest they were.

"This has to be it!" Murph said.

"Lead the way."

She marched down the alleyway and gathered some distance from Evan. He was too busy thinking about how he never explored Dallas nearly as much as he traveled around Denver in this single day.

"Found it!" she said, throwing her arms into the air like she was being scrubbed down in a decontamination pit.

"Found what?" Evan asked as he closed the gap between them.

"The final flyer, silly."

Evan noticed the door with the flyer taped to it.

It looked similar to this:

you
found
it
!

"What the fuck?" Evan said.

"What's the matter?" Murph asked.

"That is the ugliest thing I've ever seen."

"I'm sure it's like that on purpose. Shall we?"

Evan reached out and pulled on the door handle. It swung outward and revealed a dimly lit interior.

Murph walked in and quickly turned back to Evan. "It's a fucking bar! Do you believe that? All that walking for a stinking bar. They better have some food here!"

Evan knew from her tone that she wasn't upset, just trying to play it up for the audience that was watching.

He fell in line behind her and confirmed that it was a bar . . . and a pretty basic one at that. Upon first glance, it seemed like they were going for a dive bar feel. The lighting was practically nothing, a jukebox sat in the corner that flashed an obnoxious series of colors, and the pictures on the walls looked like they were ripped from any grandmother's attic. There were several customers who floated around the fringes of the bar and all looked mangled to a degree as if they just spent a week wandering the wastelands after the apocalypse. Evan found it odd that a place like this went to such extremes to lure in customers or maybe they were the idiots for following the signs. In all fairness, they were just pieces of paper tacked up to poles around the city, so the effort on their end was minimal. But what were the odds that the few streets they pass by to and from work would have one of the fliers to would set them on their quest? Evan understood why Murph wanted to track it down—there was a coincidence they couldn't ignore. It had the potential to be nothing though.

They elected to settle into two seats at the bar instead of a table.

"So this is *it*, huh?" Murph said to no one in particular as she glanced around the bar.

"Based on what you said earlier, this is the *it* for right now. I'm sure there will be others. Be on the lookout," Evan said with a smile.

"Wise words, dude."

The bartender strode over, rested his elbows on the bar top, and leaned across the gap separating him from our friends. "Welcome to It—"

"Oh, you have got to be fucking kidding me. The name of this bar is It? Doesn't Stephen King have a monopoly on that word with that giant ass book of his?"

"No, he does not," the bartender said. "Didn't you see the sign above the door when you walked in?" he asked, pointing to the front entrance.

"We actually came in through the back alley," Evan said.

"Yeah, we walked all around downtown chasing these arrows. I was convinced we were being lured in by a serial killer so imagine my surprise when it turned out to be a bar—and a pretty ordinary one at that," Murph said. "I could see a serial killer hanging out in here a few times a week though."

The bartender stared her down briefly, relaxed his demeanor, and said, "Just so you know, I was the one who put up the fliers. I thought it would be a cool way to entice people to come here, but my partner told me no one was going to follow random signs with just an arrow and a weird cryptic message. He is a man of little faith! I can't wait to tell him how I suckered you two in," he finished with a grin.

"What was the point of doing that though?" Evan asked.

"We are a relatively new bar and you need to get creative with your marketing these days. As you can see, our clientele doesn't seem to be overly active on social media, so we needed to change our strategy a bit," the bartender said, attempting to rationalize his decisions.

"Well," he continued. "I have neglected my bartender duties. What can I get you two?"

"A drink menu would be great. Also, please tell me you have food," Murph begged.

"You're in luck," he said while reaching for the menus under the bar. "Take a look and let me know what you want. I'll give you a few minutes." He retreated to the other side of the bar to tend to his other customers.

"Really? Really!" Murph yelled as she buried her head in the food menu. "They really named the bar It and my dumbass thought it was some sign from above."

Evan didn't know what to say, so he sat there and found an acceptable drink from the menu.

By the time the bartender came back, Evan had his drink in mind and Murph ordered both a drink and food.

As the bartender walked away, Murph called out, "Dude, what's your name? I feel like we have gone through a mild journey together since you had us running around town." If she knew much about Kurt Vonnegut, she may have considered the bartender to be a part of her *karass*. If she knew more about Stephen King, she may have considered the bartender to be a part of her *ka-tet*. Murph knew neither of these words. Evan had heard Vincent use them before, but he didn't believe in such silly things, so the thought never occurred to him.

The bartender turned back. "I'm Francisco or Franco for short. I respond to whatever," he said with a short laugh.

Evan and Murph extended the same pleasantries and passed along their names.

Franco welcomed them again to the bar and promised to come back as he hurried off again to assist the other patrons.

"Seems like a nice dude," Murph said without a true understanding whether he was nice or not. It's something people told others when they didn't actually know how to describe someone.

"Hey," she continued. "Do you think we will be here a while? I was going to tell Elliot to join."

"I don't see why not." Evan would have rather been at home, but the social interactions would do him good. He liked Elliot well enough too. It was clear why the two were together: they were total compliments to each other. Murph was more aloof while Elliot played it straighter. Elliot wanted to decompose complex topics while Murph would rather surf Instagram (which made the somewhat depressing conversation earlier about her father's last words so surprising).

Murph was halfway through her sandwich when the front door creaked open and Elliot stepped through. The dying light of the fading day shined against his back and gave him a heavenly look. He walked to the bar and gave each of them a hug.

Elliot rattled off the details of his day and then Murph reciprocated. She explored every nook of their travels and shared each piece with Elliot.

Evan was listening with half an ear when his phone repeatedly vibrated in his pocket. He pushed it out with no urgency and glanced at the unsaved number. The area code was familiar though.

He answered it on the fifth ring. Murph and Elliot continued their conversation.

"Hello?" he said, adhering to normal phone call etiquette.

Evan listened. He listened briefly as the sentences poured out from the voice, but he tried to stop it.

"No," he said urgently and hung up the call.

"No, no, no," he kept repeating to himself as he moved from the chair and to the door that led back to the alleyway.

He was met with a rush of cold air and the sounds of the city. A siren played its song in the distance.

Evan tried to stop his hands from shaking, but there was no use.

"What the fuck was that?" he said to himself.

The phone began to vibrate again.

He didn't want to, but an unseen force guided him to answer. The audience was waiting for the payoff. They were patient but wouldn't be sated for long.

The voice on the other end spewed out all the words in a mass jumble. Evan tried to listen again, but his mind flooded with too many questions.

A mere mutter into the phone, Evan eventually said, "I can't do this right now." He ended the call for the second time.

He returned the phone to his pocket, hoping it wouldn't start vibrating again. He walked across the width of the alleyway and leaned up against the wall, staring back at that atrocious yellow sign.

Murph soon came through the door and momentarily replaced the flyer in Evan's field of vision. She looked blurry at first, but soon came into focus.

"Dude, what's the problem? I get that Elliot's stories are boring, but I didn't think they were that bad . . ."

"I—uh—I'm . . . at a loss."

"What happened? Just spit it at me."

"My father called and invited me to Thanksgiving dinner."

seven

THANKSGIVING NIRVANA (PART I)

The meal Ann prepped came together with the synchronicity only found when your car hits a bump at the exact moment the song on the radio comes to a crescendo. The turkey was cooked to a beautiful golden-brown color, the mashed potatoes didn't get stuck to the spoon when you scooped them out the bowl, the cranberry sauce wasn't touched at all which is how it should be, and all the food finished close enough together so nothing got cold at the table. In comparisons to other years, the four plates set aside in the dining room were minimal. Neither of her children were there. Vincent was flying back from Hawaii with Athena and Jagdish, and Leigh was spending her first Thanksgiving with Lorenzo at their apartment in New Brunswick. The two remaining plates for this year belonged to Ann's mom and her husband. Jim had been a total sweetheart and driven over to Bethlehem to pick them up. It became unspoken between all of them that it's for the betterment of humanity if they avoided driving as much as possible.

Ann sat down at the table where the rest of the clan was situated. _So this is what it would have been like every year if we didn't have kids_, she thought. Who was she kidding? If they didn't have any kids, they would travel the world each holiday with the overflowing supply of cash they'd have. Of course, she would need to crush up some Xanax and swirl it into Jim's drink before takeoff, but that's the sort of thing you did for love.

She loved being a mother, so the notion of not having kids was not so much of a notion. Now that they were older though, her job was mostly done. Watching Vincent find success and move down to Dallas after college was equally rewarding and devastating. Seeing Leigh find happiness with another person when she carried herself as if the world was hellbent on her destruction was shocking. At the end of the day though, she and Jim raised two respectable children who are creating better lives for themselves than she ever had.

She was consciously aware how much she thought of her children. It was her curse.

Ann picked at the food with minimal interest. There was something about cooking all the food (and the prospect of all the dishes that would linger afterwards) that didn't make it seem as appetizing.

A part of her brain reengaged in the conversation at the table until she realized it was Jim talking about work.

She had choice words about that topic, but Thanksgiving wasn't the time to bitch about it to her mother, so she crawled back into her head.

Speaking of work . . .

Nah, let's skip over those paragraphs of certain drivel. By this point, it should be evident that Ann was not feeling too hot about her current work situation. Listen: there are a dizzying number of stories that could be rehashed to provide more depth and clarity to Boob, the work environment, and so on that would all feed into why her disdain for Bridgewater was at a nauseous level, but what's the point?

Listen again:

That is the side hustle to this story. The filler and the unnecessary time waster in order to provide more motivation for Ann Besser.

Listen once more:

The main hustle of this story is quickly approaching. Reading a novel involves some serious foreplay with a potential money shot at the end, but if you are anticipating it too much, you will be left disappointed and ashamed.

Let's return to Ann and see what she's thinking about . . .

Leigh.

Of course.

It wasn't overly surprising given the context that her kids were on the short list of topics that coursed through her mind frequently.

Following the disaster on Halloween, Ann pulled back. She stepped away from Leigh's life for the last month. She watched from afar as Leigh packed up a majority of her belongings, shoved them into boxes, and moved out the house she grew up in. There wasn't much fanfare from her. The stoic nature that always resided on her face was glaringly present as she drove away for the last time. Of course, she would be back, but it was a defining moment. Jim and Ann were finally empty nesters.

Ann still hadn't received a call from Leigh with an invite to the apartment. They exchanged several text messages when Leigh managed to snag a job at the hospital in New Brunswick, which meant she wouldn't need to crash at the house on the weekends. Besides that, though, Ann hadn't spoken to Leigh. Ann knew that Leigh made several requests of Jim to construct some furniture for them, which wasn't surprising. Jim always caved to Leigh and it constantly made Ann look like the villain, but that was imbedded in the job description of being a mom.

What truly hurt Ann during that stretch after Halloween was the thank you note from the wedding. It was clear Leigh wrote them given the flowery flow of the writing with its wide arcs and spaced out letters. Ann and Jim each got their own. Ann's was appropriate enough with all the right words and pleasantries passed along, but hers was just another that Leigh needed to complete. Jim had left his on the counter half-opened so that the contents were teasing a wandering eye. Ann walked by it several times before the gravitational pull of the card forced her into its orbit. She skimmed the contents and placed it back. She immediately went upstairs and cried. Leigh wrote about how close she was with Jim and that the wedding wouldn't have been possible without him. Quite frankly, it broke her heart because that's what she wanted: the validation that all she had done was good enough to cement a strong relationship with her daughter.

In a more present time, Ann's phone rang.

It radiated out through the kitchen and caught the attention of all three dogs. They ran toward the noise and began to howl like they were in an elementary school choir. They were horribly off-key and didn't know any of the lyrics.

It was Vincent.

A lightness passed through Ann as she answered the call in as cheerful a manner as she could muster.

Vincent called to wish her a happy Thanksgiving and tell her that he'd made it back to Dallas safely. She insisted that he go on speakerphone to talk to the rest of the group. He obliged the request.

The next half hour was spent hearing about his travels around Maui. The group elected to only go to one island for . . . well, there wasn't an exact reason, but it seemed to work out regardless. They spent time at the beach. They drove the Road to Hana and all agreed it seemed more like the Road to Hell. They woke up at an absurdly early time to catch a bus to the top of the volcano and watch the sunrise. They subsequently biked down the volcano in the early morning glow. And so on.

The group at the dining room table in Easton, Pennsylvania listened intently to the rehashing and asked questions during his slight pauses. None of them had ever been to Hawaii and likely would never make it there.

Once the call ended, Ann's mom said, "He sounded happy!"

"He did. I don't think that was always the case," Ann chimed in.

"Moving to a new place is never easy," Walter said.

The conversation continued in a fashion where no one said anything relevant for a while.

Ann left the table at some point to prep dessert and begin the process of cleaning.

The remainder of the day was inconsequential. Ann went out to participate in the shenanigans of Black Friday even though she could have completed her shopping from home. She enjoyed watching the systematic decay of the sliver of moral fiber left within society as each store, parking lot, and shopping center became a breeding ground for chaos. It was like watching a nature documentary that showed the carnivores stalking their prey. People had no issues running through others to get what they wanted. She managed to stay on the fringes and remain unharmed during her adventure out.

At some point she made it back home and it crossed her mind that Leigh hadn't even called to wish them a happy Thanksgiving.

Oh well, at least she had Vincent.

eight

THANKSGIVING NIRVANA (PART II)

The chest-high brick wall that encapsulated the front yard made the house look like a fortress.
   It was not.
   At two-bedrooms and one and a half bathrooms, the house was modest enough for a couple to live in but would be cramped for an entire family.
   The shrubs scattered across the front lawn looked neglected as branches shot out in oddball directions. Most of them were decayed and dormant due to the colder weather. The paint on the shutters was flaking and showing the pale wood underneath. One of the gutters hung down slightly like a jigsaw piece that wasn't put all the way into place.
   Evan recalled that the house didn't look quite as bad when he was one of the occupants of it. That was a lifetime ago—or a different chapter as the audience would have referred to it.
   He stepped over to the gate that was squeezed in-between all the brick and finally noticed the car in the driveway. He had been in that car numerous times—even driven it himself.
   It was all the confirmation he needed: Kieran still lived in that house.
   See:
   Evan was back in the Greenville area to spend his illustrious Thanksgiving holiday with the father he hadn't seen in nearly a decade and a half. It took a massive number of conversations with Murph and others for Evan to feel comfortable in going. A constant state of dread settled into his body as flashes of what his life used to be when his father was around came into focus. He talked to his mom at length about it and her stance boiled down to the idea that Evan was an adult and could do what he wanted. His mom had also heard throughout the years of his father's attempts to tip the scales back to him being a decent person but seeing she had been remarried more times than average, she always found herself too preoccupied to contact him.
   The coincidence of Kieran, his former long-term boyfriend, and his father living in close proximity to each other was not lost on him. It was as if the audience that was always tagging along wanted a clash to occur. They wanted Evan to stand at that front gate and have Kieran come out of the

house and see him. It would lead to a confrontation or reconcile. Evan wasn't one to forget the past though, so all those memories of their time together in the house would rush back in. The weird occurrences, Kieran's deteriorating mental state, and all those sleepless nights. His nightmares stemmed from what happened in that house, so he would never see himself reconciling with Kieran, regardless of what the audience wanted. If anything, Evan was hoping to get a glimpse of Kieran with a younger man, grooming him in the same way for confirmation that Kieran hadn't changed. He wondered if Kieran still taught high school and approached the openly gay kids to pretend to provide support only to turn around and use them as an object to fuck. Wasn't that illegal?

The house looked quiet that morning. It was likely that Kieran and whoever he occupied the house with wasn't even home. Evan walked back to the car and cried.

He missed Vincent. That relationship felt more genuine. Sure, Vincent didn't always know how to vocalize his feelings, but they had honest conversations that brought them closer. It was a relationship that could have lasted if they tried harder, if they didn't give up so easily . . . if Evan hadn't run away to Denver. The guilt of that decision pressed into him.

"Not now, not now," he said to himself.

It washed over him like water crashing into a jetty. If he didn't move quickly, he would drown in the thoughts.

What Evan never realized is that there is never a good time to have a mental breakdown, to have all those terrible memories bubble up.

Going to Kieran's house was his own choice though, part of it was a natural reflex since it had been the cornerstone to his life for a while.

In regard to his father, there was one thought that he kept running away from, which was likely part of the reason he found himself in Greenville: he didn't remember any of the emotion attached to the actions of his father. Evan remembered the events—the yelling, the destruction, the general shitty attitude that his father had—but he had long since forgotten how he felt in those moments. He was a kid after all. Books, television, movies, and so on told him he should carry a grudge and continue to be a traumatized gay man because that's what the masses wanted. Tragedy was the selling point of anything successful. But he knew on some level he had forgiven his father a long time ago and that's how he moved on, and to have him back in his life again would not be a sign of defeat or weakness, it would be a second chance for his father.

He turned the car on and punched in the address to his father's house.

After the initial call from his father at the bar, Evan started to smoke pot more. Given its abundant availability and his job, convincing himself to do it wasn't too difficult. Murph was satisfied with his decision as well. It helped to even him out and give some much-needed relief mentally. He noticed that the nightmares decreased or weren't as severe and it also helped him to think rationally about his upcoming trip. When he called his father back and told him he would fly out, the voice on the other end was elated and confessed how he didn't expect Evan to accept the invite. Evan made it clear though that he had to work on Wednesday, so he wouldn't be out there until Thanksgiving morning with plans to fly back home that night. The voice agreed to his terms.

That was two weeks ago.

In a more present time, he was pulling into the neighborhood. He parked three blocks away from the condo and started his walk over. He used the extra time to unnecessarily contemplate about life.

His father's condo was situated between several others, giving it a feeling like Grimmauld's Place from *Harry Potter*. Nothing about it seemed out of place or extraordinary, just a dull looking chunk of land for someone to rest their head each night.

Evan rang the doorbell and the sound of footsteps stomped down the hall.

His heartbeat spiked. He glanced back beyond him. He still had a couple seconds to run for it. No one would have given him a—

The door opened with one of the hinges giving a loud squeal.

"Hi, Evan. You look—well, you look grown up," his father said.

"Yeah."

"Come in, please."

Evan stepped inside and dropped the bag he was carrying. There was nothing vital inside, but he felt weird walking to the door empty-handed.

"Who else is coming today?" It was something Evan hadn't thought to ask beforehand.

"My wife is here and two of her kids are joining. I hope that's okay."

"It is."

"Can I get you anything?"

Ignoring his question, Evan asked, "Is this awkward for you too? It shouldn't be awkward to see your father, but it's been . . . it's been a long time to put it mildly."

He stared back at his father, waiting for the answer.

Evan was slightly ashamed for the majority of his life that he was named after his father. The *Jr.* that most people would have expected to be attached to his name was never included on his birth certificate, which made it easy to never tell anyone about it. He had always found it selfish of parents to name their child after someone else. It seemed as if their future was predetermined for them based on what that individual had done. They would always live in the shadow of another. Evan's future likely won't be wrought with alcohol abuse and other qualifiers for destructive relationships, so he could rest easy at night. Instead, he would be plagued with nightmares and regrets and feelings of displacement and the constant tug of sadness, which essentially made him about as fucked up as a "normal" person.

"This is awkward for me too. I think all we can do is just sit down and talk. We both know there is a lot to go through."

"Okay."

Evan followed his father into the kitchen. A brunette woman was hunched over at the island peeling potatoes.

"Oh my goodness! You must be Evan because you don't look like any of my kids!" she laughed like an engine revving.

"Do you need any help?" he asked.

"Going light on everything this year, so I should be fine. Your father did most of the work already. I'm just doing the potatoes since he has a knack for cutting himself, don'tcha hun?"

"It's true," his father said with a shrug. "Shirley, you didn't even introduce yourself."

"Oh my goodness," she said, each syllable was stretched out in her midwestern drawl. She dropped the potato onto the counter and extended a hand. "I'm Shirley. Nice to meet you."

Evan walked over. "It's nice to meet you too."

"Hey Ev," she called out to her husband. "What should we call you for today? What a silly question, huh?!?" She cackled at her question, but Evan didn't find much humor in it. He was still overloaded by the situation. "I just don't want you two to be staring up each time someone calls out Evan."

"You can call me Ethan," our Evan said. He had never used his middle name before, but it would be nice to separate himself from Work Evan and Son Evan and Friend Evan and all the other instances where his name was a defining characteristic. Was he overthinking this? Absolutely, but let him have his moment.

"O-okay," his father said with a slight smile.

Shirley gave a wide grin to show her approval. She resumed her potato peeling, which was a subtle hint for the other two to go somewhere else.

Ethan followed his father into the dining room.

"Where should we start?" his father asked.

"What do you do? I know practically nothing about you. Mom hasn't told me anything."

He gave a long sigh. "Your mother and I should have never been together. The military was tough for us with the constant moving. When you add kids to that, it complicates—" his father stopped and stared at the wall. He eventually refocused his attention on Ethan. "Look, I can sit here and apologize to you for the way I was and the failed relationship I have had with you, but it'll sound hallow. It'll be that *too little too late* type of deal, so I will spare you from that. You must know how deeply I regret my actions. Each day I wake up and realize I keep moving further away from that time in my life and I should be happy about it. I should also be happy that those memories are becoming foggier. There's probably an absurd amount I don't remember because of the drinking. But the thing is," he leaned in closer and lowered his voice so it could barely be heard over the thumping of the Christmas music Shirley had going, "I am far from happy. I love my wife and the life I have stumbled into now, but the guilt—the deep, endless pit—keeps gnawing away at me. I can't move past it. I'm not looking for sympathy from you. That would be a shitty thing for me to ask. I guess the reason I told you that is . . . I . . . I don't why. It's just the guilt resurfacing I suppose."

"It's okay," Ethan said. What else could he say?

"I love you three so much. Even though your mother and I didn't work out, as you could imagine, I don't regret the joy of being a dad. Not a very good one, but . . ." he trailed off.

"It's fine. How did you end up in Greenville?"

"There's likely a long story, but I have forgotten most of it. I doubt it's very exciting anyways."

"I lived twenty minutes away from here during my last year of college. It's strange to think about how close you were. Of all places to end up, you know?"

"I knew you were out here. Your sister kept me informed. It was foolish of her, but she was the only one that stayed in contact with me before and after rehab. I understand you two aren't close, but you know how she is. She told me many details about you, so in a sense, I watched you grow up from afar. I drove by the house once or twice. It seemed so intrusive to even get that close to you when you made it clear how you felt, but I couldn't stop myself. I was sorry to hear about your breakup with him. I guess you have moved around a lot since then, huh?"

"I have," Ethan said.

Ethan always assumed his father knew about him being gay and was happy to see it was a nonissue. There wasn't anything more to say about the topic than that.

"How long have you been sober?" Ethan asked.

His father clasped his hands together on the table and brought them up to his chin. "Eight years. I know it right down to the day." His hesitation was noticeable even though there was confidence in his answer.

"What changed?"

Another long sigh. "You'd think getting a divorce and effectively losing my kids would have been the kick in the ass I needed, but that just sent me down deeper. I dabbled with drugs for a bit until I recognized how those would kill me faster than the alcohol. That's the thing about alcohol: it's a slow death. Yeah, you risk the chance of an accident or if you're dumb enough to drive drunk . . . what I'm trying to say is that you start to decay. Your body is greedy and wants more of it and your brain is messed up enough to rationalize the need. You continue this endless loop until someone rips you from it. One night, I found myself walking on a bridge and I just stopped. I had probably finished a bottle of vodka by that point, so I was feeling it. I looked around me and realized how alone I was. There was no one to save me, to tell me I was wasting my life. It's not like I would have listened anyways. I walked over to the edge and wondered what was down below. I don't exactly recall what happened next, but I woke up in a hospital days later. I had fallen off the bridge and onto the road below. Destroyed most of my body. Took me a year to piece myself back together. Shirley was one of the nurses. She, uh, she ripped me from it. She knew a better person was in there waiting to be released. I mean, there's more to the story than that, but I don't like to talk about it too much."

"I understand," Ethan said with no emotion. He suppressed any shock at not knowing how his dad almost died. "Do you miss it?"

"Everyday."

"Why did you call me that day? What changed?"

"When you were a kid, you asked so many questions. They always started with why. Why this or why that. It frustrated me so much. I never had patience with you three. Your mom bought you a book that had all these answers and it made you stop asking questions. I sometimes wonder if we stifled any of your creativity by giving you a book instead of listening and answering. I read a lot more these days and found myself at the bookstore, looking for nothing in particular. Propped up in one of the sections was this book called *The Giant Book of Why: Everything You Need to Know* . . . or something like that. I immediately thought of you. I picked it up and skimmed through it for a while. All these emotions came back to me. That night, I talked with Shirley. I wanted to respect where you stood with our relationship, but I also wanted to fight to get my son back. Your brother has lost his way and I'm not sure we will ever get him back on the right track, so it killed me to think I would never be close with either of my sons. Shirley was supportive and suggested I call and invite you for Thanksgiving. More neutral setting, she said. She also told me to respect your decision and understand that your life has moved on from me being a part of it. That hurt to hear, but of course I knew it was true. I've had your number for years and just never knew what to say. I guess I just got tired of being scared of my own son and the potential idea you wouldn't want anything to do with me."

Ethan sat back in the chair. He couldn't find the words to respond. He continued to process everything his father said.

"I'm going to see if Shirley needs anything," his father continued. He got up from the table and disappeared into the kitchen.

Ethan was still sitting and staring out the window when the doorbell rang, signaling the arrival of the rest of the dinner party.

Introductions were made ("This is Ev—Ethan!" Shirley said excitedly) and soon dinner was spread out across the table. It was a modest feast that everyone enjoyed.

Ethan waited.

He waited for the reason not to stay in contact with his father after today. He was anticipating his father to snap and the yelling to spew from him. It didn't happen though. Ethan watched as his father laughed throughout dinner, told stories about the random things that happened at work, and urged Ethan to tell everyone how Denver was. He waited for his father to open up a liquor cabinet and pour himself a drink and start down the avenue of becoming the belligerent drunk he once was. It didn't happen though.

It struck Ethan that maybe people could change, or as Vincent would have said, that they could get better.

Several hours later, Ethan gathered himself and said his goodbyes.

"I love you so much," his father said as they hugged.

"I know. This is going to take time, but we will get there. I love you too, dad."

Later on, the flight back home was virtually empty. He sat in an aisle seat and looked toward the darkness outside. He wondered about many things. He eventually settled into thinking about how he had finally gotten his dad back.

Ethan took an introductory accounting class back during his undergrad. He struggled to understand some of the concepts, but there was one that stuck out to him: the idea of debits and credits. If you add something, you must subtract the same amount to even it out. Simple, right?

For him, it felt like he had been gaining more than losing recently. He appeared to have gained a relationship with his father and made several friends quite quickly in Denver. On the flip side, he kept moving around the country to sate a feeling of . . . well, he wasn't entirely sure about that. He had effectively lost Vincent, which—not to harp on it too much—continued to bother him every day even though he didn't like the idea of one person having that much influence over him.

He leaned his head back and listened to the rumble of the engine as he continued to soar above it all.

Give it time, he thought. *It'll balance out in the end.*

nine

HOMEWARD BOUND

Ann left work early to escape the nonsensical rambles of Boob and his constant dour outlook about the business, but more importantly, she left to go pick up Vincent!

The commute was a winding route down the turnpike and skirting around the fringes of Philadelphia to get to the airport. It wasn't an enjoyable ride.

The first breakdown happened when a truck forced its way into her lane and scraped the side of her car. It sped off before she could look at the license plate. Ann choked back the anger, but it boiled over when the exit she always took for the airport was closed for construction. The GPS struggled to update as she cruised by her normal route. By that point, Vincent's flight had landed, and he was making his way to the pickup area. Ann did not thrive in situations beyond her control. She was having a full-blown explosion of frustration and tears by the time Vincent called asking where she was.

"Vin, I don't know where I am. There was construction and now I'm driving around. The GPS won't update!" she yelled into the phone.

Vincent responded with almost as much frustration as Ann.

She hung up the phone in a hurry and continued to hurl profanities.

As it would happen, Ann miraculously made it to the Arrivals section of Philadelphia International Airport ten minutes later. All of the frustration she released seemed trivial, which was almost usually the case for her.

She pulled up to Terminal E and found the Southwest area. Standing with minimal concern for his surroundings was Vincent. He looked the same as when she'd last seen him at the wedding.

Her heartbeat spiked at having her son back home for a week. She wished it was longer. She wished he lived on the East Coast or at least within driving distance instead of the 22-hour bullshit drive to Dallas. She wished he was at least happy.

But something told her he wasn't.

What she didn't know is that Vincent had never been happy. That true, no qualms about it sort of happiness that people sometimes find, but he wasn't one of them. In a sense though, isn't being unhappy all the time his own slice of happiness? He had learned to lean into it and soak up the darkness. From an outsider's perspective, he did a convincing job of selling a pallet of goods that made it seem like he was satisfied. He laughed through most of his days and listened intently to others. He went through all the correct motions to pull off his con. Evan had seen through the façade and Ann did too if she thought hard enough about it. The cracks in the foundation were evident, but irreparable.

Vincent opened the door and said, "There are black marks all over the side of the car."

"Some *asshole* hit me. This has been a miserable ride," she muttered.

"Are you okay?"

"Yes. I just want to get home."

"Let me drive then."

Ann looked over, considered the demand, and exited the driver's seat.

Five minutes later, they were on the highway and away from the madness of the airport. Ann attempted to leave behind the frustration from the drive.

"You look great," Ann said. It was her customary first comment whenever she hadn't seen Vin in a while.

"Thanks. Same as always, I suspect. Probably put on a few pounds since the wedding with the whole breakup and everything," he responded.

"How's everything going with you two?" she asked, feeling compelled to inquire about the carrot he dangled in front of her.

"We don't talk much."

"Are you upset about that?"

"I was, but enough time has passed now that it's foolish to still be upset. I have other things to worry about or at least occupy my time with."

"How is everything else going then?"

"It's fine." He was a good liar but tended to stick with the same verbiage whenever he did.

"I hate when you say that," Ann said, moving her gaze to the passing traffic outside. They merged onto I-476, which would be the majority of their drive back to Easton.

"I'm sure you'd love to hear the inner workings of what I do at Southwest, but since it doesn't excite me, I doubt the details will excite you either."

"Okay . . . you can talk to me about anything though."

"I know," he said. He was focused on the road. Vincent never enjoyed driving at night.

"We need to start planning our trip for next year. I love the idea of a national park. They can get crowded, so we have to go at the right time. There's . . . Yellowstone and . . . Glacier . . . oh . . . what about Yosemite?

67

We could stay in San Francisco. You know how much your dad and I loved going out there."

"Seems like you already know where we should go. I'm down for whatever, assuming I don't have to plan for anything more than the flights. Just tell me when and I'll be there."

"Sometime in March of April. I'll have to make sure I can get the time off at work," she was telling herself more than Vincent.

"Any luck with finding another job closer to home?" he asked.

Vincent was hyper aware of Ann's current distaste of her job and the half-baked effort she was putting into finding another one. He also knew the neighborhood gossip, the happenings within the extended family, the current status of Ann's relationship with Leigh, and, even sometimes, Ann and Jim's financial future. Ann shared various details with him during their weekly calls. It was therapeutic for her to tell someone.

"No luck yet," she said.

"If you are serious about this, then you need to be applying constantly."

"I know. It's been busy with Christmas, so I'll start it back up again after New Year's."

Vincent didn't respond. The music hit a melodic groove and occupied the dead space between them.

Ann either had to keep talking or she would begin to worry about something. An idea would carve itself into her head and expand for the remainder of the ride home. The next week with Vincent home needed to be relaxing, so she elected to keep the worries away.

"Leigh is all settled into the apartment. Now she is asking your father to build furniture for them. She hasn't even started to pay back the loan we gave them for their honeymoon. Of course, he is going to do it . . . I just don't understand."

"Mom, I don't know what to tell you."

"It's not your concern, I suppose."

"It seems to be since you tell me things like this all the time."

"You're right. I shouldn't be saying anything."

"I don't have the answer for you on how to fix it. You two need to figure that out together. With me so far away, it would be foolish for you two not to be close."

"Let's talk about something else," she said, waving a hand to dismiss the topic.

The struggle of her relationship with Leigh occupied her thoughts often enough that it was becoming a daily hinderance, but the notion of confronting it directly was difficult. Instead, she agreed to let it linger in the shadows and control her from a distance.

"What would you do if I died?"

"Vin!"

"I'm serious."

"Why would you ask me that?"

"Because I want to know," he said.

"It's not something I intend to think about."

"Fine, but it seems unfair since I have to think about what it would be like to lose you and dad."

"That's the way it goes though."

"Says who?"

"What do you mean? It's common that a child has to see their parents die. In a way, that's life."

"Born to die. What a depressing thought," he said.

"Why would you ask me that?" she repeated.

"Just curious. You'd be surprised with the questions in my head."

"Vin, is everything okay?"

"Oh yeah. I expect to be around until I'm at least thirty," he said with a toothless grin.

"That's not funny."

"I wasn't trying to be, but I do have a somewhat funny story to share."

"Okay," Ann said. She was distressed by this and needed it to move on.

Vincent told a story about a guy on his flight that sat across the aisle from him. He was a burly man and struggled to get comfortable. At some point, his wife (even more burly than he was) boarded the plane and plopped down next to him. They talked about the things burly men and women do (cutting down trees, hunting squirrels, reading picture books, and condemning the federal government for not doing a *got dam* thing about so and so or such and such) and Vincent overheard the entire thing. Normally he would be sitting in the window seat and staring out into the void, but something compelled him to grab an aisle seat. Seize the moment or something silly like that. The plane took off after the rambles from the flight attendants that no one listened to and as they reached cruising altitude, the burly man beside him took off his shoes, which looked like concrete slabs ripped from the foundation of a building. Vincent expected an atrocious smell like all those times he passed the mushroom farm on his way to baseball games as a kid, but the odor never came. Instead, the burly man grabbed his foot and hiked it up onto his other knee. That leg pushed into the unoccupied seat in front of him. Vincent squirmed as he could feel the discomfort from across the aisle.

Ann listened, but failed to see what was funny about the story so far. She voiced her confusion.

"Hold on," Vincent said. "This story requires patience."

With the man in the ready position, his wife removed the nail clippers from the satchel she carried and began to hack away at his massive toenails.

"Oh c'mon. That did not happen," Ann cut in again.

"I do not tell lies," Vincent said, throwing his hands up in a fake surrender.

As the burly woman smiled and trimmed down her husband's nails, she scooped up each one and placed it into a vial that was propped up in-between her legs. She caught Vincent staring and yelled across the aisle, "He has the best toenails. I've seen some nasty ones in my day, but his are too perfect to go to waste. I'm going to create the next Moaning Lisa with them." Vincent nodded and chastised himself for having a wandering eye. Once the nail clipping was complete (important to note: she only did the one foot, commenting that the other one wasn't ripe enough yet), she leaned down to suck on his digits like a newborn drawn to their mother's breast. Vincent's wandering eye glimpsed most of the event. Like a train wreck, he had trouble looking away. When finished, the woman sat back up in her seat and wiped her mouth as if she just polished off a steak dinner.

"That was not funny. At all!" Ann said.

"Yeah. I lied about it being funny, but I needed someone else to be stuck with the same images I am."

Ann smiled, but refused to laugh.

Of course, the story was a complete lie. It was Vincent's specialty. What the lie did achieve was that Ann no longer wondered about why he would make a comment about only being around until he was thirty. Vincent had a habit of saying troubling things that were masked by the flood of monologues that would follow. He threw people off his path. And when he said troubling things without the monologues, nobody seemed concerned enough to inquire more.

They pulled onto Cornwallis Drive. The Christmas season was evident in the ways it had been and would always continue to be.

Ann watched as Vincent went into the house and was mauled by the three dogs. He collapsed to the floor and let them overtake him.

Her heart was full. Her son was home.

Everything was as it should be.

Everything was better.

ten

SHARP EDGES

"What are we doing?" Evan asked.

Murph inhaled the pot smoke that billowed up in the bong and gave an excruciating exhale after several seconds. Her eyes stumbled around before refocusing on Evan.

"Sorry, what did you say? I was preoccupied," she said, reaching down to pet Sasquatch.

Annoyance passed over Evan's face as he repeated, "What are we doing?"

"As I see it, I am sitting here getting as high as a space opera and you are sitting there being a little ninny."

"A ninny?"

"Yes. I watch British television sometimes. They have the best insults. All we have here are shitface, cunt (which is more of an Australian thing—giving credit where its due), moron, doofus—"

"Murph. Please," Evan said.

"Okay, fine. What are we doing? I . . . I have no idea. Why don't you tell me?"

"I'm tired of coming over here and smoking pot every night."

"We can go over to your place and smoke," she suggested.

"That's not what I mean. I didn't move here to be stagnant. This was supposed to be the next step in my life, the place where everything would finally make sense and I . . ." He wasn't sure how to finish the thought.

"You're being dumb. You have been here for two—almost—three months and from what I've seen, they have been rather successful."

"How so?"

"Let's see . . . you met me! We hang out with each other every day and still manage to be friends. I think Elliot is starting to get jealous. And . . . you are kicking ass at the job. In my humble opinion of course. You have a newfound relationship with your dad! Who would have expected that? Seems like your life is pretty sweet right now." Murph leaned back into the couch and tried to burrow herself in-between the cushions.

Evan hadn't spoken much to his dad since they met up on Thanksgiving. They weren't at the point where weekly conversations made sense.

"I expected more. I left a lot behind in Dallas."

"I'm sorry, but you didn't," Murph stressed. "You left behind an ex that you won't even talk to me about. That's it. You lived there less than a year."

Evan didn't respond.

"Do you want to go to It? Maybe a few drinks will help to unburden you from this . . . this burden you have. We won't even have to pay if Franco is working. And Franco is always working. Goodness, sometimes I think that man doesn't leave the bar," Murph said.

"No. My mom is coming tomorrow for Christmas and I need to clean up the apartment."

"Fuck. I need to pack. First Christmas without my dad. That's going to be a real motherfucker, isn't it?"

"Probably," Evan said.

"Let's hope you don't go through that anytime soon."

"I'll cross my fingers."

"Well, I'm too high to function. This is upsetting."

"Are you good if I head out?" Evan asked.

"Oh yeah. Yeah. I'll be fine. I'm just going to melt here for a bit. Come give me a hug."

Evan got up and obliged her command.

"I'll see you soon," Murph said. "Keep an eye out for somewhere to go on New Year's. You're much more of a planner than I am."

"Will do. Get home safe."

"But I'm already home . . ."

"You know what I mean."

Evan left the apartment and during the short walk to his, thought about how he wished he was going back to Dallas to visit the friends he never made or see the boyfriend that was nothing more than an ex he never communicated with. It was a great reminder of why he left. You'd think Vincent was the one who broke up with Evan considering how often he thinks of him.

Izzie paraded around the apartment upon Evan's return. She spun in circles as her eyes bulged out like a guy choking on a mozzarella stick at a restaurant.

He gave her all the attention her poor soul needed until she wandered off to some other portion of the apartment.

It's not like she had many places to hide. The apartment was a similar layout to the one in Dallas, except this time he had a true bedroom where he could close himself off from anyone else in the apartment. Given his extreme lack of visitors, he hadn't been able to practice this tactic, but that would change with the arrival of his mom in the morning. While he loved her deeply, he knew there would be a point during her stay where closing the door to his room would be the simplest option to avoid any blooming frustration with her.

Evan told Murph that he needed to clean, but as he surveyed the apartment, everything was mostly in order. He scooped up the few dishes that laid in the sink and placed them in the dishwasher. He folded up the blankets that were scattered across the couch and straightened the presents under the Christmas tree. Evan told himself that soon he would be in a house where he could properly decorate and make the space his own, but when would that be? His constant moving negated any effort to make a city his home. For now, the tiny tree in the corner wrapped in the multi-colored strands of lights would have to do.

He moved into the bathroom and pretended to tidy up as if there was somebody watching him. In one of the drawers of the vanity were the razor blades. They sat without a purpose next to the floss Evan didn't use and the bottles of pills to cure numerous ailments. He picked up one of the razor blades and examined it. Several specks of blood were crusted onto the edge. He tried to remember the last time he used one.

See:

The problem with cutting yourself, at least Evan thought, was that you had trouble remembering afterward why you did it in the first place. The euphoric release as the blade ripped open the skin was enough to make you forget. It was enough to ease you into the false notion that everything would be okay, that there wouldn't be a need to do it again. And yet, there they were. Not just one, but four different blades. It's amazing how cheap they were at any hardware store.

Evan put the razor blade down and checked his arms. The scars that once laced them were now a faded memory. He understood how to be discrete and made shallow cuts there. What concerned him more was the area where he hadn't been careful. It felt strange that he saw himself naked every day, but never took the time to notice any of the potential scars that graced his body. To him, it wasn't abnormal. It was a way to cope.

With his pants off, he sat on the toilet and checked the inside of his legs. The scars there were high enough to be covered by most boxers (unless he was wearing something skimpy!) but they were apparent. Twelve horizontal slices on each side. They sat evenly spaced, creating a mosaic. They were deeper than the ones on his arms and all were beyond being scabbed over.

That was a good sign.

He put his pants back on and grabbed the four razor blades from the vanity. He didn't need them hanging around in the apartment, especially with his mom visiting. They were a reminder of a time he couldn't even recall anymore. And yet, he brought them with him from Dallas.

He dropped them into the toilet. It took several attempts to get them properly flushed.

"That wasn't the best idea," he said.

In any case, they were gone.

It was another step forward to distance himself from any former semblance of who he was. The past was the past or some cliché shit like that. People may mistake his cutting problem as him being weak, but he understood it differently. Evan believed it came during a time where everything about his life was inward facing—his thoughts, needs, wants. He kept all the information bottled up inside and the cutting became a way to exhale.

He returned to the living room and put on *Golden Girls*. He had watched the series so many times that he had to stop himself from repeating many of the lines. He started the episode where Rose was addicted to her medication.

Everybody has a vice, Evan told himself.

His dad was a reformed alcoholic, which was nice to consider how some vices could be overcome.

His mom was hellbent on always being in a relationship and turning any serious ones into marriage.

Other people ran through his head as he tried to determine what their vice was. Eventually, when the thought turned to him, he didn't find the game as much fun.

Evan's vice was still manifesting.

He fell asleep before the episode ended, never getting to see how Rose overcame her problem for the fiftieth time.

Evan woke up the next morning around the time his mother was beginning her descent into Denver. He shook himself awake and made himself look presentable. The next three days were going to be a chore, but it was better than spending the holiday alone.

eleven

MIDNIGHT

Ann dropped her son off at the airport and cried for the first twenty minutes of the ride home. It was better than the day she and Jim unloaded Vincent's stuff into the college dorm at Temple for the first time. She cried the entire way back then. It was also an improvement from the time they began their drive back home from Dallas. She recalled crying for several hours straight that instance.

It came down to not enjoying seeing her son go. Ann suspected she wasn't the only mother who felt that way.

Once she composed herself, she considered how the week had gone. In her mind, it was another successful Christmas. The kids seemed happy with their gifts and there were no big blowouts, which was a miracle. Leigh was diplomatic and even upbeat during the times she was up at the house, but it was likely due to Lorenzo being nearby. Vincent looked preoccupied for most of the week, but Ann attributed it to her sense of worry and overanalyzing any situation, so she hadn't bothered to ask Vincent about it.

It was a stark difference from the year before when she had spoken to Jim about Vincent's sexuality and the tension in the household grew to an uncomfortable size. She didn't miss those days and was thankful everyone had moved past that. She had enough conversations with friends and family about how Vincent was gay to last her three lifetimes, but as his mother, she decided it was her prerogative to be his press secretary and let everyone know. The conversations were unnatural at first, as if she was talking about a historical figure or a man that passed by her on the street. It wasn't until Ann told Colleen that she finally felt at ease with telling other people. There was something about confiding in a friend that had lost so much that seemed to put everything into perspective. It made sense why Vincent didn't want to be a martyr or looked upon as someone in need, because there were people who actually needed the sympathy. How could Ann have ever looked at Colleen and told her how her son was gay with tears streaking down her face when Colleen lost her husband for no reason? It clicked with Ann that Vincent was no different from the rest.

If anything, she loved him more, which seemed impossible.

The rest of the drive back to Easton was uneventful as most things were in life.

Once home, Ann perused through the channels and stopped at *Golden Girls*. She hadn't watched the show in years, but it was the episode where Rena . . . no, Reilly . . . Rose, definitely Rose (her memory was still able to recall useless information on occasion) was addicted to her medication.

◊ ◊ ◊

A normal New Year's Eve for Ann and Jim consisted of claims they would stay awake until the ball dropped, but they hadn't since Vincent was in high school. Each year, their snores could be heard over the distant boom of the fireworks being set off somewhere in the neighborhood.

Their plans for the current year consisted of the same proclamations except they had dinner plans with Colleen and her fiancé. It was a last minute, cobbled together plan that Ann had to drag Jim to considering his disdain toward most social encounters.

They went to a mid-level steak restaurant that served their dishes with the elegance of a fast food chain.

Colleen and her fiancé, Stuart, were recently retired and enjoying their expansive free time. Colleen had worked at a bank and Stuart was the police chief for the town over.

The meal carried on into the night. Stuart shared his stories from the job in random bursts. Colleen spoke of the beach house they bought down in Ocean City and the boat Stuart was pleading to get.

"He wants this . . . what is it? Twenty-footer? I don't understand how boats work," Colleen confessed.

"Actually, it is a twenty-five-foot boat." Stuart said.

"In any case, he has been begging me for months and saying how I'm going to love being out on the water. Jim, would you ever get a boat? Please talk some sense into him."

Jim shrugged as he chewed on a piece of steak.

"You're no help!" Colleen said.

"Honey, I'm just trying to lay all the cards on the table now. You have time to back out of our arrangement if you want," Stuart said with a grin. "Anyways, I need a boat to get away from the madness in this country."

Nervous laughter trickled throughout the table.

"You can have your boat if you promise to take me to Italy. Bryan always promised he would after he retired from the CIA," Colleen said.

A steady silence overtook the table and the entire restaurant. To hear his name out loud was still a jab to Ann. A misplaced sense of dread filled her as if mentioning the name was taboo. Colleen continued on with her meal, hiding the twitch at the corner of her mouth, which was how the grief for her late husband now manifested.

"I'm sorry. I didn't mean to sour the mood," Colleen continued.

"You didn't, honey. We all miss him too," Stuart said, squeezing her hand.

Ann and Jim nodded from across the table. There was nothing for them to say.

"Did, uh, did I ever tell you guys the story of the tweaker who stole the police car and crashed it into the strip club? No! Oh man, it's a great one . . ."

Ann and Jim listened. Their brief contributions to the conversation came in the form of clarifying questions. They didn't have exciting details to share about their lives or plans once they reached retirement. It seemed so foreign to find themselves in that place where money wasn't a worry and leaving their home in Pennsylvania for long stretches of time wasn't burdensome.

It made sense why a majority of Ann's thoughts centered around Vincent and Leigh. She wanted them to retire at a healthy age and live comfortably. She wanted . . .

Her wants could go on for quite some time.

Still, Ann and Jim enjoyed themselves. They laughed more than did during a normal week and it was a pleasant reminder of how close their friends were to them, physically and socially.

Dinner ended after Stuart cried out that two desserts would be plenty.

○ ○ ○

Back at home, Ann and Jim settled into the couch and watched the coverage from Times Square. The weight of dinner came into full effect as Jim was asleep within twenty minutes. Ann fought the urge to drift off.

Forty minutes until midnight.

Ann focused on the television and the sweeping shots of the crowd who had been standing outside in the steady rain for the entire day. She wondered why being there was any more enjoyable than being snuggled up next to her snoring husband.

The lights from the ever-blinking strand on the Christmas tree casted her shadow out across the room and highlighted the sleeping forms of the three dogs, who managed to snore almost in sync with Jim.

Thirty minutes until midnight.

What would the new year have in store for her? It was impossible to know, of course. She wasn't one of the lucky people that scammed others for claiming to have the gift of sight. Ann had to rely on her own intelligence and determination to carry her through life. Maybe she would have a new job, finally freeing herself from the solitude of that place. Maybe she would lose those last ten pounds, which proved to be the most stubborn. Maybe. That was a stubborn word in its own right. A word that people counted on when indecision was the simplest choice.

Predicting the future was about as useful as reminiscing about the past, so she did a bit of that too.

The year had been kind to her. Leigh's wedding happened without the slightest issue. Her and Vincent's relationship was stronger than ever. She even got to meet his boyfriend, though that proved to not be such a pleasant weekend in Austin.

Fuck, her entire existence did revolve around her children. Has it become an obvious theme at this point?

Twenty minutes until midnight.

Ann was asleep.

Ten minutes until midnight.

Rigby lifted her head up off the dog bed, scanned the room, and fell back asleep.

Five minutes.

The television continued to blare with excited screams and an intense desire for a fresh start.

One minute.

The fireworks started.

Five seconds.

Ann's phone lit up on the table beside her.

Four seconds.

It was a text from Vincent.

Three.

It read: "Happy New Year's from Texas! Love you!"

Two.

One.

The time on the phone changed to midnight before snapping to black.

○ ○ ○

Ann responded back the next morning to Vincent and the other texts that piled in throughout the night. At some point, she meandered upstairs to bed with the dogs following her as if she was the mother duckling leading them to water. She slept straight through the night, which was rare considering her bladder started screaming after several hours.

Once she picked herself out of bed, she went through the same motions as any other day.

Downstairs, Jim was at the kitchen table doing one of his crossword puzzles. He was a certified wizard at them and completed half a dozen on a morning when he wasn't working.

"Good morning," Ann called from down the hall.

No response.

She moved closer, the dogs racing by her and heading right to the door to be let out. She noticed the issue: Jim had his headphones in. Ann tapped him on the shoulder, which prompted him to remove the left earbud.

"Hi," she said like a teenager on a first date.

"Happy New Year," Jim said, repeating the customary phrase uttered by millions that day.

"Can you help me take down the Christmas decorations today?"

"I suppose."

"A majority of the tree is filled with the Hallmark ornaments you *had to have*. Anyways, I don't think you'd want me packing those up. I'll just bend the boxes . . . and maybe on purpose."

"This is true," he said, still concentrating on the crossword at hand.

In a movie, this would be the point where Ann starts to walk away, and Jim asks her some variation of the question *What's a [number] letter word for [some stupid thing no one cares about]?* Jim never asks for help with the crosswords though since he knows every answer.

Instead, Ann took care of the dogs and began to bring up the boxes from the basement. She laid them out on the kitchen table and disassembled the stacks of smaller boxes from inside. They were piled high on the kitchen island by the time Jim dislodged himself from the crosswords and joined in.

At some point, the house phone rang.

"That never happens," she pointed out to Jim as she walked over to get it. He just shrugged as he picked up one of the completed boxes and moved to the basement stairs.

Ann tried to quell the dogs as best she could, but they were howling at the phone. It was a nice trick Vincent had taught them a while back.

"Hello?" she answered.

The voice mumbled a question.

"Yes," Ann responded.

More words from the voice.

"Just say it. Just fucking say it," she yelled into the phone.

She started to shake as the voice continued. She felt herself lose control. Every emotion she ever suffered from crashed into each other.

The voice asked if she was okay.

Ann brought the phone away from her ear and threw it directly into the television. The phone exploded into numerous pieces of plastic and wiring. The dogs scattered, running as quickly as they could for whatever quiet place they could find.

She screamed. She continued to scream as she collapsed to the floor. What else was there do to?

Ann didn't hear Jim race up the steps to see what was wrong.

Ann didn't feel him shake her and repeat the same words again and again.

What happened?

What happened?

What happened?

twelve

MUCK AND GRIME

It was five minutes to midnight, but let's rewind several hours.

Evan's New Year's Eve turned into a wild spiral of events. He did his due diligence and found a respectable spot for him, Murph, and Elliot to crash for the evening. The cover charge was only $30, which was beyond moderate considering the occasion.

The plans shifted when Murph demanded the pre-game at her apartment wasn't adequate enough and how they needed to make a pitstop at It.

"But why?" Evan asked.

"Follow it. That's why."

"Okay. Elliot, are you good with the change of plans?"

"The lady speaks. Do we have much say in the matter?" Elliot said.

Murph shot him a menacing glance.

"Let me amend my last statement: Murph, that was a wonderful idea and we would be foolish not to *follow* your suggestion," Elliot retried.

"I'll grab my coat and we can go!" Murph said.

Evan wished he was wearing several coats as he stepped outside the apartment building and felt the rush of air plunge into his face. The massive snowstorm from earlier in the week graced the city with seven inches, which was more than Evan ever enjoyed handling, thank you very much. The remnants of the snow were piled high on the sidewalks and turning a murky gray color as the trio maneuvered to the bar.

Franco had enlisted their help a month back to scrounge up all the ugly yellow flyers that remained around the downtown area. Naturally, he couldn't recall where half of them were, but their job turned out to be wasted effort as they were only able to recover two. The rest were taken care of by some unseen force. Franco had deemed the experiment a mild failure on account of their business staying flat in terms of clientele and money, but he was appreciative of making three new friends. Of course, they had yet to see him outside the bar, and when questioned about it, Franco admitted to having an air mattress under the bar. It took Murph several minutes of explaining to Elliot that Franco was only being sarcastic and how he likely had a wonderful apartment or home or some sort of residence he slept at.

They had the path memorized to It even without the flyers and after fifteen minutes of navigating the growing crowds filling the sidewalks, they entered the bar.

The patrons were sparse as the only song anyone knew by Joan Jett thumped from the jukebox. The few who were listening to the music swayed in a drunken way and made it clear they couldn't follow the beat whatsoever.

Evan, Murph, and Elliot took up residence in their normal corner of the bar. Like any reputable sitcom, our three leads had their seats and continued to adhere to the script provided by the audience that watched from afar.

"The trio of doom! Happy New Year's Eve to you all," Franco said as he approached them.

"Fran, my man. Can you hook us up with something light and fluffy? I need to make it to at least midnight, and if I stop drinking now, I will fall face first into this bar top and snore until the morning light," Murph said.

Elliot shook his head in agreement.

"I know what you need," Franco said. He disappeared back to the dimly lit section of the bar and began to work with the three glasses he pulled out of his magician's hat.

He returned two minutes later.

"Will three vodka Red Bulls do the trick?" he asked.

"It's a safe choice. I expected something ballsier from you Fran, but we will accept your gifts with grace and gratitude," Murph said with a mutated curtsey from her seated position.

"You never fail to entertain me, Murph. So," Franco continued, "where are you three heading tonight? I'm sure you don't want to see my balls drop in here at midnight."

"You are correct," Elliot said.

"We are going to Howl at the Moon," Evan said. "Not the most glamourous choice, but it was cheap for whatever reason."

"Do you not know what happened there a month ago?" Franco asked.

"No."

"Someone took a shit on a table and flung it out into the crowd. The bar has been shut down since then. Tonight is the grand reopening. There have been murmurs that the turd tosser may strike again."

"They forgot to mention that on their website when I looked them up," Evan said.

"You don't really think the fecal flinger will show up again, do you?"

Murph asked.

"No, of course not. They put the poo pelter in jail for the next six months. They caught him brown handed, so to speak," Franco said.

"Thank you for the imagery," Elliot said.

Evan looked over at Franco and asked, "What are your plans for the night?"

"Oh c'mon. What do you think? The captain always goes down with the ship."

"Come out with us," the trio said.

"No. I can't."

"Sure you can. Just kick out the few drunks over there and you're in the clear," Murph said.

Franco's face distorted in thought. He looked at the people scattered amongst the tables and seemed to have made up his mind. He stepped from behind the bar and approached each one. The conversations lasted mere seconds, but when he was finished with the last person, they had all moved toward the exit.

When we came back over to the bar, Elliot asked, "Are you some drunk whisperer or something?"

"Something like that. Give me ten minutes to clean up here. I hope you don't mind if I go dressed in my work clothes."

"As long as you have a jacket, you will be fine," Evan said.

After cheering him on for ten minutes, Franco finished behind the bar and proclaimed the rest could be dealt with later. (He had refused help from our three friends or else it may have gone faster.)

"One last thing!" Franco yelled out and ran back behind the bar. He poured out four double shots and handed them out to the group.

"To another year in paradise," he proclaimed.

"Cheers!"

"Okay, leave the glasses. Let's get the fuck out of here!"

After he ushered them out, Franco hit the lights and locked the door. They were finally leaving it behind . . . at least for the night.

The walk to Howl at the Moon was brief. It took them longer to get inside the bar as the line snaked down the block.

At the front, Franco had to pay $40 since he was not one of the cool kids.

The gang made liberal use of the open bar once they were inside. They had two hours to kill before midnight and they spent most of the time drinking.

They also peppered Franco with questions. It was surprising how little they knew about him given the number of interactions they had.

The breakdown of his answers went something like this:

- He was a West Coast baby where most of his family still resided
- He moved to Denver because all the economic trends showed the hospitality industry was going to boom due to the likelihood of weed becoming legal. Franco opened the bar with his best friend (whom he often referred to as his partner, much to the confusion of the group) in order to capitalize on the market
- Things weren't going as planned so far as business was slow to take off
- Yes, he took days off
- Yes, there were other bartenders that worked. He felt it was important to put in his time at his own business hence why he was there so often
- He turned thirty a month ago and was rude in not telling the trio (according to Elliot)
- He lived at Skyhouse. (At this point, Murph gave her drink to Elliot and ran around the perimeter of the room. "What the FUCK are the chances of that? Dios mio!" she yelled, somewhat out of breath)

Franco also tossed questions over to them. Evan didn't learn anything new about Elliot and Murph. He answered the questions directed at him but shied away from spilling any personal details about the recent events in his life. It took time for him to open up to someone. He hadn't even told Murph anything of value yet about his relationship with Vincent.

After the questions died down, they pried themselves from the bar and went out to the dance floor. The space for dancing was limited, which made them feel less awkward as they stood there in a lumpy circular formation as if they were worshiping some reincarnated creature in the middle.

The televisions changed to a countdown from the continuing coverage of the celebrations on the West Coast. Denver existed in a strange bubble where no one particularly cared that the city was in the Mountain Time Zone, so they were the bastard child of the coasts.

The countdown flashed again.

As the mantra goes . . .

Ten minutes until midnight.

Franco told the group he had to pee and hauled it to the bathroom. If he was lucky, he would make it back in time.

Evan turned his attention to the crowd. They weren't an exciting bunch, but it kept his mind from turning inward. He didn't see the need in examining how his year was. He already lived it and stressing over past transgressions would lead to delayed satisfaction in his present life.

He rejoined Elliot and Murph's conversation.

"I really don't think so," Elliot said.

"Go for it anyways. I give you my blessing," Murph said, touching his shoulders with her pointer finger.

Evan didn't care to be brought up to speed.

"So, got any prospects for a midnight smooch?" Murph asked.

"Can't say I bothered to look," Evan said. He stared down at his feet and noticed all the muck and grime that clung to the floor. He felt like that sometimes.

At least it wasn't shit down there.

Five minutes until midnight.

"You have"—Murph checked her phone—"five minutes to midnight. Let's find you the gayest person in this bar."

"I'll pass."

"Fine. Kiss me instead."

"What?"

"I didn't stutter. I only do that after eight drinks. I have o-o-only h-had nine. F-F-F-FUCK!" Murph shouted.

"Mind over matter. You will be fine."

"Kiss m-me."

"What about Elliot?"

"He is taken care of."

Two minutes until midnight.

"Fine," Evan said.

A smile spread across Murph's face. Evan knew the kiss would be innocent. There would be no emotion behind it.

He turned his eyes skyward. The ceiling was cradled with balloons. They were eagerly awaiting their release in the unlikely scenario where balloons could await anything given their inanimate status.

"I'm back!" Franco said, clasping onto Evan's shoulders.

"Just in time," Elliot said.

Thirty seconds until midnight.

The anticipation from the crowd rolled into cheers. Evan didn't understand the excitement. It was just time. Nobody's life would change drastically in the one second left in 2018 to the first second in 2019. Come to think of it, Evan didn't believe life could change drastically in twenty seconds or even a minute. Things took time to build—and sometimes—to crumble.

What a naïve thought.

85

Ten seconds.

Murph stepped closer and craned her neck toward Evan. She only came up to his chin, so he would need to do most of the work.

Five seconds.

Elliot grabbed Franco by the waist and pulled him in close.

"What the fuck?" Evan managed to say.

"It's f-f-fine," Murph said.

Three.

Two.

One.

Evan leaned over and kissed Murph. It was quick like saying goodbye to an aunt.

The balloons were released from their captivity and floated in a lazy manner toward the muck and grime.

Elliot and Franco exited their embrace. Evan had questions, but his mind was hazy, and the answers didn't seem important in his current state.

It was past midnight and the gang decided that home seemed better than the bar, so away they went.

Time skipped as it tended to for drunks, addicts, and the emotionally drained.

Back at home, Evan pulled out his phone. His head was swimming as he laid down in bed but managed to read several of the texts that came through.

There was only one that interested him. It was timestamped at midnight.

From Vincent:

"Happy New Year's! Been thinking about you. I hope everything is going well."

Evan fell asleep with the phone on his chest and a smile plastered to his face.

○ ○ ○

Evan returned to reality sometime late the next morning. A headache was the immediate source of pain. He pressed his palms against his forehead like he was flattening pizza dough. No luck.

Izzie scurried out from under the covers and jumped off the bed. She was ready to start the day.

Evan was not.

He laid there for several more hours until he willed away the headache. It was an acquired skill.

He forced himself to shower and start a load of laundry. No sense in wasting the entire day he had off doing nothing. Evan texted Murph to make sure her and Elliot made it home okay. The response was immediate. She was fine, but "hungover like a fucking whale ate my liver and stole my kidney to sell on the black market." Evan didn't bother to respond.

With the laundry in progress and a microwavable pizza being cooked to perfection, Evan grabbed his laptop and navigated to Facebook. It was a force of habit he regretted falling into the trap of. Given it was the new year, his Facebook feed was littered with posts about how people would be stepping it up at the gym and finally getting the *x,y,z* thing they wanted. It was nauseating and yet he was still part of the problem since he had an account and continued to feed the masses with his time and occasional likes.

He scrolled past it the first time because it was just a text post—a rare sight on the site. Something clicked in his brain, a flash of recognition. Some of the letters within the post stood out, mainly the RIP.

He didn't want to, but Evan scrolled back up. Dread consumed him.

He read the post. "RIP. Thoughts and prayers to your family. Gone too soon!"

"No," he said. "No, no, no."

Evan clicked on the profile. A dozen posts dominated the page.

"RIP."

"This is so sad ☹"

"I just talked to you last week! How could this have happened??? RIP."

They continued on.

The posts all tagged the same name.

Police Report:
> Vincent Besser, aged 25, died in a single car crash in the early morning hours of January 1, 2019. No other passengers were in the car. While exiting off the highway, appearing to head in the direction of his home, Vincent lost control of the car where it careened into the guardrail, flipping and rolling into a ditch. The airbags did not deploy. When paramedics arrived on the scene, there were no signs of life and he was pronounced dead before removing the body from the car. Early indication on the cause of death—and confirmed by the autopsy—was blunt force trauma to the head. He sustained other injuries, which were amplified by the airbags not deploying. His chest cavity was fractured. His femur was shattered. His left arm was cut—almost severed, and his right clavicle split in half. The internal injuries were numerous. Paramedics found his phone in his pocket, which likely ruled out any distracted driving. The toxicology report showed he had an elevated BAC, but it was well under the legal limit. No illegal substances were found in his system. It would be impossible to determine, but Mr. Besser was likely traveling at a high rate of speed as he made contact with the guardrail. The car has been impounded with no intention from the family to take ownership of it. The remains of the deceased have been transported back to Pennsylvania.
>
> So it goes.

interlude

1-1

QUINN'S LETTER

Q-Man,

Writing something like this to you feels like it's violating the terms of agreement to our friendship. We were never sentimental with each other except for the times when I'd tell you to imagine where we'd be a year from then. You'd stomp your foot on the ground and say, "Goddammit! I don't want to think about that." But we had to. We were seniors and life was going to drastically change whether we wanted to or not. For most of that year, I didn't know where I would end up. I had the safe option of returning to Lockheed Martin and spending a good chunk of my twenties in a dying culture that meant nothing to me. Or the harder option that would rip me away from my friends and family. You know the rest of the story. You were the first person I told about the interview down at Southwest and I vividly remember you laughing your ass off at the sheer randomness of the situation.

Anyways, this letter isn't meant to be about me, except for the next few sentences.

By the time you read this—if you ever do—I will have told you that I am sick. Maybe saying I'm sick isn't the right word to use since it implies I will get better which I won't. How about this instead: I am dying, and you will be aware. It sucks to know your own mortality is a mile up the road, but I am lucky to be surrounded by goofballs like you who continue to text me random pictures of mullets and your weird dinner choices.

The only thing I ask of you—if I'm even allowed to do that—is to never change. It's a tall order, I know even though I don't believe people are capable of change. You have this beautiful level of blissful ignorance and fierce compassion that mix together to make you the best person I came across during my college years.

I didn't talk about you too much in the writings I've done about my life, and I wouldn't want you to get offended by that. Not every detail needed to be shared of our mundane (but spectacular) existence.

We had a ridiculous amount of fun in college, but the ones I still miss the most are the countless times you'd quietly knock on my door as if you would be disturbing a hibernating bear or something. I'd tell you to come in, but you'd open the door and just stand in the doorway. You'd ask me how my day was, and I would usually give you a stupid non-answer. You didn't know at the time how much I was struggling internally and how the idea of telling you or anyone else in the house made me physically sick. You would just shake your head and dive into these long rambles about something you saw on campus or the meal you got from the bodega down the street. Each story was inconsequential, and the details are lost to time, but I loved every moment of it. You always ripped me from the downtrodden attitude that became a staple of who I was during college, who I have been since. I'll never forget that.

And then, I remember the night I told you I was gay. The buildup for me was years in the making and I took longer than I should have to get the words out. Eventually I did, and you just stared over at me and said, "Are you happy?" and I said yes to which you replied, "Then I don't give a fuck. You're still the same person to me." I told you all about Evan that night and you would always text me asking about what we were up to for the weekend and how things were going with us. You did this for someone you never even met. I can't think of another person who would do something even remotely close to that with the sincerity you had.

When I look back upon it all, I feel guilty. You have always been the one who texted me first. You were always the one to knock on my door. If it wasn't for your constant barraging (in the best way possible!) we would have stopped talking the moment I moved down to Dallas. I have found it incredibly hard to stay in touch with friends, family, or otherwise when you live so far away, which doesn't make much sense considering how connected we all are. I guess it's me never feeling like I have anything to talk about. I always viewed my life as one monotone note on a keyboard that drones on until the end of time. Maybe that was never the case at all.

You had to know there wouldn't be any massive revelations in this letter; it was meant to be an easy way to tell you what's swimming around in my brain since writing appears to be the only way for me to dump out the excess.

There's one last thing that I want to ask of you. I know, I know. I have been quite demanding, but hopefully you can indulge me one last time. Let me preface it by saying how you aren't going to like it.

Just think about this time next year. Where do you think you'll be?

How about we step it up a bit?

Just think about this time in *five years*. Can you picture that? Not to be morbid, but there's a good chance I'll be dead by that point, so I'll live vicariously through you for a moment.

I see you living in a big city. I'm not entirely convinced it'll be where you are now. Philadelphia has always been your first love, but I've learned how first loves aren't always the best or the last. You'll be in an apartment where you'll have an amazing view of the skyline. You will be able to walk to work and breathe in the culture of the city and its inhabitants. Your life will be simple because you have never been concerned about the trivial shit that occupies so many of us.

Now, go disregard that last paragraph and live your own life. Don't ever let people make choices or set expectations for you. Take whatever plan you have and set fire to it. You're going to figure things out in your own way, and I can't wait to hear about it.

You're a great friend, an awesome person, and too diehard of a Sixers fan for your own good. I certainly never want to see another Philly team win a championship again, but I'll be thinking of you when they do.

Take care,
Vin

1-2

THE WEDDING
(Sometime in the future)

It was an inevitability that Quinn would end up here.

Jacob and Sasha had been dating for so long that it was just a formality for them to spend thousands of dollars on a night to confirm their love with two hundred of their closest friends and family they never saw.

As mentioned previously in another source, Quinn and Jacob met during their freshman year of college. Yada, yada. They became friends. Obviously. Then Vincent, who is now dead, came into the picture during their sophomore year. Quinn and Vincent witnessed the relationship between Jacob and Sasha bloom into an inseparable bond for the next two and a half years. Yada, yada.

Quinn knew it had been a point of contention for a while as to where the two would get married. Jacob was from Yonkers, New York, which was a fun name to say. Sasha was from Chambersburg, PA where the most titillating thing to do was ride a tractor through downtown. Her family moved to Kentucky which further muddied the situation. The two couldn't decide which place to have the ceremony at, so they instead opted to do it in Philadelphia.

They were married in a church. It was nice.

The wedding congregation then ventured across town to the venue where they would eat and boogie (another word for dancing) until they were contractually obligated to stop eating and boogieing.

Quinn was seated at a table with familiar faces. Over the years, he had met Jacob's childhood friends on his multiple visits to Yonkers. There was Three-Sided Goose who owned several pizza joints called *You Want a Pizza This?* that he inherited from his father. Their special ingredient was love and water from the Hudson Bay—unfiltered. Next to him was Round Ball who was shaped like a triangle—an isosceles triangle to be exact—and played the oboe for the New York Philharmonic, which never had an oboe player before, but Round Ball was a damn fine oboe player. People had been known to shout "Oh, oh, oh your boe" when he passed by for whatever reason. To Round's immediate right was Sinister Secret or SS for short. SS had the unfortunate initials of a raving group of dickheads (to put it mildly). SS was a stripper at the local strip mall where half the stores were abandoned and stripped clean, and everything was always on sale! SS sat next to Silent Tim who was jabbering away and the most talkative of the group. He told a gripping story about his ascent of Dalatila Crest, which was actually the highest land mass on earth. People always confused it with Mount Everest because there wasn't a single geography book written since the troops came home from Vietnam. Nobody believed Silent Tim's story. The last person at the table was Angelo Michel who had no artistic ability whatsoever but was commissioned to repaint the Sistine Chapel to something more contemporary since religion died a long time ago.

Quinn wasn't nearly as exciting as the other members of the table. It's okay though because the Sixers just won their first championship since the moon landing and he was higher than the heroin addicts he went to high school with.

He spoke when necessary and drank constantly. He blended in just fine.

The hours slipped by and it was nearing the end of the extravagant celebration.

The bride and groom found Quinn alone at the table. He was looking out into the void, which meant it was dark out and he couldn't see anything. Beyond the glass was a pond home to a family of swans, which were angry creatures hellbent on the destruction of the human race. The pond was also the low budget swimming pool for the poor kids in the city. There was an abundance of poor families because money was only something you got more of when you already had it.

"Why aren't you out there dancing?" Sasha asked, pointing out toward the floor designated for dancing. Bodies jived and twitched and tushies shook. The disc jockey played "Wicked Passions" by December Sun because it was the most popular song on the radio. No one actually listened to the lyrics or else they would have realized the song was about the vile behavior of someone like Vincent Besser.

"You think he would have been here?"

There was a sense of dread that coursed through Quinn. It could have been the alcohol, but he figured the dread was from the idea he had forgotten about Vincent. It had been years already and Quinn no longer remembered his face. He had a hard time recalling their time together in college. It was as if he had been blurred out from any memory and replaced by a static creature. He felt guilty he had moved on from his friend.

He felt grief—the cyclical, powerful wave of it.

"He absolutely would have been here," Jacob said.

They remembered their friend in the only way friends do: with stories.

"Remember the time Jacob dropped the whole tray of cupcakes on Vin during Q's birthday?" Sasha asked. "I mean, Q, you probably don't recall since you were so drunk and passed out on the couch. Vincent laughed so much and walked around wearing those shoes for weeks that were stained with the different color icings."

"My favorite part about Vin was the ridiculous things he would say just to get Q riled up. The talks about mullets and hobos and the general state of chaos around us in that part of Philly. I miss the absurdity of what life was like back at 1912," Jacob said.

"He always wore that Temple sweatshirt. All the time. It was already ripping apart by the time we graduated," Quinn chimed in.

They continued to volley thoughts and vignettes back and forth with no structured narrative. It's what grief looked like for them.

After that night, Quinn wouldn't think about him for a while because the living has enough to worry about than carrying the burden of the dead.

"To Vin," Sasha proposed, wiping away her tears.

All three raised their glasses, chugged it, and returned to the dance floor.

They had important stories to get back to.

PART II

CIGARETTES & GUARDRAILS

thirteen

THE EPCOT FROWN

The house was filled with the sounds of strangers.
 Ann tried to stay away from them for as long as she could. She hadn't said much in the four days since Vincent collided with a guardrail and his life was ended. She replayed the moment over in her head from various angles and outcomes. Sometimes Vincent walked away from the crash, other times he made it home safe and woke up the next day to his average life. Did it hurt for him? Did he lay in the car and scream for help before slipping away? Did he have any final words that no one got to here? Maybe he said something about loving his family or wishing he traveled more. Ann's worry about his last moments catapulted her inward to seek shelter from the realization she would have to continue her life. She would need to keep paying her taxes and filling up the gas tank and shopping for overpriced groceries and commuting to her tiresome job.
 How was it that her world ended but it didn't for anyone else?
 Her project for the last day was to sort through all the pictures they had of him to create a collage. It would be something others would stand in front of at the viewing and cry at since it would be a closed casket. The funeral director had been blunt that it would do no good to let the friends and family see him in his final state. It would scar the view they had of Vincent.
 Most of the pictures she had of him stopped around high school. He had looked the same since then so Ann didn't think anyone would mind.
 Her crying came in unidentifiable waves, but usually seemed to be predicated when someone new knocked on the door to his room, which had become her sanctuary since the event. She cried for an hour when her mom came. She cried for two hours when Leigh came and told Ann how her and Jim would handle everything. She cried because the outlet of her emotions was the only thing to keep her sane. Her mind tried to drift to all the moments she would never share with Vincent, but the mountain was so steep that there wasn't even a good place to start.
 She arranged her favorite pictures out on his bed. They created a trajectory of life he had. From the numerous family trips to the sporting achievements, Vincent seemed to embody the happy kid who enjoyed life

to the fullest. Ann ran her hands over them and tried to recall as many of the moments as she could.

She didn't want to forget a single one.

Birds chirped and the sun shined in through the windows to remind her that life did exist—would continue to exist—outside the bedroom. She ignored the distractions as she began to recognize a pattern amongst the pictures.

Each one was of Vincent—naturally—but what was surprising was how he displayed a massive grin in every photo. He must have known how powerful his smile was because he flashed it any chance he could. His eyes would scrunch into nothing and his big front teeth would dazzle. Nothing about that had changed from the time someone behind the camera told him to say cheese to the last pictures from his high school graduation.

There was one exception though.

It took Ann a while to spot as it was hidden in the top left corner of the bed. They say pictures are worth plenty of words, but this story should be contained to less than that.

The photo was of the Besser clan plus Doris standing outside Epcot in Disney. The family made the required pilgrimage down there after Vincent's fifth birthday. Jim argued with her that they should wait longer so he would remember the trip, but Ann was adamant he would and how they had delayed the trip enough already. Jim relented and the five of them flew down for a week to Orlando.

Nobody was expecting Vincent to fall in love with Epcot as much as he did, and he begged them to go back there each night. For the most part, they gave into his demand. Except for the last night.

"Vinny, we have been to Epcot every night. Your sister has been really nice about it, but she wants to see some stuff too, okay?" Ann recalled saying to him.

"One more time. Please!"

"I'm sorry sweetie. How about this though: let's take a picture in front of Epcot so you can always remember it."

"No. It's not the same."

"C'mon on Vinny!" Leigh cried out from beside Ann.

"Fine!"

"Mom, go stand over there with Vinny and Leigh. I'll take your picture," Ann directed.

"What about you and Jim?" Doris said.

"I . . . uh—excuse me! Would you mind taking our picture?" Ann asked the woman who was passing by.

"Of course! What a lovely family you have! Go on and stand over there with them, sweetheart."

They arranged themselves and stood in front of the glowing golf ball.

"Okay. One . . . two . . . three!" the woman said and snapped the picture.

It wasn't until the roll of film was developed back in Pennsylvania that Ann noticed the excessive frown Vincent sported for the picture. It was the only photographic evidence she had of such a frown even though she had seen it plenty of times in person. She loved the photo so much that she framed it and kept it on the bookshelf in the family room for the past twenty years.

She missed that frown. She wouldn't have minded being stuck in an infinite loop where all her life consisted of was replaying that moment. The outcome would never change, but she'd get to spend more time with her son.

Ann collected up the pictures and attempted to preserve them in the correct order though it didn't matter much. Who cared about a fucking collage that would be sitting in the same room as her son's dead body?

She took a deep breath and winded her way downstairs. Before she hit the bottom step, Rigby peered her head around the corner and watched Ann the rest of the way.

In the kitchen was a smattering of neighbors and family. Trays of food sat out on the countertops. They had more leftovers than they'd ever eat.

The room quieted for a moment before realizing Ann was not some Russian doll. Her grief was strong, but she was not fragile, and others did not need to tiptoe around her.

"Here are the pictures. Hopefully they are enough," Ann said, passing the photos to Leigh.

"Thanks," Leigh whispered.

Ann didn't say much else as she turned around and went back upstairs to get ready for the viewing. Rigby followed closely behind.

fourteen

CLOSED CASKET

"Miss, excuse me? Would you mind signing the book?" the man said. His aged face and slanted stance made it seem like he would soon be occupying a casket within the funeral home.

Ann stopped and turned toward him. "My son is in the casket down the hall. Is that really necessary?"

"Yes, we like to keep track of everyone who shows up for a viewing," he said with his eyes half shut. "You get to take the book with you following the event."

Ann stepped over to the book that laid open. It was empty, which made sense since she was at the funeral home long before anyone else. She picked up the pen and hesitated at what to write. She hadn't been to a funeral in a while and forgot the etiquette. Something told her she shouldn't be forced to sign anything though.

She looked behind her and found the old man had wandered off to the corner and stared at a vase of flowers as if they held the key to interstellar travel.

Hey Jim, it's been a year since Vincent died. Let's dust off that book from the viewing and sit down to read it and have a few laughs. She chuckled at the ridiculousness of the thought.

Ann closed the book and pocketed the pen.

The hall opened to the main room, which was lined with chairs and flowers of a modest variety. She walked slowly down the center aisle and took a seat in the second row. Music of a melancholy sort played overhead, just loud enough to be heard, but not distract.

She clasped her hands together like she intended to pray but remained still with her eyes focused to the front. The casket was propped up with the lid closed. It was the closest she had been to her son since she hugged him goodbye after Christmas.

In a sense, she was lucky. The last time they saw each other ended on a dull note—a normal conversation finishing up as they arrived at the airport. What they talked about was long forgotten to her since the short time it occurred. Yes, she cried for part of the way home in the usual bout of sadness that followed Vincent leaving, but it hardly seemed like it would be the last time she would have seen him.

That's life though.

Vincent never mentioned anything about how he wanted to be buried, so the family had to take a guess. Leigh and Jim settled on a mid-level priced casket as if the dead cared about how they were buried. It was adorned with tassels and a whistle that someone could blow that had a 0.00000000000000000000000000000001% chance of bringing Vincent back from the dead. Nobody believed it was possible until a dead man in Russia rose out of his casket after his sister blew into the whistle for three months straight. After that, the casket became a top seller on Amazon and, with the free shipping, it was quite the steal!

The funeral home had a sign at the parlor entrance that read:

> *Please do NOT blow into the whistle. It is reserved for family ONLY!*
>
> *Thank you for your patience!*

They only charged the family an extra thousand dollars for the thoughtful sign.

Ann stood at the casket for a long time. She ran her hand across the treated wood. The tassels and whistle weren't there.

"You must be Ann," a voice behind her said.

She turned around. "Douglas?"

"Yes. I'm sorry we haven't met sooner. I understand this has been difficult for you." They shook hands.

"Somewhat of an understatement," she said.

"I know," Douglas said, placing his hand on her shoulder.

"Can I see him?"

Douglas looked past her. "I'm not sure that's in your best interest. We did the best we could, but he was . . . in poor shape."

"Please."

Douglas gave a deep sigh and signaled his arm in the direction of the casket.

Ann returned to it. Her hand shook as she found the groove to lift open the lid. It resisted at first like a warning against her next action. She continued to lift and closed her eyes. She wasn't ready to see him just yet.

Ann reached into her purse, pulled out the picture, and held it tightly in her hand.

She took a deep breath and opened her eyes.

"Vinny," she whispered.

Ann stared at his peaceful face (what remained of it) for a long time, expecting him to jolt awake and pronounce the whole thing to be an elaborate joke. His lips never moved; his eye never fluttered. He remained motionless the entire time.

The trauma from the accident was erased, or at least that's how Ann viewed it.

To be so close to him was tragic. To be right next to the lifeless body of the baby she held and sang lullabies to was . . .

"He looks beautiful. Thank you," she said to Douglas. He sat in the front row and nodded. "I think we should keep it a closed casket viewing though."

"I agree," he said in a whisper.

Ann looked down at the photo in her hand—the infamous Epcot frown. She loved the picture enough to know she could never look at it again. She didn't need any reminder of that frown.

"I just don't want to forget his face. I just—it happens right? I needed to see him one last time," Ann said.

"I know," Douglas said. "Your family is waiting for you."

She turned around and saw Leigh, Jim, Lorenzo, Doris, and Walter waiting at the threshold of the parlor.

Ann slid the photo into the casket and said something lost in the sound of the music that played overhead. It would stay between her and Vincent.

She went back to meet her family.

"How does he look?" Leigh asked, attempting to hold together her emotions.

"He looks like the kid he always did. Go say goodbye to your brother," Ann said.

Leigh walked down the aisle with Lorenzo. They stayed up at the front for a while.

Not a word passed between the rest of the group as they continued to stand in the back. Once Leigh and Lorenzo came back, Doris and Walter made their way to see Vincent.

Finally, Ann led Jim down the aisle.

"I don't think I can," he said.

"You have to. It's the only chance you'll ever have," Ann told him.

Jim took off his glasses and rubbed his eyes. "I don't know what to say to him."

"You don't have to say anything."

Ann sat in the same seat in the second row as Jim walked the rest of the way. Ann watched as he stood three steps back from the casket before deciding to move in closer. His posture was stiff. It was clear to Ann that he was holding in every emotion from the past week, every thought that tore into him about things he could have done differently. They had talked about it enough to know Jim had regrets with Vincent, but the best thing a parent can do is learn to accept the past and continue to build for the future. What happened when there was no longer a future though?

"Ann," Douglas said as he took the seat beside her. "There is something we didn't know what to do with. I asked Leigh and Jim about it and they suggested to give it to you."

Douglas opened his hand and showed off the gold chain with a crucified Jesus hanging from the end.

"We are lucky it wasn't lost," he continued.

The chain needed to be cleaned. She doubted Vincent ever went through the effort of doing so, but she knew for certain he'd worn it every day since his twenty-first birthday. He had cherished the gift from his grandmother.

"Thank you," Ann managed to say.

Ann understood the chain didn't belong with her. She would find another home for it someday.

Douglas retreated back to the corner of the room and Ann was left by herself again as she continued to watch her husband.

Jim didn't move for quite some time. Ann wondered if he had said anything to Vincent, but it was something she'd never find the right moment to ask.

Jim eventually retreated back to the group.

Ann said one last goodbye to her son and closed the casket. She returned to her family and waited for the others to arrive.

<u>fifteen</u>

KIND WORDS

Vincent was buried under a cloudless sky.

People said kind words about him during the service—the type he would have rolled his eyes at. Vincent never excelled at taking compliments or enjoyed being the center of attention.

He never realized how many people cared about him enough to show up that day and listen to the stories others told.

He never understood how rare his empathetic spirit was.

He never knew his smile was the first thing anyone noticed and how his boisterous laugh was the reason people kept coming back.

He never heard about the tiny moments people remembered with him—the moments that were nothing more than a dot in the existence of someone's life.

Vincent never knew any of this because people save kind words for funerals and forget they are worth sharing with the living.

sixteen

INHALE

Ann insisted on driving by herself to and from the funeral.

Following the burial, she began to worry.

Ann didn't understand the point of renting out a large room to house people after the funeral, so she insisted on everyone coming back to the Besser household. There was enough food to feed the entire tri-state area, so the occasion would serve at least one purpose.

Would there be enough though? Was the house clean for fifty people to just stomp all around it? Would she have to talk to each person and pretend to be okay?

Her mind turned over each question like they carried actual significance. Her worry began to intensify. She gripped the steering wheel and made a sharp turn out of the parking lot. It didn't matter to her if she was late. She was the main attraction, the person everyone wanted to share their condolences to.

Ann checked the passenger seat and found the book from the viewing was still there. The old man really wasn't kidding when he said she would get to keep it.

She had one stop to make before she went home and was greeted by the mass of sad faces. Ann needed something to level her out.

Several miles up the road from the Besser residence was a convenience store with the unfortunate name of Chubby's. It had been her go to place for many years. She would leave the kids in the car and run into the left entrance, which was designated just for adults. On the rare instances where she brought Vincent and Leigh inside, she had to use the door on the right side. She would let the kids wander around the aisles while she bargained with the underpaid cashier. Ann would motion to the same pack that sat directly over top of the cashier's head. Their movement was slow and uninspired. By the time Vincent and Leigh returned to the counter, the transaction would be complete and Ann would usher them back outside. The hardest part was always the drive back. She had to resist the temptation until the car was in the garage and the kids were in the house.

It was a vicious cycle that consumed her life . . . until it didn't.

See:

Ann always told everyone she quit cold turkey, but that wasn't entirely true. She did have the abrupt chest pains except those hadn't scared her enough to quit. It was worrisome enough that she went to the doctor though.

Upon explaining her symptoms, he stopped taking notes, spun around in his chair, and said in a coldness Ann never experienced again in her life that she was killing herself. Each cigarette she had was taking minutes off her life and that one day those little kids would grow up and watch their mother die in hospice as she became a husk of what she once was.

Ann shuttered at the thought and had no reasonable response.

After the doctor left, she cried in the exam room until a nurse knocked on the door and asked if she was okay.

"Just figuring out my life," Ann said.

"Oh, well that's alright. Take your time."

Once outside, Ann smoked one last cigarette and threw the rest out the window on her way home.

It was the only time in her life where she condoned littering.

Looking back upon it, Ann wished the doctor was right. She wanted to be dead if that meant having Vincent make it past the age of twenty-five.

Ann pulled into the Chubby's parking lot and the craving for a cigarette crashed into her for the first time in fifteen years. She was powerless against its relentless pursuit. There were moments during the fifteen years where she felt broken and beaten down by the obstacles, but nothing compared to the emptiness she felt as the casket was lowered into the ground. The emptiness from knowing where her son would be for the rest of her life. He would never be busy—just always waiting for someone to come by and visit. Eventually, he wouldn't be there anymore after the bacteria and worms and earth reclaimed him. She wasn't sure if Vincent believed in going to heaven, but she hoped he was there because the thought of him eternally rotting in the ground was far too much.

The puppeteer controlled Ann as he led her through the left entrance of Chubby's and directly to the counter where the prize waited behind the plexiglass.

The audience watched in sustained silence as the events unfolded in front of them.

"What do you need?" the voice croaked from behind the glass. If the woman had any reaction to Ann's funeral attire, it was too subtle to notice.

"A pack of Marlboro Lights." The words rolled off as easily as they did fifteen years ago.

"My favorite. Great choice. How many packs a day are you? My personal best is four, but I average about one a day now," the woman said, showing the gaps in her smile.

"Rediscovering an old habit."

"You're the third one today! I tell everyone that smoking will be popular again and stop being *to-boo* or however you say that silly word."

"I need a lighter too."

The conversation had dragged on long enough that Ann could have left numerous times, but the puppeteer wouldn't allow it. The thoughts of Vincent's decaying body covered in insects kept her frozen in place at the counter. Or his head smashing against the steering wheel as the airbags of that stupid fucking car didn't deploy.

"Of course, sweetie. That'll be twelve dollars and twenty-seven cents."

Ann dug around in her purse until she came up with the exact change. The gold chain from the night before laid amongst the loose nickels and dimes that always took up space in her purse.

"Have a great day," the woman said.

Ann grabbed her two items and fled from the convenience store without saying another word.

She stood near the door of her car and ripped open the pack. She turned the first cigarette upside down and put it back in the pack for good luck. The second one she grabbed felt heavy in her hand. Ann opened the car door and threw the pack onto the passenger seat. It landed on top of the book.

It took three tries with the lighter before the tiny flame burst from the top. She held the cigarette between her lips and cupped the lighter with the other hand so the wind wouldn't knock out the flame.

It was a familiar motion—one any human had seen before given the prolific stranglehold smoking had within society.

The cigarette lit and Ann inhaled like she was emerging from underwater. The nicotine flooded her lungs; the slight buzz pulsed its way up to her head.

For a moment she was relaxed.

For a moment her son wasn't six feet under.

For a moment she didn't feel anything at all.

It didn't last and when the emotion came racing back into her, she threw the cigarette on the ground and grinded it out with her foot.

"What the *fuck* am I doing?" she asked herself.

The audience shrugged. The puppeteer shrugged. No one quite had the answer as they faded into nothing.

She marched back into the store and came out two minutes later with a pack of gum.

On her way home, it was only the second time in her life that she condoned littering.

There wouldn't be a third.

seventeen

LOBOTOMY

The neighborhood was clogged with cars. Ann parked four houses down and walked at a steady pace.

She never noticed how ugly the shade of green was that graced all the shutters or the chipped curb at the edge of the yard or how degraded the fence was. It was the tiny details that she clung to. It would likely be the tiny details that would push her over the edge one day.

Ann walked into the house through the garage. The Christmas tree was still standing in the corner of the living room. Half the ornaments remained.

People were flooded in each room of the first floor and down in the basement. The noise that came from each conversation collided and became a garbled mess. The scene was more reminiscent of a frat party, not a . . . was there even a word for this? People loved the phrase *celebration of life* as if, yet again, a life was only worth celebrating after someone was dead. Ann viewed this activity as a lobotomy of sorts. By stepping into her own home, she entered the operation room. The first person she'd talk to would place the ice pick gently against her eye socket. *Nice and snug*, they would say. Each person after that would take a whack with the hammer until she felt nothing at all. Complete freedom from the burden of emotion.

"Ann. I am so sorry. Vincent was such a special soul." It was the mother of Vincent's high school friend. Ann hadn't seen her in so long that she forgot her name.

"Thank you," Ann said like she'd just received a cup of coffee from a barista.

The mother came in for a hug and Ann had no choice but to accept it. The intention was meaningful, but Ann didn't care for people expressing condolences about her son when they didn't know him at all.

Behind the mother was the high school friend. He looked dazed and as if he had never experienced death before, which was odd because Ann knew he had. Maybe he was thinking about all the times he called Vincent a faggot. Or maybe he was imagining what his funeral would be like someday and if anyone would bother to show up.

"Jordan, get over here," the mother scolded her adult son.

Her son stepped forward lightly. "Mrs. Besser, I'm sorry for your loss," he said as if a mallet had struck him on the head.

"Thank you," Ann said.

Nice and snug.

Knowing there wasn't anything left to say, Ann moved on.

In the kitchen, she found most of the neighborhood friends. They were gathered around the piles of food and picked at it without much appetite. As she approached, the attention turned toward her like she was a puppy. Everyone said their peace and gave her a hug. It was undeniable how fortunate their family was to have spent so many years in a neighborhood where each house was filled with exceptional people. They all shared in the triumphs and tragedies of one another.

Whack, whack, whack.

Ann's mother was sitting at the dining room table with her siblings. She repeated the same tired process.

Whack, whack.

Jim was down in the basement playing pool with Ralph. There was silence between them as they focused on the game or just didn't have anything to say to each other.

"Ralph, thank you for speaking today. Everything you said about Vinny was perfect. You know how much he cares about you," Ann said.

"The son I never had," Ralph said, shaking his head as he leaned up against the pool stick. He wiped the tears away with a handkerchief. "I'm seventy-three years old. I didn't think I needed to worry about stuff like this anymore."

Jim lined up his shot and smacked the cue ball. It scorched across the table and knocked in a stripe that sat on the edge of the pocket. He wasn't paying much attention to the conversation. Much like Ralph, this was never an outcome he foresaw in his life, so he was running from it.

"I know," Ann said.

A few others lingered around the bar and Ann did what she had to.

Whack, whack, whack.

Having completed her host duties and hearing the sympathies from everyone, Ann retreated to Vincent's bedroom. There was a man in the room staring blankly at the books Vincent had left behind when he moved to Dallas.

"Hello," Ann said.

"Oh, hi. Mrs. Besser? I'm sorry to intrude."

"Call me Ann."

"I'm Xander," he said. They shook hands.

"How did you know Vinny?"

"We met a few years ago when I was visiting a friend in Dallas."

"Oh. Where do you live? I imagine you are far from home."

Xander nodded. "I live in Boston now."

Recognition swept across Ann's face. "Are you the person he stayed with in Provincetown?"

"That's me," Xander said with a light smile.

Ann sat down on the bed and Xander followed her lead. Ann noticed how sterile the room felt. They'd never do anything to it, but what about when they moved? No, no. Ann and Jim could never leave this house now.

"He was up there when he told me," she said.

That was enough for Xander to know exactly what she was speaking about. "I remember that. I don't think I understood how important it was to him at the time. Coming out was a non-event for me, so sometimes it's been hard for me to accept that others struggled with it. He had said some stupid shit to me the day before he told you, so we weren't speaking much. I could sense the relief in him afterward."

"I know. I have always wondered why that place though."

"He felt at peace up there. Provincetown is unique. I learned a lot about myself in the years I lived on the island."

"There is so much I didn't know about him. I wish I asked him more questions," Ann said.

"You should visit. Maybe that could answer some questions for you. I have friends on the island still. They would be happy to have us."

"I . . . I would typically give an excuse as to why I shouldn't, but there really isn't one in this case. I would love to retrace his steps and help to see why Provincetown was important to him."

Xander gave her his number.

"You are welcome to stay the night," Ann continued. "It's a long drive back."

"Don't worry about me. I don't mind the drive. It's going to help clear my head," Xander said.

"Can I ask you something?"

"Yeah."

"Why are you here?"

"Because he was special. As dumb as that sounds. I couldn't tell you why. He could be a pain in the ass, but I truly cared about him. And I know he would have done the same."

115

"Did you love him?"

"No. He would have broken my heart."

Ann stood up and went to the bookshelf. Nothing but historical fiction lined the row. She pushed two of the Steve Berry books back into place to match the rest.

"One more thing," she eventually said. "Do you think he was happy?"

"I don't think so, but I know he loved you so much. He talked about you quite a bit."

Whack, whack.

"What was there to say about me?" Ann asked.

"How close you two were and how hard it was to move to Dallas. I left my family behind in Kansas City, so we had common ground there. Speaking for him now seems disingenuous though. There's nothing I could tell you that you don't already know."

"But why?"

"Why what?" Xander asked.

"Why wasn't he happy?"

"Are you?" he said casually.

WHACK!

The ice pick pierced her brain and severed any connection to the prefrontal cortex. It didn't hurt as much as she expected.

"I was happy at some point. You could imagine why I'm not now," Ann said.

"I understand. Again, I hate to speak for him, but I think for Vinny it was a matter of *when* he would be happy. He was going to get there."

She felt an uncomfortable wave of energy pass through her. "I should get back downstairs. Stay in here as long as you need."

"Okay," Xander said. "Thank you."

Ann disappeared from the room and went back downstairs to pretend the lobotomy worked.

eighteen

THE BEST MEDICINE

After the waves of people left, there was a stillness. A sudden end to it all.

Jim was the one who proposed taking down the Christmas tree, and while no one particularly agreed to help, everyone chipped in once he brought up the boxes.

With the tree gone, the furniture was rearranged in the living room to its normal look. A boring, each-day-is-the-same type of look. Ann craved that normality again, so she didn't mind it as much this year.

"Let's play Uno," Ann suggested. Leigh, Lorenzo, and Jim sat at the kitchen table passing blank stares across to one another. Ann didn't see the purpose in continuing to soak in the misery. The day had been long enough already.

"I'm really tired," Leigh said.

"Maybe another night," Jim said.

"We don't have another night. They are driving back to Jersey tomorrow and who knows when we will see them again."

"Mom, we have a life down there. We can't just come back here every weekend."

Ann hesitated briefly. "I, uh, I am going to grab the game. I'll be right back."

The few board games that the Besser's did own were tucked away in some ancient cabinet. Ann pulled out Uno. It was a family favorite growing up, especially when they were at the beach. After roasting in the sun all day, they would come back to the pink house and settle in for a long game. Someone would end up in tears after the inevitable bombardment of draw fours. The loser would claim the booby prize, which, depending on your preference in life, may not be such a bad prize after all.

The version of Uno they had was old school. Ann pulled out the plastic tray and shuffled the cards. No one said anything. She fumbled several times with the shuffling but was soon satisfied with the outcome. Ann placed a majority of the deck in the right pocket of the plastic tray and began to pass out seven cards to each person. No one said anything. She added the leftover cards to the pile and flipped over the first one.

It was a green seven.

No one said anything.

"I'll go first." Ann added a green five on top of the first card. "Lorenzo, you're up."

This cycle repeated until Jim won the hand.

No one said much of anything.

The cards were shuffled and dealt again.

Leigh won the second hand.

The cards were shuffled and dealt . . . again.

Ann won the third hand after rebounding from a late game draw two that set her back substantially.

No one said much of anything until Lorenzo declared his intention of getting a soda from the fridge. He didn't bother to ask if anyone wanted a drink.

Normally, there would not be soda in the house. Ann had given it up several years ago to help with the diet and Jim survived on water, coffee, and rock n' roll. But it was there, stuffed into the fridge, amongst the trays of food leftover from the celebration of death.

Lorenzo grabbed the bottle and attempted to place it on the counter. In an unmatched feat of stupidity, Lorenzo missed the counter and dropped the bottle five feet onto the tile. The cap exploded off as a fountain of soda drenched him and the surrounding cabinets. He looked up in confusion with a red mark on the center of his forehead.

No one said anything.

In another time, there may have been anger that part of the kitchen would need to be scrubbed. On any other day, Ann may have mumbled under her breath that she'd have to be the one to clean it up.

But those would have been days where Vincent wasn't dead, and she was able to worry about the trivial bothers of life.

Instead, she laughed. Jim and Leigh felt the contagion and joined in as well.

They all laughed until their sides hurt and couldn't breathe much. They laughed until their eyes watered and cheeks hurt.

They laughed until they were better. At least for the moment.

Everyone helped to clean up including the dogs, who particularly enjoyed mopping up the floor with their tongues.

"I still want a soda," Lorenzo said when they were all back at the table.

"If you spill it again, you are walking home," Jim said.

They were coming down off the high. The chuckles became sporadic until they died out.

The room returned to silence.

"I miss him so much," Ann said and looked over at Leigh. Ann needed their relationship to be repaired. Weren't there stories of families becoming close after tragedies? Did that outweigh all the families who became more fractured than before? Ann didn't have the answer.

"Me too," Leigh said.

Ann cried. She buried her head deep into her hands and let the uncontrollable sobs run free. Fuck the lobotomy! It wasn't bound to work anyways. To deny herself the emotion was foolish.

"Mom, it's okay. We are going to get past this," Leigh said, resting her hand on Ann's forearm.

"Are we? That bedroom is going to be empty forever. I'm never going to get a Mother's Day card from Dallas again. We are never going to get a surprise visit from him. We are never going to see him happy. All we have left are memories of what was and most of them I can't remember. It's not going to be okay. It's not. It's not," Ann said, still crying into her hands.

"You still have us."

"Really? You can't stand me. I was never enough for you or I was always too much. I can't really decide at this point."

Leigh's surface cracked as she began to cry. "Why would you say that?"

"I wrote you off, Leigh. I told myself I would let you live your life. I'd stop interfering, stop telling you what I thought since I was the goddamn devil for doing so. I'd focus on Vinny. We would keep doing our trips and having a somewhat normal relationship. But now he's fucking dead. Now he is rotting away, and I'll never get to hear that laugh again or see that smile—"

"ENOUGH!" Jim yelled. He got up from the table and disappeared down the hallway.

"I'm sorry I wasn't as good as Vinny," Leigh said.

"Don't you dare say that," Ann said, pointing at Leigh. "You are my daughter. You will always be good enough. And don't you ever try to insinuate I loved Vinny more than you."

"But you do."

"NO. If you honestly believe that, then you are never welcome in this house again."

"She doesn't mean that," Lorenzo said. "Leigh, c'mon. We are all upset and exhausted. Please don't let this happen."

"I don't care anymore. Mom, we will be gone in the morning," Leigh said and got up from the table.

"Leigh," Lorenzo said, chasing after her. "This is ridiculous . . ." his voice faded away.

Ann heard the footsteps above her and go down the hall. A door slammed. It was the last time she saw Leigh for a long time.

○ ○ ○

By the time Ann unglued herself from the table and went upstairs, Jim was already in bed. He was still awake since the CPAP machine wasn't turned on yet.

"I'm going to fly to Dallas tomorrow," Ann announced.

"Okay."

"You have no interest in going, correct?"

"Don't fucking start," Jim said. "I can't fly. You know that."

"Even for your son," she mumbled.

He ignored the jab. After thirty years of marriage, you learned to take a few without retaliation.

"I need to go back to work. I have been gone since before Christmas," he said.

"You just buried your son. I think you can take a few more days. God knows you have given more than enough time to that place."

"And what am I going to do here, huh?" he spat out. "Just sit around and be miserable. You are going to cover that for the both of us."

"Fuck you. This is how it happens. This is how we turn into every other family that loses a kid."

He didn't say anything.

"This wasn't our fault," Ann continued. "Vinny dying wasn't our fault and we can try to place blame on someone or something but it's not going to help."

He didn't say anything.

"I'm going to sleep downstairs. The nonstop to Dallas is early, so I'll be gone before you get up."

"Okay."

"Do you think I'll still have my job when I get back?" Ann asked as she finished packing a bag. She planned on traveling light.

"I don't know."

"No matter either way. I'm not worried about it now, which is surprising."

"I love you," Jim said. Ann knew the sincerity in his voice was genuine.

"I love you too. Please remember to give the dogs their pills each morning. I don't know when I'll be back."

"Okay."

Ann went to the door and shut it behind her. There was a moment of longing to knock on Leigh's door and make things right, but it passed once she hit the stairs.

She sat on the couch for a bit and watched the news. People died all over the world. More genocide, more natural disasters, more shootings and rapes and murders.

The world was turning to total shit, wasn't it?

To Ann, her world already was.

nineteen

YOU'RE OFF TO GREAT PLACES

Her first stop in Dallas was the police station.

"Hi. I spoke to an Officer Baez on the phone. He said I could come down here and pick up my son's things."

"Sure. What's the name?"

"His name was Vinny Besser. He went by Vin. His driver's license probably says Vincent though."

"The last name is fine, ma'am."

The officer stepped away from the desk and returned with a plastic bag.

"Okay, here it is. There wasn't much left at the scene."

"I see," Ann said. The officer handed over the bag. It was light.

"I'm sorry for your loss."

"Thank you," she said as if thanking someone for saying that made any sense.

Back at the rental, Ann opened the bag and sorted through the contents. His glasses were in there or what was left of them. The lenses were destroyed, and the frames were severely bent, but she would keep them regardless. His phone was also there and in perfect condition. There were several other items, but nothing carried much importance. Ann told the officer to keep the keys. She never wanted to see that car again.

Vincent's address was saved in her phone, so her navigated there and eventually pulled up to the leasing office.

It was a mild day in Dallas. Their winters were a stark contrast to the snow and miserable nature of Pennsylvania.

Ann stepped into the office.

"Hi. Welcome to Axis!" the woman said.

"Hi. Yeah, I'm here to get the keys to my son's apartment."

"Uh, okay. We can't actually do that."

"What do you mean? I just called here an hour ago and explained the situation."

"Who did you speak to, ma'am?"

"Jessica."

"That's me!" she said like a dog getting excited at hearing its own name.

"Do you not remember our conversation?"

"What conversation?" she asked.

"My son. He is dead. And I am here to get keys to his apartment so I can go through his things. Are you—" Ann stopped herself.

A manager came in from the side room.

"Mrs. Besser, I apologize for that. Jessica is our newest model and we haven't worked out all the kinks yet. Follow me."

Ann looked back one more time at Jessica and saw her licking her palm like she was getting ready for a shot of tequila.

The manager made quick work of getting the key for Ann.

"My apologies for the confusion."

"It's okay," Ann said. "He hated this complex and I could see why. I'll have his stuff out within the next few days." Vincent always joked about the leasing office employed by soulless beings, but Ann assumed it was an exaggeration.

As Ann left the office, Jessica was flossing her teeth with several strands of her hair and seemed to be experiencing pure bliss.

○ ○ ○

Ann had made two calls when she landed in Dallas. The second was to the apartment complex, which led to the confusion just rehashed. The first call was to Daniel. She had met him several times throughout the years and understood that he'd want to know she was in town. Not much was said between them except how he would leave work to come over and see her.

Ann texted Daniel to let him know she was at the complex. His response was immediate: he would be there in twenty minutes.

"You can do this," she said as she stepped to apartment 134.

Her hands were shaking. It took several attempts for the key to find the lock.

Once inside, the apartment looked as she remembered except that it was more lived in. It was a snapshot of a living space where the tenant wasn't expecting guests. The dishes were piled high in the sink and random objects were scattered across the countertop. Ann didn't know it, but it was all the stuff Vincent intended on cleaning up when he came back from the party. For when he woke up the next day and lounged around playing video games.

We know that reality never happened.

Ann walked over to the counter and grabbed his work ID. She stared at the picture of Vincent from 2015. He was clean shaven with a smile as wide as the skies. Ann wondered if he knew when he took the picture that he would die in Dallas, that taking the job at Southwest Airlines potentially sealed his fate years in advance. *Don't be ridiculous*, she thought. *But that's how I'll always be.*

Ann didn't make it through the whole apartment, instead she sat on the couch and cried. It was her first time in any of Vincent's apartments without him there to entertain and talk about nonsensical topics to pass the time.

The apartment was dreadfully quiet. The sort of silence you only heard at funerals.

She sat in the silence until Daniel called her. She didn't bother to wipe away the tears. It would have been a feeble attempt to seem okay, to seem better.

Daniel waited at the door to the complex with a large bundle of flowers.

"I'm so sorry," he said as Ann approached. "I wanted to be there, but we couldn't get flights and normally we would have gotten must ri—"

"Daniel, it's okay," Ann said and gave him a hug.

"These are for you." Daniel presented her with the flowers.

"Thanks."

They wove through the hallways of the complex and made it back to his apartment.

"Can I get you something to drink?" Ann asked.

"Actually, I think I know exactly what I need," Daniel said. He reached up to the cabinet above the fridge and pulled out the bottle of scotch. "I always had a stock at his apartment just in case. This seems like an appropriate time. Do you want some?"

"I'll pass for now."

Daniel poured himself the drink and returned the bottle to the cabinet.

"Is there anything you know about where he was going that night?" Ann continued.

"No. We didn't talk much over Christmas. Danielle and I were in Australia."

"Oh, okay. Just searching for answers that aren't there."

"I'll be right back." Daniel darted out the door.

Five minutes later, he returned with a small box. "Here are his things from work."

Ann looked into the box and found a miscellaneous batch of items. A small bottle of Fireball, a fake liver, all of the figurines they had gotten for Vincent over the years, and his notes. Three notebooks sat on the side of the box. She pulled one out and skimmed through the pages. His writing was calm and stretched from side to side and top to bottom on each page.

The jargon made little sense to Ann, but it was still his.

"I could use your help," Ann said.

Daniel nodded.

"We need to clean out the apartment."

"You want to do that now?"

"No. I am going to take the day to try and figure things out, but would you be able to help?"

"Of course. I'm sure we could get a bunch of other people too."

"That's okay. I think we will be able to handle it." Ann didn't want to say it, but she didn't need three or four other people stomping around the apartment.

Sensing that Ann wanted time, Daniel poured the remainder of his drink down the drain. "I'll be available for whenever you need me."

"He really cared about you," Ann said. "You always came up in our conversations. Whatever advice you were giving him, some of it stuck."

Daniel smiled. It quickly cracked as the unavoidable tears rushed to the surface. "I—he meant a lot to me too. I was never expecting to make such a good friend the day I first met him. He was a special person."

"You're not the first one to say that," Ann said straight-faced.

"Please let me know if you need anything else. We are all thinking about you and your family."

"Thank you."

Ann gave him another hug and ushered him out the door.

Back alone.

She pulled Vincent's phone out of the bag and clicked the power button several times. Nothing. Ann plugged in the phone and soon the familiar logo popped up onto the screen. As she waited for the phone to charge, she opened his laptop that sat on the coffee table. Nothing as well. She found the laptop charger and plugged it in.

There had to be something on his laptop or even a text message on his phone.

There needed to be something to provide her closure.

Ann sat on the couch and waited. Vincent would have put on music to defuse the silence, but she wanted to sit in it for a while longer.

The books were crammed onto the bottom four shelves on either side of his television. Ann forgot how much he loved to read. After reading him the first two *Harry Potter* books, Vincent demanded he could read anything on his own. She'd find him in his room sitting in the corner with his head buried in a book. For hours at a time, he would riffle through the pages without a care of what was beyond them. Sometimes Ann would catch him zoned out at the kitchen table or in the car and likely drifting back to the worlds within the books.

She envied him. Ann was never able to take the time to read. Exhaustion showered over her each day that watching television after work was the only viable option to preserve her sanity. It was odd to her that parents could envy their kids in traits and habits they helped to develop. Ann was the reason Vincent read so much. Ann was also the reason Vincent wasn't happy . . . at least that's what she convinced herself.

Ann noticed one book on the bottom shelf. The spine was wrapped in colorful stripes. The gravitational pull of curiosity and familiarity lifted her off the couch. She bent down (her knees cracking in displeasure at the movement) and pulled the book from its home.

Oh, the Places You'll Go by Dr. Seuss.

She remembered giving this to Vincent after his high school graduation. Everyone who came to his graduation/going-away-to-college party signed it with well wishes and praises.

Ann opened the book and several leaflets of paper fell out. They were the instructions for his graduation day. A laundry list of do's and don'ts for the students to follow. Behind that sheet were copies of letters teachers wrote for his college admissions. They surged with kind words and strong recommendations about how Vincent would be a wonderful addition to any school.

It could be said that funerals *and* letters of recommendations are the only times people say kind words about another.

Ann replaced the pieces of paper and continued to flip through the book. Messages were scribbled in random corners of each page. Neighbors thanking him for all the times he watched their houses and mowed their lawns. Distant relatives wishing they had seen him more even though they lived less than an hour away. Friends from the fringe who attempted to write out kind words but couldn't help themselves from making a sarcastic joke or two.

The book was reinforcement on how great of a person he was even though Ann didn't need any further convincing.

With the book back on the shelf, Ann walked over to the counter and clicked the home button on the phone. The screen lit up with an array of notifications. Even in death, Vincent was still connected to the outside world.

She skimmed through them. Familiar names like Athena, Jag, Daniel, and

Quinn were all there, but one stuck out more than the rest.

Dylan.

Something told her the name was important, which may have been due to the quantity of messages he sent.

Her memory conveniently dislodged a piece of information about Vincent mentioning his passcode to her one time: Rigby's birthday.

"It's only a few days after dad's," he would always tell her.

Ann tried 0223. The phone shook it off. "Dammit."

She bumped up her next attempt by one digit to 0224 and the screen unlocked.

"How could I forget her birthday?" she scolded herself. Ann was right the first time though. Vincent was the idiot who didn't realize Rigby was born on the 23rd.

She found Dylan's number, copied it into her phone, and immediately called him.

He picked up on the second ring.

twenty

QUESTION & ANSWERS

Their phone call was brief.
    Dylan's voice cracked and sounded as if he expected the call to happen. Ann asked if he was able to meet up, and barely audible, he said yes.
    Ann followed the same route Vincent had when he left El Fenix the night he told Dylan that death was slowly tracking him down. The parking lot to the Tex-Mex restaurant was empty besides an idling black BMW that had been put through the woodchipper. Dents lined the driver's side and paint was chipping off from several spots near the trunk. One of the taillights was cracked and blinking at an uneven pace.
    Ann parked several spots away from Dylan and stepped out of the car. He did the same.
    "Dylan?" Ann asked, already knowing the answer.
    "Yeah."
    "It's nice to meet you."
    "Yeah."
    Ann led the way inside the restaurant. They were quickly seated at a table, which happened to be the same one Dylan and Vincent sat at months earlier.
    A coincidence neither of them realized.
    The waitress came by and ran through her checklist of what drinks they might want and if they would be interested in any queso or guacamole. No, not this time.
    "How did you know Vinny?" Ann asked. There was only one question Ann was interested in asking Dylan, but she needed to ease into it. She needed to understand some other things first.
    "We met a few years ago," Dylan said, his eyes darting between Ann and the people seated at the table beside them.
    "Okay, but how?"
    "On Grindr."
    "The hook up app?"
    "Yeah."
    "Why were you on there?"
    "Because I was lonely."

Ann didn't respond.

"I had just gotten out of a relationship—a long-term relationship—and I thought I'd find something on there to distract me," Dylan continued.

"Why was Vinny on there?"

"Because he was lonely too. We talked for a long time the night we first met. He just kept asking questions. It took me a while to realize he wasn't asking the questions to know every detail about my life, but to help me talk through how I felt. Vinny was good in that way."

"Did you two date at all?"

"You are asking questions I didn't think you'd care to have the answers to," Dylan said with a nervous laugh.

"I want to understand what he was to you. It's not like I can ask Vinny anymore. I'm finding he met a fair amount of people in Dallas and he spoke about none of them."

"Would you really have wanted to hear about his hook ups? All of the random people he encountered?"

"It was that many?"

"It's all relative I guess, but it didn't seem like a lot to me. He would have told you differently though."

"I see," Ann said. She took a sip of the water. The taste was slightly off.

Worry began to weave its way into her. She worried that the angelic impression she had of her son was a lie. Had he spent his entire time down in Dallas encountering strangers? How many other people would magically show up and claim to have known Vincent? Ann dominated the conversations with Vincent about her distaste with her job, the gossip of friends/neighbors/family, and the worries that plagued her. She failed to ask him the questions that would have elicited a meaningful response. Did he like Dallas? If he didn't, why? How could things change? For a while, she didn't have to worry about him. He was in a relationship with Evan and everything seemed to be tracking along. Evan was a nice enough person (though not the one she would have expected Vincent to end up with).

The waitress returned for their food order. Ann didn't particularly enjoy Tex-Mex, but she powered through it anyway.

Within a minute of walking away, the waitress returned with two plates of food. They had perfected the art of microwaving their frozen meals.

The food would sit there untouched, which was yet another coincidence to the last time we found ourselves at El Fenix. No need to continue to point these out as they are abundant.

"Do you know the one thing that didn't get damaged in the car accident?" she asked.

"N-n-no," Dylan said, clearing his throat.

"Vinny's cell phone. It was in perfect condition."

"Oh."

"I'm surprised you haven't asked how I got your number or why I wanted to meet you."

"I just—"

"I saw the text messages you sent him after the accident. The guilt you had. You were with him that night, weren't you?"

"Yes."

"Was he drinking?"

"He promised that he was okay to drive," Dylan said. He was crying. It's all anyone seemed to do anymore when Vincent was mentioned.

"The officer told me they are working on a toxicology report, but that it would take weeks. I would rather hear it from you first. Did Vincent drive drunk that night?"

"N-no."

"Where were you two?"

"Out toward Fort Worth at my friend's place. She decided to have people over for New Year's and I knew Vincent could use the distraction."

"What does that mean?"

"Things, uh, things had been tough for him since the breakup."

"Why didn't you two drive out there together?"

"I don't know. We . . . we could have." Dylan's face registered with recognition. The idea hadn't occurred to him until that point.

"Did you stay out at your friend's place that night?"

"Yes."

"Why didn't he?"

"I don't know."

"Did you two have an argument or something?"

"No, we were happy. Things were going well."

"I don't understand. Were you two dating or something?"

"Maybe. We were there for each other. I wasn't thinking that far ahead, and I doubt he was either."

"He should have stayed that night," Ann said to yourself.

"You're right. I have this guilt pressing into me that I could have stopped him from leaving. I wish I had."

"I didn't mean to point blame. I'm just trying to find answers. We won't ever know what exactly happened, which is the hardest part." Now Ann was crying.

The waitress made a beeline for the table, saw that both occupants were crying, and immediately fled back the other way. She had no intention of dealing with that mess.

"I'm not even hungry now," Dylan said. He pushed his plate toward the center of the table.

"You cared about him, didn't you?" Ann asked.

"Of course," Dylan said like it was the most obvious thing to him.

"I'm sorry for your loss. I have been forgetting how other people lost him too."

"Mrs. Besser, I lost my stepdad a few years ago and it still sucks. Grief doesn't spare anyone. To be honest, you won't ever be the same again."

"I'm beginning to feel that way. I need some sort of positive from all this."

"There won't be. This isn't some cheap movie. Your son died. Nothing positive can come from that."

"I guess you're right. It's barely been a week . . . I can't imagine how it will get easier."

"I don't know."

They sat still for a while. Once the check came, Ann grabbed it and they went toward the exit.

Things had a way of abruptly ending.

The clouds covered the sky in a mosaic of shapes and shadows. Neither of them paid any attention to it. Why would they? The sky would always be there and most of the time it displayed nothing of value.

Ann considered thanking Dylan, but that felt contrived. There wasn't any logic in thanking him. Instead, she gave him a hug. His body went rigid.

"Is everything okay?" she said, stepping back from him.

"No."

"I—what's wrong?"

"There's one thing I haven't told you. Vinny mentioned he was going to tell all of you at some point, but from the way you talked, I got the impression you didn't know."

"Didn't know what?" Ann's anxiety climbed rapidly. Worry settled in like the old friend it was.

"He was sick."

"Dylan. C'mon. What does that even mean?" Her mind was trying to guess before Dylan could give her the answer.

"He was diagnosed with Lee Gerber's disease."

"Wha—you mean Lou Gehrig's disease?"

131

"Yes. Sorry. I'm not good with names."

"That is impossible," Ann said.

"No. He told me it is extremely rare for someone his age to get it, but it does happen. Like one in a billion or something."

Like Vincent, Ann had watched their family friend deteriorate to nothing during the seven years he fought the disease.

"Dylan."

"It's true. I'm so sorry. He found out a few months ago."

Ann stared up at the clouds. Nothing was interesting up there, but it kept her from dealing with the information that had been handed to her.

"Why didn't he tell us?" she asked.

"He mentioned not wanting to burden himself on others. Vinny knew how devastated all of you would be. Part of me wonders if he wanted to die. It was the better alternative."

"*Don't* say that!" she yelled. "All I wanted was more time with him. I'd give anything for that."

"I'm sorry. I . . ."

"Did he tell anyone else?"

"Do you not believe me?" Dylan asked. "And no, I don't think he did. Before you ask me, I have no clue why he told me of all people."

"I need to go," Ann said.

"Mrs. Besser, I'm sorry. You needed to know. I'm not sure you would have found out any other way."

Ann said nothing as she moved toward the rental. Dylan stood there watching. Eventually, he walked to his car and drove off.

Ann sat in there for a while. She screamed several times and slammed the steering wheel with her palms like it was the source of her pain.

Losing Vincent was bullshit to begin with and now she was told he was dying. He seemed fine at Christmas. She knew that was a foolish thought. The disease took its time to eat away. It was a slow-moving entity that crawled its way toward you until it finally latched on.

Her natural instinct was to consider whether Vincent had purposely . . . no. She pushed the thought aside. There was absolutely no way that could have been the case. He was happy, right? Xander hadn't thought so, but Vincent would never have done that.

It was foolish to think happiness was the sole factor in a decision like that.

She came to the conclusion that no one would ever know what Vincent was thinking that night.

And that would be the worst part.

[twenty-one](#)

WHAT WAS LEFT BEHIND

Everything was reduced to dots.

Ann began the process of tagging Vincent's belongings. Red dots meant it could be sold. Green dots meant it needed to find its way back to Pennsylvania. She hadn't thought through exactly how that would happen yet.

At first, it was easy. The furniture was given red dots. There wasn't space for them at the house. Ann went around and added red dots to things like the lamps, televisions, and video game consoles. While some of the objects were important to Vincent, they didn't carry much value to Ann.

It became more difficult when Ann dug into more minute things like his books. To Vincent, they were portals. To Ann, they were an endless flow of words that didn't weave together into narratives worth exploring.

She picked up one of the books and turned it over in her hands. The front cover had a cutout of a dog flipped upside down because it looked edgier than having the dog right side up. Ann read all the praise printed on the back cover and wondered if anyone actually bought a book because some author or publication they never heard of claimed the book was "amazing" or "graced with the level of detail Picasso could have only dreamed of achieving." Where were all the books that printed the shitty reviews?

Ann put the book into the box she had laid out on the floor. The process became methodical. Sometimes she would examine the book closely to try and understand why Vincent had it; other times she would quickly deposit the book into the box, willfully unconcerned about the meaning of it.

At the top of the bookshelf were the scrapbooks. Ann had forgotten that Vincent made the one during high school and the other was created by Leigh. She pulled the beige colored scrapbook down and stared at the photo of a grinning Vincent who was proudly displaying his age to the camera. She wanted to open it and look through the pages, but instead, she dropped the scrapbook into the top of the third box.

Once Ann finished packing the books, she turned her attention to the kitchen. Almost nothing in there was worth keeping, so the several boxes she filled up with kitchenware were slapped with the red dot.

The laptop sat on the countertop, fully charged. Ann moved toward it and flipped open the screen. She was greeted with a prompt for a password.

"C'mon Vinny," she said and closed the laptop in a fury.

How many of those things would she come across? Accounts locked by a password she didn't have. The spiral began. What about his credit card? Or his Hulu subscription? Or the money he had in his 401(k) or bank account? (Ann would never discover his premium membership on Pornhub, thankfully.) Vincent had spread himself out so much because there was no reason not to. The stress of the details—the meaningless details—continued to lean into her. If it was going to be this hard with him, what about her own life? She had a house stacked with containers of nonsense and sentimentalism that did nothing but occupy space. The answer would be for her to simplify, to remove the excess and focus on what mattered.

She pulled herself out of the spiral by taking out the trash. It had steadily filled up during her afternoon of perusing through Vincent's wares.

"Are you a new neighbor?" the voice asked as Ann stepped outside the apartment.

She looked and found the source. A young woman was standing at the next apartment over.

"No. Moving out actually," Ann said.

"Oh no!"

"Yeah. This was my son's apartment. He died a week ago in a horrific car accident. They said his head was crushed, but when I saw him at the viewing, he looked like he always did—that big freaking head of his."

"Oh," the woman managed to say.

"Anyways, it was nice talking with you," Ann said with a smile.

The woman fumbled with her keys and quickly tried to work them into the lock. Ann didn't stay to watch and turned the other way to rid herself of the trash.

○ ○ ○

The next day found Ann finishing up tagging the rest of the apartment. It took her until early afternoon to discover the pantry in the kitchen. It sat in plain sight the entire time. She opened the door and found it stocked with miscellaneous items. Old cards, billing statements, pins from Vincent's work anniversaries, the box for the wand from his trip to Universal Studios the year before, and a dusty beer bong were the majority of things in there.

Ann swept most of them into the trash after it became clear their value was minimal. (She did keep the pins and letters of acknowledgement from

Southwest.)

She moved to throw out a yellow notepad in her hand when she noticed what was written on the page.

Vincent had decent handwriting, so it was immediately noticeable that it was his scribbled note across the top that read *Should the names change?*

There were other notes scattered across the page. None made sense to Ann, but dear reader, Vincent was asking himself questions about the books he wrote. There was a hearty helping of doubt within those scribbles. He was never confident in his writing and it showed on that tiny yellow page.

Ann moved to the couch and flipped back to the front of the notepad. Nothing significant was on the first few pages. One was dedicated to Vincent laying out his battle plans for one of the trivia nights he hosted at work. Another was a tally of points for a game he and Evan played. Assuming the objective was to have the lower score, Evan won by a massive landslide.

Ann came to a page with a list of all the books Vincent had read. She didn't know it, but it was how he tracked his New Year's resolution from a few years ago. The list was long and extended for several pages.

She continued on and found a sketch of Vincent's tattoo. It was remarkably faithful to what ended up going on his arm. Ann hadn't been a fan of it when he first told her, but now it seemed like such a trivial thing to get worked up over.

Deeper and deeper she went, peeling back the layers of Vincent's inner workings. Who knew they would have been buried on a notepad within the pantry? Ann passed the page with the rhetorical questions and came to another with a bunch of names crossed out. Similar to the texts on his phone, she recognized some of the names, but not all. Who was Allen? And Red? Further down, she saw ~~Mom~~ and ~~Dad~~ and names of other family members.

The next few pages were titled CHAPTERS and had one list that went from 1 to 50 and another that started back at 1 and ventured to 42.

Ann couldn't look at it anymore. More riddles and a continuing trend of no answers.

She tossed the notepad onto the coffee table and leaned back into the couch. Her phone began to vibrate in her pocket, but she ignored it. The texts and calls had piled up since she got to Dallas. People were concerned that Ann ventured down to Dallas by herself to deal with Vincent's things. She guessed many of the texts were poetic novels about how strong she was, and that so-and-so person was there for her if she needed anything at all. The same trite nonsense that gets spewed each time someone dies. Ann wanted someone to tell her she was a fucking idiot and wasted all the time she had with Vincent due to her incessant worrying and fear of expanding outside her comfort zone. Ann and Vincent never did that trip to New Zealand he kept talking about because she was worried about the long flight or how she could swing the time off at work. And now he was gone.

Ann reached for the notepad and tore out the page. She ripped it to shreds. And the next one. And the one after that. She didn't need his fucking riddles.

She got to the last page and hesitated long enough on tearing it out to read the following:

This is probably what you're looking for: rigby0224

Ann walked over to the laptop and input what she found. It worked.

Vincent's desktop only had one folder tucked away in the upper right corner. She clicked on it and a screen popped up with one document and several subfolders.

Ann didn't know what she was looking for or if she even needed to be looking for something, but she felt compelled to understand what Vincent left behind.

Obeying the instruction, Ann selected the document which had a title of **Start Here**.

The Microsoft Word icon at the bottom of the screen jumped with joy and displayed the document.

It was a letter.

It said the following:

Dear Whoever,

Somehow you managed to bypass the tight security that encased this laptop and now you are prying into my personal business. You must have found my password within the notepad. I didn't want to make it too hard for you. (Disregard if you found out some other way.) Well, guess what? This letter is meant for you, so I'm happy you found it.

If you are reading this, then I'm dead. I'm just kidding, I hope. That is such an overly dramatic line that gets used way too much. I find it to be about as annoying as someone who constantly points out things they find annoying.

Anyways, I am likely not dead, but I am most certainly dying. You should already be aware of that though, so I will skip the details. The circumstances why you find yourself reading this may be hard to predict, so I won't bother to try. But let's move into the point of this letter.

I never enjoyed writing as I was growing up. I preferred to bury myself in a book and let someone else's creativity guide me. I also found myself getting frustrated at the subjectivity that writing has. My teachers never rewarded my hours of effort because of silly grammatical issues or that the third sentence in paragraph four didn't support the main argument.

So, I continued to read. All through high school and college. With each book I put back up on the metaphorical shelf after completion, I kept expanding upon the notion that I would be capable one day to craft my own story and find a way to enthrall readers.

As you may be aware, one day I stumbled into Dallas. And what a fine city it is(n't)! I have spent the last four years here and along the way, I have fallen face first into a wide variety of people and experiences. You may know some, but I doubt you know them all because I have never shared all my stories.

I can't remember the exact rationale I had for it at the time, but I eventually told myself I could do it. I had read enough and understood the pacing, the character development, the idea that story is more important than plot, and all the nuances that writing a novel entailed. But a major problem stood in my way: I didn't have an idea. I imagine some writers just go without having much of an idea, but I figured I should at least try to tackle this correctly. I sat for a while and picked at my brain to discover something that would be unique and funny and engaging, and I got . . . nothing. Inspiration doesn't work that way. You actually need to go live some life to find it. And that's when I realized my story would be good enough.

See:

I don't believe my story is unique or funny or engaging, but it was the easiest thing for me to write at the time. And there is something to be said for writing that touches upon personal aspects. (I don't know what should be said about it though.)

I opened a Word document and took off.

Months later I sat back and thought one would be enough.

I thought the second would have a happy ending.

Listen: books write themselves. It sounds like something a college professor would tell their students, but it is true! Trust me. You may be wondering how a book about my own life could write itself when I know how things happened but let me level with you: I lied. I won't tell you when or how often, but I will tell you why.

I'm ashamed of some of the things I did, so I decided to mask the truth behind a shifting veil of deceit.

In some aspect I feel like I cheated myself, but then I think about the book(s) I wrote being on store shelves and someone stumbling upon it. They probably wouldn't want to read about some random bloke's life, so I had to polish up the turd a bit. The funniest thing about it though is that these books were never meant to leave the confines of this laptop. But now that you have access to them, feel free to do with them as you wish.

I believe I have lost the thread of this letter, but I will continue to ramble nonsensically until I get tired of writing.

Let's get the logistics out of the way.

Within the folder you clicked into, you found this document. I sure hope you started here as instructed. Beyond this letter, you may have noticed the subfolders. One of them will have a variety of letters (we will circle back to that in a moment), another will have the two books, and the last one will be home to my other book ideas I never took the time to think through.

I have been given the rare insight into my own demise, so I wanted to make sure I won't be forgotten or that the countless hours I spent writing will at least give one other person something to pass the time with.

Back to the letters!

With the clarity I have now, I tasked myself with . . . you know what? It is pretty self-explanatory. I'll let you see for yourself. You can decide what to do with them.

I think we are getting to the closing of all this.

This hasn't served as dramatic of a purpose as I was hoping, but reality tends to be a real boring motherfucker compared to the lofty expectations we set.

Sometimes I find myself zoning out and thinking about what's next after all this. It scares me. Actually, it terrifies me. Many people put their belief and worry in some higher power so they can sleep easier at night, but I am not convinced. What if all of this is for nothing? What if it isn't even worth fighting this disease because we all end up in the same void? I try to stop myself from thinking like that, but it's hard. We all accept death like it is the wave of a hand, but it actually is. So many people come and go from this earth with barely more than a whisper that I can't help but feel like there has to be something more out there. This is where I start to spiral. I try to rationalize my existence and I just can't. Eventually I get tired and stop.

I wish I had the answers.

I wish I understood why I'm stuck with this bullshit disease. I wish I could stop others from suffering worse fates than I could even imagine. I wish my parents wouldn't have to watch me die.

Wishing is for people who don't understand reality.

So, I will be here for as long as I possibly can. I will try to make each day count, but I will fail. I will try to laugh instead of being angry, but I will fail. I will try to outrun the shadows and spirals, but I will fail.

I am beginning to see that failure is unavoidable (and that my pessimistic attitude will never change).

I hope you get something out of the things I've written. I intend to be selfish and want someone to enjoy it. I want someone to laugh or groan or cringe or express any sort of emotion. But most importantly: learn from what I did (or didn't do). I am harder on myself than needed, so you likely won't see the fault in my actions, but I promise they were there. Don't hate me too much.

But, at the end of the day, who doesn't like a good story?

It is the one thing that will live on after I die.

Take care,
Vin

Ann shook her head. Every word sounded like Vincent. She could hear him reading out each sentence with the sarcasm and dry wit that became a staple of his personality.

Ann realized that the letter would unravel and make more sense over time, but it did give her confirmation that Vincent was in fact riddled by a disease. It was interesting how he didn't mention it by name as if he didn't want to give it any life or identity.

Ann bypassed the subfolder with the letters and clicked on the one with the books instead. She was greeted by two documents. The first one was titled **Definitely Not a Book.docx**. She doubled clicked it and the Word document popped open.

```
        I Wanna Get Better

                by

          Vincent Besser
```

She scrolled through the document and saw how he framed it like a book. Chapter titles, page breaks, the whole works. Ann felt a swell of pride. Her son had written a book!

Not just one though.

She closed out the first book and opened the second (the Word document was titled **Might Be a Book.docx**).

```
          The Good Side

                by

            Vin Besser
```

The second one seemed shorter. Was Vincent able to finish it? Were either of them technically completed or just rough drafts? Always more questions.

Ann moved to the letters next. They seemed endless and full of names she did not recognize. She clicked on the one that said **Lee**. Vincent wrote about how excited he was to hear of Lee's adventures as a doctor someday.

Another letter to someone named Antonio.

One to Arturo.

One to . . .

The list went on and Ann didn't pay much mind until she found hers.

Mom,

    For many of the letters I wrote, they were done out of need to tell someone how I felt because I failed to do so in person. I would drone on for paragraphs about how things should have been different or that I was sorry for the numerous things I never said.

    What I have to say to you is quite simple:

    I love you very much.

    You already knew that though.

    I don't want you to be upset with the brevity of your letter. To me, it's a sign that there isn't anything left unsaid between us and that our relationship was one of the things I actually figured out.

    It's okay to be sad that I am wasting away. It's okay to be sad that you'll have to bury me one day.

    But it's not okay if you let it get in the way of you continuing on. It may block your path for a while, but please find your way back.

    I hope we have enjoyed the time we have left with each other. And while there will be tears, I know we will laugh and talk about the places we want to go.

    Promise me you'll make it to all of them.

    I hope the list is long and plentiful, but it may be daunting on where to start.

    I have a suggestion though:

    Find your perfect place and begin there. You may not know where that is yet but think of me when you make it.

Love,
Vinny

Ann closed the laptop and pressed a hand to her chest and felt the cross underneath. The tears never came, which had been a staple of her life for the past week. Instead, she left the apartment and explored the neighborhood. It was quiet besides the occasional car that whipped by.

    Dallas appeared to be in a state of transition where everything was attempting to decide if the brief spurt of winter was there to stay or would pass by without much interference.

    She ventured far away from the apartment. Each building blended into the next, but Ann was certain she could navigate back. That was Vincent's specialty though. They had talked about what would happen if they joined *The Amazing Race*. The consensus was that Ann would get them lost and

Vincent would lose patience within the first leg, which would result in them seeing a quick departure from the game. Ann believed they would have been fan favorites due to her talkative personality (which is more common when she isn't dealing with a death) and Vincent's somewhat pessimistic view on life and his insatiable need to self-deprecate.

The light began to fade and dip beneath the height of the buildings.

Ann liked Dallas and didn't understand Vincent's disdain toward it. Once you got beyond the main roads, things calmed down and morphed into a crowded suburbia that grew eerily quiet after rush hour traffic.

She found a bench, sat down, and did nothing for a while. To a passerby, Ann may have looked dead, but that was only on the inside.

The feeling wouldn't last forever.

As the darkness crept in more, Ann pulled out her phone.

"Hello?"

"Hey, it's me," Ann said.

"H-how's everything going out there?"

"I found out some stuff."

"What do you mean?"

"I thought about waiting until I got home, but I don't think I could look at you and say it."

"Tell me what?"

"Jim, Vinny was . . ."

Ann spoke for a while. Jim listened, no hint of cracks in his titanium exterior.

Darkness overtook her with the lampposts being the only guide back home. Still, she continued to sit on that bench.

The last surprise of the day was that she still had tears left. As she hung up with Jim, they flowed openly and blurred her vision as she walked back to Vincent's apartment.

twenty-two

VIVIDH STORIES

Ann laid in bed for a week.

Without the need to entertain guests or fly to another city and set Vincent's affairs in order, she had time to grieve.

It was an ugly time. It was a time that has been recounted endlessly in various forms of entertainment. Television shows tried to show grief; books attempted to explain the abnormal process of grief; countless songs have superficial lyrics about losing the love of your life and the heartbreak that ensued.

Complete bullshit. All of it.

No one understood grief. There wasn't a handbook that could discern why Ann felt the need to shield herself from the outside world or sit alone for so long and cry. Lots and lots of crying.

Of course, it would be a massive disservice to believe grief won't be explored in this book, so it's common for everyone to fall victim to deciphering its meaning.

See:

Ann's grief was strong during this time—pure, unfiltered, and wicked. She thought about the wedding Vincent would never have or the Christmas presents she no longer had to get. She thought about how she'd never find him down at the kitchen table on his laptop again or that any future trips to Dallas seemed unnecessary. She thought about how she would go back and do it all over again. Every moment, every mistake, every triumph. She would do it again just to see him, even if the outcome was the exact same. She thought about her marriage. She thought about her daughter. She thought about how she was in an elite club of people who have experienced the shattering reality of losing a child, but at least she had twenty-five years with her son. Some didn't even get a day. She thought 2+2 most certainly did not equal 4 because if it did Vincent would still be alive. She thought about how global warming couldn't come and kill them off any faster because they were a dumb species that ruined everything. She thought maybe Vincent smashed into that guardrail on purpose and how it didn't do much guarding from killing him. She thought she should be angrier that the airbag didn't deploy on the car, but how everyone overlooked what was right in front of them. She thought about her childhood and being the youngest sibling. She thought about how she hadn't eaten in two days. She thought about how she could remarry if Jim died, but she couldn't go out and find another son. She thought about . . . everything.

The pain was unimaginable. A cyclical wave of nausea would pass through each time she recounted what happened that night. She should have been there. She should have been there. The guilt was disgusting and unfair. Was it pre-determined? Was Vincent always meant to die in that city in a pathetic car accident? Was she being punished? Was she a bad mother? Why couldn't Vincent have been happy? Not a single answer came to Ann.

It was exhausting.

Jim kept his distance because the right words never bubbled to the surface for him. Rigby though, she stayed close by. For all her quirks and oddities, the dog seemed to know best the pain Ann was going through. An impossible reality, but if dogs could talk, Rigby would have told Ann how the pain was only the thing before the thing.

After her week-long prison sentence was up, Ann stopped thinking. She finished her deep dive into the unknowns of the universe, discovered that the meaning of life was 42, and finally got out of bed.

We'd never fully understand what Ann went through. It's one of those things we'd have to experience for ourselves if such a thing was possible for entities like us any longer. Empathy died a millennia ago.

Ann took a shower because of the societal pressures of not doing so.

She walked downstairs, grabbed the flash drive off the counter, and drove to Staples.

Because that's what people do when the grief graph starts to trend downward.

◌ ◌ ◌

"I have this flash drive with a substantial number of documents on it and I want them printed. Is that possible?"

"Yes ma'am," the employee said, briefly staring up at the sign that read PRINTING.

"Great. Do you take this then?" Ann asked.

"You can use the computer over there and select the documents you want to print."

"I have never used a computer before," she said.

"I'd be happy to show you," he said without missing a beat.

"It was a joke. I'm not that incompetent."

"You got me there," he said. A nervous laugh echoed throughout the empty store. No one had ventured into that Staples in six years.

"What's your name?" Ann asked. She was hunched over the computer and trying to navigate the terrible UI of their printing service. No wonder Staples was as relevant as Flappy Bird, Danity Kane, or the guy who ate a hundred and twenty-seven tacos in twenty-seven minutes, only to live out his days in a taco-induced coma due to the tacos he ate without any regard for his health or sanity.

"Vividh."

"Vivid?"

"Close enough."

"That's a unique name."

"So I've been told."

"How'd you get that name?" Ann asked.

"I never asked my parents. We lived in India for the first few years of my life. Then London. Minneapolis. Dallas—"

"My son lived in Dallas. He wasn't a fan."

"I was only there for high school. I moved out here for college and landed this sweet part-time job, which essentially functions as a paid study hall."

"Which college?"

"Lafayette."

"Oh, that's nice." Ann continued to click away.

"Where did your son move after Dallas?" Vividh asked.

"He came back home."

"I hope he is liking it. Moving back home is never easy."

"It isn't. What are you studying?"

"Political science."

"Do you intend to whip this country back into shape?"

"It would be an uphill battle until I become a US citizen."

"Oh, I wouldn't have thought . . . you speak English really well!"

"A lot of green card holders do."

"I didn't mean that in a condescending way," Ann said, looking up from the computer.

Vividh was smiling back at her. "I know."

"I grew up in New Jersey and then moved here when my son was born. I have always been surrounded by white people. We live in a diverse community, but the neighborhood is quite sterile."

Knowing there was more to be said, Vividh listened and waited for Ann to keep going. She clicked the mouse several more times.

"My son was gay and it was an intense realization that there are people who live in the minority and struggle to feel accepted in this country. I hope you . . . I hope you get your citizenship."

"You said *was* . . . your son *was* gay?"

"He passed away recently."

"I'm so—"

"Sorry. I know. You share the same condolences as everyone else. I started to wonder why people said sorry. Were they sorry because I was sad? Were they sorry because they actually cared? Or were they sorry because we are conditioned to say sorry when we feel uncomfortable? I have been to plenty of funerals where I wasn't sad or even knew the person well, but I still told the family I was sorry. It was the unconscious reflex."

"It is empathy. People are trying to relate to you."

"Maybe."

"My parents divorced when I was in middle school. It was clear my mother wasn't happy, but she hung in there for a while. I didn't talk to her for a while when we left. I missed my father and it wasn't until a few years later I realized how vindictive he was toward her. I guess the reason I said I was sorry was because you telling me your son died tapped into that buried memory of what it felt like when my parents divorced. It's amazing how quick a memory can resurface, and you can draw on it."

"You're very insightful."

"Thank you. Do you need any help?"

"I'm about finished. Too many documents to click through."

"What are they for? I'm actually not supposed to ask. Company policy."

"I don't see any management here to reprimand you. Occasionally, my son would surprise us by coming home for the weekend when he was living in Dallas. He had a knack for always catching me off guard with that and the gifts he would give at Christmas. Anyways, none of that matters. The point I'm trying to make is that he liked surprising me, and I like to think all this was his last chance to. He left behind . . . let's see . . . I'm counting twenty-seven letter, two books, and all his other ideas for novels."

"That's incredible. You had no idea?"

"None."

"What are you going to do with them?"

"I have thought about that a lot this past week. I like the idea of tracking down who these people were that he wrote the letters to and surprising everyone with them. It seems like something Vinny would have done."

"Vinny and Vividh. We would have been a dynamic duo. What about the books?"

"I just hit print," Ann said, ignoring the questions. "How long do you think it will take?"

"Twenty-seven minutes. At least that's what it says on my monitor."

Ann wandered around the store for the twenty-seven minutes and looked at the dusty merchandise.

When she came back to the counter, she asked Vividh, "When did Staples start selling cigarettes?"

She noticed them in aisle twenty-seven, which was essentially the contraband section. Used needles, blood diamonds, endangered species, pebbles from North Korea, soil from Hawaii, the spines of two hundred and twenty-seven Congressmen, and Vladimir Putin's disgustingly large forehead lined the shelves. An entity dressed in a Grim Reaper outfit guarded the supplies. Ann asked how much for a pack of cigarettes—the itch was still there. The entity croaked and choked and said they would cost Ann her life. Not a bad trade. She considered it briefly.

"No deal, Howie," she ended up saying. (It was a funny enough line that it deserved to be directly quoted for authenticity and remembrance.)

The entity screamed in rage and collapsed in on itself.

"You're talking about aisle twenty-seven? Yeah, it was something Staples did to try and bring in new customers. For some reason corporate thought that bringing in the Grim Reaper was a selling point. He's a bit moody if you ask me."

"Anyways," Vividh continued, "your documents are ready. I arranged them in four different boxes. One for the letters, one for each the books, and the last one for his miscellaneous ideas."

"Thank you so much Vividh."

"I snooped a bit. *I Wanna Get Better*. That's a heavy title."

"It is."

"Do you think he got better?"

"No, but I guess I'll need to find out."

"I hope he did."

"Me too. How much do I owe you?"

"Two hundred twenty-seven dollars and twenty-seven cents."

"Printing is expensive," Ann said.

"Mhmm," Vividh said as he took her credit card.

"Sometimes I forget everyone has a story worth sharing. Thanks for telling me a piece of yours. Good luck with the rest of school and getting your citizenship. I will expect big things from you."

"Thank you—I never caught your name."

"Ann."

"Thank you, Ann. It's okay to be sad."

"I know. I'm ready to not be though," she said with a smile.

Ann grabbed the four boxes and carried them out of Staples. She looked back at the store as she closed the gap to her car and saw nothing there except for an abandoned storefront.

<u>twenty-three</u>

NEW YORK TIMES BESTSELLER

There is the unprovable notion that we exist in one of a limitless number of realities. The realities can be strikingly similar to each other or wildly different. Our reality is likely no more than a dot on the back of a giant turtle they barfed up a million billion years ago.

In one reality, JFK didn't get a bullet to the head and continued to wave at the crowd in Dallas. Stephen King already explored that reality and it looked pretty grim.

In another reality, the idea of paper money is nonexistent, and people trade for goods with blades of grass, which means people fought over land to the point that a civil war broke out and decimated that entire reality. The turtle's back got a tiny bit lighter that "day." (There is no concept of days in the land of the giant turtle, but that term is used to appease the people of this reality.)

There are many realities where humans don't exist, which allows for Earth to sigh with relief—as if Earth was capable of such a thing.

One interesting reality involved a group of "scientists" who discovered the ability to peek into other realities. They became so disenchanted with the disastrous reality they were inundated with that they built a time machine, went back in time, and killed themselves so they would never live in the future reality that waited for them. Some of these realities are gnarly.

Believe it or not, there is one, lonely reality in which pharmaceutical companies charge a respectable price for their products and the C-level employees aren't evil twats who shove their money in the most convenient orifice they can find (which is usually their mother's outrageously large asshole). The reality is a stable one where people can afford the medication they need. Everyone lives to see their grandchildren and the sun shines only half the year.

You and Ann happen to live in the most boring reality as voted on by the Committee of Realities and Cones (CRaC). For as long as anyone could remember, the committee had a mild obsession with cones of any sort—traffic cones, ice cream cones, mathematical cones, cone cells, pinecones, gluconeogenesis, falconers, conenoses, and so on. It was a long vote considering the number of realities, but yours took home the booby prize due to "their con(e)tinued insistence on creating shitty remakes to films and rebooting old television shows that no one wanted." CRaC took their entertainment seriously and was bored with the lack of creativity. The committee did not take any rebuttal and as punishment, your reality is set to be erased in 2030.

Onto more serious matters . . .

The reality we care about is not one in which Vincent makes it home safely from that New Year's Eve drive or lives his life without the burden of ALS, but the one where Ann reads the books and decides they need to be shared with the masses.

She stumbles into a literary agent, which is usually an impossible task since those individuals have their head lodged so far up their ass that the small intestine is insisting the head starts paying for half the rent.

In any case, the literary agent sucks off every publisher in the free world until one agrees to sell the book.

Time passes and *I Wanna Get Better* is thrust upon store shelves worldwide.

Many copies are used as kindling and sex toys, but some people decided to read the book . . . and they loved it.

Enthralled by the unbeatable charm and sharp writing, the book becomes a bestseller. Ann goes on a press tour to promote the book and people always ask: does she know the inspiration for the story?

No, she'd say. Ann enjoyed perpetuating the lie because it wasn't a harmful one. It allowed her the freedom to makes oodles of money but preserve the secrecy of her son's story. Of course, some people knew because some of those people were in the books, but Ann sued them for defamation and other legal jargon until they died from stress and constipation.

As the money poured in, Hollywood executives maimed each other in the bidding war for movie rights. For a while, she considered that making the book into a Netflix show would have been great, but they would have canceled it and instead thrown more money at season twenty-seven of *Stranger Things*.

A deal was eventually struck with V27—premier studio for gritty films—and Ann made more money. Money she didn't share with anyone. She had rediscovered a meaning to her life but became a mingy asshole in the process.

The movie was a massive hit and was cast with a bunch of unknowns to add to the authenticity. The impact of the film was large enough that everyone became gay and agreed how people don't change.

From there, the world descended into chaos. No more children, no more AA, no more reason to fight the failing war on drugs. People were going to do what they wanted.

The second book was released and became mandatory reading for every child in the broken education system. They would be the last generation. Podcasts were formed to dissect the meaning. Reddit threads clogged server space as people tried to figure out what the third book would be about. There had to be an end to the trilogy, right?

See:

Ann always told the publisher there were three books and how the third was the best. She never anticipated anyone would care or read his piss pile.

The mob grew outside her mansion as leaks about the unwritten third novel began. People stopped believing in change because of this. And turned gay! They demanded restitution! They demanded she write the book.

She did.

It wasn't a long book and it began like this:

This is where I will begin writing this book. So it goes.

It ended like this:

This is where I will stop writing this book. So it goes.

The book was approximately twenty-seven pages long or the equivalent of an eleven thousand word essay. Ann enjoyed playing with the theme of how people/things/cones/squids/carbon don't ever change by starting and ending the book with similar sentences. People cried at her genius. (People seemed to forget how the first book also employed this tired tactic. People were stupid.)

If it can be believed, the last book sold more copies than the Bible ever did, which would have made the Church uber angry if everyone wasn't gay. It was especially nice for all the priests who could now fuck each other and not the innocent altar boys who had been taking it up the ass. People didn't seem to mind the ever-apparent rape that occurred within the Church. People were *fucking* stupid and stupid *fucking*.

Ann died some years later having amassed a beautiful fortune she'd gift to the sea turtles of Papua New Guinea. Life was great for her. The money, the notoriety, the divorce, the estranged daughter, the dead son, the dead son, the dead son. Life was so great for her. People loved her because she found it in her heart to publish her dead son's work. People were stupid.

Rumor has it that Ann's last words were uttered into a cow utter and she said *So it goes*. Thus, was the rub of life. To live was to die.

In your boring reality, Ann never did any of those things. Thankfully for you. Instead, she hid the books for those first few months. They collected dust on the highest shelf in her closet. She wasn't ready to share what Vincent had wrote yet.

Shit, she wasn't even ready to read them yet.

His work would never become a *New York Times* bestseller. He would never find posthumous fame or the validation he wanted.

Reality was a real boring motherfucker, wasn't it?

twenty-four

REDISCOVERING THE PATH

Two things became clear to Ann in the undisclosed time after her trip to Staples:

1. She still had a job
2. Sending the letters wasn't going to be easy

Let's dissect those bullet points in alphabetical order.

Probably the least exciting plotline of this story is the brief exploration into Ann's hatred for her job. It is understood that the investment isn't quite there, so for now, it will be boiled down to this: Ann continued to hate her job even though everyone was exceptionally nice for the first month she was back. Paperwork was completed without repeat requests. Carpenters and installers finished their work in a timely fashion and with great precision. Designers actively sought out new clients and followed through on the appointments.

The great steam engine of Bridgewater Lumber was alive and lumbering (ha!) ahead.

You know that it isn't going to last, but that happens later.

Onto the next bullet, Ann had this wonderful idea of sending out the letters as a surprise. It wasn't her objective to read them all, but she imagined they all had meaningful words in them, which would make each letter a cherished memento to the recipient.

Vincent helped out in some regard with this task. Ann continued to use his phone and she eventually figured out he had put in addresses for some of his contacts. Overly convenient, but there is no need to question it.

With the newfound information, Ann was able to knock out some easy targets.

She sent Quinn, Jacob, and Sasha their letters. In each envelope, Ann included a brief note to preface the letter.

Ann enjoyed crossing the names off the list and seeing the stack of letters reduced and returned to their rightful home. She understood the task was always meant to fall to her. From the moment Vincent wrote those letters, she would be the executor. It gave her something to do and helped her work toward getting back to the path.

As implied, some of the letters were hard to track down the recipient. For all of them, Vincent identified the person by their first name and when she would cross check that in his contacts, there would be nothing. Those were the ones that lingered. She agonized about each one.

By the end of that first month of Ann being back at work, she had delivered ten of the twenty-seven letters.

Evan's letter was the last one of the ten she sent out. The note to him was longer, more detailed. She considered calling him and trying to see how he was handling things—if he was even bothered at all—but she had only met him a couple of times and didn't want to seem like the overbearing mother she was.

<u>twenty-five</u>

PRIORITY MAIL

The snow and dullness of winter finally decided to give up and make way for spring. The flowers bloomed and the trees regained their color palette. Ann's favorite season used to be fall. She got to watch Vincent's football games and Leigh's field hockey games. That portion of the year flew by because the family was always moving. Things began to slow down as they left for college and moved on with their lives. Fall didn't carry the same urgency anymore. Her attention turned toward spring as it was a renewal of sorts. And that was something she desperately needed.

On the first day of spring, Ann and Jim got dinner with Doris and Walter. They decided on an Italian restaurant not far from Doris's place in Bethlehem.

They stuffed the two walkers into the trunk of the car and loaded in the cargo. The drive was short, and the conversation was light. Ann spoke with her mom multiple times a week, so it's not as if they didn't know what was going on with each other. The meet up was more intended to get Doris and Walter out of the apartment, and likely the same for Vincent's parents.

Once the caravan was seated and drink orders were taken, Doris asked, "How are you two doing?"

"A bit better each day," Ann said. Jim nodded along in agreement.

In terms of their marriage, nothing much had changed for Ann and Jim. The distraction of work served as conversation starters. Once they got home and settled in after work, they dispersed into their separate areas of the house. Jim went to play the guitar or work through his crossword puzzles. Ann would go watch television or if she was feeling particularly anxious, she would do some more digging with the letters. Still though, the books sat in the closet.

Some may have believed the separation at home was worrisome, but after thirty-three years of marriage, Jim and Ann learned they didn't need to be by each other's sides every moment of the day.

"And how is Leigh doing?" Doris asked.

"Mom, you know I haven't spoken to her since she was up for the funeral. We just need time and I am determined not to interfere in her life," Ann said.

"She is doing fine. Finally settled into the apartment. They are thinking of getting a puppy," Jim said.

"Oh. That's wonderful!" Doris replied.

Ann condensed her emotions and took a long sip of her water (with extra lemon!). She didn't know Jim had spoken with Leigh. It's not like they had a pact not to, but there was a deep throb of pain that shot through her. She had been the one to take care of Leigh as a baby and worried constantly for twenty-seven years in how she would find her way in life. Why was she surprised though? Ann always had a much stronger bond with her father until he died.

"Did Doris tell you about karaoke from the other night?" Walter asked.

"No."

"Every month we do karaoke, and Walter and his son always sing." Doris said. "I think you know that already. Anyways, this time, Walter wanted to sing the song *Alley Oop*. Do you remember that song?"

Ann and Jim nodded.

"So he made me and several others come up on stage and start singing the background vocals. We kept saying 'Alley oop, oop, oop-oop' over and over again until Walter walked out wearing a wig and carrying a huge stick. He looked just like the caveman from the comics! It was hysterical. Everyone got a kick out of it."

"I have been trying to get Doris to sing for years and that is how we finally got her to!" Walter added.

"I promised to sing if there were other people. I wanted my voice to be drowned out," Doris said.

"You two seem to be fan favorites," Ann said.

"Except when we play Bingo. We win too much, and people start booing," Doris said with a laugh.

She was eighty-seven years old. Walter was seventy-nine. They were in relatively good health (no more hospital trips for Doris since the brief adventure months back) and seemed to be enjoying life.

But the end was near for them.

It was undeniable.

Every human who had lived before them was proof that immortality was unattainable and that they would eventually . . .

Ann couldn't think about that. It was too soon. The idea of losing someone else—her mother nonetheless—was . . .

"What else is going on in the building? Any exciting gossip?" Ann asked.

"Well, there were three ambulances at the building yesterday. One of the residents died."

"Oh goodness. I'm sorry."

"We are used to it at this point," Walter said, casually cutting away at his spaghetti.

"We have a friend who sits at the window all day and reports back on what she sees, so we tend to be some of the first to know what is going on with the residents," Doris said with some pride. "It is unfortunate though to see so many people pass away. I guess I never considered the apartment would be the place I would die."

"Don't say that," Ann spat back.

"What? It's true."

"Somebody took our spot at dinner yesterday," Walter said, changing the topic. "We have sat at the same table for three years now."

"Is there assigned seating?" Jim asked, a rare contribution to the conversation.

"Well, no. But everyone has their spot."

"What did you do?" Ann asked.

"We sat somewhere else."

"So no big argument or anything?"

"Just a few dirty looks," Doris said.

"Why that table?"

"Every day they switch how they serve the food," Walter continued. "One day they will start from the front and the next day they will go from the back. So we sit in the middle," he said with a grin.

"When the meals take up six hours of your day, you have to make them worthwhile," Doris chimed in.

Ann appreciated the simplicity of their lives. It was something she had been working on as well.

The rest of the meal consisted of idle conversation about the extended family. They were as boring as the reality the cast of characters found themselves in.

Back at the building, Ann lugged the walkers from the trunk and set them up outside the car doors. Doris and Walter latched onto their walkers and started toward the door.

"Mom," Ann called out. "Did you finish that thing for me?"

"What? Oh. Oh yes. I did. Want to come up and get it?"

"Yes." Ann turned to Jim and told him she would be a few minutes. She grabbed her purse and followed them into the building.

Once in the apartment, Doris rummaged around for a few minutes until she returned with a little black book.

"I wrote down all my accounts and details about how everything should be divided up amongst you kids. The arrangements for the funeral are in there—right down to how I want to be dressed," Doris said.

She handed Ann the book. Ann flipped through it quickly and saw less than ten pages of it were filled. Doris's entire life condensed down to almost nothing. It didn't seem right.

Ann had been asking Doris for years to let her know about the assets she had—in case something happened. After Vincent died, there was a reignition of purpose to get that information from her mother. You never knew. You never knew when someone was going to be gone and Ann didn't have the capacity to do what she did again.

Vincent's things had arrived a few weeks earlier on the truck about the same time the toxicology report came back.

He was under the legal limit with his BAC and there were no illegal drugs in his system at the time. Ann was relieved he wasn't driving drunk or under the influence of anything else, but the nagging thought returned if the accident had truly been an accident.

More questions than answers.

As for his belongings, everything survived on the truck ride from Dallas. The movers unloaded the items into the garage and drove off to their next delivery. Vincent's life was reduced to practically nothing. It's almost as if he never existed.

Ann flipped back to the present and thanked her mom for the book.

"Also," Ann said. "I have something for you both."

"Oh yeah?" Doris said.

Ann reached into her purse and pulled out two envelopes. One said *Grandma* and the other *Walter*.

"Vinny was sick when he died—"

"What do you mean?" Doris asked.

"He was dying. Of ALS. It was a recent diagnosis. He hadn't told anyone yet. When I went down to Dallas, I found a series of letters on his laptop addressed to different people. You each had one. I'm sorry I didn't give them to you earlier. Some have been hard to pass along."

Ann handed over the envelopes. "You don't need to read them now. I didn't read what he said but thought it would be nice to fold them up and make it more formal."

Doris and Walter couldn't find the right words.

"He also wrote two books," Ann continued. "About his life down in

157

Dallas. I haven't read them yet."

"I didn't realize he enjoyed writing," Walter said.

"Neither did I," Ann said. *What else didn't I know about him?*

"Did he leave anything else?" Doris asked.

"Some ideas for books, but they weren't detailed. So, no, there wasn't much else."

It clicked for Ann in that moment why she hadn't read the books. There was a finality that she would have to face. No more secrets from Vincent. No more details to uncover. Once she finished her read through of the books, there would be nothing left to explore. She wasn't quite ready to face that.

"Are you . . . are you wearing the gold chain?" Doris asked, pointing to Ann's neck.

"I am."

"I—I thought it was lost in the accident. Actually, I wasn't sure if he still wore it." Doris sat down on the couch to steady herself.

"He wore it every day. I thought I would hang onto it for a while if that's okay."

"Yes. Of course." Doris covered her face and muffled the sound of her crying.

"Are you okay?" Ann asked, sitting down next to her.

"Can I see it one more time?"

Ann nodded and unclasped the chain from her neck. Doris held it lightly in her hands. "There was never a time I saw your father without this. He was religious, but in a quieter way than most people were back then." She thought a moment and continued. "I know Vinny wasn't religious. He wore because it meant something to me and that it was the only piece of his grandfather he'd ever know. I loved Vinny so much. At my age, you never think . . ."

Doris trailed off, not able to finish the thought.

"I know, Mom."

"It's moments like these where I'm ready. I feel like I have lived a full life and I'm ready to see the ones we have lost."

"I hope that's not true. We need you here."

"I know. Just promise me that if things ever get bad to let me go. I don't want to be on a ventilator or in a coma. I've lived a good life—no need to burden the rest of you."

"I promise."

"Ann, it's okay to be sad. We all know loss. I'm here if you need anything."

Did Ann keep giving off the impression she wasn't sad? It was everyone's favorite thing to give her permission to be.

Doris gave Ann the gold chain.

"I better get going," Ann said.

"Okay," Doris said.

"Okay," Walter said.

"Okay," Ann said. She gave each of them a hug and moved to the door. "I'll call you two sometime this week."

"Okay," Doris said, one last time.

Ann pulled into the garage twenty-seven minutes later. Jim's car had been out in the driveway for weeks. His side was piled high with boxes. Some of them were Vincent's things, others were the junk the Besser clan was getting rid of. Ann started her sweep of the house in the basement and was working her way through the first floor. The summation was that they had enough useless crap to furnish another house. It was stuff they didn't want or need. It was her first defiant act in simplifying her life.

Once inside and after the dogs finished launching their attacks, Ann looked over at Jim and said, "There is something I need to give you."

"What's that?"

"Just wait here."

Ann came back with another envelope and handed it to Jim. "Vinny left this for you. I'm sorry I didn't give it to you sooner."

Ann had already told Jim about the treasure trove she found in Dallas, but never told him about the letter addressed to him. Even though Jim never asked any questions, Ann was sure the thought crossed his mind at least once.

Jim sat down at the table.

"I'll leave you for a while," Ann said and moved to the stairs.

"Did he write one to you?" Jim called out.

"Yes."

"How was it?"

"It helped."

"I could never figure him out," Jim turned around and said. He stared through Ann and then quickly diverted his eyes downward. "I didn't ask him enough questions to see what really drove him. I failed and I have to live with that."

I got Vinny and he got Leigh, Ann thought.

"You are a great father. Just read the letter," Ann said and went upstairs.

The dogs followed closely behind.

It was one of the few letters she had read. She understood that Jim would need time to digest it.

An hour later, she came back downstairs, and the sounds of Jim's snoring permeated from the living room. She grabbed a drink from the fridge and, for no reason whatsoever, began to clean portions of the kitchen. A pile of junk that belonged to Jim was laying on the counter. She opened up the drawer and stuffed it in.

Ann caught a glimpse of the envelope, unopened and laying at the bottom.

twenty-six

NEIGHBORS

Around the time Ann would have taken a few days off to fly to Dallas and then to some exotic location with Vincent for their annual trip, she found herself in Easton.

She always found herself in Easton.

Besides her job and finding someone to take care of the dogs, there wasn't anything that stopped her from traveling.

To make the traveling more compelling, Daniel had contacted her and said she and Jim would have access to free flights for the length of Vincent's tenure at Southwest, which rounded out to three and a half years.

Southwest flew to over a hundred destinations, most of which she had never even thought about going to before.

It was her chance to enjoy her life, to enjoy the benefits she never took advantage of when Vincent was alive.

Instead, she sat at home and continued to simplify her life. The boxes continued to stack up in the garage. Rooms were cleared out. The pantry was reduced from five boxes of pasta down to one.

Neighbors constantly came by to ask if they needed any help. They saw the mounting pile in the garage and wondered what the ultimate goal was. The conversations with them would skirt around the subject (or anything that would remotely relate to Vincent) even though Ann would eventually explain what the purpose of the pile was. It wasn't that the neighbors didn't want to ask about the pile or see how Ann and Jim were doing, they just didn't know how. No one ever wrote the manual for consoling grief. Actually, there probably was, but who would take the time to read that?

There were two neighbors who approached Ann and Jim differently.

Ralph appeared at their door one morning. He stood outside patiently as Ann unlocked the door and swung it open.

"I noticed that stack in the garage the other day. Is Jimmy finally giving up on the carpentry? About fifteen years too late if you ask me."

"Hey Ralph. No, we are getting rid of some stuff. Want to take a look?" Ann asked.

He stepped inside and followed Ann to the garage.

Over half the garage was scattered with boxes and miscellaneous objects shoved in the empty spaces.

"You guys having a sale or something?" Ralph asked.

"I don't know."

"Is there anything left in the house?"

"Some things."

"Do you want to talk about it?" Ralph said, rummaging through one of the boxes. He pulled out a book, *Slaughterhouse-Five*. "One of Vinny's?"

"Yes."

He put the book back and closed up the box. Ralph noticed the *V* that was labeled on the side and nodded to himself.

"Are you going to leave his things here?"

"I haven't had the motivation yet. I come home from work and just want to sleep. I lay awake all night and think about having him back. Not for long. Maybe a minute or two. I thought it was going to get easier. I thought I had made it past the worst, but the pain and sadness are still following me. Stalking me."

"Ann, I was lost for a long time after Vietnam. I came home and was rejected by so many others because I fought in a war people didn't believe in. It didn't make sense to me. I held pieces of my friends in my hands and had to keep moving forward as if nothing happened. Some days I wondered if dying over there would have been a better fate than living with the steady reminder of what I saw. Time eased some of it. The flashes still exist. The moments of recollection I hide away . . .

"I . . . I got married. I had a kid. They leveled me out. I got to meet people like you—like Vinny. And it all made sense. I fought for you. For him. For my family. I did everything I could to ensure you would have a good life. Sure, my part wasn't much, but I did something. There isn't a day that goes by where I don't hear the artillery or the gunshots that buried themselves into the helmets of my soldiers. I'm waiting for a peaceful night of sleep. An end to my suffering. And when my time comes, I'll know I did some good.

"It doesn't ever go away. I'm not going to pretend like I know how it feels to lose a child, just like you wouldn't pretend to know what it's like to be in combat. Your sadness is real. The weight of your loss is real. His things . . . they are real. Remember that."

Ralph walked over to another box and looked inside. "Hey! I could use this." He pulled out a tape measure. "Mind if I take it?"

"Go ahead. We had about ten of them."

"Should I be worried with this spring cleaning of yours?"

"No," Ann said, shaking her head. "Just trying to simplify. You never know when something could happen. I'd hate for Leigh to . . ."

"Ann, I don't see anything happening to you guys for a long time."

"I thought the same about Vinny."

Ralph took a deep breath, realizing he had ensnared himself. "I'm sorry. I didn't mean anything by that."

"It's okay."

"I miss him too."

"I know you do."

"How's Jimmy doing?"

"You know how he is. It's impossible to understand how he is feeling. We are doing okay though. It's just gone unspoken between us."

"Tell him to call me sometime for breakfast."

"I will."

Ralph moved to the garage door.

"There's something I need to give you," Ann said and together they went inside the house. She returned a minute later with the envelope. You know the routine by now.

"What's this?"

"Vinny's last surprise."

"That kid was special," Ralph said, waving the envelope.

"I don't know if I've ever said it to you but thank you for your service. I should tell you that more often," Ann said.

"I didn't do it for the recognition but thank you."

Ralph gave Ann a hug and walked out the front door.

○ ○ ○

There reached a peak during the wet season of spring where the lawn needed to be mowed twice a week. Before the heat of summer killed all the grass, the steady downpours helped to grow it to jungle-like heights.

With a sloping backyard that consisted of hills on either side, Ann did not enjoy the task of cutting the grass. Jim had trouble doing it due to his bad knees, bad shoulder, bad ribcage, bad pinky toe, bad male pattern baldness, and other maladies.

Thankfully, she had completed the backyard and absentmindedly pushed the lawnmower through the front yard. (Okay, but why is backyard one word and front yard two? This is why kids hate English class and half of America can't even form a coherent sentence.)

Ann missed the days when she could schlep the kids outside to do the yardwork.

She considered how it had been three months already since she heard from Leigh. Three months since—

A hand waved near Ann's face. Startled, she released the grip and the lawnmower powered down.

"Hi. Sorry. I saw you out here and we hadn't spoke for a while, so I—"

"It's okay Colleen. How are you?" Ann stepped away from the lawnmower, distancing herself from the chore.

"I've been better, but I'm more concerned about you."

"Almost everybody seems to be."

"Almost?"

"I haven't spoken to Leigh in months and I'm not sure what I should do."

Colleen shook her head in recognition. "She probably doesn't know what to do either. My guess though is that she wouldn't mind hearing from her mother."

"You're right. I have been keeping my distance. I don't want to interfere in her life."

"I get it. I really do. The kids and I bickered about the most senseless things after Bryan died. It's the nature of losing someone. Doesn't mean it needs to continue to be that way for you and Leigh."

A car passed by and pulled into Colleen's driveway. A burly man in a suit stepped out from the driver's side. He looked around and spotted Colleen. He gave a sad smile.

One minute, Colleen indicated with her hand.

"Who's that?"

"One of the CIA agents Bryan worked with."

"T-today is the anniversary isn't it?" Ann asked.

Colleen nodded. "Twelve years. It always feels strange how we acknowledge the day he died. Such a terrible day and I have to relive it each year."

"I'm sorry. I . . ." Ann said, reaching out to grab Colleen's shoulder.

"No need to apologize. You have enough to worry about."

"Are you afraid you're going to forget him someday?"

"Of course not. You shouldn't be afraid of that either with Vincent. He's your son. You don't just forget someone that important to you."

"He wrote two books before he died. I found them when I went to Dallas. I printed them out and had every intention to read them. I wanted to celebrate what he did, the story he told. But the books are about his life, and I'm scared of what I'm going to find . . . and when I'm done, there is nothing left to explore. No more secrets or surprises. I've been holding onto the feeling he isn't completely gone yet. I don't think I'm ready to give that up."

"Ann, read the books," Colleen said, grabbing her arm. "He meant for you to find them. He wanted you to read them. You know that."

Colleen gave her a hug and walked back toward her house. She greeted the CIA agent and they disappeared through the garage.

Ann stood still and felt the first drop of rain hit the bridge of her nose. A cool sensation ran through her body. Another drop hit her arm.

She laid in the grass and stared up at the dark clouds. They moved rapidly across the sky and ready to release the full force of another storm.

Ann waited for something to happen, waited for something to change.

The gap between the drops shortened until it was a steady flow and then a downpour. She continued to lay there. She clasped her hands together and laid them on her chest like she was in a casket.

The rain soaked through her clothes and drenched the uncut grass around her.

In a different time, Ann would have been annoyed that she didn't finish cutting the grass before the storm.

In a different time, she wouldn't have done something as absurd as laying in the yard for the entire neighborhood to see.

Ann didn't have the propensity to care any longer.

I have to read the books, she thought. No sense in running from it.

Ann picked herself up from the ground and brought the lawnmower back to the shed. She would finish the yard some other time.

The chore didn't seem as important anymore.

twenty-seven

THE GOOD SIDE OF WANTING TO GET BETTER

The patio in the backyard was recently redone.

Before, the bricks were sloped and walking over them felt like you were involved in some low-tech rollercoaster ride.

With the power of money, Ann and Jim hired some contractor to fix the mess.

As you may guess, the job was completed. Gone was the moss between the bricks and the random divots. Ann had an area she could enjoy again.

It's where she decided to read Vincent's books.

On a regular Saturday morning, Ann grabbed the books from the highest shelf in her bedroom and carried them outside.

The Adirondack chair groaned as she sat in it. The chair didn't get much use anymore and began to crumble after the steady rain they had received over the past week. The only upside was that everything seemed alive. The trees were adorned with bright green leaves, the flowers proudly displayed their multitude of colors, and a variety of animals belted out their springtime mating call for the enjoyment of others.

She began to read *I Wanna Get Better*, slowly and with the explicit intention to absorb each word.

It took her a while to make it through the initial pages. The exploration into Vincent's mind was unpleasant and jarring. He wrote in a scattered, almost manic style that was vastly different from the conversations she had with him.

There were moments where she had to put the book down and walk into the house. Vincent warned about the false information, but Ann had a tough time distinguishing the two sides.

The apprehension to continue kept swelling as she dove deeper into the book. Her emotions toppled over one another in a chaotic spin. She was sad at Vincent's sadness. She was angry at the staggering number of hook ups he alluded to and his wanton attitude toward meeting strangers. She cracked a smile at some of his jokes, but probably not as many as he would have liked. Melancholy engulfed her as Vincent recapped the trips they had gone on with the undeniable fact that they wouldn't have the chance to do any again.

It is important to tell you Ann's feelings during this time because they are something she shared with no one else.

After two weekends of dedicating herself to reading the first book, she closed the final page and wondered if it was always midnight for Vincent. The same, repetitious cycle seemed to plague him. She wanted to rip him free from it. She wanted to shake him loose from the reality he wrote so scathingly about. She wanted him to see that life was worth living, even the shitty parts that felt endless.

How could she have told him those things if she didn't believe them herself?

And anyways, it was a moot point. There wasn't anything to tell Vincent.

Ann placed the first book on the highest shelf in her bedroom. She would revisit it in future times (when things became dire), but she never shared it with the general population. She didn't need Vincent's image tainted.

She hated how he wrote about some things. The fractured relationships he described and events he must have misremembered. Was it all part of the lying game? Ann looked like a monster in that first book. She refused to believe Vincent viewed her that way. The idea could sink her forever if she let it, so she fought hard against it. The lying only made sense if he did it all for show, but who would have been the audience?

She began the second book the following weekend. With the second one being shorter and somewhat lighter on the dreariness (at least until the end), Ann sat outside underneath the clear sky and finished it in one weekend.

Several truths came out of reading that second book with the largest one being that Vincent was sick. He had mentioned it in the letter, but to see it explicitly stated was unbearable. Her son's life was reduced to deli meat where the expiration date was quickly approaching.

And that ending. He stood on that ledge and seriously thought of stepping off. Was that proof enough that the accident wasn't one . . .? No, never. That was one of the exaggerated portions. It had to be.

All the buildup. All the worry about the finality of reading his books was reduced to rubble. When she put the second book back on the highest shelf, she understood she couldn't be the only one to read it. It wasn't meant for her. The ideal reader was hundreds of miles away, even if his view of Vincent would be forever changed.

Her thoughts remained scattered on the books for months. Random comments would pop into her head and lead to frustration. Like the drugs. Really Vincent? She hadn't raised her son to be so careless.

Ann's image of Vincent didn't shatter, but it did morph into something more grotesque, more human.

Vincent didn't remain the angelic presence she once believed, but it also didn't take away from all the great things he ever did. She beamed with pride at his insistence to truly understand people and ask them questions that would often get overlooked. That's the son she knew. That's the son she would remember, regardless of what he had written.

Ann understood that Vincent never got better. He wasn't afforded the luxury of time.

She had time. Ann could get better and do the things he didn't have a chance to.

Ann would find her perfect place and learn to ask better questions. She believed people could change. She didn't subscribe to the belief that it was always midnight. It would have been easy to sink to that level, but she had to be different. Ann owed it to Vincent.

Ann needed to rediscover the good side of life.

What more was there to say? You have read the books and understand the ebbs and flows of it. It would be impossible to distill Ann's never-ending surge of thoughts regarding the content. Most of it was stuck in her subconscious anyways and locked away from us.

After returning the second book to the highest shelf, Ann found her iPad in the kitchen and navigated to the Spotify app. A quick search landed her on the page for Bleachers. As expected, "I Wanna Get Better" was their most played song.

With headphones in, she sat at the table and listened to it. One, two . . . five times before she decided it was enough.

She repeated the process and found "The Good Side" by Troye Sivan. It made sense. She understood why Vincent chose it.

The puzzle wasn't entirely over yet if Ann chose to dig in deeper and find all the songs from the chapter titles. There were nearly a hundred chapters across the two books, so her time would have been occupied, but she felt detachment. Reading the books were enough for her at that time. To burrow in further would cause her to drift even more into Vincent's psyche. She needed to start pulling herself out of it.

Ann added the two songs to her Spotify playlist and returned to them often.

twenty-eight

PERSPECTIVE

It was Ann's last day at work before Memorial Day weekend. A time-honored tradition in the United States where people spent more time getting trashed and stuffing their assholes with food then recognizing what the holiday was actually for. People spent so much of their lives at work that when a federal holiday rolled around, they lost their goddamn minds and reverted back to a state of primal instinct where the hierarchy of needs was avoided in order to get fucked up and relax for once.

Of course, that is a gross generalization, but generalizing is the hip new fad, so we are just trying to stay relevant.

The Richter job had been a grueling multi-month affair. The affluent Richter family came to Bridgewater Lumber for a complete remodel of their kitchen. It was moderately priced at just south of one hundred thousand. One of the designers worked up a beautiful sketch and worked tirelessly with the family for their approval. The materials for the job were currently being shipped out in chunks to the home with the installers beginning work where they could. Things had been going well, which was a pleasant surprise to Ann.

Ann sat at her desk and reviewed the paperwork for the Richter job. She reminded herself to give them a call today for the last twenty percent of the payment.

The office was quiet—actually, the entire building was. She still had time before anyone else showed up.

Ann got up from her chair and meandered around the building for fifteen minutes. She paced up and down the aisles, realigning merchandise on the shelves and putting things back to their rightful place. That was Vincent's job once, but not anymore.

She walked to the back office and strolled past the rooms that splintered off from the main corridor. It always amazed her how some of the employees were hidden away from the madness of the other departments. They squatted back there day after day, never seeing anything more than the fluorescent glow and hearing the hum from the desktop towers.

Ann continued to the kitchen in desperate need of a remodel. For a place that specialized in such things, it didn't quite click with her why they had failed to do so.

Back through the store she went and ended up near Jim's office. She peeked in and found him sitting at his desk. His head was tilted back slightly as he attempted to read an email off the computer. He began to peck at the keys, using only his pointer fingers.

"Hey," Ann said.

"Yeah?"

"Are you sure about all this?"

"You need to let Bob know today and start working on your replacement."

"Okay. I was thinking Laura would be a good fit."

"That—I don't know," Jim said, thinking through the suggestion.

"She has a great relationship with the guys out in the field and can get stuff done when she has the right motivation."

He nodded. "Something to consider."

Sensing the end of the conversation, Ann left Jim's office and returned to her desk. She still had twenty minutes to think through how to deliver her two-week notice to Boob.

See:

Ann came to the decision about two months after Vincent died that she would leave the company by year's end. Part of her wanted an explosive event to happen that gave her just cause to leave. That didn't happen, but she finally recognized how she was too far gone. Ann didn't need any more justification to hang around. Jim listened as she laid out her plan the week prior. He peppered her with questions about if she would find another job or what she would do with all her time if she didn't. Never once did he tell her it wasn't a good idea or not support her decision. Ann stressed she didn't want to leave him to fend for himself at a job he didn't particularly like either. Jim shook off the comment and repeated a number which was the amount of time he had left before retirement. She saw it in his eyes that he wanted her to move on. He wanted her to find the peace and happiness she needed to continue moving forward. Ann loved him all the more for it. That wasn't to say Bridgewater Lumber was the banana peel she kept slipping on, but without the stress of the job, Ann had a more defined path.

"Morning," the gruff voice said after his morning cigarette.

"Bob, I'm putting in my two-week notice today." Ann convinced herself that bluntness would work best with him.

"Hmm. Okay." Boob sat down and spun around in the chair to face Ann. He rested his hands on the protruding gut that stored the years of excess.

"Okay," he said again. Boob hoisted himself up and left the office.

By lunchtime, the news spread across the company like measles through a group of unvaccinated children. Coworkers asked Ann if it was true like she'd really have the mental stamina to bolster up such a meaningless lie.

She was surprised by the response due to the shitty behavior many of them displayed on a day-to-day basis. The nepotism claims always followed her around as some suspected her four-day weeks and extended vacations were due to who occupied the GM chair. Other employees were just needless dicks because they had nothing better to do than be needless dicks. The yelling and rudeness and constant dour demeanors always bothered her, but the worst was the notion that Ann received special treatment. No one else had to deal with the countless drives home where Jim ripped into the employees (and by extension, her) and threatened to quit on a semi-regular basis over the past few years. The fear that he would follow through stalked Ann. He wasn't the sole provider for the household, but without his income, they were fucked without a paddle.

Ann believed Jim continued to force himself to stay at that job because of fear he wouldn't be able to find anything else at his age, but also because it was his lot in life. Jim was supposed to work ridiculous hours and drive himself into the ground to atone for the scorched earth his family left behind, for the daughter he abandoned. An absolute exaggeration, but sometimes people blamed themselves without cause.

Sometime after lunch, Boob came back to the office and had questions for Ann.

"Why?" was his first one.

"Time for something different. I need to be closer to home," Ann said.

"Do you have another job lined up?"

"Not yet."

"What about Jimmy?"

"He will be fine. Or at least he keeps telling me so. He only has a few years left until retirement."

"It's going to be a shame to lose you. You're one of the few who had any sense around here."

"Thanks Bob."

"Was it me?" he asked.

"What do you mean?"

"Am I the reason you're leaving? I know I'm difficult to work with."

"No." The question didn't deserve a longer response than that.

"Is it because of Vinny? I'm sorry. I don't know what it's like to lose a child, but it must weigh heavily on you all the time."

"Losing Vinny helped me gain perspective, but it's not the reason why."

Bob nodded. Calling him anything otherwise that this point seemed childish.

"That kid was sharp. He was going places," Bob continued.

He had no idea. Most people didn't. Ann kept Vincent's illness a secret, not for any other reason than the further stiff-arming of sympathy she would have needed to do was not worth it. Vincent's illness was well documented in the letters and second book, so others already knew.

(Illness? ILLNESS? Vincent was dying from a debilitating disease not the common cold. Sometimes Ann's thoughts didn't correlate well to the boring reality you live in.)

"He was," Ann said.

They sat together for a while. The conversation drifted into reminiscing about the odd jobs and people who had come through the store.

It gave her peace knowing her time spent there wasn't for nothing. She helped complete a respectable number of remodels and sent away a lot of satisfied customers (along with some disgruntled ones as well).

Two weeks later, there was a cake and hugs and even some tears.

On that final car ride home, they sat in traffic for over an hour as a blue shell hit a car and knocked them out of first place.

It gave Ann time to think about the surprise visitor they received the prior weekend.

twenty-nine

SEEING RED

Memorial Day Weekend passed by without much fanfare. Ann and Jim didn't participate in any of the events—the golf tournament, binge drinking sessions, barbecue, and general social banter. Ann couldn't speak for Jim, but she didn't enjoy the idea of seeing friends of friends and other strangers that would whisper if she was the one with the dead son, if she was the one who was sad, broken, and on the long path to getting better. Ann didn't need any more whispers in her life.

Instead, they watched television and caught up on all the shows bound to get cancelled.

The following weekend—the last one before her big departure from Bridgewater Lumber—Ann and Jim were outside doing yardwork.

It is common knowledge that yardwork is about as enjoyable as a rogue finger up the ass, but what made it worse for Ann and Jim was that it was mulching season.

Once a year, the Yard Fairy comes around to all the houses and decrees that in order to keep the weeds at bay and the sparkle of the flower beds radiant, a new dusting of mulch is required. If the residents do not comply within twenty-seven business days, the Yard Fairy will return with a hundred farm animals to eat every blade of grass that exists in the yard and every blade that will ever grow for eons to come.

The threat didn't bother Ann too much considering climate change would wipe out the planet by 2050 regardless of what the elephants believed.

They ordered twenty-seven yards of mulch. It covered the entire width of the driveway and leaked out into the street.

Normally, one of the kids would have been around to help, but that wasn't an option this time around. Neighbors casually strolled by and asked if they needed assistance, but they politely declined. There was something to be said for two old farts completing the task by themselves.

They started in the front yard where the flower beds were easier. Jim loaded up the wheelbarrows while Ann spread the mulch to the desired location.

This process was repeated until the sun began its descent down the gigantic parabola.

They were well into the backyard when a voice called out to both of them.

"Mr. and Mrs. Besser?"

They both turned around, cutting short their discussion of which shrub would work best in the open area.

Ann wasn't proud of it, but a wave of nervous energy passed through her.

A black man stood in front of them with a sweeping smile and a pair of overalls on.

"H-hi," she said.

"I'm Red. I don't know if Vinny ever mentioned me before." He didn't realize how close he was to stepping in dogshit with the weird side shuffle he was doing.

"I know all about you," Ann said, a hint of sadness behind her eyes. She took off her gloves and stood up to greet him.

They hugged like they were long lost siblings. Red was ranked highly on Huggr, which was an app where you met up with strangers and gave each other hugs. Some shouted to the void claiming it promoted weird fetishes, while most others didn't give a fuck if strangers wanted to hug. Red's rating was 27 squeezes out of 25.

It was surreal to meet someone from Vincent's books. Red was a just a character on a page with a biased story written from one perspective.

"Do you need any help?" he asked. Without waiting for the answer, Red grabbed the wheelbarrow and pushed it back to the driveway.

"Wait—wait," Ann said, moving after him. "You don't have to do that."

"But I want to."

Ann stopped. She watched Red scoop up shovelfuls of mulch and dump them into the wheelbarrow. He did with ease like he had prepped for the task beforehand.

"Where to?" he asked as he wheeled past Ann.

"Over there," she said, pointing to the empty patch next to where Jim stood.

This process repeated for the next hour until the pile out front diminished into nothing, appeasing the demand of the Yard Fairy. The three of them focused on the job and didn't exchange much conversation.

After loading the equipment back into the shed, Ann begged Red to come inside. She paced through the pantry to find something to make him. Ann hadn't been prepared for visitors since the funeral.

"Mrs. Besser, I'll just take some water." He reached down to pet the dogs that were huddled around him. They were excited for the change of pace. "Which one of them is Rugby?"

"Rigby is the middle one."

"Oh, hi Rugby! You are very cute!"

Red lived in his own world where names were a matter of opinion.

Ann sat down at the table and passed him a glass of water.

"How did you find our house?" she asked. The question sounded more accusatory than she wanted.

"Facebook. I was surprised no one had deleted his yet, so I looked around his friend's list and found Leigh. We had a nice chat and I explained the situation to her. Here we are now!" he said with a clap of his hands.

A total stranger has spoken to my daughter more than I have, Ann thought.

"Where did you drive from?"

"Baltimore. I was visiting my family and it reminded me how I needed to visit Vinny's."

"That's a far drive. Thankfully we were home," Ann said with a smile.

"Leigh assured me you would be."

Ann nodded.

"Did Vinny ever talk about me? You mentioned something earlier," Red said. He wrapped his hand around the glass but left it on the table.

"Indirectly. I knew he went to Key West when he first moved to Dallas, but he told me he went with friends. I knew he went to Nashville, but he lied about the reason for that as well."

"How'd you find out about me then?" Red asked, stretching his face into a confused look.

"The books."

"The books?"

"Yeah. You didn't know?"

He shook his head. "I do know how secretive he could be. He never told me anything. Probably the case with everyone else too."

"Vinny certainly told a lot in the books. It chronicled his time since moving down to Dallas."

"Did he say kind words about me?" Red asked. He laughed as he finally took a sip of the water.

"Kind words? He was very critical. Sometimes of others, but mostly himself. There weren't many kind words in the books about anything. His mental state was in distress."

"He carried burdens he didn't need to. No different from anyone else I guess."

"Tell me something about Vinny I don't know," Ann asked.

"You're is mom. You probably know everything."

"Reading the books taught me how I don't."

Red stretched out his hands across the table and Ann noticed the tattoo on his finger. WWMD. Weapon Weapon of Mass Destruction. No, no. What Would Michael Do?

"You actually have the tattoo," Ann pointed out.

"This?" he said, holding up his finger. "Did he mention it in the book?"

Ann nodded. "Vinny talked about how some things in the books were fiction, so it's nice to know a small detail like that wasn't."

"Why would he make anything up?"

"I wish I knew."

"Did you know he could whistle?" Red asked. "Like that screeching, annoying kind."

Ann flipped through the filing cabinets dedicated to Vincent. No results were returned.

"No," she said. "I wasn't aware."

"My band had a gig in Key West the first time he visited me. I brought him up to the balcony of this cute little house converted into a bar for him to watch. I tried introducing him to some of the locals, but he wasn't as outgoing. Vinny always carried around this nervous energy like he wasn't sure if he belonged. Anyways . . . toward the end of the show, I catch a glimpse of him with this massive smile spread across his face. It was enough to push me through the last few songs. Now that I think about it, that might have been the moment I fell for him. Certainly didn't last long, but the feeling was there. As we finished the last song, the cheers started flowing and I heard this extremely loud whistling above everything else. I looked over, and sure enough, it was Vinny. It's the little things you always seem to remember."

It was a familiar story to Ann, but with new details from a fresh perspective.

Ann absorbed the information, stood up from the table, and moved to the sliding glass door. "Let's sit on the deck."

"Okay." Red followed her.

They settled into two of the chairs on the upper part of the deck. Being at the top of the hill within the neighborhood meant they had a great view. The Blue Mountains rolled in the distance, covered in a shroud. Houses blended into the canvas as did the sounds of cars, kids, and the occasional airplane from the nearby landing strip.

"What a beautiful sunset," Red said.

It truly was. Ann turned around to face it and inhale the beauty. She'd seen a sunset like that a hundred times, but she was always too busy to care.

"I remember all the times I would find Vinny out here reading during sunset. He'd be hunched over and squinting at the pages. I'd tell him to just come inside, but he would tell me how there were too many distractions in the house. I always admired his ability to step away from all this and get lost in another world. After reading his books, I'm not sure he was able to escape his reality much after moving to Dallas."

"I know it wasn't easy for him," Red said.

"Do you think he killed himself? It's been bugging me for months. Much of the acci—"

"He didn't . . . he wouldn't," Red stressed.

"None of it makes sense. He wasn't drunk. Never had an accident before. And on that night—a night that carries so much significance in his writing—he loses control of the car. Red, you see why I'm having trouble rationalizing this, right?"

"Yes. You're having trouble because your son died." He paused and looked beyond Ann. "I'm sorry I wasn't there. At the funeral, I mean. I'm sorry I didn't see him more. I got so wrapped up in the music. I always assumed he would be there."

"I thought he would always be there too. Maybe not in Dallas, but somewhere," Ann said.

"I have something for you," she continued. Ann left Red behind on the deck and moved into the house. The dogs congregated like an angry mob and Ann pushed her way through. She went upstairs to sift through the letters. There weren't many left, so she found the desired one quickly. Ann heard the noise dribbling out from the guitar room as she left the bedroom. The door was closed, and she wondered briefly what Jim was doing in there.

Back outside, she handed over the letter to Red.

"From Vinny," Ann said.

"Do you mind if I read it now?"

"Not at all."

He opened the envelope and pulled out the letter. Red read at a steady pace. Ann watched as his eyes scanned further down the page. He laughed at one point and shook his head at another. At the end, he flipped the page over, looking for more. It was a sentiment Ann could relate to.

He muttered something to himself.

"What?" Ann asked.

"He told me that I should do a cover of 'Like a River Runs' by Bleachers. All he ever talked about was that band." Red rolled his eyes. "I never saw the appeal."

"Why that song?"

"I don't know. Want to listen to it?"

Ann unlocked her phone and navigated to Spotify. Several clicks later she found the song. She set the phone down on the table.

They listened.

And they understood.

"I agree. You should cover it," Ann said.

"When I do, you'll be the first to hear it."

"Where do you think Vinny is right now?"

"You don't want to know what I think."

"I do. That's why I asked."

"Okay . . . he is nowhere. This is it. The time we have here is all we get. I don't think reincarnation is a thing or a paradise we all go to. His body is in the ground, which makes it all the worse."

"I hope that isn't true. I'd like to see him again."

"I hope you do too."

"Are you planning on driving back to Baltimore tonight?"

"I have a friend a couple hours away."

"You can stay here."

"I figured that was the case, but I do need to head back. The music calls me."

"Don't forget about any of us when you make it big one day," Ann said.

"How could I? People like Vinny are the reason why I have the confidence to push forward. He was extremely supportive and always asked about how all of it was going."

Ann smiled. It never got old hearing the small things that Vinny did.

Red continued. "Oh, he could be a major asshole, but after setting him straight a few times, he didn't try that nonsense around me again," he laughed.

"You are welcome back anytime," Ann said.

"I appreciate that. You have a very nice home. Thanks for letting a stranger crash here."

"We don't get many visitors anymore, so it was a pleasure having you."

Red grabbed her hands. "It's going to be okay."

"I know."

They moved back into the house and toward the front door.

"One more thing," Ann said. "Did Vinny ever talk about someone named Ochi?"

"Ochi? No. It doesn't sound familiar. Why?"

"No reason. Just a name I had come by."

He nodded. A thought bubble formed on his face. "Remember: keep moving forward li—" Red said.

"Like a river runs," Ann said calmly and with understanding.

They hugged and Red moved out into the fading light.

Ann watched from the window until the car moved down the street and out of sight, knowing she would never see Red again in this life.

thirty

LETTING GO

It wasn't until that first Sunday night where the dread of work wasn't setting in that Ann finally realized how free it felt to no longer work at Bridgewater. She remained stoic around Jim, but she felt like that kid who just walked out of school on the last day of the year. There was the overwhelming sense of freedom, but also the constant jab that she wasted so much of her time being unhappy there. Ann had dragged herself through the mud for years because of all the fears that surrounded leaving the job, and now, none of them seemed so bad.

She slept with ease that night.

The next day, with Jim at work and the warm glow of weekday sunlight, Ann looked for another job. Secretarial work was the goal—preferably at a school district, given their above average benefits—but she would settle for anything remotely quaint with a short commute.

With several applications submitted and not feeling confident about any of them, Ann took the dogs for a walk. The trio bounced with excitement at the mention of the w-word. For a group of dogs who didn't go on many walks, they got overly excited when the rare opportunity presented itself.

They winded through the neighborhood. Nothing ever changed. The people, the houses, the cars, the dead patches of grass, the dilapidated mailboxes, the waves from neighbors she didn't know. It was all so domesticated. It was all so perfect.

No one saw the storm that surged inside her. The plague of thoughts that corrupted her every movement. The doubts, the insecurities, the sorrow.

Ann was no different than her son. She may have even been the reason he was so fucked up.

Of course, Vincent wasn't fucked up. No more or no less than the average person. Discovering who the average person was could be largely subjective, but who cares at this point?

Of course, Ann wasn't fucked up either. Just displaced. Dislodged from the narrow path she walked down for so many years.

As they returned to the house, the foursome squeezed past all the boxes piled inside the garage.

"This has got to go," Ann told anyone that cared to listen. The audience listened and mumbled in agreement. She had grown tired of the stacks. Removing all the junk from the house and leaving it in the garage was like painting three walls in a bedroom.

Ann ushered the dogs into the house as she stayed put in the garage. She grabbed the first box and pried open the top. It was stacked with cards. From birthdays, anniversaries, or otherwise. Unaware why they were out in the garage, she began to sift through them.

It didn't take long to figure out that they were all from Vincent. Of course they were.

As Ann dug deeper into the box, the handwriting devolved into childish form, but the message was always the same: Vincent had kind words to say in the cards. Well wishes were abundant. Sometimes they were squeezed into the bottom of the card, other times they stretched across the centerfold.

Another reminder that kind words aren't saved just for funerals and letters of recommendations. What a naïve thought that had been.

Ann cried as she dumped the cards into the recycling bin. Years and years of words, thoughts, reflections, and more would be whisked away to the trash land.

Those words wouldn't bring back her son. Neither would the books nor the letters nor the power of necromancy.

She marched onward. Box after box was briefly sorted through to make sure nothing of extreme value was in there. Ann avoided the ones marked with a *V.*

Ann's first trip to the Salvation Army location was with a trunk so packed with boxes that she couldn't see out the rear window. She pulled up to the back dock. A woman was up a flight of steps and leaned against the railing.

"Whatcha got today?" she asked.

"A lot."

"Need a hand?"

"That would be great," Ann said.

The woman treaded carefully down the steps, leaning hard on her left leg. As she reached the bottom, her gait turned into a pronounced limp. Her head bounced back and forth with each step.

"I'm sorry . . . I can get these—"

The woman held up a hand in protest. "It's not a problem. You ain't the first or the last today."

They each took a box and carried it up the steps. They dropped them near the door where another employee was likely to grab them and begin sorting through the contents.

After they were done, the woman said, "Are you going to need a receipt? For taxation purposes."

"No, that's okay. I'll be back soon with more."

Not one to lie about such trivial things, Ann returned later with another carful of boxes. The woman was still perched up against the railing, her stare drifting out beyond the tree line.

"I told you I would be back," Ann said with a smile.

"That you did."

Halfway through part two of their adventure together, Ann asked the woman, "How long have you been working here?"

"Oh, I'd say something like twenty-seven years. I don't get no medal or nothing, so I stopped keeping track. That number sounds nice though, so I'll go with that."

"Are you from the area?"

"No, ma'am. The South raised me, and my late husband uprooted me from the comfort of it. I can't be too mad at him. We had some babies, but now they are all grown with their own worries and such."

"Do you get to see them often?"

"No. No I do not. There are enough young folks that come through here that I get my fix. These kids got more problems today than we ever had to worry about." The woman shook her head at the thought.

"Do you think we messed it up too badly?"

"I'm not sure, but I do know that people like you make it a bit better."

"Why do you say that?" Ann asked.

"Because you take time to load up your car over there and bring us your belongings. Not everyone could be bothered to do so. They'd rather hang onto all of it."

Ann nodded. She didn't find herself to be noble in bringing her excess to the Salvation Army. It was a place to deposit her junk, a place for someone else to sort through it all. There was no making the world better by pushing your shit onto someone else. Unless that person didn't see your stuff as junk.

It wasn't a thread worth exploring so she let the thought go.

"That's it for this trip. I'll be back one more time," Ann said with hesitation in her voice.

"Alright now. See you soon, dear."

The last carload was the hardest and the smallest amount. Ann could see perfectly fine through the rear-view mirror the entire drive to the Salvation

Army. There were only four boxes.

"Welcome back," the woman said. She began to walk toward the steps, but Ann stopped her.

"I only have a few this time. I can grab them."

The woman limped back from the steps and returned to her post at the railing. She watched Ann intently as she walked up with the first box.

"Over here?"

"Just like all the others," the woman said.

She repeated the same process for the next two.

As Ann reached the top of the steps with the last box, she hesitated. The *V* on top faced skyward. To the woman, it must have looked like an unfinished *A*.

The woman took two painful steps and took hold of the box. "You can let go now. I have it."

"Thanks," a sad smile worked its way onto Ann's face.

"I remember when I lost my oldest. You don't truly know loss until it happens." The woman placed the box with the rest.

"How'd you know?" Ann asked.

"A mother's intuition, I guess."

"What happened to your child?"

"That's everyone's favorite question."

"I'm sorry—"

"It's quite alright. You'll find that it gets easier to talk about with time." She paused for a moment, moving her gaze back to the tree line. "He was three. He always told me he was a 'big bird' and didn't need help with anything. Too smart for his own good, like most kids I suppose. One day he was playing upstairs, and I heard this awful crash. The noise disappeared as quickly as it started. My baby boy was lying face down at the bottom of the steps. Dead before he landed at the bottom."

Ann brought her hands to her face. "Oh my God."

"You are acting all surprised like that story wasn't going to end in death."

"It's just . . . he was so young."

"I know. Some days I think about the type of man he would have been. If he would have ever grown out of that big bird phase. He would have been a good brother I know that for sure."

"What was his name?"

The woman spoke. The word took a while to register in Ann's mind. Ann felt unsteady and reached out for the railing and clutched it with force.

"Are you okay?" the woman asked.

"I'm fine."

"How old was yours?"

"Twenty-five," her mind still swaying slightly.

"A lifetime," the woman said with benign envy. The pain had never left her, only transferred to more present matters.

"Thank you for all your help today," Ann said abruptly. She needed to move on from this.

"My pleasure. Get home safe." The woman seemed unconcerned with Ann's sudden departure and continued to watch her as she got in the car and rounded the corner.

Ann fought off the surge of tears and focused on driving home. She passed by guardrails that sat idling on the side of the road. She quickly slipped back to that night and tried to piece together what happened for the thousandth time. No new evidence, no different explanation for the events. Vincent still crashed into that guardrail. Vincent still came out of that car in a body bag.

Back at home, she pulled the car into the garage for the first time in months. Jim's car was already there.

"All the stuff is gone," he keenly said as she stepped inside.

"Yeah."

"What happened?"

"It felt like it was time."

"Are you okay?"

"No. No, I'm not. I feel like I just threw away every memory of our son. Those boxes had clothes and toys and things we would have never touched again, but why would it have mattered? They were his. Now they are going to be used and worn by some fucking stranger. They'll never know Vinny. They'll never know how much we loved him, how much we miss him. How much I wish it was me in that car instead of him. They'll never know. They'll never know . . ."

Jim walked over and gave her the most meaningful hug of her life. She relaxed at his embrace and felt all the emotion pour out of her. The wave wasn't as severe as it would have been even a month ago. The graph was still trending downward.

Ann didn't let go of Jim for a long time.

<u>thirty-one</u>

MARSHALL, MARSHALL, MARSHALL

Part of the difficulty of writing this account of Ann's life is attempting to capture the happy moments. There were plenty—they just occurred in another time.

Each chapter has felt like another punch to the jaw. How much more downtrodden could this possibly get? Which punch would be the fatal blow?

See:

Happiness—like any other emotion—is fleeting. Sometimes it hangs around for an extended stay at the local Holiday Inn, while other times it fucks right off to Tibet for a yearlong sabbatical.

You know this, right? You've been around the block. You've taken in the sights and sounds. You've basked in your happiness and pushed away the anguish. You've been punched in the jaw before and realized pain is no less fleeting. You can sympathize—maybe even empathize. You've been in the audience before. There's a reason you're here.

You want to see Ann get better. You wanted to see Vincent get better. You want to believe people can change.

Maybe you want to change. All those times you've said you'll pick up that new hobby or escape the confines of that miserable job, and yet, you haven't done anything about it.

This isn't a self-help book though.

This is all about your boring reality staring back at you.

And the grief you'll never be prepared for.

○ ○ ○

Ann was fifty-three years old when Vincent died. Her birthday was a month later, which—assuming the math was accurate—she upped her stats by one and completed another rotation around the sun. People will say that age ain't nothing but a number, but people don't know shit. She aged a great deal over the last six months.

The wheels began to turn on this subject when Ann flipped open the case to her iPad and the black screen greeted her. The wrinkles in her face stood out like a comedian stepping into the spotlight. Her tired eyes darted around the borders of the screen, finding it hard to make direct eye contact with what was staring back.

If Ann ever won the lottery, she would buy a first-class ticket to California and waltz into the most glamorous doctor's office and get all the punctures, knife hacks, and rejiggering needed for her to pass as one of the elite women in their fifties.

In the boring reality she lived in, there wasn't a need to go and buy lottery tickets considering her chances of winning were on par with blowing on that whistle attached to Vincent's coffin to bring him back from the dead. The Pennsylvania lottery claimed to benefit older Pennsylvanians every day and yet her mother had to spend hundreds of dollars on medication. Something seemed fishy there, but Ann forgot about it as her mind turned to Vincent's books.

There wasn't a logical jump to the new topic; the thought just appeared. Ann was torn. She wanted to be more upset about the books. She wanted to decree Vincent's behavior as adverse to how she understood him, but Ann had to realize that maybe she didn't understand her son much at all. A level of detachment formed due to her not knowing all the characters within the books and never being quite sure what was true. Someone observing Ann's life may have seen the introduction of the books as a turning point in the plot of her life. What a foolish notion! Expectations must be cast aside when dealing with real people. They don't always adhere to the clichés admired by the masses. With that in mind, Ann occasionally contemplated the content of the books but never obsessed over the details. Vincent's choices were his own and any shouting or ranting Ann could have done would have fallen on deaf ears. She liked to believe he found love in Evan. She also liked to believe that they could have worked out if Vincent fought more for him. At least Vincent got to experience what love was like before he smashed his face off the steering wheel.

Ann shook her head and brought herself back to the present. She unlocked the iPad and began searching for flights. She had narrowed down her itinerary and needed to lock in the specifics.

Flying always made her nervous and she insisted on having a window seat, but now her concerns seemed trivial. All those years that Vincent was down in Dallas and she visited him once or twice a year. What a waste. She wouldn't make that mistake again.

The doorbell rang. It seemed distant like in another house entirely. Ann didn't move from the kitchen table as the dogs flooded into the hallway toward the noise pollution.

She heard footsteps on the tile and the sound of the door opening. Ann didn't look up from the screen to see who it was. Probably just another neighbor checking in to make sure the two of them had a pulse.

"Mom?" the voice said.

There were only two people in the world who used that name for her and one of them was long dead.

Ann finally looked up from the screen. Leigh stood in front of her with an honest smile. She held out the golden retriever puppy in her arms. "This is Marshall."

"Oh my god. You got a dog?"

"Yeah. Last week. We did a lot of research and found this breeder up in Portland. She wouldn't tell us which puppy we'd get until we met them all. Everyone was jealous that we got Marshall," Leigh said.

"He's a terror," Lorenzo chimed in from behind.

Ann darted her gaze between Leigh and the puppy. Her daughter was actually standing in front of her. It had been three . . . no, four months since Ann last saw her.

"Why are you here?" Ann asked, a poor question to ask so quickly.

Leigh's shoulders sagged as she took a long exhale. "We wanted to see you."

Marshall began to squirm and attempted to break out of Leigh's embrace. His tiny whimpers were a sign of protest. Leigh bent down and set him loose. The other dogs chased after him with intense curiosity at the little bundle running across the floor.

Ann collapsed the iPad and got up from the table. She gave Leigh a hug that lasted for quite some time. Ann whispered something to Leigh, but we will never know what was said. It wasn't our moment to intrude.

She repeated the same process with Lorenzo.

"How is work going?" Ann asked him.

"Actually, I got some good news. They are giving me a full-time position at the end of my contract. I don't have all the details yet, but my boss was adamant that it's a done deal," Lorenzo said.

"That's great! I know that was a big worry for you both. Also, can I get you anything? I can make some lunch. I'm sure Dad wouldn't mind grilling."

"We are fine for right now," Leigh said. She moved over into the family room and scooped up Marshall. "He probably needs to go out."

Ann followed Leigh outside. Marshall zipped around the yard and explored every corner of it.

"You've lost a lot of weight," Leigh said as they were standing out in the grass.

"You think so?"

"Yeah. Have you been dieting?"

"No. I haven't."

"Dad told me you left Bridgewater."

"You've talked to Dad since January?" the pain was obvious in Ann's voice.

"Yes, Mom. You need to understand that we have all been grieving too. I have a large amount of guilt toward the whole situation. I should have been there more . . . I should have done a lot of things differently. The anger and frustration toward you weren't fair. I recognize that now. I also recognize that we are never going to see eye to eye on everything. And that's okay. I need you in my life though. I don't want the three of us to drift apart. It can't happen. Vinny wouldn't—"

"I know. I know. I just felt like I had tried everything I could think of to repair and build our relationship and seeing as that didn't work, I decided to pull away. Leigh, I love you more than I could ever describe. You have to understand that. Sometimes I try to insert my opinion in places where I shouldn't, but I only want what's best for you. You are at a major turning point in your life and I don't want you to make the same mistakes I did. Marriage is tough. Being happy with your career choice is just as hard. Soon you will be thinking about having kids and there are things you need to discover about yourself and Lorenzo before doing so. I would have absolutely dissuaded you from getting a dog, so I'm glad it turned out to be a surprise," Ann said and scanned the yard until she found some shrubs wavering. Marshall burst from them with a stick twice his size.

"How's it going so far with him?" Ann asked.

Leigh explained the highs and lows of puppy training. Ann remembered those days all too well, especially the time her and Jim raised a litter of puppies before the kids were born. It was a whirlwind experience and having to say goodbye to all the puppies was easily the hardest part.

". . . Vinny was the last one to raise a puppy so I'm sure he would have had some advice," Leigh said.

"Yeah, I hadn't thought about that. He wrote about it in his book."

"What book?"

"Vinny chronicled his time down in Dallas. He . . . he was brutally honest. It was hard to get through. I didn't understand many of his decisions and now I don't have a chance to ask him. Part of me is happy though that he wrote what he did. It shed light on the fact that Vinny wasn't okay. He struggled with many things. When I think about that it makes me extremely sad, but I know we were a bright spot for him. He valued the time he spent up here after moving to Dallas. That doesn't bring much consolation to everything that has happened though."

"I'd like to read it sometime," Leigh said.

"Yeah, it would be great if you did. Also," Ann continued, "there are a few other things you need to know."

Ann told Leigh about the letters Vincent wrote. The stack Ann had been hiding away upstairs was dwindling to a thin number. Ann also explained Vincent's illness. Leigh's stoic demeanor held up as she listened to her mother tell her the news.

"Remember that night around Christmas when Vinny, Lorenzo, and I went to the brewery?"

"Yeah."

"Vinny wanted to tell us something, but he stopped himself and said it wasn't a big deal. That must have been it. We would have lost him either way," Leigh said.

Ann nodded. "I haven't told many people about it. Just didn't seem worth sharing."

"Do you think he was scared?"

"Yes. He was. After reading the books, it was clear he was more introspective than I ever knew. We would have been here for him though, but I think that scared him the most."

"What did?"

"Being a burden to us," Ann said.

"He wouldn't have been though."

Marshall returned to Leigh and started biting at her shoelaces. "Let's bring him back inside," Leigh said and scooped him up in one swift motion.

"Are we okay?" Ann asked.

"Yes."

Ann didn't believe the affirmation but decided not to challenge Leigh on it. There was a sense of surrealism that Leigh magically appeared at the house with the puppy as some sort of peace offering. Things weren't exactly okay. It would take time and numerous conversations to repair whatever was damaged. Leigh and Ann would never have the quintessential mother-daughter relationship. It just wasn't in the cards, but that doesn't mean they should ever go four months without speaking to each other again.

Ann reached out and grabbed Leigh's arm. "I need you."

"I'm not going anywhere," Leigh said and walked back into the house.

Lunch was spread out on the table an hour later. They sat in their usual spots—Jim at the seat closest to the front door, Ann with her back to the kitchen, Leigh across from her, and Lorenzo filling the void of Vincent's spot next to the bay windows.

The dogs were passed out in an oblong crop circle. Marshall gave the others more exercise than they'd seen in months.

Back at the table, Leigh told her gross stories from the hospital. Jim plugged his atrocious dad jokes. Lorenzo gave a detailed account of Marshall's quirks. Ann listened. She listened to her family laugh and forget the pain for a brief moment. She would be the one to carry it. Always. Ann didn't mind the burden.

It would be Vincent's birthday in a few weeks. He would have been twenty-six—one year away from that magic number.

There wasn't a need to fixate on that now, so Ann returned to the present and enjoyed the time with her family.

thirty-two

EXHALE

Ann left for Boston on Vincent's birthday. She thought about the cake she didn't have to make, the presents she didn't buy, the birthday cards she didn't fill out . . .

The clear skies in both Philadelphia and Boston made for a smooth take-off and landing.

We are familiar with the arduous nature of getting to Provincetown, so let's skip the drivel.

Ann stepped off the ferry in the early afternoon.

"Got everything?" Xander asked as he made his way off the ramp and onto the boardwalk.

"I think so." She surveyed the area and saw the blend of people filtering off the ferry and heading toward town. "This feels like what I was expecting," she continued.

"It's such a cute place. I actually miss it," Xander said.

"How far away is your friend's place?"

"Like a fifteen-minute walk. Follow me."

She did. Xander weaved his way through the crowd that grew thicker as they moved onto the main drag. Ann tried to keep pace, but his long legs propelled him forward at a faster rate. She felt winded just from the walking.

The house was unoccupied when they arrived. Xander's friend was out of town for the weekend, which is likely the reason why he agreed for them to come up then.

Ann settled into the living room and began the process of spreading her things out.

"Vinny slept on that couch when he was here," Xander pointed out.

"Oh really?"

Ann hoped the trip wasn't going to turn into some recollection of every moment Xander and Vincent had spent together. The details from the book were enough for her.

Xander had laid out some ideas of what they could do over the next few days. He suggested places to eat and bars to frequent. Ann wasn't opposed to any of the ideas but wasn't exactly comfortable with getting thrust into the gay culture of the town. She was bound to feel out of place as she didn't imagine many middle-aged women were spending the weekend in Provincetown.

Nothing of importance happened the first two days. Ann and Xander explored the town and had numerous conversations spanning a wide variety of topics. They visited the restaurant he worked at previously. The place didn't have much charm and seemed run-down in Ann's opinion based on the wobbly furniture, rusted utensils, and the constant static that blared from the TV behind the bar. She learned much more about his upbringing and the current status of his relationship, which seemed to be extremely complicated.

Ann had a hard time understanding the appeal of Xander. He was a perfectly fine person, but he felt safe. She had always envisioned Vincent attracted to someone bolder and more driven to rip him from the normality of his life. Ann had the same notions about Evan, but realized it wasn't her place to pass judgment on who her son dated (even though it became a habit while reading the books).

What became very apparent about Provincetown in those first two days was that a hierarchy existed within the town. Xander was often leaning in to whisper about so-and-so and how they were married to such-and-such. He would pass by people and exchange pleasantries, but it was clear they were meaningless words being said between two strangers. It was exhausting to watch and likely even more exhausting for Xander to directly be a part of.

"Did you get tired of always having to be 'on'?" Ann asked at dinner the second night.

"What do you mean?"

"It seems like you have to build up this persona within the town where you are overtly friendly to everyone even if you don't like the person."

"Yeah, well, it comes with the territory. Considering I was a bartender, I needed to be nice or else the tips wouldn't be great. Tips were the only way to survive the winter months out here since the only people in town during that time were the locals."

"Did that play into why you moved away?"

"No. I'm still bartending in Boston. I'm trying to figure out how to get into the management side of a restaurant, but I don't know enough people in the city yet. I realized that P-town is a fantasy. This isn't what life is like. Expensive dinners every night. Drugs and drinking in the afternoon. Trying to be flirty with the old guy who has lots of money. It was fun for a few years, but I knew it wasn't sustainable."

"Hopefully I didn't force you to come back here," Ann said.

"Not at all. I know Vin enjoyed coming to P-town so I can understand why you'd want to see it for yourself."

"Can we go to the beach tomorrow? The one where he called me from the first time he visited?"

"Yeah, I'm guessing he was at the one by the hotel. Sure, we can do that."

"Great."

"Did you want to check out anywhere tonight?"

"Xander, you know I wouldn't fit in at any of the bars here," Ann said.

"But no one cares."

"I do."

"Fine. We don't have to go anywhere tonight but get mentally prepped because we are going somewhere tomorrow."

"I'll be sure to get a good night of sleep then," Ann said with a smile.

○ ○ ○

The walk to the beach was a straight shot up the road toward the end of the island. Ann kept pace with Xander as the sound of his flip flops bouncing off his feet radiated with each step.

It was early enough that all the drunks and druggies from the night before were still sleeping off the hangover.

They picked out a spot near the water and marked their territory with towels.

"I haven't been to a beach in years," Ann said. "It's not much of a beach though."

The sand stretched for a quarter mile along the shore until it faded into tall, wiry grass. On the other end was the hotel home to an unhealthy amount of illegal activity during the summer months.

"There's a nude beach, but it's a bit of a walk from here."

"Oh, I think I'm okay to skip that."

"It's not that great," Xander said with a cheeky smile.

"So, this is it, huh? This is the place where Vinny called me from."

"Apparently. I was at work that day. He didn't tell me until later that night."

Ann didn't understand the appeal. It was just a beach. No different from the ones they went to at the Jersey Shore, but she was forgetting who Vincent was surrounded by when he was at the beach. The space had been littered with gay men of every variety and they all seemed to be happy. It was a rash generalization on his part, but he went along with it because he wanted to believe he could make it to that place.

Ann should have remembered this. She read the books. She didn't absorb them though like Vincent would have wanted.

Xander took off his shirt and exposed his skin and bones.

"Oh my goodness. You are extremely skinny," Ann keenly pointed out.

"A blessing and a curse. One of these days my metabolism is going to slow down, and I will be fucked."

"As long as you don't have any kids you should be fine."

Ann had the one-piece bathing suit on underneath the other clothing, but a massive wave of insecurity washed over her. She didn't know anyone for hundreds of miles in any direction and yet she was afraid of the judgment and whispers about a middle-aged woman on the beach who wasn't in perfect shape.

Over the last six months, Ann lost a significant amount of weight and she barely noticed. Her priorities had shifted, and she no longer worried about the way she looked because it seemed like such a trivial matter. Because it was. It always should have been.

But now, the insecurities resurfaced without logical reason.

Lucky her.

"I'm nervous," Ann said.

"About what?"

"Taking off my shirt."

"Pshh," Xander said, flicking his wrist and scoffing at the comment. "No one is looking at you here. I can tell you with certainty that you are the least desirable person here and it's not because you aren't attractive. You just have the wrong anatomy."

They both laughed at the comment.

It was the confidence boost she needed. Ann took off the shirt and shorts and tossed them aside. No one ran away screaming at the (supposed) ghastly sight and she didn't spontaneously combust.

"What do we do now?"

"We can lay here for a bit. Maybe walk the jetty over there."

"Right. I remember Vinny wrote about that too."

"Are you just retracing his footsteps from what he wrote about in the books?"

"Not entirely. I have just been really interested in why he came out when he did. He told me afterward how he never had any plans to, so what exactly about this place made him change his mind?"

"I wish I had the answer for you."

"I don't expect much answers anymore about Vinny. I am lucky he wrote the books even though they were a somewhat dour account of his life. Was he always negative when he was around you?"

"I mean . . ." Xander paused. "Probably. His inclination was to always be slightly pessimistic. One of the things I liked about him actually."

"I—"

"XANDER! Darling, how are you?" the voice said in a completely manufactured accent.

He looked up and found the source.

"Oh. Edgar. How are you?"

"About as well as you'd expect. Where have you been? I don't ever see you at the bars anymore."

"I live in Boston now. I wanted to move closer to my boyfriend."

"How cute. I swore off relationships years ago. Now I just fuck whoever I want!"

"That's great, Edgar. Really great to hear."

Seemingly not hearing the comment, Edgar continued on, "And who is this wonderful woman with you? Is this your mother?"

"No. No, it's my friend's mom."

"And where is this friend of yours? I know you don't hang around with anyone who isn't ripe for the taking," Edgar said with a strange grin.

"He's dead," Ann said.

"Oh," Edgar said, clutching his hand to his chest. "I'm so sorry."

"Is your full name Edgar Allen Poe?" Ann asked. Of all things she could have remembered, this outrageous character was one of them. "Or otherwise known as Fred Fisty?"

"Y-yes. I don't go by that name anymore," Fred Fisty said in a triumphant manner.

"Oh, of course. My mistake. My son met you last year when he was visiting Provincetown."

"I don't reca—"

"Vincent Besser. From what I was told, you two had a memorable experience."

Edgar/Fred grew red in the face.

"It wasn't anything like that." Ann said. "Do you think I'd want to rehash a sexual experience my son had with you?"

"Well, n—"

"Are you flustered, Edgar?" Ann asked.

"Well, n—"

"He wrote about you differently than you're portraying yourself right now."

"He wrote about me?"

"Yes. Keep up," Ann said.

"Why though?" Edgar asked. He was still standing with his back to the water and staring down at the two of them.

"That's a great question. Unfortunately, I can't ask him, but my guess would be that you were a part of his story. I would have figured you to be one of the many lies he told. You seemed . . . a bit fantastical."

"Oh goodness," Edgar cried out. "He didn't write about the fisting, did he?"

"He sure did," Ann said with a vigorous nod.

"Vinny!" Xander shouted as if he was cursing his name.

"It's okay. He didn't say kind words about many people. I looked like a complete monster in the books," Ann said.

"Are you going to the tea party this afternoon?" Edgar asked, trying his damnedest to change the subject.

"It's a possibility," Xander said. "Do you think it'll be crowded?"

"Of course, sweetie. It's the tea after all!"

"If we go, we will try to find you."

Edgar dismissed himself with a small wave and wandered off to the nearby pool.

"What were the odds of meeting the one person Vinny wrote about from Provincetown?" Ann asked.

"Pretty high considering this is all made up," Xander said with a sigh.

"What did you say?"

"I asked if you wanted to walk to the jetty."

"Yes. That sounds nice."

The jetty was a series of huge stones placed in a somewhat logical sequence at an unknown time. The need to build up the jetty was to stop the waves from coming into the shore. Now, it served as a mile-long platform for people to traverse to get to the curl of the island. Does this sound familiar? It should because it has been explained to you twice before.

Ann took several steps out into Vincent's proclaimed perfect place before she noticed the turtle hanging out on one of the rocks.

"Is that normal?" she asked Xander.

"Probably not."

"Should we toss it back in?"

"Probably not."

They continued to walk across the sloped rocks that cut into one another. Several other people strolled across them without much of a hurry.

Halfway across the jetty, Ann looked back and noticed the town shrinking into nothingness. The chaos and crowded streets seemed like a distant memory.

"Is there any reason for us to keep going?" Ann asked.

"Probably not."

"How is the beach at the end of this?"

"Probably not—I mean, it's okay."

"Let's just turn around then."

They retreated back, following the same path.

"I just don't understand," Ann said as they closed the gap to the shoreline.

"What don't you get?"

"Vinny talked about this being his perfect place and there's nothing perfect about it."

"Maybe not for you. This was the first place he went to after he came out. I bet that carried more significance for him than we'd ever realize. Why are you so concerned on trying to figure this out?"

"I—I don't know," Ann confessed. "I felt like I had to."

"I promise that you don't. It is impossible to understand every thought or feeling someone had—even when that person is your son. Ann, you just need to live your life, and maybe find your own perfect place."

"Did he ever talk about someone named Ochi?'

"Ochi?"

"Yeah."

"No. He didn't. Why?"

"Just another mystery . . . Did you want to go to that tea party thing?"

"If you feel like being surrounded on all sides by gays."

"It's worth experiencing once in my life," Ann said.

The walk to the tea party brought them closer to the center of town as the thickness of people in the street began to clog. They veered off to the right and down a slight hill. After paying twenty-seven dollars each to get in, Ann and Xander pushed through the pockets of people and found an open space near the edge of the pier.

Ann wasn't aware that Dick Dock was right below her and the sounds of pleasure would begin in a few short hours.

"Do you want a cigarette?" Xander said, dangling one in front of Ann's face.

"I . . . I don't smoke."

"Oh. I thought you did for some reason. Do you mind if I do?"

"No. Go ahead."

"You know," Xander said with the cigarette between his lips, "your wonderful son shamed me quite heavily for smoking. I'm still somewhat bitter about it. Did that fun tidbit make it into his acclaimed novels?"

"I don't remember."

One, two, three . . . twenty-seven times of flicking the lighter before the flame caught and lit the cigarette. Xander took a deep inhale, let the smoke penetrate every curve of his lungs, and let out a long exhale that sent the smoke wafting up into the sky.

The sight disgusted Ann. The sight that she herself had mimicked thousands of times throughout her life.

Ann observed the shifting mass of people around her. Wild stints of laughter and garbled conversations all blended into one blob of noise that pierced her ears. She didn't necessarily hate her time on that pier, but it wasn't particularly memorable either.

That was an accurate summation of her entire experience in Provincetown. Whatever powerful draw Vincent had to the place was lost on her and that was okay. He never understood why she liked to sit and read trashy celebrity magazines or why the windows needed to be washed exactly three times a year.

Sometimes the answers just didn't answer much.

thirty-three

NODULES

"What's your secret?" Ann asked.

"I don't have any secrets," Ann's mom said with surprise.

"Of course you do. You are in your upper eighties and have lived a relatively healthy life. What tips have you got for the rest of us?"

Ann sat across from her mom at The Palace—a restaurant that thrived on the aging clientele. Their cheap meals and dinnerware from the 1980s brought in massive waves of people that lived through many wars and presidential fuck ups.

"Well . . . I . . . I don't ever curse. Maybe that has something to do with it?" Doris said.

"I never thought about that. It's a minor miracle you didn't considering you raised four kids."

"Your father did enough cursing and yelling for the entire neighborhood."

"He had plenty to be mad about. I can think of so many stories where we were just absolute nightmares," Ann said.

"All part of being a parent, I suppose. You have to get through the bad times. We were lucky to have four healthy children who grew up and had families of their own. I know he'd be proud of you all."

"Do you think about him often?"

"More and more now than ever before," Doris said, picking at the rest of her food.

"Why?"

"Because I don't have much time left here and I want to see your father again. I try not to feel guilty about it because I know Walter wants to see his wives too."

"I don't know what I'd do if I lost you. Especially now."

"You'd move on with your life because there isn't any other choice. I've lived a good, good life. Better than most I'd guess. I would leave behind four kids that graced me with grandchildren and even a few great grandchildren. That's all I could possibly ask for," Doris said. This was the part where the tears would flow, but they never came. The truth wasn't always sad.

"Do you think you'll see Vinny up there?"

"I hope so. I really hope so. I have some things I want to say to him."

"Like what?"

"What a beautiful letter he wrote me. In it, he talked about one of the books that always stuck with him. I don't remember the name now . . . Loud? . . . Loud Alter? . . . Crowd Antler? . . . Hearts in Atlantis? He said there was a phrase in there repeated several times: *death is only a door*. He wondered whether that was true or not. I know Vinny wasn't very religious, but I think he was special enough for an exception to be made. I wish I had the answer for him before he died, but if death is only a door, I imagine I'll find him on the other side of it soon."

"Not too soon I hope."

"Of course not."

They sat in silence as the waitress came back and slapped the bill down like a poker player proudly showing off a pair of pocket aces. She cleared away the plates and grunted something in Yiddish about paying for the bill up at a mall in Nova Scotia.

"I want to read his books," Doris eventually said.

"Mom, you can't."

"My eyesight isn't that bad."

Ann laughed. "No. No, I meant that they are . . . crude and littered with spelling mistakes."

"I'm not a snob. I read *Fifty Shades of Grey* for goodness sake," Doris said with pride.

"But it's about him and, quite frankly, the poor decisions he made over the last few years," Ann said.

"What does it matter now?" Doris asked.

"I—I never thought of it like that. I guess you're right."

"Regardless of what Vinny did, he is still my grandson. I am so proud of the fact that he wrote novels! I could have been the grandmother of a famous author!"

"He never intended to publish them," Ann said.

"Oh. Why not?"

"I don't know."

"Why don't you publish them?"

"I don't see the point and I wouldn't even know where to start." In other words, Ann couldn't because the reality of the boring reality she existed in wouldn't allow her to do such a thing. The universe demanded her compliance in suffocating the atrocious writing that Vinny had the gross audacity to spend his time vomiting up on his laptop.

"Something else to ask him about then," Doris said with finality.

Ann reached for her purse at the same moment Doris did. They locked eyes and both froze.

"No. Don't even bother Ann. You got lunch the last time we went out."

"Mom, we have this argument every time."

"I'm going to write you out of that little black book if you don't put your purse away."

"Now that's just awful," Ann said. She relented though and the purse returned to the seat beside her.

Doris thumbed through the cash and pulled out a twenty-seven-dollar bill. It would be enough to cover the food and the tip. She ripped a fourth of the twenty-seven-dollar bill off and dropped it onto the table.

"Do you think that's a big enough tip?" Doris asked.

"That should be fine."

Once outside, they shuffled toward the car. The October air rushed into them like a linebacker. It was cold. "I'm going to be late for the doctor's appointment," Ann muttered to herself.

"What did you say?"

"Nothing. Let's just get you settled into the car."

The ride back to Doris's luxury apartment was short. They managed to talk about a multitude of topics that have no bearing on this story. It's easy to forget that characters live outside the words on these pages—even the fictional ones manufactured for your enjoyment.

Ann offered to walk her mom upstairs to her apartment, but she declined and stated with gusto about how she was more than capable. As Ann retreated back to the car, Doris turned around and reminded Ann on how she expected a copy of the books next time they saw each other.

Ann nodded and added the task to her list. It seemed like another trip to Vividh was in her future.

○ ○ ○

The exam room had a window, which was rare. Ann had been in that office numerous times before throughout the twenty plus years she lived in Pennsylvania and had only been an exam room with a window two other times.

She stared out beyond the glass panes and watched the cars zip by on the road. Beyond that, rolling hills that led into a freshly developed neighborhood. It was evident that the rolling hills wouldn't be there much longer as the neighborhood would continue its push and consume everything within reach.

Ann didn't plan to be around long enough to see that happen. The more likely scenario was that she wouldn't get a room with a view again for a very long time.

A sliver of her brain kept dissecting the conversation with her mother, but that wasn't anything new. Ann tended to cycle through the filing cabinet of her life. If you didn't know that by now, have you even been paying attention? Better yet: where the fuck is Evan and why has this part of the book been unbearably long?

She asked herself questions like that and more until she was rudely interrupted by Dr. Vonegat.

"Hi Ann! Another year on the wheel of life has passed by. How are things?" he asked.

Dr. Vonegat had been her primary care physician for quite some time, and they had developed a cordial relationship. He was the doctor for their entire family, so it was only a matter of time before it was brought up . . .

"How is the family? What are the kids up to?" he continued.

That didn't take long.

"The family is fine. Thanks for asking." She looked out the window. Ann figured if she looked out there long enough she could stop herself from crying.

It worked.

"So," Dr. Vonegat said, flipping through her chart, "it looks like you've lost . . . fifty-four pounds in the last year. That's amazing! What have you been doing?"

"I don't know."

"Have you been exercising and dieting?"

"Not that I recall."

Dr. Vonegat raised his eyebrow that her response. "Well, let's run some tests and make sure everything is okay. Given your history of—"

"Smoking."

"Yes. Of smoking."

"I haven't smoked in years though." A lie, technically.

"I know, but let's grab some bloodwork."

"Okay."

Dr. Vonegat stayed in the room for another five minutes checking her blood pressure, listening to her heart, and doing other doctorly things. He wrote down the occasional note within the chart. He muttered something about adding a chest X-ray too.

"The nurse will be by to take you back to the other room," he said.

"Is everything okay?" Ann asked.

"Yes. It should be." Dr. Vonegat left and moved to the next patient.

As expected, the nurse knocked lightly on the door and asked Ann if she was ready. Of course she was. Her only ways out of the room were the window with the five story drop to the pavement below or through the door. Considering how death was only a door, there shouldn't have been much to fear with that option.

Ann completed the series of tasks described by the technician in the X-ray room. A room that sounds much more intimidating in concept than the boring reality Ann occupied.

Following that, she sat in a chair in some other room. Ann squeezed the ball in her hand to help the nurse find her vein. Several vials of blood were taken.

Ann was deposited back into a room without a window. She read the signs that warned about the risks of having high blood pressure and what the first symptoms of a stroke were. Ann waited patiently for twenty-seven minutes before Dr. Vonegat came back into the room.

"Hello again."

"Hi," Ann said. She knew he didn't have good news.

"We won't have the bloodwork for a few days, but I took a look at your X-ray and compared it to one that you had a few years ago . . ."

Dr. Vonegat took off his glasses and placed them on the counter.

". . . your lungs have some nodules on them."

"What does that mean?"

"I'm not sure yet. And I don't want to postulate."

"But it's your job to make guesses and not be held legally accountable for them."

"True, but I'm going to refer you to an oncologist. She is a great doctor. I have known her for many years."

"An oncologist?"

"It's just a precaution."

"Sounds like more than that."

"Do you recall when I said if you didn't stop smoking you would die?"

"Yes."

"Your decision to do so may have just saved your life."

A chill ran through Ann and then a thought: *What if I want to die? What if I want to see my dead son on the other side of that door?*

"I hope so," Ann said.

"The receptionists at the front will help to schedule your appointment." Dr. Vonegat leaned in and grabbed Ann's hands. "It's going to be okay."

"And what if it isn't?"

"Then we do everything we can."

"Take as much time as you need." Dr. Vonegat stood up, adjusted his jacket, grabbed his glasses, and left the room in a collected calm only a person who was used to delivering potentially bad news could do.

What bad news did he give Ann though? Nothing was certain yet besides her need to go to the oncologist. Things would be fine because everything was always fine. Fine as nine sipping on a bottle of wine looking exquisitely divine.

Ann didn't sit in the room long. The windowless view was enough to drive her over to the receptionist's desk where she was given a phone number to call and the wonderful news that her co-pay was waved for the visit.

Everything was turning out beautifully for Ann today.

Instead of taking the stairs to the first floor, she briefly considered slamming her full body weight into the windows of the waiting area until the glass gave way and she descended quickly down those five stories.

It would have saved her years of pain.

Her rational side won out and she navigated down the stairs to her car.

She thought about what remained on that highest shelf in her closet. She thought about if she should tell Jim about this or behave like Walter White and turn to dealing meth.

She thought about how it would all turn out fine.

It had to.

There wasn't any other option.

thirty-four

EVERYTHING IS FINE

Weeks passed as the appointments came and went. The doctors and nurses were vague about the results of everything. Ann would be herded into a room and reappear in the outside world sometime later without much knowledge of what had taken place.

Jim drove her to some of the appointments, but he had this pesky thing called a job that required his attention most days. Thank goodness Ann still didn't work at Bridgewater (or have any job for that matter) because she would have been fired. Employers don't like when the underlings use excuses like "I may have cancer" or "I need to get a biopsy of my lungs" instead of feeding the corporate machine.

When Ann told Jim about her slew of upcoming appointments and the reason behind them, his only reaction was a slight tilt toward the kitchen island. He stuck out his hands to steady himself. The silence spread out between them like a thick fog.

"Are you okay?" Ann asked.

"You're all I have."

"Everything is fine. It has to be."

Ann looked back at him. The lenses on the glasses had expanded throughout the years and were getting into the realm of retired secretary that moonlighted as a librarian. Ann had never seen Jim without a mustache in all the years she had known him. Currently, he was sporting a full beard due to the decreasing temperatures. His eyes were sunken in slightly from the years of waking up at the unholy hour he did. There was a wart on the edge of his nose that wasn't noticeable unless Ann stood at the right angle.

Ann had known no other person for the past thirty years. Sure, they suffered through their ups and downs like any other couple, but they never quit on each other. And Ann knew that now would be no different.

She hadn't bothered to tell Leigh, her mother, or anyone else who may have given a damn. Why churn up concern for other people? Everything would be fine.

Between all the appointments Ann had, she managed to take a side trip to Staples and plugged the flash drive into the computer again, repeating the same process she had done eons ago. Vividh no longer worked there said The Reaper that took up his mantle behind the counter. He had graduated college and moved down to Dallas, apparently. All roads lead to Dallas, The Reaper said with a crude smile that Ann couldn't see beneath the hood.

She ignored most of his comments and clicked through the prompts. Once the order popped up on his screen, The Reaper grabbed his scythe and began hacking away at the printer until a perfect copy of each book slid out.

The Reaper began to hand over the box with the copies inside but hesitated. That'll be [insert some amount of US currency] he said. Ann flashed the credit card and swiped it down the magnetic strip.

Satisfied with the outcome, The Reaper handed over the box.

Ann turned toward the exit, but I thought ripped through her. "Wait. I want another copy of each."

Reaperfucker, he said. Allegedly that was some sort of insult that Ann should have blushed at.

The Reaper returned to the computer and smacked at it with the scythe. He then turned to the printer and continued to smack at the machine like Chris Brown would do to his girlfriend.

(Seriously though, fuck Chris Brown.)

The Reaper handed Ann another box with the two books. If Vividh was still working there, he would have given Ann a box for each book, but it was just impossible to find good workers these days.

○ ○ ○

It wasn't until the afternoon of Halloween that Ann and Jim found themselves driving over to the oncologist. The results from the biopsy took several days, which delayed her final appointment. Ann was still sore from the needle that was driven into her chest.

The music coming from the Sirius XM station sat at volume four, which did nothing except break up the silence between Ann and Jim. What was there to say? "Oh hey, I hope you don't have cancer!" or "It sure is chilly outside today. Global warming must be a hoax! Har-har-har." or "Everything is fine because it just has to be."

In the backseat, a familiar box from Staples sat idly. Ann had yet to hand off the copy of the books to her mother. She had purposely been avoiding Doris for fear that she'd spill the details of what has been happening over the past few weeks.

The other copy of the books was halfway to Denver.

Hard cut to Dr. Phening's office. (If they can do that in screenplays, we can do that here, right?)

Ann and Jim sat motionless in the chairs

The door opened and shut quickly. "Hi Ann. Is this your husband?" Dr. Phening said.

"Yes."

"Hi, Dr. Phening." She extended a hand.

"Jim. Nice to meet you." He reciprocated the offering.

"How are you both today?" she asked as she settled into the chair across from them.

"Fine," Ann said.

"Fine," Jim echoed.

"I have the results of the biopsy. No need to keep you waiting any longer." Dr. Phening flipped open the manila folder and reread what was on there. Her eyes dashed across the page.

With a cold certainty that reminded Ann of the phone call she had gotten on New Year's Day, Dr. Phening said, "You have stage 3 lung cancer."

Ann's mind flashed to the cigarette she had after Vincent's funeral. That was it. That was the cigarette that kick started the tumors in her lungs.

What a foolish thought.

No, of course it wasn't that one cigarette; it was the thousands that came before. The tick marks kept adding up and climbing until the scale couldn't take it anymore and toppled over. Her body succumbed to the pressure and the abuse and the trauma.

When Ann quit smoking a decade and a half ago, there was a fear that her choices would catch up to her, but as time limped forward, her fear receded into nothing. Instead, she went to her daughter's field hockey games and her son's football banquets. Instead, she raised two kids and kept her marriage working. Instead, she lost her only son.

"What does it mean?" Jim asked. Ann continued to look beyond Dr. Phening.

Jim and Dr. Phening exchanged more questions and answers. None of which Ann was concerned with and neither should you be.

Past Dr. Phening was a window. Large and grandiose for whatever reason. Outside the window was a man walking. He had a strange gait that left him leaning to one side. He passed by the window at a methodic pace and Ann understood everything about him: what he was, what he would be, what he would never achieve.

It's what her father looked like during his last days.

That's when she cried.

"Here, here," Dr. Phening said, passing several tissues Ann's way.

"I'm sorry," Ann said.

"Don't be."

Jim grabbed Ann's hand and held onto it. He looked from Dr. Phening to Ann. "What is the survival rate?" he asked.

Dr. Phening considered the question and returned a non-answer. "It is hard to say. Age and current health play into it considerably. With that in mind, I'd say there is a 27 percent chance that Ann survives this. We will need to be aggressive."

A 73 percent chance I get to see my son soon, she thought.

Jim squeezed Ann's hand tighter and asked the simplest question that carried a monumental weight.

"What now?"

interlude

2-1

JIM'S LETTER

Dad,

I'm not sure if there is anyone you have ever come across who has truly understood you. My guess is that Mom has been the closest, but there will always be a tiniest barrier that separates any married couple from knowing one another completely.

I won't try to make a case for me being that one exception, but I think it is worth noting that I view you differently than most. Whereas people at work may view you as the hard ass that has a propensity to yell, I see it as you caring immensely about the success of the business and the people who work there. (You may want to tone down on the yelling though. You're getting too old for that needless shit.) Whereas the folks in the neighborhood may see you as the quiet one who doesn't enjoy social settings, I remember all those nights at the dinner table where you'd make some joke (they weren't always funny) that would get you laughing so much that you'd have to get up and leave. We could always hear your laugh echoing through the house. You just needed to be around the right company to feel comfortable, and I can relate to that more than you'd ever know.

It makes me miss being at home.

In some ways, I was always meant to leave and the fact that I did shows how well you two raised me. I don't know many other people who were able to pick up and move to a foreign place right after college.

Anyways.

It's not that I have an exact agenda with the letters I'm writing, but I guess I should actually move into the things I wanted to bring up. That does sort of sound like an agenda then, huh?

First of all, I wanted to apologize. By the time you read this, I will be a shell of the person I once was. I don't know where I will be living, but I imagine I will have to move back home at some point. I'm also assuming I will eventually need to be taken care of, so I apologize for being a burden. You took care of me enough as a kid that it seems spiteful for me to need just as much help as an adult. I also want to say sorry for not being the person you wanted. Listen: I'm going to skip the cliché theatrics right now.

I know you have accepted me for being gay, so this apology isn't aimed around that. I will always feel bad for not taking a stab at playing the guitar or following you around the workshop more to learn. It took me a long time to realize that your passions run deep on certain things and to not have invested more time in them was foolish. There is a trap that parents sometimes fall into where they feel their passions need to be absorbed by their kids. I never felt that pressure from you, but I do wish I made more of an effort.

Secondly, I wanted to say that you were enough. I fully understood as a kid that you weren't at every baseball or football game not because you didn't want to see me play, but because you wanted to provide everything you could for me and Leigh. What more could a kid ask for? Let me jog your memory with other things to prove you fulfilled your fatherly duties in case you aren't convinced yet. I still remember the times you would take me up to the park and throw me batting practice. I hit you in the shins so many times with line drives that I'm surprised you can even walk. As a form of punishment, you'd make me run around and pick up all the balls scattered across the field. Or what about the times when you would stand outside and lob baseballs as high as you could so I could practice catching pop-ups? I always noticed how much you'd have to ice your shoulder after that and, yet, you continued to do it. Or how about when you sent out my resumé to a THOUSAND companies by snail mail? You knew how stressful finding a job had been for me and you dedicated yourself to helping. Of course, we received almost no replies back because companies no longer look at paper resumés, but I approved of your resolve regardless. Or how about every year you slave away on creating those ridiculous letters from "Santa" that Leigh and I read? I have no clue how that tradition started, but if it was another life and I would be able to have a family, I would have continued doing that forever.

I may have been aggressively aggressive with proving that point, but I didn't want to leave any doubt for you.

Thirdly, I want to take us back down memory lane for a second to the night we talked after Mom told you I was gay. I recapped this elsewhere, but I wanted to call attention back to the first thing you said. You sat on the edge of my bed and fiddled with the water bottle you were holding the entire time. You unscrewed the cap, took a drink, put the cap back on, and viciously repeated the process for the whole conversation. You didn't look at me much, but it wasn't out of disgrace or shame. You just never thought you'd have a gay son and you needed the time to process. I told you earlier

I would skip the clichés of talking about my coming out, but I have fallen for my own trap.

Anyways.

The first thing you said to me was "What could I have done differently?" I remember laughing at the time because the question felt so silly. You knew you couldn't control who I liked. It wasn't until recently that I recognized you meant it in a completely different context.

I'll answer it the same way now as I did then. There was nothing different you could have done. I'm proud to have you as my father. I hope you continue to see that.

I'll only ask one thing of you and it requires an ugly, but quickly approaching circumstance. When I'm gone, make sure you are there for Mom. She is more reliant on you than you may realize.

As for you, I know your grief will be scattered, and you may not stare it down for a while, but don't run from it. It's okay to be sad. It's okay to lean on others for help. It's okay to be angry. There are some days where I can't see the sunshine to all this and it makes me frustrated, but it's the path my life has taken, and I have to accept that.

You will have it in writing that I give you permission to use my old room to store your extra guitars since I doubt you'll ever stop buying them. Feel free to throw in some tools from the workshop while you're at it!

One last thing:

Quit that fucking job already! You deserve better. You are better.

Love,
Vin

2-2

THE PLAQUE
(Sometime in the future)

Jim was jostled awake.

He had been up for hours already but in a sense, he had just woken up. He reoriented himself and realized he was down in the workshop. Located in the basement, this became his place of sanctuary on the weekends and the only reason any of the house projects were completed in a timely manner.

The amount of money they saved because of his handiwork was staggering. It is also worth noting that working for a lumber company and general home suppler helped immensely as well.

There was a constant film of dust that covered all the tools that hung from the walls. Various wrenches, hammers, saw blades, drills, and an assortment of other items that no person would understand what their purpose was occupied every inch of available space. Cans of stain and paint lined the shelves, many of which hadn't been touched in years but were kept on the off chance that a wall or piece of furniture would need to be touched up.

Jim wasn't concerned about the dust or the number of items that had been sitting there for years; he was primarily focused on finishing out this bitch of a project that had consumed him for months now.

It was a rocking horse. Simple in nature, difficult in execution.

Being the self-taught person he was, he never relied on how-to videos. It was an intuition. One that started back at the first house that he and Ann got together. They were married within a year and a half of meeting each other and moved in together shortly after returning from their honeymoon. It was a dinky two-bedroom house in Brick Township. Every aspect was dated, so he decided to take a sledgehammer to the bathroom one day and try his hand at remodeling. There were missteps and times where he questioned whether he was in over his head, but each task he completed connected another dot. The sequential nature of demolishing something and putting it back together newer and better clicked with him and it became an outlet. So much of his life was an aggregation of pent up frustration and anger but being able to step back from that bathroom for the first time and see all the work that *he* did was proof he wanted to keep going.

So he did.

The dinky two-bedroom house in Brick Township turned into a refreshed two-bedroom house that sold at a higher price than when they bought it for by the time they moved to Pennsylvania.

Jim and Ann knew the house on Cornwallis Drive in Pennsylvania would be their home for a very long time. They knew the country-style kitchen that came standard in each house in the neighborhood would eventually fall out of taste or that the wallpaper in a majority of the rooms would lose its appeal. Jim was patient and homed in on his craft until the time was right. He built end tables and chairs and trinkets for the kids. He took his time and made sure each cut was perfect, the sanding was even, and the stain spread evenly across the surface.

Eventually, it was time.

His first major remodel in the Pennsylvania house was the basement. He built the bar and the entertainment center. He tiled the floor and wired the ceiling with the sound system. He created the recessed shelves that would house the sports memorabilia from the kids.

It was the first of many major projects for him and certainly his finest.

They had parties down there. The kids had sleepovers. They played pool. They watched the Giants win the Super Bowl . . . twice!

The basement became the epicenter of activity for so many years.

And now it was practically dormant.

Age began to cripple his hands with arthritis. The cuts he'd make with the saw were becoming increasingly crooked. The even strokes of the paint brush were becoming harder as his hands shook and ached.

He didn't spend as much time down in that workshop anymore doing what he loved because he couldn't.

Sure, the primary reason was the growing arthritis, but he also had to walk past those recessed shelves each time to get to the workshop.

Jim was never an emotional person. That luxury was ripped away from him at a very young age and he always clung to the idea that emotion was nothing but wasted time. He held onto that belief throughout his teenage years and young adult life. He clutched to that mindset all throughout his marriage to Ann.

But then something funny happened: his son died.

Jim had lost his parents had a somewhat young age. His mother was a tortured soul who lost her way; he felt no remorse when his father died six months later though. He knew what it was like to lose a parent and tried to prepare his own kids for that inevitability from afar.

No one ever told him he'd have to worry about losing his own child.

The judges would have given him a 10/10 for his performance during those initial months after the car accident. He suppressed every single emotion that attempted to break through the surface. He continued to bury himself in a job that was more meaningless to him than ever before and tried to stay connected to Ann even though she was rightfully broken. He had never been an outwardly loving person so that was no easy task to show her the proper affection and know how to pull away when she needed time.

But it was those stupid fucking bookshelves that gnawed away at him for years. He avoided looking in the direction of them each time he went down into the basement because he didn't need to be reminded. See, unlike Quinn, Jim still remembered his son's face. He still recalled his laugh and his fierce sarcasm, but he wanted to forget. The pain was too much. The knot inside him grew at a steady rate for years and it was ready to burst.

Today would be different.

He put down the sander and stepped back from the rocking horse. He still had time. Even if it took him another six months, the gift would only be symbolic and not yet practical. He just hoped they wouldn't ask him to make a second one. They'd have to learn to take turns.

Jim didn't bother to clean up any of the mess from his progress. He shut off the lights and closed the doors to the workshop as he exited the room.

He wanted to gravitate toward the stairs, toward the sanctuary that awaited him up there, but he had to do this. It was long overdue.

Instead of heading left to the stairs, he went right and walked past the end of the bar and into the section of the basement with the entertainment center, couches, and recessed bookshelves.

He stood in front of it numbly.

Eventually, he reached his hand out and grasped the baseball that read:

VINNY'S 1ST NO HITTER
April 10, 2003

He recalled writing that. He recalled actually being there for the game. Most of his games were too early after a workday for him to make and anything over a weekend usually conflicted with a remodeling project he would have been working on with Ralph. But he was there that time. It was one of the few instances where he had succeeded as a father, at least that's what Jim believed.

He spun the ball in his hand for a little longer and then put it back.

Next, he grabbed one of the plaques off the highest shelf from Vincent's days of being on the traveling baseball team. They were never particularly good and would get stomped by the Bally Bearcats each time they played them, but they got far in several tournaments. The plaque detailed their third-place achievement and had a picture of the team.

It took a moment to find him. Vincent was in the second row.

Anger swelled inside Jim.

He took the plaque over to the bar and held it high over his head. He brought it down in a swift motion and the wood from the plaque cracked against the surface of the granite countertop. The noise echoed across the basement. Ann was gone, which meant it was just him and the dogs. He heard the patter of paws on the basement steps and soon a glowing face peeked around the corner. Rigby stared at him briefly before deciding that going back upstairs was the preferred option.

His hands ached. His eyes were flooded with tears.

He lifted up the plaque one more time and brought it down with even more force upon the granite. Jim let out a scream that pierced every corner of the basement. The plaque splintered off into two pieces. He continued to hold the bottom half in his hand while the top half had flopped onto the floor. He bent down to pick it up. Jim ran his hands across the picture, across Vincent's smiling face, across the face of a kid who never realized he would be dead at twenty-five. In the moment the picture was taken, Vincent was surrounded by friends and the adrenaline of getting third place in the tournament and not the abstract thoughts that Jim was fighting with.

The burst of anger still hadn't subsided.

"WHY?" he shouted with considerable force.

"Why?" he repeated more solemnly.

As he waited for the answer that would never come, he sat in one of the bar stools and cried. A deep, terrible, endorphin releasing cry that lasted for a long time. He clutched the top half of the plaque the entire time and focused his eyes on Vincent's face.

He cried because he missed his son.

He cried because he thought he should have been a better father.

He cried because there was finally no reason not to.

After some time, Jim left the plaque on the bar and went upstairs. He fished through the drawer that was filled with his endless junk and found the envelope buried in the back.

Jim tore into it, pulled out the letter inside, and rediscovered that he had been good enough.

PART III

LIP-SYNCS & DEEP CUTS

thirty-five

SEE YOU SOON

Evan closed the laptop with reserved calmness and went back into bed.

Sleep caught up to him in short order. The exhaustion stemming from the night before and the realization of what he'd just seen collided in a frustrating tangle.

A small house was built into the side of a mountain. The peak was not far above and had enough space to cater to an entire community, but it remained barren. Evan's vision was hazy as he knocked on what appeared to be the front door. It opened after several locks disengaged. A warped face stood in the doorway and motioned for him to step inside. Evan hesitated. The warped face motioned again and opened his mouth, blood leaking out and dropping to the floor. It pooled around Evan's feet and began to move up his legs. Evan took two steps back, his feet reaching the edge of a steep drop. The warped face cocked its head and extended a shattered arm. Evan spoke but it came out in a language he couldn't understand. "Where are you?" the warped face asked in return. "You should be here," it continued on. "I . . . n-need yo-u. It hurt. H-elp-p." The blood crawled up past Evan's stomach. He felt the heaviness as it pressed into his body. The warped face moved into the full light of the porch. The entire body was mangled like a dog's chew toy. The body staggered forward and groaned with each step. "It hurt. It hurt. It hurt," the shape kept repeating. Evan moved past it and into the house. The blood snaked its way up his chest. He was barely able to breathe. Evan slammed the door shut and bolted it. He slid open the slot that was situated at eye level. The warped face looked sad as it shuffled several steps back until it was flush with the edge. "See you soon," the warped face said. It fell back and disappeared off the edge. Evan watched until the blood reached his eyes and suffocated him fully.

Evan jolted upright in bed and squinted his eyes at the light that seeped through the windows. He hadn't had a nightmare in a long time.

Evan noticed the puddle at the bottom of the bed.

"Izzie. What the fuck?" he asked her.

Her tail flicked back and forth. Izzie stared back at him with her protruding marble eyes.

Evan pulled himself together and took her downstairs to shamble around the moderately sized patch of grass outside the complex.

A man was bundled up and waiting patiently for his dog to finish taking a shit. The dog roamed around in tight circles; its nose buried in the snow.

He turned and noticed Evan walking over.

"Hi, h—" was all he managed to say before chunks of his breakfast were vomited out onto the ground. His eyes widened in embarrassment. After wiping his mouth with the coat sleeve, the man said, "I'm so sorry about that. Partied a bit too hard last night."

Evan had no desire for conversation, but he felt cornered as he stood in the open field.

"Are you feeling better?" Evan said in an attempt to tap into his empathetic side.

"Yes. Yeah, I'm probably going to die of embarrassment but beyond that, I feel renewed."

Evan extended the leash and allowed Izzie to peruse the area. Neither dog cared for the other and kept their distance.

"That's good to hear," Evan said.

"H-how was your New Year's Eve?"

"Saw some balloons drop and kissed my best friend at midnight, so very engaging."

The man nodded. "Are you hungover at all?"

"I'm not much of anything at the moment."

"That's . . . cryptic," the man said with a half-smile.

"I can't tell a stranger all my secrets."

"I puked in front of you on our first meeting. That's more intimate than anything I've done so far this year."

"Oh. Clever. I wouldn't advise you in using that joke too many times. It grows stale."

"Of course," the man said, sensing the conversation had nowhere else to go.

"Do you think any of the hardware stores are open today?" Evan asked.

"This is America, where capitalism thrives due to the greediness of the conglomerates that step on the backs of the lowest class citizen every chance they get."

It was the start of a monologue right out of *Mr. Robot* except it lacked coherence and that sense of anarchy.

"Okay, so is that a yes?"

"Yes."

The man bent down and scooped up his dog's shit. "Well, it was nice talking to you. See you soon."

Evan stood still and watched as he scampered back into the building.

See you soon.

See you soon.

See you soon.

He repeated the phrase in his head all the way up to his apartment.

○ ○ ○

Evan drove to the fringes of Denver and found the monstrosity. It was surrounded by a nearly abandoned parking lot that was more expansive than the Dead Sea.

Once inside, Evan was greeted by a half-dead employee. She looked like she'd rather be anywhere else.

"Hello sir. Happy New Year. Need any help today?"

"Yeah." Evan then told her what he was looking for.

She blinked several times. "Can I ask why you need those?"

"Seeing as you already asked, that question doesn't make sense. And no, it's none of your business."

"But Evan," she pleaded, "we here at Home Depot—the world's premier depot for homes if you weren't aware—know all about your tendencies. While we can't stop you from making the purchase, we can give you disapproving looks as you walk throughout the store and pay."

"Fine."

"Fine?"

"Fine."

"Fine?"

"YES! It's all fine," Evan said. He began to walk away but turned back. "Which aisle?"

"Twenty-six," she said.

"Thank you."

"Evan?"

"What?"

"Why are you just wandering around the aisles of Home Depot having make believe conversations in your head?"

Evan snapped back to his boring reality. He was halfway down aisle twenty-five. A variety of ceiling fans dotted the walls. His interest was elsewhere, so he moved over to aisle twenty-six.

The razor blades came in a multitude of shapes—stars, elephants, circles, cones, octagons, etc.—but Evan gravitated towards the run-of-the-mill straight-edged razors. They were a family favorite.

He sifted through the packs. His options were limitless. A buy one, get one free sign dangled over his head. Evan dawdled in the aisle for several minutes before grabbing a box of twelve straight-edged razor blades.

At the checkout counter, the employee asked him if he found everything okay.

"I did. Thanks."

"Doing a home improvement project?" she asked as she dragged the box across the scanner.

"How'd you know?" he said with a wide smile.

"What kind of project?"

"Cutting picture frames." It was the first lie that popped in his head.

"Be careful! These look sharp!"

Evan laughed at the obvious observation.

"Receipt in the bag?"

"That'd be great," he said.

"See you soon!" she said and returned to scrolling through her phone.

Evan left the radio off for the drive home. The sound of wheels bumping along potholes was enough to keep him company. The phrase kept recycling itself in his head.

See you soon.

See you soon.

Evan had no intention of seeing the warped face soon, but why did he go buy those razor blades? They certainly weren't for an art project or to peel some paint.

Just in case, Evan told himself. *Just in case.*

After Izzie completed her spins around the apartment to show her excitement for Evan returning home, he placed the unopen box of razor blades on the second highest shelf next to the albums and framed picture of him and his mom.

"See you soon," he whispered.

thirty-six

DISTRACTION

"Evan. EVAN!" Murph yelled as she rounded the corner into their cubicle.

"How'd you know I was here?" he asked.

"Since you had the audacity to walk without me to work, I made the correct assumption you were already here. Anyways, why did you ignore me yesterday? We had things to discuss."

Evan had noticed the string of texts from Murph, but never replied. After his trip to Home Depot, Evan did nothing except chores around the apartment to keep himself occupied. He kept *Golden Girls* on in the background for the occasional laugh.

"What things did we need to talk about?"

"Are you upset? You look upset," Murph said. She eyed him from head to feet and scrunched her face in thought.

"I'm not upset."

"You are and I know why."

"You don't know why I'm upset."

"So you are admitting to being upset? I knew it!"

"Murph, chill." Ever since becoming friends with Murph, Evan had gotten in good practice for perfecting his dad voice—the one that shows he's serious about a topic coming to an immediate halt.

"Whatever man. You are so wound up sometimes. You need to get laid."

"I never understood that logic."

"Sometimes when Elliot and I are super stressed, we will just rip—"

"Thanks. I'm okay with not knowing," Evan said.

"In all seriousness, if there is something you need to talk about, I'm here for you. If not, I will review my talking points."

"Go ahead," Evan said. He took a long sip from the coffee mug on the desk.

"I'll start off with the more exciting of the two . . ." Murph unearthed a folded piece of paper, smoothed it out, and slapped it on the desk. "Check it out."

Evan leaned forward and read through the flyer.

> THE CITY OF DENVER PRESENTS:
>
> THE 27th ANNUAL
> LIP-SYNCHRONIZATION COMPETITION
>
> JUNE 27th @ BELLCO THEATRE
>
> Ideas must be submitted by April 10th
>
> The theme is DUETS!

"Where did you find this?" he asked. "Also, who spells out lip-syn*chronization* like that?" The second question was more for himself. "Did a toddler make this?" The third question was free to be answered by anyone in the audience.

There were no takers.

"Attached to one of the light poles while walking to work. This city is so active with placing flyers on their light poles. It's great!" Murph said.

"Mhmm."

"Are we going to do it?" Murph leaned forward and rested her elbows on her knees. "It wasn't as much a question as it was a demand."

"Wait . . . no, no. Absolutely not. I have no interest in doing that."

"I know that, but you're going to do it anyways because you're my friend and it'll be fun."

"How does being your friend—actually that doesn't matter. Go ask Elliot or Franco or someone from the office."

"Oh Evan, you naïve soul. I can't ask Elliot because that's in the middle of baseball season. He is going to be muy, muy busy. As for Franco, I just don't feel that chemistry required for an outstanding lip-sync performance. Imagine if Lady Gaga and Brandon Cooper—"

"Bradley," Evan said.

"—Bradley Cooper didn't have that sexual tension during *A Star is Born*. And that also plays into why I can't ask anyone here. I don't need that tension with coworkers."

"Are you implying we have sexual tension?"

"I'm saying it outright: we have sexual tension."

"Can we stop saying sexual tension please?" Evan asked.

"You didn't feel something during that kiss on New Year's?"

"No, Murph. I did not."

"What a shame. Still, I stand by my rationale. Let's do this. Please."

Evan saw the strain on Murph's face. He didn't understand why the event was important for her, but sometimes you do things for people you care about without questioning too much.

"Sure," Evan said.

"Awesome! This is going to be great! We only have six months to prepare so we should probably get started. Maybe with a list of great duet songs. I think Elliot could help . . ."

Murph continued on and Evan stopped listening. A deep, unsettling wave of guilt passed through him. It made him shutter. *None of this would have happened if you were there. You had to leave. Always running from an uncomfortable situation.* It wasn't his fault. He knew that but convincing himself otherwise was a chore. The same outcome may have happened whether Evan was there or not.

"Hey? Hello? Try to pay attention," Murph called out to him. Evan looked over at her. "That was the first order of business and it took less convincing than anticipated, which is a minor Monday miracle."

"It's not Monday though," Evan pointed out.

"I know that! But any day that is the first workday of the week shall be considered a Monday."

"If you insist."

"Anyways, you seemed very confused about the events of New Year's Eve. I texted you several times yesterday to come upstairs and discuss it over some tea, but your silence was quite the indication you weren't interested."

"Didn't we already talk about this? I was busy."

"No worries. We can discuss it now since there doesn't seem to be an HR emergency around here."

"Okay," Evan said.

"Elliot is bisexual."

"Oh. I wouldn't have guessed."

"Are you being sarcastic?"

"No."

"That's a very sarcastic thing to say."

"How long have you known?"

"Since he decided to tell me a couple years ago. I had no clue before then. I guess some people would make the assumption since he does have some queer tendencies, but it was always part of the charm for me."

"Does it bother you?" Evan asked.

"Not at all. And if I did, it's not like I could change him."

"Has he experimented with other guys?"

"There's been a few times where we brought a third into the relationship for a one-time encounter, but I think that's the extent of it.

"I tell you all that," Murph continued, "because I need for you not to be weird around him. He had asked me several times if I thought you'd be bothered if you found out."

"Why would that have been a problem?"

"Do you want me to be honest?" Murph asked.

"Of course."

"You're a bit . . . stuffy."

"What does that mean?"

"You do things by the book and being bisexual straddles multiple lines. For some reason, within the gay community, that orientation is looked down upon. Elliot didn't want anything to change between the three of us."

"He has nothing to worry about."

"Hindsight and all that I suppose. Anyways, it was just an innocent kiss. We weren't even sure if Franco was gay."

"I've seen him on Grindr," Evan said.

"Oh, awkward. And wow! I'm impressed. You're actually getting back out into the dating scene."

"Not quite. I need some more time."

"Evan, that's a tired excuse and you know it," Murph said. She spun her chair around and began checking emails.

It was a lame excuse, but the only one he had.

thirty-seven

RUN

Nothing happened for a long time.

It's not as if Evan ceased to exist, but his life filtered into the monotonous routine of going to work and coming home to occupy himself with some project.

The nightmares continued. The warped face seemed to always be a part of it.

Evan read the obituary; he even contemplated buying a ticket to Pennsylvania to pay his respects, but he didn't work up enough courage.

Instead, he checked the Facebook page periodically and saw new posts come in from complete strangers. It was bizarre that people would write to a dead man; it was even weirder that they were from strangers to Evan.

The strangers would write messages claiming how great of a person Vincent was and rattle off a list of memories they shared together. Evan couldn't imagine how he had a life outside of their time together. It was as if the first day of his existence was the moment he and Evan met. A ludicrous thought. Evan knew about the previous hook ups, mistakes, regrets, and everything else. He talked about them somewhat incessantly.

Evan continued to run from Vincent because it's the only thing he knew how to do.

He ran from the grief until he forgot Vincent existed.

Vincent.

Evan always thought it was such a refined name for an unrefined individual. It added to the convoluted charm he had.

Evan's mind was far away from Vincent and his death when he found himself sitting in Murph's apartment. Snow was falling and sliding down the windows outside. Everything was covered in that white sheen that would soon fade to slush.

"Okay! Let's start brainstorming some songs. We have procrastinated long enough," Murph said. "Elliot, whatchu got?"

"I have done some research on this event and it's actually quite a big deal. A Denver tradition so to speak. People are going to bring their A-game. The performance will be important—no doubt—but the song . . . you will win if we pick the right one."

"Is there a prize for this?" Evan asked.

"That's a great question," Elliot said, pointing at Evan. "No, there isn't. BUT! All of the proceeds go to charity so if that doesn't warm your heart than I don't know what would."

Evan shot a glance at Murph.

"What Elliot is trying to say is that it's our civic duty to compete in this. I know that competitive spirit is buried down inside of you. We just need to tap into that," Murph said to Evan.

"I said I'd do it. You can stop trying to sell me on it," Evan said with a laugh.

"So, I have gathered the definitive list of duets. The best of the best. Shall we start at the top?" Elliot asked.

Evan and Murph nodded.

Elliot clicked several times on his laptop and sound burst from the speakers around the apartment.

Evan didn't recognize the song until Elliot yelled out the title.

"A bit of a dark horse. 'Who Says You Can't Go Home' by Bon Jovi and Jennifer Nettles."

"No. Definitely not," Murph said after listening to the first verse.

"Okay. Okay, I was expecting rejection but not that quick," Elliot said. "How about this one?"

Elliot clicked again and the song changed. Rhianna's voice filled the room.

"Pass," Evan said. "It is a boring song."

Another click.

"'Broken' by Seether and Amy Lee," Elliot announced.

"Absolutely not!" Murph said. "Do you want the audience to slit their wrists and drop dead while we are up there?"

Evan winced at the comment, but it went unnoticed.

"Let's try for something that isn't as modern," Elliot suggested. An Elton John song belted out across the apartment.

"Someone else is definitely going to pick that. We need something unique," Murph said.

"Give me a minute," Elliot said. He leaned in close to the laptop and began scrolling through a long playlist.

"I'm getting the sense that he is a music aficionado," Evan said to Murph.

"Yeah. His parents were roadies for The Grateful Dead back in the day and he absorbed their love of music. You should see his family's house. Filled with so many albums and different music memorabilia."

"I would have expected him to have the perfect song right away then," Evan said with a smile.

"Give him time. Elliot, any luck?" she called out.

"No. I need more time. Sorry."

"We still have"—Murph checked her phone—"two months until we need the song finalized, so plenty of time!"

"I'm going to head out then if that's okay." Evan stood up and finished the last of his beer.

"See you soon!" Murph said.

"See you soon," Elliot echoed, still not looking up from the laptop.

Evan stepped into the elevator and hit the button for the first floor.

His mailbox was stuffed with countless advertisements and other garbage. Evan pulled out the pile of papers in two attempts. He leaned against the long row of mailboxes and sifted through the junk.

He tossed a large stack into the trash and was left with four envelopes.

The first two were his internet and electric bills as described in massive print across the front of each envelope.

The third was from work. It looked unimportant.

The last envelope was addressed to him in an unsteady hand. Evan's name and address slanted across the front. He was surprised that anyone knew his address. It wasn't information he had given out except for a couple people.

His eyes shifted to the top left. There was no return address.

Evan turned it over and found a sticker pressed to the back with the usual information.

A name was there. One he was familiar with.

Ann Besser.

thirty-eight

RETURN TO SENDER

The elevator ride back to the eighth floor took an excruciating amount of time.

Residents piled in on the first floor and hit every button.

Silence spread out amongst the group of strangers. Everyone stared directly ahead and tried to occupy as little space as possible. As people began to get off, the remaining horde moved to unoccupied corners and continued their hundred-yard stare.

Evan flipped the envelope around in his hand several times.

Many questions floated around in his mind with several of them cresting the surface.

Why?

What could possibly be in there?

Evan knew the answers would be inside the envelope and, yet, he hesitated.

The envelope sat on his kitchen counter for several hours. He tried to busy himself around the apartment until he ran out of chores, which weren't many considering he had used the excuse of busying himself with chores three other times that week.

Evan really needed a hobby like trolling people on the internet. That would take up his time for sure.

After he walked by the envelope for the twenty-sixth time, Evan snatched it off the counter and tore it open.

He pulled out two pieces of paper. He started with the handwritten note.

> Evan,
> By now, you are aware that Vinny died. I'd like to not be as blunt about it, but it's the unfortunate reality we find ourselves in.
> I'm devastated and I don't quite know how to keep pushing myself forward.
> I hope this letter makes it to you, but I can't be certain I have the correct address. When I went down to Dallas to collect Vinny's belongings, I found a series of letters he left behind. Twenty-seven letters for twenty-seven different people.
> And you were one of them. Enclosed is the letter he wrote to you.
> He had your address programmed into his phone within your contact

information. I doubt you care to know the details, but I'm allowing myself to write freely without stressing about each word.

I have done my best to not read the letter he wrote for you. Part of me wanted to examine each line and word of every letter because it would help me to understand how he felt about others. I'd learn about the relationships he worked hard to create, and in your case, the ones that fell apart.

I was sad to hear you moved to Denver. You were a great compliment to Vinny's style and demeanor. You were the first true relationship he was invested in.

It won't be easy but read the letter. Moving on is a difficult process; the longer you avoid it though, the harder it will become.

I hope you find success and happiness in this world. It's something we all deserve but only a few are lucky enough to find.

You are always welcome at our house if you ever have a strong desire to travel to Pennsylvania. I don't see our address ever changing. We have lived our best years here and would like to continue that trend even after what's happened.

With love,
Ann

Evan placed the note on the counter and picked up the letter. It was several pages long.

Evan,
You are long gone. I said my last goodbye to you—

He stopped reading, folded the letter up, and placed it back in the envelope. Evan wiped the tears from his face and put the envelope under the unopened box of razor blades.

The words were going to hurt. That was a massive understatement. The words would drive him to the edge where the slightest change in any variable would send him careening into the abyss. The letter would be filled with regrets Evan didn't want to confront.

His dad was coming to visit in a few weeks. He was partaking in a massive lip-syncing event. Evan had things to look forward to. He didn't need to keep burying himself in the past.

Their relationship had been less than a year! Evan had dated Kieran for seven years—a failed relationship that actually hurt when it ended.

Vincent was a dot within his life. Dead or not, a few years down the road, he would be forgotten. Nothing but a hazy memory from a previous life.

Fucking Christ, Evan, he told himself. *Vinny meant way more to you than that. He's dead! It's okay to be sad. It's okay to want him back. It's okay to wish things were different.*

Evan needed to keep moving forward.

"Not today," he said aloud and walked away from the shelf. "Not anytime soon."

thirty-nine

EVEN

Evan had another week to prepare for his dad's visit to Denver. In the meantime, Evan, Murph, and Elliot took a weekend road trip to Breckenridge to partake in some skiing.

None of them had skied before that day. It made sense considering Murph and Elliot spent their lives in the flat, putrid wasteland of Dallas. For Evan, it was slightly bizarre since he had migrated around the country more often than a buffalo caravan.

After an hour of lessons and words of encouragement from the instructor, the trio found the easiest slope of the bunch. The results were mixed. Evan found himself sliding down the mountain more than he was actually skiing. Elliot was the most skilled but complained about how boring the activity was. He didn't enjoy the five minutes of skiing and then having to spend four times as long getting back up the mountain to do it again. As for Murph, she was the most determined. Each time they went down, she improved and would walk over with a huge smile and ask if they could go just one more time.

Elliot and Evan finally tapped out after hearing Murph's mantra six times. The guys retreated to the lodge while Murph continued on her journey to Olympic gold.

"Do you think we can smoke in here?" Elliot asked.

Evan looked around. "It would probably be best to do it outside."

"Wanna join me as I freeze my ass off?"

"Of course," Evan said.

They passed through the lobby of the lodge and out onto the balcony. A few others loitered in the corner, but they seemed to be uninterested in the new inhabitants.

Elliot lit the blunt and took a deep inhale. He handed it to Evan.

The process was repeated until they agreed they had enough.

"Do you ever get tired of smoking?" Evan asked as Elliot placed the stub of the blunt back into the plastic bag.

"Not at the moment. It's not something that's going to be a lifelong habit. I'm sure once Murph and I get married, we will grow out of it."

"I figured the Rockies would be strict about that."

"I'm not a player, so they don't give a shit. We have a 'don't ask, don't tell' type of policy. I could easily point out the potheads in my office. Like any place, they are always evident."

"More importantly, you seem confident you and Murph are going to get married."

"Why wouldn't we?"

Evan finally felt the blunt course throughout his body. He leaned against the railing and let the lightness pass through him.

"I just never took Murph as the marriage type," Evan said.

"That's fair. I'm probably more monogamous of the two of us, but I know she'd marry me."

"When are you going to propose?"

"I'm glad you asked," Elliot said. "I bought the ring last week."

"Really? That is exciting!" Evan gave him a slap across the chest.

"I'm nervous," Elliot confessed.

"Anyone would be. It's a huge step to take in a relationship."

"I called Murph's mom a few weeks ago to talk about it. She was so happy. I'm going to get them up here for the proposal. I think it's important to celebrate with family after an event like that."

"That's a great idea."

"I have a favor to ask."

"Go for it," Evan said.

"Would you take our photos that day?"

Evan's love of photography declined once he got into the relationship with Vincent. The last time Evan used any of his cameras when during their trip to Tallulah Gorge, which was the weekend of the memorable pillow talk. It was a massive signal of what was to come and kick started the series of conversations that drove the two of them deeper into chaos. Evan began focusing more on stitching together the relationship rather than the things he enjoyed. The cameras collected dust on his shelves and after he moved to Denver, he hadn't thought of using them even once.

Finally, he had a reason to get himself back into it.

"I'd love to. It's cool of you to ask."

"To be honest, we don't know many people out here and I know you enjoyed photography, so you were the logical choice," Elliot said.

"The pictures will be good. I promise."

"I know they will be. Anyways, what about you? I'm talking about getting married. What's going on in Evan's love life?" Elliot asked, gesturing toward Evan in a circular motion.

"It's nonexistent. Just focused on other things, I suppose."

"You must have had a rebound after . . . uh . . . what was hi—"

"Vinny."

"Right. Vinny."

"And no, I haven't been with anyone since."

"I don't believe it."

"Why's that?" Evan asked.

"Because everyone in the gay community is into hook ups."

"Says who?"

"Says . . . well, Twitter and all the hook up apps out there."

"Elliot, that is a massive generalization. Not every gay guy likes hook ups. I certainly don't. That's never a good way to form a connection with someone."

"But sometimes you got to let off some steam."

"I have myself for that. I could go the rest of my life without having sex again."

Elliot looked over in shock. "There is no way."

"Having sex is messy—both physically and psychologically. Have you ever had sex with another guy before?"

"I did once, but Murph doesn't know about that."

"I don't intend on telling her. Didn't you think that fucking a guy was more of a chore than having sex with a woman?"

"I never said I did the fucking. And you're right, having sex with a guy can be a hassle."

"When did you figure out you were bisexual?" Evan asked, shifting the subject slightly.

"It's a boring story and one I don't have the cognitive ability to recall right now. Is this pot hitting you as hard as it is me?"

"Probably."

"Okay, good. It's no fun being alone on High Island."

"Do you consider yourself a part of the gay community?"

"Since when did you start asking all these questions? For a long time, I didn't think you liked me. Sorry. It's just that you are so . . . safe. You are so even that it's difficult to get a read on you. Sorry again. Even Evan. That has a nice ring to it."

"Why do you keep apologizing?"

"Who knows, man. Just a pathetic way to avoid confrontation I suppose."

Evan's previous question would go unanswered. Elliot slowly moved from the railing to the sliding door. They seated themselves by the fire and waited for Murph.

They both fell asleep within minutes.

Evan was back at home. Not his apartment in Denver, but the place he shared with Kieran—his last true home. He walked into the kitchen and noticed the rice scattered across the floor. Evan stepped on it and grabbed his phone from the table. The screen was bright and displayed the Grindr logo:

He scrolled through and found that each square showed the warped face. The doorbell rang. Evan appeared in front of it without taking a step. The door opened. The warped face stood on the other side. "R-r-r-ready for our d-d-date?" the voice sputtered. "Yes," Evan said. The warped face extended a hand and Evan took hold. They stepped off the porch and fell together into the darkness. Evan floated slowly to the ground and regained his footing. The warped face was nowhere around. Evan called out to it and received no response. A sign lit up in the distance for a sushi restaurant. Evan never cared for sushi, but he moved toward it anyways as it seemed to be the only option. He was inside the restaurant and the warped face greeted him with a wide smile that showed all of its missing teeth. "S-sit," it said. Evan sat—

"Dude! Dude! Wake up. Goddamn, how high did y'all get?" Murph asked. Evan returned to his boring reality.

He tried to remember the dream, but any remnant of it fluttered away.

Evan opened his eyes and stretched his neck to shake away the tightness.

"Finally!" Murph said in rejoice. "Let me tell you both about how I conquered the mountain out there . . ."

She spoke for a long time in strenuous detail about her experience. Elliot and Evan nodded, laughed, and cried when needed.

Following Murph's Shakespearian monologue, the trio headed back to their room.

The weekend continued on with more skiing and eating and drinking and smoking and idle conversations amongst them and the strangers they came across at the lodge. It was a relaxing escape from the normal buzz of Denver.

Evan sat in the backseat during their trek home and thought through what Elliot said. Well, more like considered how it was strange that he hadn't gone on any dates. It had been plenty of time since ACL and the breakup. It had been plenty of time for him to get settled in Denver. It had been plenty of time for him to . . . forget Vincent. That last one becomes easier when the person you dated ends up dying shortly after you break up with them.

It wasn't that simple though.

Evan still couldn't wrap his head around Vincent being dead. Evan still felt unsettled in Denver. Evan still worried that any date he'd go on would end up being a complete waste of time.

He wasn't in the right head space yet.

Starting over with someone new was always the worst part. Having to relive those tedious conversations where every detail is covered and examined just to understand the basic qualities of a person. The thought of Evan having to constantly open himself up on dates with the false hope that one would turn into something was exhausting.

That was how it worked though. He could either complain about the process or dive into it.

For the time being, he decided that complaining and contemplation was the best option. He'd think about it more in a few weeks, which essentially meant he'd think about it nonstop. There was no off switch for Evan.

The mountains receded into the distance as the skyline of Denver took shape. The weekend was never long enough.

"Should we end this weekend with a night cap at our favorite watering hole?" Murph asked.

"I'm down for one drink," Elliot said.

"Sure," Evan said.

Twenty-six minutes later, they walked into the empty bar and were greeted by an excited Franco. The trio took their place at the bar and ordered the usual poison.

Evan wouldn't realize until much later that the answer to some of his problems was right in front of him.

forty

A VOID DANCE

It was Saturday evening. Evan's father strolled out the hotel and into the car.

"Get everything done you needed to?" he asked.

"Yeah," Evan said.

Evan's father had been in town since Thursday. They checked off all the touristy things to do in Denver and the surrounding area, many of which Evan had yet to see.

Evan spent the afternoon doing "chores" around the apartment. It was a convenient excuse he came up with to get a few hours to himself. Too much human interaction sent him into a spiral where he needed alone time—and that was most apparent with his father. Sure, the trip was going well, but there were pockets where they had nothing to say to each other. It was frustrating considering they had a decade and a half of time to catch up on.

It'll work itself out, Evan continued to tell himself. *Rebuilding a relationship takes time.*

"Are you good with having burgers tonight?" Evan asked.

"Yes. Where is this place?"

"On the other side of town. I've been to it a couple times," Evan said.

"Hey, by the way," his father said, turning to look at him. "Thanks for organizing this weekend. I've had a great time. You live in a cool city."

"Of course. Glad to have you here. Maybe I can come by to visit you and Shirley sometime soon."

"I'd like that," Evan's father said with a wide smile.

The restaurant was a tight space. Tables were placed haphazardly throughout. Evan and his father waited twenty minutes until their name was called over the intercom. The hostess shuffled them over to their seats in the corner.

"At least the view is nice," Evan's father said.

Out beyond the window was a view of a street performer. She was standing with an acoustic guitar and belting out some tune they couldn't hear.

"It's too cold out there to be doing that."

"Gotta make a living somehow. Speaking of which, how's your job going?" Evan's father asked.

"Very tame compared to my old one in Dallas. People just do what their supposed to, so that doesn't leave much for Murph and I to do."

"Who's Murph?"

"My friend down here. I haven't talked about her at all?"

"No."

"That's surprising. She lives in the same building as me. Quite the firecracker. She is constantly ripping me out of my comfort zone."

"Good friends will do that." Evan's father said.

The waiter came over and asked what they wanted to drink. Two waters.

"So," his father continued, "do you see Denver as the place you'll be at for a while."

"Yeah. I could see myself buying a house and settling in."

"I hope that happens for you. Establishing your roots somewhere is extremely important. I think it lends itself to being mentally stable too. I roamed around for far too long."

"Are you satisfied with where you are now?"

"I am."

"Why?"

"I finally found the things we all want—a home, someone that loves me, a stable job, and a relationship with my kids."

"Life tends to be more complicated than that," Evan said.

"You're right, but if you've managed to figure out those basic things that carry a huge weight, let me tell you, you are headed in the right direction."

"Have you ever lost someone?"

"What do you mean?"

"Have you ever had someone close to you die?" Evan asked.

"Yes. I hope you remember that your grandparents died before you were born."

"I remember."

"I have been close to many people who have died. One of the downsides of battling an addiction—not everyone makes it out the other end."

"How did you grieve?"

"I didn't . . . most times I never did. I was so drunk or drugged up that I couldn't ever focus on that. I guess you could argue that's how I dealt with it," his father said with a shrug. "I'm not proud of it, but if I always held onto regrets from the past, I wouldn't be sitting in front of you right now."

The waiter came by to refill his father's glass of water.

"Why do you ask?" he continued.

"I'm worried about when that time comes for me. How am I going to handle it, you know? You can think you have it all planned out in your head about how you'll react or move on, but I just don't know."

"It's not something to stress over now."

Evan wanted to tell him. He wanted to tell someone, but his avoidance of grief didn't allow him to do so. Instead, he steered the conversation away from such morbid things and allowed for his father to tell stories—happy ones.

The warped face sat three tables away, staring back at Evan and shoveling food into its open cavity.

It was waiting.

forty-one

SOBER, OR SOMEONE'S VIEW OF IT

Evan's phone lit up at the end of their meal.

"Looks like someone is trying to get a hold of you," Evan's father said, pointing down at the phone.

It was a call from Murph.

"I'll call her back when we're done." He clicked the side button and sent the call to voicemail.

"Anything else planned for the evening?" his father asked.

It was already dark outside, which eliminated many options.

"That is the one thing I didn't think through. I assumed you'd want to head back to the hotel early since your flight is in the morning."

"I'll be alright. I can sleep on the plane. What's a normal Saturday night look like for you?"

"If I'm not at home—which is the case some weeks—then I am probably out somewhere with Murph and her boyfriend. We generally avoid the crowded bars. Our favorite spot is a dive bar not too far from here, but I don't know if you'd—"

"Evan, it's fine. I don't mind going to a bar."

"Are you sure?"

"Yeah."

The check arrived at the table and Evan's father immediately grabbed for it. "Don't even bother," he said. "I had a great weekend here with you, so this is the least I can do."

As his father pulled out cash, Evan texted Murph and said to meet them at It. She responded back saying they were already there.

A short time later, Evan and his father walked into It. The bar had an unusual number of people loitering around the tables.

Evan found Elliot and Murph at the end of the bar and went through the necessary introductions. Murph gushed at finally getting a chance to meet Evan's father even though Evan hadn't spoken much about him since Thanksgiving.

Francisco came over with four waters and they repeated the introduction process again.

"It's busy in here tonight," Evan noted.

"Yeah. I put up those flyers again and people seemed to notice."

"Please tell me you didn't use that ugly yellow color this time," Murph said.

"Of course I did. That's a power color. It draws the eye," Franco said.

"A . . . power color? You make no sense sometimes, Fran."

"I'll take an Old Fashioned," Evan said to Franco.

"What do the rest of you want?" Franco asked.

Evan didn't hear their replies as he left for the bathroom, but he could guess that Murph and Elliot didn't stray far from their normal poisons.

The bathroom was surprisingly clean. It was likely from the lack of use and not necessarily from the uneven cleaning schedule. Of course, Evan was no bathroom specialist, so his best guess was pure speculation.

He stood in the mirror and fixed his hair. Evan cut off most of it the week prior, so there wasn't much to work with. He took a long inhale and held it. He was okay. Life was okay.

"Get over here! We are about to cheers," Murph called out as he left the bathroom.

Evan hustled over and grabbed his glass.

"To what?" Evan asked.

"To all the stray cats. May they find a home," Murph said. She raised her glass and waited patiently.

Slowly, the others raised their glasses in recognition.

Evan's father took a long sip of his drink and sat back in the chair. "How did y'all find this place?"

"It's a long story," Elliot said.

"But one worth sharing," Murph started off. "It was a cloudless night in the cool embrace of October. The year was . . ."

Evan tuned her out as she devolved into a detailed—and mostly false—story about how they came across It. Murph conveniently left out the meaning of the posters and how they related to the dying words of her father. Evan realized how little she had spoken of him since then. Maybe she was better. He considered asking her about it, but that felt intrusive. Murph was open enough that she'd feel comfortable telling him if she needed to talk.

Evan looked across the bar and saw Franco laughing with another customer. Franco was cute—no doubt there—but . . .

He turned his attention back toward his drink and noticed his father's glass.

"What did you order?" Evan asked him, cutting off the final piece of

Murph's story.

"A Jack and Coke," his father said with minimal concern.

Evan's eyes widened. "Are you joking?"

"No," he said with a chuckle. "What's the problem?"

"You're a fucking alcoholic. Are you kidding me? What the fuck are you doing?"

"I'm having a drink. Didn't I tell you? I limit myself to one mixed drink a week."

Evan shook his head incessantly. "No. No. That's not how this works."

"Evan, what's the problem?" his father repeated.

"This isn't how sobriety works." Evan tried his best to not yell. Murph and Elliot stared over at him, watching how it would all unfold.

"I'm still sober."

"No, you aren't!" Evan yelled. "Dad, this is called a relapse. How—what are you thinking?"

"I have been doing this for two years now."

"Two years? You gave me that sob story at Thanksgiving about how you almost died. And I believed you! I thought you had changed."

"I did change. I'm still sober," his father repeated.

"Recovering alcoholics don't drink. Do you not understand that?"

"Evan, you have never been addicted to alcohol, so please don't try to tell me what I can and can't do."

"Are you two listening to this?" Evan asked Murph and Elliot. "Better yet, you both know about my dad. How could you let him order that drink?"

"Evan—"

"This is crazy," Evan said to himself.

"I have changed. I got better," his father said. "I stopped with the abuse. No more of the yelling or the excessive drinking. I'm finally better, but life is hard sometimes. I get stressed and that one drink helps to take the edge off."

"You realize that's what an addict would say?"

"I'm not an addict," his father said.

"What are you even stressed about now that made you get that drink?"

"More than I could possibly tell you."

"Try me," Evan said.

"Okay . . ." His father reached for the drink and began to take a sip.

"STOP!" Evan swiped at the drink and glass shattered against the bar top. The drink spread out and began to slowly drip onto the floor.

Franco ran over to clean up the mess. "What is goi—"

"TELL ME!" Evan said. "Tell me why you're stressed."

"Because you are impossible to read. I can't recognize whether you love me or not—or even if you want me around. And I get it. I wasn't around and you learned to live without me. I have been trying so hard though. I want to have my family together again."

"Are you seriously blaming me for your drinking problem?"

"I don't have a drinking problem."

"Yes, you do. Have you told anyone . . . have you told Shirley or my sister?"

"N-no."

"Why?"

"Because it's not a big deal."

"Are you still getting sobriety coins?" Evan said.

"I stopped going a while back."

"So, you haven't told anyone else and you stopped going to AA meetings, but you think it isn't a problem?"

"Evan, you brought me to this bar. If you thought my sobriety was so important, why would you bring me here?"

"I-I asked you and you said it was okay."

"Of course, I did. Would you offer a drug addict a bump of cocaine? No. This is your fault."

"Fuck you. Fuck you for saying that. Your two years of drinking is your fault. You did this to yourself."

"I'm still sober. I'm better. I'm better now," he said quietly. "You don't understand."

"You know nothing about me. I shouldn't have let you back into my life."

"You don't know what it's like to wake up every day and have this desire tugging at you. I couldn't think. I couldn't function without it. Now, I'm able to. Now, I'm able to enjoy a drink without abusing it," his father said.

"YOU KNOW NOTHING ABOUT ME! You have no idea the struggles I have. They should have left you on that road to fucking die."

His father rubbed a hand through his beard. "I'm sorry," he said in a hushed tone. "I didn't mean to hurt you. Please don't say something like that. I'm better now."

"Stop saying that. You're not better. You'll never change. I was so stupid. I shouldn't have ever listened to any of you," Evan said, pointing to his father, Murph, and Franco.

Evan stood up from the table. "Find your own way to the hotel. And don't contact me again."

"You don't mean that. I love you Evan."

"This isn't some fucking joke. I only met up with you because you said you were sober. You aren't sober now and weren't at Thanksgiving."

"Evan—"

"Goodbye." Evan grabbed his jacket and rushed to the door.

No one came and tugged at his arm to stop him from going. It wasn't a veiled threat Evan would retreat from given more time.

No, it wasn't the case at all.

forty-two

CHANGE

Evan sat on the gray couch with his head pressed into the cushion.

He had been listening to the monologue for quite some time but hadn't been paying attention for most of it.

"So yeah, that's why I think people don't change," the monologist finished saying.

"That's really interesting," Evan observed. "But people do have the ability to change."

"Sure, they do. For every person that buys a gym membership after New Year's and actually gets healthier, there are ten times more that burn out and never follow through."

"How can you say that? That is a sweeping generalization."

"I don't think you can prove me wrong."

"Well, you can't prove yourself right," Evan said with a smile.

"This is my apartment, which means the burden of proof lies with you."

"I don't make such demanding rules when you're at my apartment."

"A missed opportunity on your part. You also don't like to have these deeply intellectual conversations with a deeply intellectual individual like myself," he said with a smile. It was a simple smile compared to how warped it would become.

"I just don't agree with you. People can change. Sometimes it is subtle, other times it can be extreme."

"How have you changed?"

"I . . . I haven't had a reason to in a long time. I like the way I am."

"Bullshit. Be honest with me, but more importantly, with yourself."

"I am being honest with you. It's not my fault you always think I'm holding back."

"Fine. I'll ask the question a different way: How have the people around you changed?"

"I don't know. Can we talk about something else?" Evan asked.

"It's Friday night! This is what we do. This is all our relationship has been. I ask you thought provoking questions and you hold back."

"Let's not get into this right now. Athena and Jag are coming over soon."

"One more question."

"Can I abstain?"

"You always do, but I'll ask it anyways: Do you think your deadbeat, piece-of-shit father will ever change? If you can answer that truthfully and with a yes, then maybe—just the tiniest dick hair of a maybe—I'd believe people can change."

"I wouldn't even care to find out if he did."

Evan was back at his apartment, in a more present time. He didn't recall the drive back home from the bar.

His phone continued to buzz with texts and phone calls until he decided to turn it off completely.

Evan grabbed Izzie's leash and brought her downstairs for a walk. He looked up at the evening sky but didn't find any stars. Nothing but total darkness up there when he was in the confines of the city.

Izzie trotted around the patch of grass and finally decided to move along with the task.

Evan's mind raced the entire time. He tried to distract himself, but he was imploding. The charges were set, and the demolition would be imminent.

Back upstairs, he walked over to the bookshelf and grabbed the box of razors. The envelope underneath fell to the floor. Evan bent down and returned it back to the shelf without paying much notice. He tore into the razors without restraint and pulled one free. Evan admired the simplicity in the destructive potential of the object.

Whether his father believed it or not, Evan understood the struggle of an addiction. The constant pull of wanting to feel better with a quick slice or two.

This time he'd have to go deeper to rid himself of the pain.

Evan walked to the bathroom sink and straightened his left arm. Several veins ran down his forearm.

It was quiet. He was alone.

In one quick motion, Evan brought the razor to his left forearm and sliced downward toward his hand.

"Fuck. Fuck. Fuck," he muttered to himself.

The pain was brief; the relief lasted much longer.

Evan leaned against the wall and slid down to the floor. He let his arm hang as the blood began to pool on the floor.

The events of the evening faded into oblivion. His concern for any of the insignificant chores of his life disappeared from view.

Evan's vision began to blur as his head fell to the side. He rested for a moment. Izzie licking up the blood from the bathroom floor was the only noise in the apartment.

He was broken.

Evan reached out to the rack and yanked down the bright green towel. He pressed it tightly against his forearm to stop the bleeding.

He let his head fall to the side again.

Izzie continued to lap at the blood.

Evan rested for a while. He was tired and didn't see the need in moving to his bed. Might as well not make a mess in two areas of the apartment.

Evan lapsed into a dreamless sleep. The warped face didn't plague him.

It was still dark out when he woke up. Izzie was asleep by the toilet with patches of dried blood stuck to her fur.

Evan pulled the towel off his arm and tossed it aside. His arm was a pattern of red streaks and the threat of an infection. He stood up and walked to the sink. Evan waited until the water was warm and began the process of cleaning out the cut.

Sometime later, he stepped out of the bathroom with his arm wrapped and the razor blade in his hand. Evan tossed the used razor blade deep into the garbage can. He walked over to the shelf and grabbed the envelope from Vincent's mom.

Evan pulled out the unread letter from Vincent. He looked at the first line several times until the words were committed to memory and then tore the letter in half. He tossed the pieces onto the kitchen counter and left them there to decay.

The glass windows showed the quiet city below. Evan wondered how many other people were awake in the city right now. Or how many other people had just cut open their arm and bled out all over the bathroom floor.

Was his father still awake? Was he contemplating the events of the night with a drink in his hand? Did he know what Evan just did?

No. No, he was likely asleep even though the guilt and absurdity of his beliefs should have kept him awake.

Evan stepped away from the windows and returned to the bathroom to clean up the mess on the floor. The pile of blood was the size of a homemade apple pie. It took Evan half a roll of paper towels to consolidate the blood and return the floor to its ugly tan color.

Izzie did not enjoy the next part. It took considerable time to wash the blood out of her fur. The process kept getting stalled by her thrashing and attempts to bite Evan with the few teeth she had left.

With everything back in order, it almost seemed as if a traumatic incident hadn't occurred within the apartment. Evan certainly wasn't giving it much thought.

He was nothing in those first few hours after the event.

There were still eleven more razor blades in that box and if Evan didn't find help, he'd burn through all of them without hesitation to avoid any of the pain buried deep.

<u>forty-three</u>

THE PATHS NOT TAKEN

Evan's life could have been different.

    Evan's crying as a baby was a near constant state. His mom had trouble understanding how to quell the sobs that would radiate around the house. One day, while she was giving him a bath, Evan began to cry again. He swung his arms wildly against the shallow water and splashed it all over her. She sat back from the tub and watched the crying episode unfold as if she was watching an octopus through the glass at an aquarium. His mom wondered how quick it would be. If she held Evan's head underwater for maybe twenty or thirty seconds, the crying would stop and the buzzing in her brain would finally end. She let the invasive thought soak and settle. After some time, she leaned back toward the tub and reached for Evan. She grabbed and lifted him out. His mom found the bright green towel nearby and wrapped Evan up within it. He stopped crying and stared up at his mother with a wide smile.

    In another instance, Evan disappeared from his house for an entire evening when he was five. He slipped out without his father knowing, who was sitting in front of the television and having another Jack and Coke. His mom came home several hours after Evan's disappearance and asked where he was. His father gave a grunt of indifference and panic began to spread through the household. She checked every room, closet, and hiding spot she could think of. Evan wasn't anywhere. His mom called the police and they quickly found Evan laying in the grass two blocks away. When questioned as to why he wandered off, Evan said he didn't want to hear his daddy yelling again and how he wanted to see the stars. Evan likely doesn't recall that event today as it was one of many unfortunate moments within his childhood. It carries significance for his mother though because that was the first time she recognized her husband had a problem. That was the day she slowly started to plot her escape.

    Evan was one of three openly gay kids in his high school. It was lonely. He felt extremely isolated from most others. While he didn't get bullied about his sexuality, there was an unhappiness that wove deep within him. Then the English class came around and his teacher felt the loneliness. He prayed upon it and kept Evan within reach for the next seven years.

What if Evan's life ended that day in the bathtub?

What if Evan's mom didn't see the decaying nature of his father?

What if Kieran couldn't feel the loneliness oozing off Evan?

Our lives can be boiled down into a series of what-if questions that could be phrased in a way to carry extreme significance. Do you notice the pattern within those questions? None of them involved Evan making a decision. The people around him were the catalyst for what happened (or what didn't). Evan has been bounded by those around him.

Here's a few more meaningless what-if questions:

What if Evan never met Vincent?

What if Evan felt like Dallas was his home? Or Michigan? Or South Carolina?

What if Evan wasn't as fucked up as the rest of us and didn't have the desire to find relief from the edge of a razor blade?

Listen:

These questions have no answers because those paths were not taken. Life shouldn't be an exploration of what could have been rather than what it is.

Listen once more:

Each time Evan grabbed a razor blade and slid it across some portion of his body, he made a choice. He kick started a path and left behind another. All those choices brought him to that bathroom floor and the desire to find freedom.

For once, he wasn't bounded by others.

forty-four

TELL THEM EVERYTHING

The banging on the door rattled Evan awake.

He struggled to pull himself out of bed, but once he did, he shuffled to the door in nothing more than his boxers.

He flung the door open and was shoved aside by Murph.

"What the fuck is wrong with you? I called you twenty-six times last night. We were knocking on the door for hours. Your dad—"

"Let me stop you there," Evan said, holding up the arm with the bandage. "Don't talk to me about my father. Not now. Not in two weeks. Not in three months when everyone forgets about what happened because I won't." He spoke as if he had several shots of vodka.

"What happened to your arm?" Murph asked.

"I cut myself."

"Were you, like, chopping carrots or something? I don't remember you having that last night."

"No, Murph. I used this." Evan walked over to the shelf and tossed the box over to her.

"Evan," she said, staring up at him.

"It was the first time I have cut my arm like this. I . . . It helps."

"You've done this before?" Murph put the box in her purse.

"Yes."

"Where?"

"Places you'd never see unless you got me naked."

"Evan—"

"Don't."

"How does cutting help you?" Murph asked, treading on delicate ground.

"When things aren't going well. When it feels like everything around me is colliding against itself."

"You could have died," she said quietly.

"Murph, you know me. I looked into this and made sure I understood what I was doing. I don't want to die; I want to get better."

"You could have died. How could I have not seen this?" she asked herself. "We should get to a doctor."

"That's not necessary. I cleaned out the wound."

"The wound? This isn't some fucking medical show. Evan, you were harming yourself. I can't just let you continue to do that."

"I don't need you to fix me. You aren't some savior." Hadn't he said some variation of that to Vincent?

"Okay. So, it's fine for you to continue to cut yourself, but you couldn't stomach your dad having a drink last night at the bar. How are they any different from each other?"

"Don't. They are not related in the slightest."

"They are!" she yelled.

"My dad was a fucking drunk that verbally abused my entire family until the day my mom decided to get us out of there. He would slap me upside the head when I was THREE YEARS OLD!" he screamed. "He was a fucking monster. I was unbelievably stupid to think the façade he put up was anything more than that. Fuck him! That fucking drunk deserves nothing more from me. Ever."

Evan sat on the bed and cried. "I trusted him. I trusted him. Murph, I wanted things to be different. It had been so long. He had to have changed, right? I want to believe that people can change, but maybe Vin was right."

"What did he say?"

"He didn't think anyone could change or that they wanted to."

"Vin sounds like a total jackass."

Evan looked over at Murph. She stepped closer to him.

"He liked to say profound things that weren't actually profound," Evan said. "I think he's wrong. People can change; my father just isn't one of them."

"How about you put on some clothes and we head down to my apartment? We can talk through everything."

"Yeah."

Evan moved methodically around the apartment and pulled together an outfit. Sweatpants and a sweatshirt were the best he could come up with. He figured no one would judge him for his basic attire.

"Shit, I forgot my keys in there," Evan said as they left the apartment.

"I'll go and grab them," Murph said.

"I don't even know whe—" Evan started to say, but Murph already moved back into the apartment. He paced outside the door and waited for her to return. Evan didn't realize being alone right now was the easiest way to fall apart.

Murph came back outside before Evan could spiral. "Found them," she announced and locked up the apartment.

○ ○ ○

A majority of the day was spent in apartment 713 with Murph and Elliot listening to Evan speak for long periods of time.

He told them more details about his father and the man he was.

He told them about the first time he had cut himself and the powerful emotion that radiated through his body.

He told them about his mom's current marriage that seemed to be heading down the exciting path of divorce.

He told them about Kieran. All of the spooky stories included.

Evan talked more than he had in months, or even years, but there was one tiny piece of information he left out.

He never told them that Vincent was dead. It wasn't like Vincent was the root of all Evan's pain over the past six months, but to lose someone suddenly was a jab to the chin. Maybe it was guilt. Maybe it was grief, which was the likelier of the two.

Regardless, Evan made his choice and kept that one secret to himself.

He thanked the two of them profusely for listening to him talk and for the unusually good pizza from the crappy local joint down the block that Elliot raved about.

Elliot and Murph stressed how important Evan was to them. For once, he believed it and considered himself lucky to be surrounded by healthy people.

When he returned to his apartment that night, Evan sat on his bed and stared out the windows toward the world beyond. He didn't know what to do next until he realized he didn't have to know.

He walked over to the shelf to throw out the razor blades, but they were already gone. He searched around the apartment and came up empty. Evan figured Murph must have snatched them at some point and he was thankful for the kind gesture.

Getting rid of the razors always seemed to be a mindless task Evan was able to do. The bigger issue was whether he'd go out for them again or resort to another sharp object already in the apartment.

He moved into bed and tried to shake off the potential spiral. Evan propped up his laptop on the pillow and navigated to Hulu. It had the drug he needed. *Golden Girls* appeared as the next show to watch. He clicked on it and eased into sleep after a couple episodes.

forty-five

SMALL TALK

Evan waited with the mass of people as random names were called out.
"Eighteen shots of expresso for Captain Underpants!"
"I got a small chai latte for Ruth Bader Ginsburg."
"A large mocha for Brain."
"Uh—do you mean Brian?"
"Grab your shit and leave, dude," the barista said.
Brain/Brian did as told and scurried off after snatching his drink. He had important business to take care of at his dead-end job.
"Order for Jett. Who the fuck names their kid that?"
An older woman stepped forward. "My last name is Enginn, so my parents seized an opportunity. Fuck you very much." She grabbed her coffee and stomped away to complete businessy things at her dead-end job.
"I have a gallon of coffee for Guy-Who-Drinks-And-Posts-It-On-Instagram-Because-He-Thinks-It's-An-Aesthetic-That-People-Think-Is-Cool." The barista took a long breath. "Please don't make me repeat that."
A self-important Instagram "influencer" with ten million followers pushed through the crowd and demanded to know why he had to pay for his gallon of coffee. The barista handed him the gallon without some witty comment, which caused an audible gasp from everyone in the coffee shop. Instead, the barista hit the kill switch under the counter, which turned the gallon of coffee into unsweetened iced tea.
"Ugh! This place is the WORST!" the self-important douche shouted. "Third time this week!"
It was only Monday.
"I love pressing that button," the barista said. "Order for Even."
"Evan?"
"I'm illiterate, but that doesn't mean I can't read."
"Actually . . ."
"Shut up and take your drink."
Unfazed by the rude barista, Evan grabbed his coffee and found an unoccupied table in the back corner. Most of the tables were vacant since everyone was running off to their dead-end jobs to make money for rich

folk.

Evan took the day off as Murph suggested and was unconcerned about rushing through his coffee to get to work at a decent time.

Sitting and wasting hours at a coffee shop was a favorite pastime of Evan's, but one that he rarely engaged in over the past few years.

He had a specific mission today. Murph allowed him to leave the apartment the previous night on one condition: Evan had to look into finding a therapist.

"I get it. You must be thinking 'Murph, I don't need no stinking therapist to tell me how to feel! All they are going to do is give me drugs and yada, yada, blah, blah, hooey.' Well, Evan, my response would be that they have been helpful for me in the past. Actually—"

"Murph," Evan said. "I have been to therapists plenty of times, so it's not something you need to persuade me to do. Talking to someone objectively has worked in the past."

"Okay good. I really think it could help."

Finding the right therapist was the longest part of the process.

There were different criteria to consider:

Should he go with a male or female? Historically, Evan had gone down the female route because of the father issues that made talking to males more difficult.

Did he want someone who was younger or older? Styles could vary depending upon the generation.

Was he interested in a large practice or something more intimate?

Evan knew he wanted to stick with a psychologist because being loaded up on pills seemed like an artificial solution to the problem. He needed to change his behaviors and the self-sabotaging nature of his thoughts.

Evan clicked and navigated through a multitude of websites for offices in the Denver area. Location wasn't a concern, neither was cost (at least he made the assumption his medical benefits would cover the majority of it). He scribbled down notes and the pages quickly turned into an orderly set of bullets, separated out by each practice he looked into.

As the morning crowd continued to be berated by the barista, Evan took a break from the search and looked up from the laptop. He had spent so much time either at work, his apartment building, or It that he forgot an entire city thrived all around him.

Part of the joy of moving to a new city was the endless possibility of meeting an assortment of people. All Evan had done so far was make a best friend out of a coworker and her boyfriend and have a half-assed friendship with a local bartender.

He could do bett—

"Evan? Evan Eaton?" a voice called from his right.

He turned and saw a shorter guy looking in his direction.

"Yes."

"I found this on the floor over there. It had been kicked under the counter." The man held up a driver's license. "You seem to match the picture," he said with a smile.

Evan checked his wallet and realized he was missing his ID. "Thank you. Wow. That would have been a major inconvenience to lose."

The man handed over the ID.

"Texas, huh? You recently moved here?" the man asked.

"Yes. Well, depends on what you define as recent."

"Within the last month or two."

"Then no. I suppose laziness is the reason I still have a Texas driver's license."

"Ah. Laziness. A valid excuse for most things. Can I give you some advice?"

"Sure," Evan said with slight hesitation. He felt as if he was about to get reprimanded.

"Go there an hour before they close. I have it on good authority that the lines are significantly shorter than in the morning. People think they will beat the crowds in the morning, but don't realize they are the crowd."

"I will keep that in mind."

"I'm debating about just skipping work for the day since I completed my good Samaritan deed of the week."

"I took the day off," Evan said.

"Any reason in particular?"

"No. Not really," Evan said, reaching for his left arm. It hurt to the touch.

"I support your endeavor, Mr. Eaton."

"What's your name?" Evan asked.

"Vincent."

"Oh."

"You seem surprised by that," Vincent said.

"I knew someone else with that name. I don't run across many people named Vincent."

"I bet he was just as cool as me and enjoyed wearing suits to work every day like I have the unfortunate pleasure of doing."

"He was cool, but not one for suits."

"His loss."

Vincent stood there and noticed how the conversation was dying out. "Okay," he continued. "It was nice to meet you Evan. Welcome to Denver."

"Thanks Vincent. I really appreciate you bringing over my ID."

With that, Vincent gave one final nod and went toward the exit.

Evan wasn't used to small talk, especially from someone who didn't have any sexual interest in him. But c'mon. Did his name really have to be Vincent? Was the universe trying to get him to collapse into another spiral?

It's okay. It's totally fine. Evan took several deep breaths and moved past the hiccup. Other people existed with the name Vincent. It's what made the boring reality so damn boring.

Evan returned to his investigation of psychologists and only thought about Vincent and that disturbing warped face twenty-six times. He figured whoever he went to could help him decrease that number.

An hour later, the multiple pages of bulleted lists were crossed out and reduced to a handful of potential options. He revisited their websites before circling his choice.

Evan called the office and set up an appointment at week's end.

And with that, he closed the notebook and sat back from the laptop. He wasn't sure what to do next. The easiest thing would have been to go back to the apartment and waste away there, but he didn't see the point.

Evan packed up his laptop, slung the bag over his shoulder, and walked out the coffee shop with no destination in mind. He meandered around the city, weaving through city blocks. He walked into a park, which seemed to be an easier task than it would have been in Dallas. Small pockets of people were playing in the melting piles of snow. Spring was making its strongest push yet.

Evan sat on a bench and looked out at the nearby river. It wasn't particularly nice, but he wasn't there to admire the beauty. He watched as joggers occasionally zipped by in front of him.

Now that was something he hadn't done in a while.

Running used to be Evan's escape. It was a hobby born out of a comment from Kieran. After a grueling semester his freshman year of college, Kieran commented on how Evan had gained significant weight. It seemed like a trivial, run-of-the-mill thing for Kieran to say, but it stuck with Evan. He stood in front of the mirror each morning and poked, prodded, and pulled at the fat that cling to his hips and stomach. He would push back the skin on his face to remember a time when he could see his jawline. For several weeks, Evan hid behind layers of clothes and didn't get naked in front of

Kieran.

The simple comment drove him mad until one soggy morning in late June when he decided he was tired of complaining about the issue.

He went for a run around his mom's neighborhood and felt . . . jolted. A sensation of elation cascaded throughout his body. It could have been the pain after the first half mile, but he continued, nonetheless.

It took Evan several months before he actually enjoyed running, but once he felt that high—the pure, straight from the source kind—he made it a daily habit.

During his sophomore year of college, Evan was running an average of five miles a day and competed in as many 5Ks as he could find throughout the area. He managed to run in a few half marathons, but the full marathon was always elusive.

He quickly shrunk down to a size he had never been before. The fat from his hips, stomach, and face all disappeared, and, yet, Kieran never said anything. They continued on in their relationship as if nothing changed.

Evan pushed further regardless and kept running as a daily activity in his life through the remainder of college and during his time in Michigan.

Things halted once he got to Dallas and met Vincent—a trend it seems.

An elderly woman sat next to Evan on the bench as he continued to dive into a plan about how he could get back into running, writing poetry, and all the other interests that had seized over the last year and a half.

"Good morning," she said.

"Hi," Evan said, ripping himself from his thoughts.

"I'm sorry to have interrupted you. You seem like you are thinking about something important."

"Just figuring out the meaning of life," he said with a laugh.

The woman smiled and said, "I discovered you don't need much to be happy. A loving relationship and some hobbies you're invested in. Everything else will work itself out."

"I sure hope so."

"Do you come out here often?" she asked.

Their conversation continued on with little significance. Not every person you meet is going to have a lasting impact even when the conversation is happening in a fictional book where words are money and there is little sense in introducing characters if they don't propel the narrative forward.

Evan left the park following the talk with the elderly woman and went to the nearby brewery for lunch. A text from Murph popped up saying to be at her apartment by 7 p.m. Evan sent back an acknowledgement.

"What can I get you?" the bartender asked.

"Just a water. Do y'all have a food menu?"

"Yeah." He reached under the bar and grabbed one. "I'd recommend the chicken fingers. Who knows what's in them, but they are hella good."

"Hella good? That's quite the endorsement."

"They don't pay me minimum wage for nothing."

"Thanks for the suggestion," Evan said, and the bartender wandered off to pretend to be busy with something else.

Evan read through the menu and agreed that the chicken fingers seemed to be the most appetizing.

"What'll it be?" the bartender asked when he came back over.

"You sold me on the chicken fingers. I'll have those."

"Solid choice." He punched in the order. "So, do you always come to a brewery for the food?"

"Only on Mondays."

"It's usually dead until people get off from work, so you're an anomaly."

"I'm flattered."

"You look like you'd be in some fancy building downtown. You don't have to work today?" the bartender asked.

"Usually, yes, but I took the day off."

"Have you made the most of it?"

"I'd like to think so," Evan said.

"You must be if you ended up in this place."

"Hey, I am enjoying the ambiance so far."

The brewery went for the overplayed industrial look with some random paintings thrown up on the walls. Evan didn't necessarily enjoy the ambiance, but it was a lie that seemed trivial.

"I hope you don't mind small talk with a stranger."

"Fine by me. I don't usually get to interact with many new people," Evan said.

"Why is that?"

"I have been sticking to the same routine and hanging with the same people."

"We are somehow more connected with each other than ever before and still find ourselves isolated. Bizarre, huh?"

"Very bizarre. You must be okay though."

"Why's that?" the bartender asked.

"You work at a brewery. There are new crowds of people in here every day to interact with."

"You're right, but can I tell you a secret?"

"Yeah."

"I don't like people very much."

"Why not?"

"People will always disappoint. They will treat you like shit for their own gain and are so absorbed in their own lives that they forget about others."

"Can't you just attribute that to the people you surround yourself by? What if you were with people who were the opposite of that? I'm guessing your opinion would be different," Evan said.

"I'm speaking from experience, I suppose, but changing the people you are surrounded by isn't easy, especially when they are family or friends you've known your whole life."

"It's okay to let go of the excess. Not everyone needs a place in your life. In mechanical engineering, they say the easiest part to maintain is one that isn't there."

"The mysterious *they* . . . You must know that letting go isn't simple."

"Yeah, I know a bit about that," Evan said.

"People love to return to what's familiar even when it's damaging. Creatures of habit and such. Hold on—" the bartender said and scurried off to the kitchen.

He returned with Evan's meal.

"Here ya go, pal."

"Thanks. So, why are you working here if you don't like people?"

"A stepping-stone to my next adventure."

"Which is?" Evan asked.

"To plant trees."

"Are you wanting to be a landscaper or something?"

"No. I want to plant trees for the rest of my life."

"I didn't realize it was a paying profession."

"It's mostly restricted to non-profits right now, but they will pay for your housing and such. You get to travel around the world and plant trees. Pretty cool, right?"

"Uh, yeah," Evan said.

"You're not convinced. That's okay. But let me say this: we have *fucked* our earth raw for centuries now and she has the worst yeast infection we have ever seen. We can try to combat it with technology, which we will always do considering our society is hellbent on tinkering with shit and solving problems with robots and minimal human intervention, which is because we ruin things, but that will only be a half measure," the bartender paused for a moment to catch his breath. "Trees though. They are our friends and damn good at what they do. If we plant enough of them, we may actually be able to not completely waste this planet. Imagine if we took all those people who are pent up in prisons and had them planting trees. What if every citizen was required to plant one tree a month? It's a monolithic task and I intend to do my part."

"You are clearly passionate about this."

"I wasn't always. I did some DMT a few months ago and spent a year on this beautiful world where I was king of a village and we valued the inhabitants, nature, and all living things with equal respect. There was so much harmony amongst everything and then I was returned to this shitstorm. I realized my bartending job was not bettering myself and society, so I started my search. I hope by the summer to have something locked down."

"I have no idea what DMT is, but good for you for finding purpose."

"We could try DMT sometime," the bartender suggested.

"I'm not really into drugs. I'm too neurotic for something that extreme."

"You don't have to do drugs to find your purpose. Maybe you already know what it is."

"Honestly, I do not."

"You'll find it. Just give it time."

Evan nodded. A cop out of an answer in his humble opinion. If all people did was *give it time*, nothing would ever get done.

"I'll let you eat. It was nice talking to you. Let me know if you need anything else," the bartender said.

"Thanks."

There was no rush, so Evan took his time eating and tried to figure out what his purpose in life was.

He came up empty handed by the time he pushed his empty plate to the far side of the bar. It was an open question he'd need to revisit later . . . or maybe it would fall into his lap without trying.

Evan left the brewery and went back to his apartment. He was tired. All of the conversations were new to him and stretched his introverted side to the max.

Before he took a nap, he scoured through his closet and found the small stack of running clothes. He pulled them free and put them on the couch for future use.

Gotta start somewhere, right?

<u>forty-six</u>

EVAN MEETS LOAF

"Elliot, you better have something good," Murph warned.

"Don't insult me with your vague threats. I always pull through, *but not out*," Elliot said with a wink to Evan.

"Never again," Evan said.

"Hey! You're the one who slipped some tongue to my girlfriend on New Year's. I'm just asserting my dominance."

"Elliot, please try and focus. We have three weeks until the song needs to be finalized and I really, really, REALLY want to win," Murph said.

"Why do you care so much?"

"Because I like to win."

"Okay, fine. Here is what I have . . ." Elliot ripped off the sheet covering the whiteboard revealing the song title.

"Did you go out to buy that whiteboard?" Murph asked.

"Did you buy a sheet specifically to do that?" Evan asked.

"Yes," Elliot said, pointing to Murph, "and I abstain from answering your question," he said, waving a finger at Evan.

"Babe, I can't read your shitty writing."

"Perfect! That allows me to explain and provide backstory. Think back. Think back to a time when you were a child and sitting for hours at the dinner table because you refused to finish your meal. All the other dishes were clean and, yet, you held out like the last men in a regiment fighting a losing battle. You stuck to your morals and refused to eat the mystery concoction that sat humbly on your plate. It watched your every move and you teased each other, wondering who would cave first. Is this a familiar image to anyone?"

"No," Evan said.

"Maybe? Tell me more," Murph said.

Evan sighed. They truly were a perfect match for one another.

"Great! Thank you Murph. Love you. So, tell me then: What was the food on the plate that made you sit at the table for hours?"

"Meatloaf," she said without hesitation.

"CORRECT!" Elliot shouted and clapped his hands.

"What the fuck is wrong with you two?" Evan asked.

"Everything and nothing. Anyways, I believe you two should celebrate the genius of the one and only . . . Meat Loaf! Remember: it is two words contrary to the disgusting food item," Elliot said.

For the uninitiated and because Evan was afraid to ask, Meat Loaf is an American musician born in the great city of Dallas, Texas. He spent his childhood and college years around the city where the assassination of John F. Kennedy happened, which is still marked on the road with a white X because that's the American way. Following his mother's death during college, Mr. Loaf isolated himself for a long period of time until his friend ripped him from his depression and shoved him onto a flight to Los Angeles. Yada, yada. Time passes and Mr. Loaf meets (ha!) Jim Steinman, who would be a collaborator on his three most famous albums known as the Bat Out of Hell trilogy. Besides being one of the most successful artists of all time (his first album, *Bat Out of Hell* (1977), still sells hundreds of thousands of records each year), Mr. Loaf is also an accomplished actor. He has been in dozens of shows and movies with his most notable appearance being in the cult-classic *Fight Club*. While there are many fables around the origin of Mr. Loaf's name, he has never confirmed any rumors thus leading to his mysterious private life.

"Never heard of him," Murph said. Thank goodness Evan didn't have to say it.

"For suck fake, how do you not know who Meat Loaf is?"

"It's simple: I listened to country music growing up. My dad was slightly obsessed."

"Murph, I have known you too long to just be hearing this."

"Elliot, cut to the chase here. What song do you think we should perform?" Evan asked.

"It's not simple. In order to understand the undeniable sound and energy of this delicious meat dish—"

"Wait, I thought you didn't like meatloaf?"

"That was Kid Elliot. Adult Elliot loves him some meatloaf."

"Jesus fucking Christ," Evan said.

"Anyways, we need to listen to his entire first album. Put simply. We shall reconvene in forty-six minutes. See y'all on the other side!"

Before any protest could be made, Elliot hit the space bar on his laptop and the opening piano riff for "Bat Out of Hell" belted out across the apartment.

Evan sat on the couch with his arms crossed, showing his displeasure to the waste of time. About three minutes into the song, Murph started to tap her foot and nod her head. She was sold. It took Evan slightly longer to feel the power of the Loaf, but he was sucked in by the time all three of them were clapping along to "You Took The Words Right Out of My Mouth (Hot Summer Night)."

They finished the remainder of the album by singing lyrics they didn't know and dancing around the apartment with reckless ferocity.

"You know," Elliot said after Mr. Loaf sang out his last *I love you* from "For Crying Out Loud," "the man is just incredible. That is one cohesive story across the whole album and for suck fake, have you ever heard so many sexual innuendos in your life? Incredible. Bravo. Brava for the ladies."

"You're a complete freak," Murph said. "I didn't realize you had this obsession."

"We can delve into the inner workings of Elliot's dysfunctions some other time. Please tell us what song we should sing," Evan said.

"It's been up on the whiteboard the entire time."

Evan looked over and strained his eyes enough to decipher the toddler-like scribble:

Paradise By the Dashboard Light
by THE Meat Loaf

"Shit, dude. Isn't that song stupidly long?"

"Eight and a half minutes."

"How would we choreograph a song that long or keep the crowd entertained?"

"I have some ideas," Murph said.

"Me too," Elliot chimed in.

"Evan, it's the perfect duet song! You know it is."

"I'm not convinced yet," Evan said.

"Fine. Let's consult one outside source and see what they have to say."

"Go for it."

Murph stepped out the room and into their bedroom. She returned a few minutes later. "Any second now."

A knock at the apartment door.

"W-who? How?" Evan asked.

Murph flashed him a smile and scooped up Sasquatch into her arms to quell his barking. "Welcome! Welcome!" Murph greeted the guest after flinging open the door.

Francisco stepped into the apartment. "Nice place," he suggested.

"Goddammit," Evan said to himself. He hadn't talked to Franco at all since the confrontation with his father at the bar.

"You said there was an urgent matter needing to be resolved," Franco said. "Hi, Evan. Elliot, how are ya?"

"Hi."

"Oh, I'm just wonderful. High on meat right now," Elliot said.

"Uh, okay," Franco said.

"Here's the deal, Fran: we need an unbiased voice to put an end to a blooming argument," Murph said.

"Got it."

"Are you familiar with the artist Meat Loaf?"

"Of course."

"SWEET BABY BACK RIBS! Franco, you are the only sane one here," Elliot said.

"Go on," Franco urged.

"Okay, so we have chatted about the lip-syncing competition I roped Evan into . . ."

"Mhmm."

"It's taken Elliot many miserable months and failed attempts, but he has decided on a song he thinks will work. I'm in agreement. Evan is playing hard to get even though he was singing along to it earlier."

Evan considered protesting but he stopped himself.

"Which song?" Franco asked.

Elliot motioned to the whiteboard.

"I can't read that," Franco said.

"My handwriting isn't that bad," Elliot said in defeat.

"'Paradise By the Dashboard Light,'" Evan said.

"Amazing song. This is supposed to be a duet, right? That is such an underrated choice. I fully approve."

"I knew it!" Murph said. "Sorry Evan. Time to embody the Loaf."

"Fine," Evan said with a smile. "Thanks Franco."

"Is that all you need?" Franco asked.

"Yes, but you are welcome to stay and hang out with your wonderful friends," Murph said.

"I . . . I . . . yeah, I can do that."

Elliot grabbed Franco a drink and they are huddled around the coffee table playing several rounds of One Night Ultimate Werewolf, the game of how well you can lie to your friends.

Turns out, Evan was deceivingly good at it and won a round singlehandedly by feigning his innocence.

There were times when Evan felt he needed an expansive group of friends to be satisfied. It was something he never had but continued to strive for. As he sat in Murph's apartment, he realized three was a great number and more than enough. The small talk with strangers was welcome, but there was no need for every conversation with someone new to try and develop into a friendship. If it happens, fantastic; if not, at least he had the people in the room with him now.

Evan did his best to bow out of the night's activities after the second round of beers were passed out, but Murph caught him by the arm.

"How'd everything go today? I don't want to be your mother, but I am concerned."

"It went well. I looked at a bunch of psychologists around Denver and I think I found one I like."

"Did you set up an appointment?"

"Yeah. For Thursday."

"Evan, that's great! I know talking to someone doesn't solve everything, so you should cons—"

"I am going to start running again."

"If you ever need a partner, let me know."

"Of course."

"We can talk at work about our practice routine for the lip-sync stuff."

"Looking forward to it."

Evan gave Murph a long hug.

"Before I leave—" Evan said and walked over to Franco.

"Leaving already?" Franco asked.

"Yeah. Hey, I wanted to apologize for breaking the glass the other night. It wasn't a good look for me to lose my mind at your bar."

"Based on what I know, it was justified."

"Thanks. You know, you live so close to us. Don't be so much of a stranger. We like hanging out with you."

"I'll keep that in mind. Thanks Evan."

Back upstairs in his apartment, Evan took off his sweater and looked down at the bandage running the length of his forearm. A dull throb still pulsated throughout the area.

He slowly removed the old bandage and replaced it with a fresh one. The cut didn't look infected, but it was going to leave a scar.

A reminder of what he did. A reminder to never do it again.

<u>forty-seven</u>

THE ROOM WITH TWO CHAIRS

Evan sprinted the last quarter mile on the treadmill.

His legs protested each stride. His lungs begged for a break. He felt his pulse in his ears, chest, and neck.

But he continued on.

As he hit the two-mile mark, the treadmill slowed down to a normal walking speed and Evan rejoiced at being done. It was nowhere near what he used to do several years ago, but it was a start. His mind cleared from the distraction and chaos of the outside world. With time, he'd go further and faster.

For now though, he was ready to have an honest conversation with a complete stranger.

○ ○ ○

Positioned on the northern fringe of the Denver city limits, the building blended in with all the other blobs plopped along the highway.

The office was quaint enough. Light music played in the waiting room and a plethora of dated magazines were lined up neatly on the end tables. Evan grabbed one and browsed through the pages, absorbing none of it.

His mind raced, wondering if Dr. Knox jump right into things or take a softer approach. The softer approach would cost Evan more money due to the quantity of sessions needed but diving directly into the heavy stuff would require Evan to immediately open himself up.

"Dr. Knox is ready to see you," the receptionist said in a whisper.

Evan put the magazine back in the pile and stepped to the door.

Inside the room was two chairs spaced out evenly from each other. Seven windows lined the walls. Dr. Knox greeted Evan near the door and ushered him over to one of the seats.

"And please, call me Kash. The doctor title is somewhat of a sham." She saw Evan's face tort in confusion. "Oh, I just meant I'm not a medical doctor, but I'm sure you knew that already."

"Yes, I did my research."

"Somewhat of a planner then?"

"I try to do what I can to be prepared. It makes things go smoother for me and others."

"Do you mind if I ask you a few basic questions? I'll be taking notes throughout."

"Of course."

Kash asked Evan his age, occupation, where he was living, and other questions you'd answer when filling out an application.

Kash kept pace with Evan's speaking and when they were both finished, she said, "The rest of this hour is yours. I know the first few sessions can be awkward for us to find our balance. Would you like me to ask some things to start us off or . . ."

"I have been to a therapist before, so I don't think we need to spend any time skirting around why I'm here."

"Okay," she said, raising her eyebrows and scribbling a short note.

Evan pulled up his left sleeve enough to flash the bandage underneath. "I cut myself this past weekend and I want to make sure I never do it again."

"Was this your first time?"

"No, but it was the worst."

"Explain that to me," Kash asked.

"For years now, I have been cutting in hidden places like the inside of my thigh. No one has ever noticed the faint scars. I think part of me wanted to get caught because it would show that someone cared enough."

"When did this first start?"

"High school. Toward the end of my junior year. It was spaced out though like months would pass between the incidents."

"Do you always refer to them as incidents?"

"No. It's the word that came to mind."

"When did these incidents become more frequent?"

"Never."

"Please explain," Kash said.

"When I cut my arm, it was the first time I had done any self-harm since I moved to Denver. So, it has been many months. Honestly, I can't remember when the last time was, but I imagine it was during my time with Vinny."

"Where did you live prior to Denver?"

"Dallas."

"Why did you move?"

Evan shrugged. "It's what I do. My parents were in the military and we moved around a bunch when I was younger. This move to Denver was my third since I graduated college."

"That must take a toll on you."

"It does."

"I'm going to press you to think harder for a moment. Why did you move to Denver?"

Evan grabbed at his knees and squeezed. "I-I had nothing there. No friends. A miserable job."

"You mentioned Vinny. Who was that?"

"He was my boyfriend."

"Did he have anything to do with you moving?"

"No." *Liar.*

"When you decided to move, were you two still together?"

"Yes."

"Did you break up with him when you finalized your move?"

"Yes."

"Do you want to talk about that relationship anymore right now?"

"Not particularly."

"That's okay," Kash said, shaking her head. "One more question about it if you don't mind."

"Sure."

"Are you still on speaking terms with him?"

"No, I am not." He still could not bring himself to tell anyone how Vincent was dead. The words were locked up; the grief was still hiding. The warped face was enough of a reminder that Evan didn't want to confront it more. Give it time, right?

"Why did you cut your arm?"

"It's complicated, but not in the way you'd expect."

"I'm here to help."

"That's something Vinny would have said. Actually, he said that all the time, but he didn't end up helping me much."

"Do you think other people can solve your problems?"

"No. He just tried really hard to do so."

"Tell me why your incident was complicated."

Evan broke off into a long but vague answer about his father. It was partially true. His father and his minimized change were a significant reason as to why he dragged the razor blade down his arm, but didn't Evan buy those razors before his father came to visit?

Kash continued to take notes as Evan spoke.

"How did you feel when you cut your arm?"

"Scared. I knew I made a mistake and that people wouldn't understand."

"What wouldn't they understand?"

"I didn't want to die . . . I don't want to die. I needed relief."

"Relief from what?"

"If I knew the answer to that, I probably wouldn't be sitting across from you now."

"Do you have any more razors in your apartment right now?"

"No, my friend took them."

"Which friend is this?"

"Her name is Murphy—prefers Murph," Evan said.

Kash nodded. "Have you ever had suicidal thoughts before?"

"Yes."

"Have they been recent?"

"No."

"Do you remember the last time you did?"

"No."

"Have you ever thought through how you would do it?"

"No, no. It never got that intense."

"Evan, there are some paths we can do down and explore, but we won't have enough time today to do so. Before we meet again, I want you to try out some techniques to diffuse yourself when anything becomes too unbearable . . ."

Kash clued Evan into some techniques he could have found in the top results of Google if he searched how to stop being depressed as if it was as simple as that.

At least she couldn't prescribe him any medication. Those were a real drag.

When the hour was up, Evan scheduled his next appointment with the receptionist and started the long walk back to the car.

He hadn't expected a miracle cure in the first session, but he did expect Dr. Knox to be more concerned about the long cut down his arm. The moment was critical for him, so it had to be for everyone else, right?

The sessions would get tougher. Evan would need to directly confront his childhood trauma and during a session right before his birthday, Evan would tell her about Vincent's sudden death and how it devastated him. It was mostly the same speech he gave to Murph.

But that's jumping ahead of things.

forty-eight

SOMETHING GOOD

Baseball season was in full tilt and it turned out Elliot was not traveling as much as Murph anticipated.

Flying extra people with the team involved additional money and Elliot wasn't worth the expense. Most of his days were spent in the front office doing stuff we don't necessarily care about. Even with the more unique setting, Elliot's dead-end job followed the same boring cadence as the rest of you.

On the other side of town, Murph and Evan were tucked away in their cubicle.

"Murph, we have gone through this form ten times. There's nothing else for us to do. Let's just submit it."

"Hold on, hold on, hold on. No spelling mistakes?"

"No."

"No ink smudges?"

"It's a PDF."

"Did we put in the right song?"

"Yes."

"Scoot over. Let me read it one last time."

Evan slid back from his deck and let Murph take up residence. "I never knew how competitive you were."

"This isn't about being competitive," Murph said.

"What's it about then?"

"I'd rather not embarrass myself in front of a crowd. I read there could be a thousand people at the event!"

"You're joking."

"Evan, I don't joke about numbers and crowd sizes." Murph continued to look at the screen and scroll through the form.

"Have you performed in front of crowds before?"

"Yes."

"Care to elaborate?"

"No."

"Okay then. I'm gonna get more coffee." Evan walked out the cubicle and down the hall to the breakroom. Someone had spilled coffee all over the Keurig. He contemplated briefly about ignoring the spill, but he reached for the paper towels nearby.

"Finally! Someone is taking care of that," a voice behind him said.

"Just doing my part," Evan said.

Birch walked closer to Evan and watched as he contained the spill better than BP in the Gulf.

"I actually wanted to talk to you about something," Birch started.

Evan braced himself. Birch was known for many things around the office—none of them redeeming.

Birch lifted off into a long ramble about the state of things and whether HR could do anything about it. Evan listened because he was cornered, but he didn't particularly care. Birch was a constant visitor to his cubicle and always rattling off some newfound concern.

". . . Are you even listening to me?" Birch asked.

"Not entirely. I was focused on this," Evan said, pointing to the wad of used paper towels.

"Between you and Murphy, you both are the most incompetent HR group I've ever seen."

"Thank you Birch. We will take that into consideration."

With nothing left to complain about, Birch left the room. Evan shook his head and grabbed his coffee cup.

Sometimes Evan wondered if it wasn't the big life events like his dad drinking again or Vincent taking a dirt nap that drew him to cutting, but instead, it could have been the tiny digs people made. They added up until boiling over to destruction caused by the edge of a razor blade.

Evan convinced himself of his competency by the time he returned with the coffee.

"Are you free tonight?" Murph asked.

"Yeah. Why?"

"Elliot texted and said we can get a tour of the Rockies stadium," she said. "He specifically mentioned for you to bring your camera."

Evan understood the signal. It was about fucking time.

The rest of the day passed by in a haze. Evan told Murph what Birch had said. Murph was dismissive of Birch's comment and played it off, but Evan knew it bothered her too.

After a quick shower, Evan grabbed his Leica and met the other two downstairs in the lobby. Elliot was pacing around and avoiding eye contact with either of them.

"What's your problem, dude?" Murph asked.

275

"I haven't given a tour of the stadium before, so I'm nervous."

"Babe, you are overthinking."

"You have no idea. Ready?" Elliot asked.

They ventured out into the night and walked the mile to Coors Field without much conversation. Evan stopped several times and snapped pictures of Elliot and Murph from behind, focusing in on them holding hands. The pictures harkened back to when he'd roam his college campus, sit on a bench, and take photos of random people. Sometimes he'd sit for an hour and never find anything worth photographing, but he always appreciated his own willingness to suffer through the mundane on the off-chance he'd capture something unique.

"There's a door over here," Elliot announced as the stadium came into frame.

"Is anybody else going to be with us?" Murph asked.

"No. Private tour."

"This is an honor I don't deserve," Murph feigned as if she were accepting an award.

Elliot swiped his ID and ushered them inside. They were in the bowels of the stadium.

"Let's head this way. I can show you where I work first."

"This is exciting! I get to see where my dude makes all that money for me," Murph said.

"Always with the jokes," Elliot said.

They walked down a long hallway toward a nondescript elevator. They took it to the top floor and Elliot went into a speech about who sits where and what their role is.

It was very informative and extremely exciting, so much so that Evan forgot everything Elliot mentioned by the time he left the stadium that night.

"Here's where I sit!"

The desk was tiny and huddled into the corner. Pictures of Murph, Sasquatch, and Elliot's family sat framed and scattered throughout. Sticky notes clung to the monitors with reminders of leftover work Elliot had to complete.

"I know it's not much, but you have to start somewhere."

"It's perfect," Murph said, grabbing his hand and squeezing. "Before we go to the next area, where's the bathroom?"

Elliot pointed down the hall and around the corner. Murph ventured off.

"How are you feeling?" Evan asked.

"I don't know if I deserve her. What if—"

Evan placed a hand on his shoulder and gave a reassuring smile. "You can't honestly think that. Murph adores you and I can see why. You two understand each other so much. You make each other better."

"Thanks Evan."

"What do I need to do?"

"Just hang back. You'll know when it's about to happen."

Once Murph returned, they walked through more of the common areas. Elliot did his best to talk through the history of the stadium and the team.

The tour ended with them walking out onto the field. Enough of the lights were on to highlight the infield.

"This is incredible!" Murph said. "I can't imagine what it's like when the stadium is sold out."

"That hasn't happened in a very long time," Elliot laughed.

Evan slowly moved back to give them space. He uncapped the lens and began taking photos. If Elliot was going to do it anywhere, it had to be here.

Elliot grabbed Murph's hand and led her out to the pitcher's mound. Evan couldn't hear what they said to each other, but their conversation carried on for a couple minutes.

Evan stepped closer when Elliot reached into his jacket pocket and removed the box. Murph was looking at the press boxes above home plate, unaware of what Elliot was holding.

"Hey, I have something for you," Elliot said.

Murph turned. "Oh yeah? Are you going to give me a fistful of dirt or something?"

"Hopefully you'll find this slightly better."

Elliot dropped to one knee.

"Wait, are you actually scooping up dirt? Don't do that."

"Murph, I'm not grabbing dirt," Elliot said, laughing

"Then why are you crawling around down there?"

"You are asking too many questions."

"I'm only asking the important ones."

"For suck fake," Elliot said. He stood back up and dusted the dirt off his knee. "You are making this more difficult than it has to be."

"What does that mean?"

"Just listen for a minute."

Evan continued snapping photos of the botched first attempt and the aftermath.

"Murph," Elliot continued, "you are almost indescribable. I know that is cheap, but sometimes I have trouble finding the right words. You are expansive. Your love runs deep, and you treat me better than I ever thought I deserved. Before your dad died, I asked him if one day I could marry his daughter and he told me yes. I knew the timing wasn't right back then, so I waited. And now we are here. We have made it through so much and I can't wait to experience even more with you. You're it. I want to spend my life with you. Murph, will you marry me?"

Elliot dropped down again to his knee and opened the box. Murph stepped closer and placed her hands on his shoulders.

Through the tears she said, "Elliot, I love you so much. Yes. Of course."

Elliot took the ring and placed it on her finger. They kissed and everything seemed right. The audience following Murph since that night at the parking garage in Dallas cheered as loud as if it was Game 7 of the World Series. Finally. Finally, something good happened. The constant drip of sadness was abated for the briefest time.

Evan captured the moment as best he could from various angles. He loved it and regretted ever dropping the hobby.

"The camera! You knew about this!" Murph shouted. "Come here."

Evan walked over and gave them both a hug. "I'm so happy for you both."

"Thank you for being here and doing what you do," Elliot said, motioning to the camera.

"Did you really ask my dad?" Murph said.

"Of course. You should have seen the smile on his face. He was so happy."

"Elliot—"

"It's okay to be sad. I wish he was here to see it."

"Me too."

"That reminds me! This way. Let's go to the visitor's clubhouse. It's the last spot to show you both."

Our trio walked off the field and away from the bright lights. The audience stayed back in their seats, munching on popcorn and chili dogs. They were sated for now.

The passageway leading away from the dugout was a dreary sight of concrete lined walls with the occasional fluorescent bulb to highlight the way.

"We just got engaged. I didn't think you'd want to murder me just yet," Murph said.

"Oh stop. It isn't that bad down here."

"It's not that great either," Evan said. The lighting created a unique opportunity, so he drifted back behind them and took a few candid shots.

"Almost there," Elliot called out. He made a quick right and walked through the open door.

Inside, the room was decorated with various balloons and candles in some of the lockers.

"What are you—"

Before Murph could finish, she was swarmed by three people. Evan snapped as many photos as he could.

"That has to be her family, right?" Evan asked.

"Correct. I figured this was an event worth celebrating with everyone. They were excited to finally visit Denver."

"What about your family?"

"We, uh, we don't get along. To be as vague as possible about it."

"I'm sorry," Evan said.

"Don't be. I just gained a new family as corny as that sounds."

"You did good. I never pegged you as a planner, so I'm pleasantly surprised."

"My stunning looks and unmatched charm get everything I need done. You know what this means, right?"

"Enlighten me."

"You're next."

"Next for what."

"To meet the love of your life and become a boring couple like me and Murph."

"I—yeah, sure. Maybe that will happen sometime soon."

"Let me introduce you to her family," Elliot said. He grabbed Evan's arm and whisked him to the center of the room.

Murph's mom was an identical copy of her—personality and all. She hugged Evan as if he was Shadow at the end of *Homeward Bound*.

Murph's brothers—Leo and Maverick—were slightly more reserved. They shook hands with Evan and exchanged mild pleasantries.

The group hung out in the locker room and basked in the happiness of the moment. Elliot had plotted out a weekend of activities for Murph's family. They invited Evan to tag along to as much as he wanted, but he found himself giving a cheap excuse. It felt like an intrusion especially since Murph hadn't seen her family much since her dad passed away.

They eventually drifted out the locker room and stadium. The walk back was livelier than the walk there.

Evan separated from the group in the lobby of the apartment complex. He told Murph he'd work on getting the pictures ready for them in the next week.

The elevator ride was quiet. A phrase Vincent told him several times repeated in his head.

The thing before the thing.

Vincent was adamant that Evan's next relationship would be the one, but Evan didn't believe in finding the one. That bullshit didn't exist; you just managed to find someone you were the *most* compatible with.

Finding *the thing* seemed like an absolute bong dream to Evan. But he wanted it. He wanted someone to cuddle up next to at night and go have fancy drinks at a quiet bar. He wanted to intertwine his life with someone else's and go to weddings, parties, and other events where they could show each other off. He wanted the support to chase his dream—whatever that would turn out to be. He wanted what Elliot and Murph seemed to have.

Evan had to put himself out there to achieve any of that, so he started at the only place he knew.

As he collapsed against the couch, Evan had a handful of dating apps downloaded onto his phone. The usernames were still saved in some cloud database on the tiny island of Galapagos. The apps began populating with his previous matches—hundreds of random faces he never interacted with.

Against his sane side, Evan downloaded Grindr again. He adjusted to make it painfully clear he had no interest in a hook up, but it took less than fifteen minutes to get his first unsolicited dick pic.

The thing wouldn't come from a simple hook up; it would take many dates and patience.

His phone pinged with more messages from Grindr. He opened up the top one:

> well, well, WELL! You have finally come over to join us bottom dwellers. Let me know if anyone gives you shit on here.
> I've met some of the gay boys in the building.

Goddammit. It was from the only gay guy he knew in Dallas. Evan frequented his bar multiple times a week.

He responded to Franco with a cordial thanks and hoped he wouldn't respond.

Franco did. Almost immediately.

Evan tossed the phone aside.

Let's say that Franco ended up being *the thing*. Evan didn't want their first one-on-one conversation outside the bar to be on Grindr. That seemed like the fast track to nowhere pleasant.

When Evan reached for his phone again, he saw the jagged cut on his arm. It was there forever and ever.

He pushed the thought aside and went through the cycle of checking all the dating apps and swiping right on only the luckiest guys.

Evan ushered out the Age of Before and welcomed in the Age of Thing. May it be filled with prosperity and good head (winds).

<u>forty-nine</u>

FAKE

Evan was in the midst of his weekly meal prep when his phone started vibrating in his pocket.
 It was his mom.
 "Hello?"
 "Hi, Evan! It's been a while. How are you?"
 "I'm fine."
 "That's good to hear."
 "Still liking Denver?"
 "It's been growing on me recently."
 "That's good to hear. How is the job going?" his mom asked.
 "I get called incompetent every month by this employee named Birch, but besides that it is uneventful. I really wonder what possessed his parents to name him that . . ."
 "That's good to hear."
 "Is there anything I could say that wouldn't be good to hear?"
 "What do you mean?"
 "Never mind," Evan said. He hugged the phone against his ear with his shoulder and continued prepping the cauliflower pizza.
 "Didn't your father come to visit? I remember you mentioning something about it the last time we spoke."
 "He did."
 "How did that go?" she asked as if she was trying to hear the latest high school gossip.
 Evan had no desire to talk about what happened. It was easier to lie or avoid the topic entirely, but Dr. Knox urged Evan to be honest with himself and others about the situation.
 "He is still drinking," Evan said with indifference.
 "What a piece of shit. Some people never change. I told you he was still a bad, bad man. I knew it. I knew it. That man is absolutely deplorable. You should have never listened to him or any of his lies."
 "Mom, you told me I should go for Thanksgiving dinner last year. I didn't make the decision to bring him back into my life on my own."
 "Yeah . . . well . . . I don't remember ever telling you that."

"Of course, you don't. You'll take any opportunity to prove you were right."

"Not true at all."

"I have no interest in talking about this further with you," Evan said.

The silence hung in the air for an uncomfortable amount of time. Evan placed the pizza in the oven and set the timer.

"Are you still happily married?" Evan eventually asked.

"Not really."

"That's goo—why not?"

"He is boring. I want to go out and have fun, but he'd rather sit at home."

"Are you working at all?"

"No."

"Do you plan on finding a job?"

"No. He makes enough money for the both of us. I will say he does enjoy spoiling me." Evan could hear the smile through the phone.

"So, you don't do anything while he's at work?"

"Sometimes, but most days are very relaxing."

"You're using him for his money then," Evan said.

"Absolutely not! I love him very dearly."

"No, you don't. You have been married four times. You know how to con the system. Mom, it's okay, you can tell me the truth."

"I would never con anyone. What a terrible thing to say!"

"Sure you would."

"Yeah? What if I am using him for his money? I deserve this! I had to raise you and your siblings on my own. It wasn't easy!"

"I never said it was."

"All I have tried to do as your mother is provide a home for you, make sure you got an education, and that you turned out to be a decent person."

"Save me the sob story. You're not special for doing any of that."

"What is wrong with you?!"

"How come you haven't visited more?" Evan pressed. "Huh? You visited me once in Denver. You never came to Dallas. My dead-beat, absent father made more of an effort to see me."

"I-I've been busy," she said quietly.

"Oh, I bet. Busy doing nothing for the past six months while you get to bask in the benefits of a one-sided marriage. Sounds like such a taxing life."

"Why are you doing this?" his mom asked in a whisper.

"Because you tell me you are so bored and yet it's been a month since you've talked to me! Because you made me feel like shit for trying to rebuild a relationship with my father!"

"I'm sorry, Evan. I didn't mean anything by it."

"Listen: I'm going to hang up now. I have stuff to do today."

"Okay. I'll call you soon."

"Fine," he said.

"I lov—" Evan ended the call before his mom could finish.

The timer on the oven beeped incessantly. Evan pulled the cauliflower pizza out and let it cool off before cutting it into slices.

Evan moved onto the next meal prep: pesto chicken with broccoli. He didn't put much thought into the conversation with his mom. It wasn't the first instance of a blow out between them. To Evan, this is what you should expect with family—the ebbs and flows pull you in various directions and sometimes they aren't all positive.

Evan wondered what his life would have been like if he had normal parents. Defining what normal parents are is tough, but Evan had a vision. It was the definition of the American Dream. The household where the fake mom does the cleaning, cooking, driving the kids to sports, and makes the executive decisions. The fake dad works the upper level job that rakes in enough money for the family to spend a week of quality time together each year in the form of a road trip to some destination that involves a lengthy drive and a mediocre result. The multitude of fake siblings in the fake family would spread out and begin to diversify. Some would turn to sports; others would turn more inward. The fake siblings wouldn't have much respect for one another until after college when they all settled down into families. They would reminisce about how poorly they treated everyone and how fortunate they were for fake dad and fake mom putting up with all of their fake bullshit.

It was all so sterile and not what the American Dream was anymore. Now, it consisted of poverty, dead-end jobs at minimum wage, divorce rates sitting at a 50/50 rate, constant unhappiness cured by tiny pills manufactured at an alarming pace, cyber bullying, high suicide rates, incompetent leaders, tone-deaf lawmakers, and so on.

People rarely changed. If anything, they only got worse.

For Evan, it summed up to this: the American dream was broken homes with broken people.

Maybe if Evan's father didn't disappear or abuse him as a child, he wouldn't be gay. Because every gay guy has daddy issues, that is a well-documented fact.

Maybe, maybe, maybe.

The worst word in the English language. It implies the desire for an outcome to be different due to not being satisfied with the actual result.

Come to think of it, that word isn't much different from asking *What if?* all the time.

Listen:

Evan understood he couldn't change the past or how he'd never have that perfect, fake family in that boring reality.

But letting his mind drift away to those thoughts removed him from any unpleasantness in the present. It was his self-medication and seemed way healthier than running a razor blade down his arm.

Evan finished cooking the pesto chicken and cleaned up the spreading mess in the kitchen. Afterward, he changed into his running clothes. His goal was three miles.

It was easily achievable and would bring in a rush of dopamine to numb the festering unhappiness for a short time.

fifty

TWENTY QUESTIONS

"When are we going out to the gay bars?" Franco asked. He leaned across the bar and rested a hand under his chin.

"I mean, you seem to be the resident expert around here, so I'd go whenever you wanted to."

"Why not tonight?"

"It's a Wednesday."

"Wednesday's are the ideal combination of crowded but not unmanageable. You can easily find a quiet corner to chat or bust some moves on the dance floor."

"I'd love to hear your breakdown of the other days sometime," Evan said.

"So, is that a yes?"

"Doesn't seem like I have much choice, but I don't intend on drinking much."

"Same," Franco said. He pulled out a bottle of cheap vodka and poured two shots. "One for the road?"

They slung back the shot and cursed at the awful taste.

"Hey Denver, you good to close up tonight?" Franco asked.

Denver gave two-thumbs up from the other end of the bar.

"Since when did y'all hire another bartender?"

"Denver has been with us since we opened. You never noticed him before?"

"No," Evan laughed. "I will attribute it to us always sitting at this end of the bar."

"Or . . . I just grabbed your attention so much you couldn't take your eyes off me. I like that answer way better."

"Just to be clear: this is two friends going out to soak in the gay culture and have a drink."

"Yes, yes. Of course. You're not really my type anyways," Franco said.

"Is that so? I figured I was desirable to everyone," Evan said with a smile.

Franco placed the vodka bottle back and asked, "You ready? We can walk there."

They went outside and walked the short distance over to the gay bars. Three of them were clustered onto the same block. Franco explained Evan's options and they all seemed similar to what he found living in Dallas. There was the club, the more relaxed bar, and the hybrid. Considering what Evan's objective was for the evening, he voted for the casual bar.

"Here we are!" Franco announced. Six Nine Bar came into view. Pride flags hung from the second story balcony and a few patrons were loitering against the railing.

"Seems chill and a good place to talk."

"First round is on me," Franco said and led Evan inside.

The lights were kept low, which hid the aesthetic of the bar. Evan's concern for that diminished once they reached it.

"Don't even bother telling me what you want. I got this covered."

"How could you know what I want?"

"You have been coming to my bar religiously for six months now. You are a creature of habit and fine taste," Franco said.

Franco ordered himself a cheap beer and snagged Evan an Old Fashioned.

They went upstairs and away from the noise pollution of the awful pop songs that were recycled every twenty minutes.

"Thanks for the drink," Evan said. "It is certainly my go-to."

"Nothing wrong with that even though I haven't seen anyone outside my ninety-year-old grandfather drink those."

Evan shrugged with indifference.

"What's new with you? How's everything been since the night with your dad?" Franco asked.

"Not much has happened there. We haven't contacted each other at all. I don't see us maintaining or rebuilding any sort of relationship."

"I'm sorry Evan. That's a tough situation for you to go through."

"It's been okay, but thanks."

Evan took off his jacket. Franco didn't notice the scar or was afraid to ask.

"I feel like I don't know anything about you," Evan continued.

"I'm an open book."

"Everyone says that until you start asking the tough questions and then they give light responses that don't mean much."

"Try me."

"Okay . . . how about this: tell me something you have never told anyone else."

Franco went through the normal cycle of telling Evan he doesn't have secrets, so they sat there for an extended time before something clicked with Franco.

"When I tell you this, you are going to wonder how I've never told anyone else. It's amazing how we can block out details of our lives that are . . . icky. Anyways, back when I was finishing up college, I understood I was gay, but wanted to explore the other side of things. Sometimes things aren't as defined as we'd like for them to be. Through my friends, I met a girl. Her name was . . . it actually doesn't matter. We hung out and you can see where this story is headed. I liked her—way more than I should have for someone who wanted to spend their life with a guy—but there was this shroud of doubt that maybe I could date her long-term, possibly even marry her. We continued on together through graduation and into that summer. She was set for law school and I had no plan. She was a constant encouragement that I'd figure out my passions and way in life. I remember lying in bed one morning and she came out of the bathroom holding that plastic stick. She tossed it over to me and I'd seen enough movies to know what the two lines went. This flood of emotion passed through me. I was . . . placated for once. Like I had finally figured out what I'd do with my life. She would become a kick-ass lawyer and I'd have a light job that wouldn't take me away from the kid—or hopefully kids as more time passed. We held off on telling anyone because of the fear of judgement. It was no secret I was gay and our whole relationship may have looked fake to someone from the outside. Why would a gay guy become so attached to this girl? I don't think people would have understood that physical appearance is the bare minimum of what I care about. We scheduled her first doctor's appointment and on the morning of, the sheets on the bed were covered in blood. I rushed her over to the hospital and they told us how she lost the baby. They left us alone in that room and we both cried. We cried about how things wouldn't be the same after that and the future I'd constructed in those few short days was shattered. We never recovered from it. She went off to law school and we drifted apart in the subtle ways that couples do. Our breakup was nothing more than a friendly conversation and the unspoken truth that it was never going to work out in the first place.

"Sometimes I think about how I could have a nine-year-old kid right now. I certainly wouldn't be a bar owner in Denver. All those what-if questions zip through my head and I get lost in them. Those . . . paths . . . all those paths not taken start to add up. I have to remind myself that I'm not special. Everyone has their story. Everybody lost somebody. Each time it happens though, we lose a bit of ourselves. We weren't built to sustain ourselves on grief; it's not a motivator. It's—I don't know. Grief can bury us without realizing it."

"I understand the last part of that more than you'd realize," Evan said. He took a sip of his drink. "Thank you for sharing. Can I ask you one follow-up question?"

"Yeah."

"Why didn't you tell anyone? About losing the baby."

"I—it was easy that way. I don't have more of an answer than that."

"I understand. I'm here to talk through it more if you ever need to."

"Probably not but thank you. I try not to think about it much. Better to run from the pain than confront it any more than I had to, right?" A few seconds of silence. "Your turn. Tell me something no one knows about you," Franco said.

Evan hesitated, knowing his answer wouldn't compare. "I hate wet socks."

"Huh?"

"The thing no one knows about me is that I can't stand wet socks."

"I poured my heart out and this is what you tell me?" Franco questioned.

"Yeah. See, I apologize about that, but my life is downtrodden enough already and I just couldn't go to that place right now. I'd be miserable for the rest of the night."

"It's fine."

"Franco, I don't want to downplay what you went through," Evan said, grabbing his hand. "Really, if you ever need to talk about it more, I'm here."

"I appreciate that, but it's fine. Really. It was a long time ago. Tell me more about this wet sock nonsense."

"There's not much to describe. It's gross to have your feet flopping around making a slapping sound with each step. That's on the extreme end, but the hatred still applies if I step into a small puddle of water or something. As soon as I feel wetness soak through my sock and onto my foot, the socks are immediately off, and another pair will be retrieved."

Franco leaned back and shook his head in confusion. "I don't have much of a rebuttal to that."

"As you shouldn't."

"Ask me another question," Franco said.

"Okay. How about some easier questions?"

"I'd like that."

"Where were you born?"

"Portland."

"Which one?"

"Oregon."

"How many siblings?"

"Only child."

"Do you like to read?"

"Not often, but it's gotta be non-fiction if I do."

"First car?"

"1998 Ford Contour. I was the envy of my all my friends."

"Is that . . ."

"Hell no! That car was awful, but it was mine."

"Night owl or early riser?"

"All the late nights at the bar answers that question."

"First R-rated movie you watched?"

"Oh, wow. How are you thinking of all these so quickly?"

"Someone once taught me the value of knowing how to ask questions and taking the time to listen to the answers. Not many people understand active listening."

"Tell me what that means."

"Active listening is like watching a YouTube video on how to make an apple pie and you following those instructions to bake your own. Does that make sense?"

"Well, no. Not at all."

"Shit. When you are actively listening to someone, you are hearing everything they say and adapt the conversation. You ask follow-up questions or understand when an empathetic response is needed. It's much different from normal conversations where the listener just nods their head but is thinking about that salad for lunch or how great that hentai porn was."

"I get it. That apple pie analogy was terrible though," Franco laughed.

"I was just making sure you were paying attention to call me out on it."

"Uh huh," Franco said sarcastically.

"I'm still waiting on the answer."

"Oh right! First R-rated movie . . . let's see . . . it was . . . *Scream*."

"Interesting. Did you watch that with your parents or by yourself?"

"My parents let me watch it with them. I'm not sure why, but that movie is way tame compared to today's standards."

"How's it been owning the bar?"

"Co-owning," Franco corrected, "but I enjoy it. Business is still not sustainable for the long-term. My business partner is adamant that things will pick up through the summer months. I have some other marketing ideas, but we likely won't make it past this year if things don't change."

"I'm sorry."

"Don't be. An alarming number of bars and restaurants close in their first year, especially those run by people who have no clue what the fuck they're doing."

"At least you got some regulars," Evan said with a smile.

"You're right. Meeting you, Elliot, and Murph has been a pleasant surprise. I don't know why we haven't seen more of each other outside of It."

"How many dating apps do you have on your phone right now?"

"It's, like, a cardinal sin to pull out your phone on a—"

"On a what?"

"A casual hangout with a good friend," Franco said.

"We aren't good friends yet, but if you keep answering my questions then maybe we will get there."

Franco pulled out his phone and swiped through the multiple pages of applications he had. "Four. Grindr, which you are aware of. Tinder, Hinge, and Scruff."

"You must be drowning in ass."

"I used to be into hook ups, but I've moved out of that phase."

"What phase are you in now?"

"I'm looking for the thing."

"What did you say?" Evan asked, caught off-guard.

"I'm looking for that long-term relationship. I want to settle down."

"Oh nice."

"What about you?"

"I want to have fun for a while." The lie seemed so natural like what any twenty-five year old gay guy was supposed to say. We all know Evan didn't actually feel that way, which made his comment even more confusing.

"You don't strike me as the type to hook up with strangers."

"I have been around. Hopefully you don't judge me for that."

"Of course not."

Evan was bombarding Franco with questions and receiving honest answers, but when the roles were flipped, Evan resorted to petty lies. Why?

"What's the longest relationship you've been in?" Evan asked.

"Three years."

"Why did it end?"

"I moved here."

"Oh." That sounded familiar.

"Of course, there were things wrong within the relationship that led me down the path to Denver, but I know things were done when he had absolutely no interest in joining me out here."

"So, this was a fresh start for you?"

"Definitely. Why did you move here?"

"I got a better job and Dallas was boring."

"Really? Murph talks highly of it."

"Murph and Elliot grew up there, so it makes sense that they'd at least somewhat enjoy it," Evan said.

"From what Murph has told me, you have had trouble finding a place to settle into."

"I didn't realize y'all talked about me when I wasn't around," Evan said with a laugh.

"Nothing bad. I just had some questions about you."

"You could have asked me directly."

"I agree. That would have been the smart thing to do, but people who are smart don't generally dump all their money into a low-grade bar in Denver."

"Very true," Evan said in agreement.

"I didn't know if you were gay for the first few months."

"Are you joking?! I figured it was painfully obvious."

"It's not like you knew I was gay either."

"That's true. I have been noticing this trend in media and real life where people who are gay aren't necessarily being defined by that. For some people, it is an aesthetic and they enjoy being in that bracket of people, but for most others, it isn't the total makeup of who they are. I appreciate not having to tell people outright because I am just a normal person after all."

"I totally get it."

"Let me ask then: Why did you kiss Elliot on New Year's Eve?"

"It was out of necessity. I didn't want to be the sole loser who stood there at midnight with nothing to do but stare down at the grimy floor. Anyways, he's cute. It was just a single moment. Nothing deeper than that."

"Makes sense."

"Why'd you kiss Murph?"

"Because I wanted to feel the embrace of a sophisticated woman," Evan said.

"Quit the shit."

"She asked me and it seemed innocent enough."

"New Year's Eve should always be memorable in some way."

Evan nodded. "Another drink?" He pointed to the empty glasses as evidence.

"Sure."

Evan grabbed the glasses and moved over to the bar. He ordered another Old Fashioned for himself and a different cheap beer for Franco.

"I took I guess at what you'd want," Evan said after he got back to the table.

"I'm not picky. I've sampled so many beers in the past year so I think I've lost my palette to know what's good anymore."

"I thought of more questions."

"Lucky me."

"Biggest fear?"

"Dolphins," Franco said.

"Are you fearful of their intelligence?"

"No. It's a long story for another day."

"What's one thing you wish you were better at?"

"Sudoku puzzles. Give me anything above a two-star puzzle and I'm fucked more than a twink at a leather bar."

"Are you happy?"

"Yes, but I'd describe it as being content with my life. Sometimes I get lonely though."

"What happens when you get lonely?"

"I converse with strangers and try to finish three-star Sudoku puzzles."

"Does the loneliness ever become too much?"

"No, but I feel like the exception to that."

"What does your fake sick day look like?"

"Discovering a new hobby like collecting baseball cards or playing racquetball."

"Do you send nude pictures to strangers?"

"Yes," Franco said. "I'm proud of the way I look."

"Worst place you've traveled to?"

"I find something to appreciate in every place I go to."

"Such a profound answer."

"It's true!"

"Have you ever run from grief before?"

"Yes. After the miscarriage."

"How long before it caught up to you?"

"I don't remember the exact time."

"What happened when you finally took time to grieve?"

"I took time for myself and started to think through how to make my life worthwhile. The most important thing was recognizing I couldn't change the outcome. I wasn't at fault for what happened. I know that gets said often, but I believe it."

Evan paused from his onslaught of questions. He had to stop running from it. He had to stop allowing Vincent from being the invisible puppeteer. The nightmares needed to end. The warped face needed to recede to nothing.

"Have you ever been to a therapist?" Evan eventually asked, tilting the conversation away from grief.

"Oh yeah."

"When's the last time you have written a letter to someone?"

"Fourth grade. You know, like, one of those do-you-like-me type letters. The response I got back was not favorable."

"Such heartbreak at a young age."

"I have recovered. Barely."

"One last question. For now, at least."

"I'm ready."

"If you were able to steal one painting and get away with it, what would the painting be and why?"

Franco cocked his head. "You are making a huge assumption I know any art."

"Oh please. Just answer the question."

Franco did. The answer was lighter than the diatribe Evan had given to Vincent a year earlier.

"Did I pass the test?"

"You should receive your invitation in the mail in three to six weeks."

"What an honor . . . my turn now with the questions," Franco said.

"Do your worst."

fifty-one

MANUFACTURED SADNESS

"Have you ever heard of *Euphoria*?"
　"Like the word?"
　"No."
　"Then what?"
　"The television show."
　"I'm not familiar."
　"It's big on Twitter, Tumblr, Rumblr, Bumble, Myspace, Ask Jeeves, Reddit, Farmers Only, and all the other popular websites everyone hates."
　"Oh. Why do you ask?"
　"Because I'm upset about it."
　"You're upset about a television show?"
　"Yes."
　"Did they kill off your favorite character or something?"
　"No. They had the chance to be different, but they fell into basic clichés of the high school drama."
　"Okay, fine. I'll bite. What are some of the clichés?"
　"Of course, the jock is an aggressive psychopath who gets all the chicks he could possibly want, but still goes on gay dating apps to fulfill some deprived fantasy of his. Of course, every party depicted in the show is some massive rager as if the police wouldn't have been called in five minutes or that people are reliable enough to show up to a place when expected or that parents of a high school student wouldn't question why their kid was out until dawn's early light. Of course, the overweight girl is the one character on the show who was the prude, finds a sexual awakening, and then gets all the attention she suddenly needs. Of course, the drug dealer that makes an appearance is a total sleazeball with face tattoos and essentially tries to rape the main character if she doesn't pay for the drugs he forced upon her. Of course, everyone in the school stares and whispers at the overweight girl as she walks down the hallway after the sex tape gets out. Of course, everyone in the school stares and whispers at the overweight girl *again* as she walks down the hallway after embracing her dominatrix side. Of course, the wine drunk mother hits on the boyfriend who isn't actually the boyfriend since he likes to play games with homegirl's

heart. Of course, the main character keeps relapsing on her sobriety because people don't change—at least not in the first season of a TV show. And you know what the biggest problem is?"

"I have no idea."

"It has only been four episodes. FOUR! Good grief."

"Why are you so fired up about this?"

"Because it's a beautiful show. So many amazing visuals, but it's becoming a gimmick."

"Again though, it is only a TV show . . ."

"What's your point? People petitioned to redo the entire last season of *Game of Thrones* because they hated it."

"And those people are morons."

"I understand it is only a TV show. I'm not a moron and recognize the need for entertainment. Whether you believe it or not, I can get passed the cliché nature of the show. But I think I figured out why it will never be popular."

"What did you deduce, Watson?"

"It's a sad show."

"That's nothing new."

"Correct, but it's a sad show that takes place in our boring reality. People love to be sad, but not when it takes place in the same rundown, fucked up world we are occupying."

"Is this a hypothesis or proven fact?"

"Proven after many years of research. People don't want to read a story about some stranger who wants to get better or some drug addict teenager that keeps relapsing."

"There is plenty of media that is downtrodden and popular."

"I stand by my statement."

"Not much of a statement if that's your argument."

"Evan, aren't you tired of being sad, of being told you have to be sad because life is so, so tough? Aren't you tired of the meme culture where kids joke about committing suicide because it would be a better alternative to this? Aren't you tired of the same cycle of news stories depicting violence, political injustice, wildfires in California, our President saying something obscene for the twenty-six thousandth time, or how Troye Sivan is really just Brittany Spears in disguise?"

"I have been talking to a therapist, so I don't have to feel sad about any of that stuff anymore, especially Troye Sivan."

"Lucky you. My point is that we are required to be sad about something.

It's like they are putting sadness in the air for us to suck in with each breath. I'm so tired of it."

"Then find things to be happy about."

"Don't be thick. I understand what I'm saying is absurd, but you must relate in some capacity. I mean, you didn't do what you did for no reason."

"That horse has been beaten, burned, thrown off a cliff, and run over by every car in the state of Colorado, so we don't need to talk about that any more than me saying this: what I did was a mistake and will not happen again."

"I'm sorry to have brought it up."

"It's fine. When is Murph coming back?"

"No idea. Am I not good enough for you?"

"Correct. You're elongated conversations about fictional television shows are too much for me. You know, you can be a total idiot sometimes."

"I'm just living up to my cliché nature," he said with a smile.

Elliot grabbed the bong and took another deep hit. "Someone has to smoke and say profound things," he declared.

Evan didn't bother to respond.

They sat in silence for twenty minutes until Murph came home.

"Murph. Murph!" Elliot called out. "My sweet, sweet fiancé. Have you heard of *Euphoria*?"

"Yes. I know what the word means."

"Gosh dangit! No. The TV show."

The conversation took the same shape as the one we just read about. Evan listened as the two bounced back and forth with their opinions.

"Murph, didn't you want to practice tonight?" Evan eventually said.

"Yes! I was thinking that we could focus on . . ." her voice drifted out. Evan nodded when needed and smiled when provoked.

He thought about telling them that Vincent was dead, but he decided to wait for another night. Evan needed to sit in his manufactured sadness longer.

fifty-two

CUE THE MUSIC

The montage sequence is a filmmaking technique often applied to simulate the passage of time. It tends to occur when the pacing of the story needs to get up and go. This technique became a staple of American cinema in the 80's during the decade of crappy action movies. Uplifting rock songs would be played over a training montage or something more mundane like the main character completing chores around the house. In any case, it is an effective, yet cliché way to keep things moving forward.

Finding a montage in a book is rare because reading one is not nearly as stimulating as watching. The passage of time is lost on the reader unless it is specifically spelled out. If anything, this trilogy of fake stories is an exception to how books should be written or structured.

Imagine after that night of *Euphoria*, Evan settled into a routine — one that most others fall into. It was a cycle of tedium and predictability. It went something like this . . .

MONTAGE - THE FINAL STRETCH TO THE LIP-SYNC COMPETITION

A.) APARTMENT - Evan wakes up looking disheveled from a sleep plagued with nightmares. Every montage needs to begin with the character's morning routine, and we will be no different. Shower, Izzie, breakfast, coffee, and head to work.

B.) OFFICE BUILDING (WORK) - Evan sits at his desk and punches random keys, trying to create something out of nonsense. Cut to encounters with Birch in the breakroom and Evan's indifferent expression each time he is told he is incompetent.

C.) OFFICE BUILDING (THE ROOM WITH TWO CHAIRS) - Evan and Dr. Knox are conversing about topics we don't have any insight into. She writes down meaningless notes (but ones that don't depict graphic visions of death) as Evan clasps his hands together to stop them from shaking.

D.) VARIOUS LOCATIONS - We follow Evan as he runs through parks, city streets, and occasionally on the treadmill.

He is running faster and further than we remember. He is embracing his inner Rocky and will soon be the boxing champion he was meant to be. Just kidding, Evan would get slaughtered.

E.) BAR - Evan and Murph learn lines, talk through potential dance options, and occasionally yell at one another for not being dedicated enough. Flash to Franco who is watching them and tries to offer suggestions in a quiet demeanor.

F.) VARIOUS LOCATIONS - Evan, Murph, Elliot, and Franco are gallivanting around Denver at some bar or restaurant. They are enjoying each other's company.

G.) SOMEWHERE - We break from the montage for a moment to slow things down. Evan's phone lights up. We pan down to see the name is MOM. He hesitates but decides to answer it. He turns away from us. We don't see his reaction, but we hear the apology from him and can assume one came from Mom as well. There will always be an inherent bond with his mother. She did the best she could and is partly why he is independent and as fucked up as he is. Evan will need to accept that.

The montage continues.

H.) APARTMENT - Evan collapses into his couch in a vain attempt to show his exhaustion from the busy days he is having.

Great, you have seen the montage once, so let's speed it up. We flash through A to F, and sometimes H, several more times, each circuit being faster and only capturing the most important details. We start to see costumes for Evan and Murph to wear and crude storyboards of how the action will be laid out. We see Evan's posture at the therapist is more relaxed as if he has unburdened himself from some of his weight. We notice that Franco's stare settles more on Evan than Murph. We can tell that Evan's encounters with Birch decrease drastically because Evan and Murph construct a 'THIS HABITAT DOES NOT SUPPORT BIRCH TREES' sign outside their cubicle to stop any disturbances. Is that an appropriate thing for HR to do? Absolutely not.

The montage continues. We need to show that with time,

Evan forgets about the betrayal of his father, the feeling of displacement from so many moves, and the unrelenting emotion of Vincent's death. Evan is stronger than that, but he will need to face the death in order to move on, to get to the thing.

We end with a sign showing us that the 27th ANNUAL DENVER LIP-SYNC COMPETITION is TONIGHT.

fifty-three

BOWLING'S BOOKS

The Colorado Convention Center was flooded with half the population of Denver.

Or so it seemed.

People loitered in the hallways, snagging one final drink or making a last run to use the bathroom before finding their seat.

The Bellco Theatre tucked within the convention center held five-thousand people. The overflow seating in the other halls held another ten thousand. It was a staggering underestimation of the mere thousand Murph had told Evan months back.

Every single seat would be filled.

Evan wasn't aware of several things: (1) the event was massive for the city, (2) Denverites went to great lengths to keep the tradition a secret, and (3) the duo was unbelievably lucky to snag one of the twenty-seven available spots.

See:

Murph had another one of her *Follow It* moments when she found out about the competition. Elliot was listening to Frank Sinatra as "It Was a Very Good Year" echoed throughout the apartment. Murph kept focusing on the one word over and over. Such a common word to be fixated over. Murph read that *it* is the tenth most common word in the English language according to COCA (not to be confused with CRaC) which meant she heard *it* dozens of times each day, read *it* in almost every email, and said *it* herself constantly. Murph learned quickly not to fixate on *it* because *it* would drive her crazy. The word only carried meaning in the unlikeliest of times and she knew when Frank Sinatra belted out his tune, *it* was one of the times to pay attention.

Murph left the apartment without an explanation and exited the complex.

"IT IS THREE BLOCKS AND TO THE LEFT!" a man yelled outside the main entrance. A kid on a motorized scooter stuck his thumb up in the air and kept riding.

Murph followed those instructions . . . somewhat. She went two blocks and made a right because sometimes you need to make your own luck.

She turned onto Easton Avenue. The street was crowded with

insignificant restaurants, coffee shops, and clothing stores. Many of them were closed due to the holiday, but Murph saw one sign flipped to OPEN.

Murph walked inside the bookstore. Mellow instrumental music played from the speakers. Book displays were scattered throughout the open area, showcasing the newest craze: self-detonation books. People were no longer interested in self-help; they yearned for miraculous ways to self-destruct in the same essence as Vincent did across the two books. There was no cashier at the front of the store; Murph checked several aisles and found them deserted. She moved deeper into the bookstore and heard excited mumblings from further back. Past the spines from books she didn't recognize, Murph moved closer to the noise.

The group was hovering around a laptop. None of them paid any attention to her as she walked up.

Murph poked the closest person. "What are y'all looking at?"

"Oh—hi! You don't know what's going on?" the older man said.

"Can't say I do. I was just wandering around the city and stumbled into this place."

"Are you new to Denver?" he asked.

"Somewhat. Moved here last September."

"Do you have any idea what today is?"

"New Year's Day," Murph said with uncertainty.

"You're not wrong, but as a fellow Denverite, you are entitled to so much more on this day."

"Do y'all give out free money or something?"

"Even better."

"In what world is there anything better than that?" Murph said to herself.

"This is the twenty-seventh year for our citywide lip-sync competition!" the man said with pride. "Every New Year's Day, they announce the date and theme. They find a new host each year with the caveat that they don't publicize this well-kept secret."

"A lip-sync competition? Sounds dumb if I'm being honest."

"You aren't the first to say so. I agree, the concept does sound childish, but we are the pioneers of this uptick in popularity. Not that we can tell anyone about it though," the man said.

"Who is the host?"

"Look for yourself." He pointed at the laptop.

Murph shifted around and looked past the bobbing heads. Conan O'Brien was standing in front of a drab backdrop and talking about how he landed the hosting gig.

"How did you manage to get him?" Murph asked, looking back at the man.

"They come to us. I wasn't kidding when I said this was a big deal."

"Is this a cult or something?"

"No, no. It's nothing like that. We discovered it's a great way to bring the community together. Everyone loves music and enough people like the idea of performing in front of a vast audience, so we get new talent each year. Actually, the winner from the previous year is the only one allowed to perform again. We have never had the same group win twice if that clues you into the level of competition."

"People take this pretty seriously, huh?" Murph asked.

"Yes."

"How do I sign up? I used to perform in front of crowds when I was younger, so this sounds fun."

"Hold on—" the man said. He pointed back at the laptop.

". . . They gave me this envelope and said, 'Conan go out there and make shit up until someone waves a white flag behind the camera and then open the envelope.' Bizarre, but being a professional, I agreed to the terms. Now, there is this poor guy vigorously waving the flag. I see you buddy. You can stop before you pull a muscle," Conan laughed. He tore into the envelope. "The two pieces of information everyone wants to know: the date and theme. The 27th annual Lip-Sync Competition will take place on . . ." Conan revealed the information we already know.

Everybody kick started new conversations in the bookstore. Apparently, they were happy with the outcome.

"Normally," the man said, turning back to Murph, "in order to participate, you have to be a resident of Denver for at least a year and get numerous referrals. Lucky for you, I have some pull and can bypass some of the requirements."

"Really? Why would you help me out?"

"There's a reason you stumbled into this bookstore today. Maybe you were meant to do this."

"Oh c'mon. You don't actually believe that?"

"Tell me then: how did you find this place?"

"I . . . I was just going for a walk."

"It's freezing outside and it's New Year's Day, so most places are closed. It wasn't by chance you found this place."

"You're right," Murph said. "But it's still slightly silly."

The man shrugged and continued on, "I'm Brett Bowling." He extended a hand.

"Nice to meet you. I'm Murphy Law but prefer to go by Murph." They shook hands.

"Hello Murph. So, what do you think? Are you interested?"

"I'm not sure I understand how massive this event is yet, but I am definitely interested."

"You likely won't realize the enormity of it until the night of. We are discreet with our marketing and promotional material since there are plenty of tourists floating around here."

"Do non-Denverites find out about the competition and attend?"

"Of course," Brett said. "Anyone is welcome to go."

"Very inclusive."

"There's no reason not to be at this point."

"Where do we go from here?" Murph asked. Conan's reveal was finally over and the group hovering around the laptop began to break apart.

"Do you have someone to perform the duet with?"

"I have someone in mind," Murph said with a wide grin.

"Perfect. Give me a few minutes." Brett stepped away from the crowd and into a side room.

Murph continued to loiter as no one else huddled around the screen paid attention to her. When Brett returned, he was holding a piece of paper.

"Like I said, we do minimal marketing for this, but I pulled together this flyer." He handed it to Murph. "If you don't want to rehash all this backstory to your friend, just show them."

Murph looked down at it and choked back a comment at the sheer ugliness of it. She reckoned that Brett did it on purpose. "Good idea. He probably wouldn't do it if he knew it was such a big deal. Thanks so much."

"My pleasure. Don't be a stranger. I'm here to help if you need it."

After exchanging goodbyes, Murph raced back to the apartment, contemplating the whole time how much convincing Evan would.

She'd figure *it* out.

fifty-four

CRITIQUES

Squadrons of people were littered throughout the backstage of Bellco Theatre. Each group was focused on perfecting their costume and makeup for a flawless performance. Assistants were running throughout and grabbing various things to make themselves look busy. Stagehands dressed in black were standing idle until being summoned. Someone had even brought a dog who was occasionally barking at anybody dressed in a costume that walked by.

It was madness except for the tiny corner that Evan, Murph, and Elliot occupied. They weren't doing much.

"Brett told me this was a big deal, but shit dude. This is insane," Murph said.

"Who is Brett?" Evan asked.

"You know . . . Brett. I have mentioned him a dozen times."

"No, you haven't."

"I have. Brett is the guy who snagged us this gig in the first place."

"Murph, I promise that you have never brought him up before."

"Now you know. Brett is a cool guy."

"How many groups are performing?" Elliot asked.

"Twenty-seven."

"Twenty-seven on the twenty-seventh. I doubt that is much of a coincidence," Evan said.

"Expert detective work, you should get a promotion," Murph pointed out.

"Oh, fuck off. I'm just thinking out loud."

"When is Fran coming?"

"Sometime soon."

"He is an integral part of the performance, Evan."

"I know that. I'm not his lackey though. I don't keep track of him at all times."

"I figured that this point you would considering how much time he has been spending with us. Our trio has evolved into a quad."

"LISTEN UP!" the voice blasted from a bullhorn. "THE ORDER OF THE PERFORMANCES ARE POSTED OVER HERE. GOOD LUCK!"

The groups all scrambled over to find their position. Evan and Murph hung back to avoid the mob.

After most of the groups walked away from the posting with a look of indifference, Evan and Murph checked it out.

Here's what they saw:

👤 THE LINEUP 👤

1.) I'LL MAKE A MAN OUT OF YOU 💪

2.) AIN'T NO MOUNTAIN HIGH ENOUGH ⛰

3.) UNDER PRESSURE ⚠

4.) DON'T GO BREAKING MY HEART 🫀

5.) PRINCESS OF CHINA 👫

6.) YOU'RE THE ONE THAT I WANT 🔥

7.) (I'VE HAD) THE TIME OF MY LIFE 🕐

8.) A WHOLE NEW WORLD 🌍

9.) THE NIGHTMAN COMETH: A MEDLEY 🚶

10.) BREAKING FREE ⛓

11.) UP WHERE WE BELONG 🧗

12.) THE WAY I ARE 🕴

13.) MY BOO 👫

14.) TELEPHONE 📡

15.) ENDLESS LOVE ∞

16.) STOP DRAGGIN' MY HEART AROUND 🦅

17.) WALK THIS WAY 🏃

18.) EMPIRE STATE OF MIND 🏛

> 19.) HATE THAT I LOVE YOU ☹
>
> 20.) PICTURES 🏞
>
> 21.) NUMB / ENCORE 💉
>
> 22.) ZERO TO HERO 🎭
>
> 23.) HAKUNA MATATA 😀
>
> 24.) BROKEN 🧩
>
> 25.) WHO SAYS YOU CAN'T GO HOME? 🏃
>
> 26.) DILEMMA 👥
>
> 27.) PARADISE BY THE DASHBOARD LIGHT

Evan stood behind Murph and looked over her head as she scanned through the list.

"Terrible choice . . . that's not even a duet . . . okay, that one worries me . . . where the fuck are we o—wait! What the fuck? Fuck the what fuck?"

"What's the problem?" Evan asked.

"They didn't give us an icon next to our song! What an injustice!" Murph pointed multiple times at the empty space after their song.

"Who cares? We get to go last. This gives us a much better chance to win."

"How do you figure that?" Murph asked, turning back to Evan.

"The judges have to sit through twenty-seven performances. There is no way they are going to remember each one even if they write down notes. We are going to be fresh in their minds."

"Or, they will be so exhausted that they won't even pay attention to our stunning performance."

"That's a possibility, but the city lives for this event. I'm sure they picked judges who are heavily invested in this or at least give enough of a shit to sit through all of these. Any idea who the judges are?" Evan asked.

"From what I was told, the Lip-Sync Competition Assembly—LSCA for short—picks judges from a list of individuals that have had an impact on the community over the past year, so the faces will be recognizable to Denverites."

"This is whole thing is so bizarre."

"What do we do now?" Murph said.

"Stretch."

"Seriously?"

"Yeah."

"Fine."

They returned to their corner and ran through a series of stretches led by Evan. He avoided injury with his reignited passion for running by being rigorous with his pre- and post-run stretches. A pulled hamstring could sideline him for weeks and that was a quick way to lose motivation.

The number of conversations dwindled in the backstage area after a stagehand announced they had ten minutes until showtime.

"I wish I had smoked beforehand," Elliot said. "It is going to take hours to get to our performance."

"We need to scout the competition," Murph said.

"What do you mean?"

"If a group goes out there and absolutely slays it, we may need to rethink our strategy."

"No," Evan cut in. "It's too late for that. We already did the rehearsal yesterday. They have the timings down for the lights and everything."

"Yeah, well, tough shit. I wanna win."

"Murph, why is this such a big deal to you? I still d—"

"Sorry I'm late," Franco said. He had a backpack slung over his shoulder.

"Where have you been?" Murph asked. "Thank goodness we weren't first or else we would have replaced you."

"Impossible. My job security is rock solid," Franco said, flashing a smile to Evan.

"Don't mind her. She's on edge. The heat of the competition and all that," Elliot said. He grabbed Murph's hand and gave it a squeeze. "We are doing this to have fun."

"I'm doing it for more than that," Murph muttered to herself.

An extended applause rippled from the audience out front.

"Finally," Evan said.

Conan O'Brien stepped out onstage and delivered his introduction. It was laced with his typical humor.

"Conan O'Brien? How the fuck did they get him? And . . . why?" Elliot asked in confusion.

"For the thousandth time, this shit is a big deal," Murph said.

"GROUP ONE! GROUP ONE! YOU'RE UP. LET'S GO. GROUP TWO, BE

READY," the stagehand yelled for everyone to hear.

Four people materialized in ludicrous costumes ripped directly from the movie their song originated.

"I'll be doing recon. I will report back my findings," Murph announced.

For the next two hours, Evan, Elliot, and Franco sat patiently as they watched the groups march out for their performance.

As for Murph, she gathered her intel and delivered it in a series of rushed, broken comments.

Performance #1 – I'LL MAKE A MAN OUT OF YOU
- "They were good. Not great, but a solid start. They had a dragon. Nice touch."
- 3.2 Murphs out of 5

Performance #2 – AIN'T NO MOUNTAIN HIGH ENOUGH
- "BORING! No stage presence whatsoever. Why'd they even bother?"
- 0.4 Murphs out of 5

Performance #3 – UNDER PRESSURE
- "They were the winners from last year . . . and I can see why. Fuck."
- 4.4 Murphs out of 5

Performances #4-6
- (Murph ditched her recon position and was speaking to someone no one in the group knew. The man handed her a book and she dropped it into her bag.)
- N/A Murphs out of 5

Performance #7 – (I'VE HAD) THE TIME OF MY LIFE
- "Holy fuck. They tried to go full Pat Swayze and the guy face planted when he jumped off the stage. I definitely saw blood."
- 1 Murph out of 5 (a Murph was rewarded for their effort and grit)

Performance #8 – A WHOLE NEW WORLD
- "Huh, I think they mastered witchcraft. They had a flying carpet. Very authentic."
- 4.2 Murphs out of 5

Performance #9 – THE NIGHTMAN COMETH: A MEDLEY
- "I appreciate the genius of the show, but that is NOT a duet. It's more like a smattering of village idiots dancing and singing nonsense

around a fire."
- 1.6 Murphs out of 5

Performances #10-14
- (Murph took an extended bathroom break.)
- N/A Murphs out of 5

Performance #15 – ENDLESS LOVE
- "That was cute. It looked like an old married couple out there, but what a snooze of a song." Murph mimed falling asleep.
- 2.6 Murphs out of 5

Performance #16 – STOP DRAGGIN' MY HEART AROUND
- "I have nothing witty or constructive to say about that mediocre performance."
- 2.5 Murphs out of 5

Performances #17-20
- (Murph watched the performances but did not report back her findings. It's impossible to always come up with something witty to say.)
- N/A Murphs out of 5

Performance #21 – NUMB / ENCORE
- "Not a duet—technically—but actually, what is a duet? Truly, do we even understand the meaning of the word? I do not and therefore I am at a loss. Anyways, the audience was super into that one."
- 3.8 Murphs out of 5

Performances #22-26
- (Murph abandoned her post and began getting ready.)
- N/A Murphs out of 5

(Disclaimer: The rating system established by Murph is not affiliated with LSCA and the personal opinions expressed by Murph are hers alone.)

The notorious stagehand waddled over to our friends and said they had two minutes.

"Does anybody need anything?" Evan asked.

Everyone shook their heads.

"Let's do this!" Murph said.

"Good luck y'all! See you on the other side." Elliot said.

fifty-five

UNBURDENED

Evan snuck out from behind the curtain and took his spot on the left side of the stage. Murph stood ten feet away from him, shifting nervously as they waited for the music to start. Evan stepped closer to the microphone stand and grabbed hold of it. He had a minute or so before he joined in on the song; Murph was the main attraction.

They had the brilliant idea of shaking things up. Murph was dressed in a white button-down shirt with overalls on. Elliot had stuffed a pillow inside her shirt to give the impression that she added on significant weight to mimic the stature of Meat Loaf. Evan, on the other hand, was dressed in a one-piece Spandex cut low to show off his undefined chest. He had a shoulder length wig on to really pull together his transformation.

Evan and Murph had watched the music video enough times to nail the look of Meat Loaf and Karla DeVito. (Interesting fact: Karla DeVito is lip-syncing in the music video as Ellen Foley provided the vocals for the song. Everything comes full circle, huh?)

"Make sure the microphone is turned off," Evan called out.

He could barely see Murph's outline in the darkness, but he saw her nodding in acknowledgement.

Applause tore out from the crowd. They were either excited for the performance or excited it was the last one.

The guitar riff started, and the spotlight kicked in, pointing at Murph. Evan watched as Murph grabbed the microphone and stepped toward center stage.

Murph mimed the manic behavior of Mr Loaf in the music video and whipped around the stage with the spotlight chasing after her as best it could. She ran over to the piano situated in the middle of the stage. Franco was hunched over it and furiously pretending to hit the keys. The audience cheered at his introduction.

Murph finished up the verse and ran up next to Evan. He leaned into the microphone and delivered his first lines.

> *Though it's cold and lonely in the deep, dark night,*
> *I can see paradise in the dashboard light.*

Things began to get hectic at this point. Evan and Murph roamed around the stage lip-syncing their lines while trying to build up the sexual tension. It consisted of Murph chasing Evan around haphazardly. The spotlight followed in swift dedication. There wasn't a moment they weren't drenched in the light. Murph and Evan made sure to face the crowd (particularly the judges), so that everyone could see their over exaggerated lip-syncing. They kept this up until the point where the radio announcer starts running through his play-by-play.

Elliot stepped out in a three-piece suit, holding an old school microphone in one hand and a fake cigarette in the other. Another spotlight flicked on and focused on him while he took the audience through what happened during the ninth inning of the baseball game. He leaned into the absurdity of the play-by-play and stressed all the right words.

Evan and Murph went through the theatrics of faking their romance for another. As the player rounded second base, Murph grabbed at Evan's chest and gave his fake boobs a firm squeeze. Evan leaned down and kissed Murph, igniting a massive cheer from the audience.

Murph continued to escalate her advances until the suicide squeeze happened. Evan pushed her away and transitioned into the next phase of the song where he questions Murph's seemingly fake love for him. They volleyed back and forth for several minutes as Murph continued to ask if (s)he can sleep on it.

Murph eventually relented and confessed to loving Evan forever just to have sex for that one night. Every light turned on and became a light shade of blue. Franco kept keying away at the piano in a frantic rhythm, where it was painfully clear he didn't know his way around the ivories. Evan's expression turned to shock and then a deep shade of admiration at the realization of what Murph just told him.

Murph—understanding her mistake—spends the rest of the song praying for the end of time. When it finally comes, the lights fade out. The audience will never know what became of that teenage romance. Maybe it lasted forever or it was only the thing before the thing or maybe it shouldn't be thought about as seriously as that. It's only a song after all.

Evan, Murph, and Franco exit stage right and listen from backstage as the cheers and praise erupt from the audience. It wasn't the loudest they were all night, but for Evan and Murph, it was good enough.

"Holy fuck! We actually did it! That was incredible," Murph said. Her face was red and sweaty. "I'm taking this damn pillow out."

"The crowd really seemed to like our passionate romance," Evan said.

"You play a convincing woman," Franco said.

"Thanks. Maybe it was my calling in another life."

"What happens next?" Elliot asked as he walked over.

As if on cue, Conan returned to the stage and asked for everyone's patience as the judges deliberated the top three. "And I want to give a special thanks to someone this community knows all too well. He doesn't need much of an introduction considering that we wouldn't be sitting here without his dedication in starting this tradition twenty-seven years ago. Please give a hand for Mr. Brett Bowling!"

Brett walked out on stage and gave a quiet wave to the crowd.

"Would you like to say anything?" Conan asked.

Brett nodded and took the microphone. "Thank you all for coming. This has been a wonderful tradition and a great excuse to bring the community together each year. When I moved here from New York City in the late eighties, I didn't think this city would still be my home thirty years later, but I'm so glad it is. Denver is filled with beautiful people that I get the pleasure of meeting every day. Thank you again for being here. And please, give it up for the performers. Another amazing year of creative performances!"

Brett gave another wave to the crowd and walked off stage toward our quad.

"The song choice was perfect and swapping the roles. Great thinking! I'm rooting for you!" Brett said to Murph and the group.

"Thanks Brett."

As Brett went to congratulate the other groups, Elliot leaned in and said, "You just happened to meet the founder of this event at his bookstore six months ago. What are the chances of that?"

"If you ask him, it wasn't chance," Murph said.

Conan announced that the judges were done, and he flashed an envelope. "Let's get all the groups out on stage. Try to squeeze in."

Evan, Murph, Elliot, and Franco were standing directly behind Conan as he tore into the envelope and looked down at the three lines.

He called out third place. It wasn't them.

He called out second place. It wasn't them.

He called out first place. It definitely wasn't them.

Evan turned and saw Murph deflate each time their names weren't called. They left the stage after all the celebrations and cheers were over and returned to their corner to pack everything up.

"What's wrong?" Evan asked. "Did you think we were going to get top three?"

"Yeah, yeah I did. I thought we were great," Murph said.

"We were, but so were a lot of other teams."

"You just don't get it."

"Then explain it to me," Evan asked.

"Not here."

"Why?"

"Because I don't want anyone seeing me cry more than I already am."

"No one cares Murph. It's okay."

"I care!"

"Fine. Okay. Where can we go?"

"Hold on." Murph stepped away and walked toward Brett.

"What was that about?" Elliot asked.

"She is upset that we didn't get in the top three," Evan said.

"Hmm. Well, I'm gonna let you handle that one. Franco and I are heading to the bar. Text me if things go awry but come over after y'all are done."

"Don't you want to know why she is so upset?"

"Honestly, I do, but she cares about you Evan. There's probably a good reason why she wants to talk to you about it. I have the rest of my life to learn everything about Murphy."

Evan nodded. He grabbed the bags and walked over to Murph.

They walked out of the convention center and toward the nearby park.

"Brett just told me we got fourth place," Murph said.

"That's great! I have always envisioned a future where getting fourth place would be a recognizable achievement. Something to work toward I suppose. Are you happy with that?"

"It's better than fifth, but I would have preferred third."

"I can't argue with that logic."

Murph laid down in the grass and used her bag as a headrest. Evan did the same.

"The only downside of living in a city: you never get to see the stars," Murph said.

"We could always leave this place and go somewhere quieter."

"And abandon our wonderful jobs? No, thank you," she said with a smile.

"How long are you going to stay in Denver?"

"I don't quite know, and I think that's good enough for right now. Dallas is always a fallback option, but I'd prefer to keep branching out before heading back there."

"Understandable. I'm sure your family would be thrilled to have you back."

"After the weekend they spent here, it's best for us to have our space. They stress me out."

"Before I forget, thanks again for forcing us to do this. All that work for eight minutes of bliss. It was amazing to perform in front of a crowd again. The adrenaline is such an unbeatable high," Evan said.

"Did I ever tell you how I used to do beauty pageants?" Murph said, acknowledging Evan's comment in a roundabout way.

"No, I don't think you have."

"Reality television has given them a bad reputation—though it is rightfully deserved in some respects—but I enjoyed my time doing them. My dad was the one who carted me around to all the pageants and did my hair and makeup. The other moms were weirded out by this and there were plenty of times where people tried to get him kicked out. It was a terrible stereotype to think that my dad wouldn't be the parent who was the one heavily involved. My mom suffered from intense postpartum depression after my youngest brother was born, so she didn't come to many of my pageants. That was okay though because my dad was always there. He would be in the second row—always the second row—with the biggest smile on his face. He was immensely proud of me for doing such a silly thing. This trend continued as I got older. I was in the school choir and he'd be there in the second row at our concerts. When I tried to play the oboe for a year, he was there. When I discovered cheerleading, he would come to the football games just to watch me. When I would go to Elliot's baseball games, he would tag along on days when he got home from work early. He was my biggest fan. I would get so nervous before any events in front of a crowd and he would pull me aside and say, '*You're doing this because you want to, not because you have to.*' Once I was out there at a pageant or a football game or a band concert, I'd always look out and see my dad and I'd be relieved. Tonight was the first time without him. Part of me did this competition because I expected to look out into the crowd and see him sitting in the second row with his wide smile. The whole cancer thing would be revealed as just a cruel joke. But he wasn't there, of course. Nothing but strangers in the second row. I still felt relieved though. I don't know why.

"I should be grateful I got as much time with my dad as I did, but I'm selfish. I wish I had more. I wish he got to see me get married and hold his grandchild and collect social security and enjoy retirement and die quietly in his sleep after living a long, plentiful life. But that reality will never happen. I miss him so much. I wish he was still out there in that second row cheering me on for whatever comes next with my life."

315

Evan stared up at the blank sky. He reached out and intertwined his hand with Murph's. "I don't know what to say."

"I didn't say all that for you to sooth me with some kind words, but I do have a favor."

"What's that?"

"You can tell me the truth."

Evan sat up and looked over at her. "About what?"

"Whatever it is. Evan, you cut yourself that night for more than what happened with you and your father."

"You don't know that."

"I took the letter," Murph said. She sat up and pulled her knees toward her chest.

"What letter?"

"The one from Vincent, the one you ripped up."

"W-why? Wh-when?"

"I went back inside your apartment to find your keys and I saw it in the kitchen. I was being nosy, and I looked. I saw it was from him. I just had a feeling I needed to take it since you were going to throw it out. If I had to guess."

"Yeah, that was the intention."

"But you didn't."

"I got . . . distracted."

"Did you read it?"

"No, Murph. I didn't."

"I did. I'm sorry that I did, but I was worried about you. I thought maybe the letter had something to do with what you did, but you never brought it up and I didn't want to force the topic."

"But now we are going to talk about it anyways?"

"Yes. Evan, when's the last time to spoke to Vincent?"

Evan looked away from her and back up at the empty sky. The dots weren't there. Evan felt incredibly small in both a meaningless and lonely way. He imagined a scalpel sitting in the grass next to him, left behind by some careless child. He would pick it up and drag it down his right arm until he had a scar that matched the one on his left. Equilibrium and balance were what he needed. Debits and credits. But the scalpel wasn't there. Instead, Evan ripped out a chunk of grass and held it in his hands.

"Today is his birthday. I tried not to think about it all day, but it was impossible not to. I thought the lip-sync competition would distract me enough; I think it was the only reason I agreed to do it. I saw the date of the event and knew I would be broken that day and this stupid competition would be the only thing to keep me sane. I texted and wished him a happy birthday, but it didn't go through. I'm surprised th—he would have been twenty-six."

"*Would have been?*" Murph asked.

"He's dead."

"What?"

"New Year's Eve or New Year's Day—I guess it doesn't really matter. It was a car accident. Can you believe it? A fucking car accident—"

"Evan—"

"That motherfucker never even got a traffic ticket before and then he goes off and crashes headfirst into a FUCKING GUARDRAIL! WHY? I had to read about it through Facebook posts from strangers he never even talked about. They were probably posts from people who didn't give a fuck about him, Murph! Can you imagine what that feels like? I sat in my apartment and wanted to disintegrate into a billion particles and float away. I felt so helpless in that moment. I-I didn't even go to the funeral. And you know what I hate the most about all this? He has been ruining my life ever since. The nightmares and the constant thoughts about him trying to worm their way into my head. I dated him for a YEAR. A YEAR! I shouldn't have my life completely dismantled by the death of someone I broke up with!"

"Evan—"

"Don't. Don't bother telling me that you're sorry. Those hollow words won't help me right now."

Murph shook her head. "Did he live at Axis?" she asked.

Evan stared through her and tore apart a blade of grass in his hand. "Yes," he whispered. "How did you know that?"

"I met him." A sudden and miraculous realization, but one she had known ever since reading the letter. Something about *it* felt familiar.

"You *met* him? You met Vin Besser?"

"Yes. Well, he never told me his last name, but I remember the conversation clearly, which is strange because I didn't any of the other times you spoke about him."

Evan let out a hysterical laugh that cut through the tears. "You're telling me of all the people in Dallas, you—Murphy Law—lived in the same complex as my dead ex-boyfriend and subsequently had a conversation with him?"

"That's what I'm telling you."

"What did you two talk about?"

"I don't—"

"Please. Murph, I want to know."

"As my dad got sicker, I either spent my time outside of work at the hospital or roaming around Dallas. My favorite spot was the top of the parking garage at Axis, which is weird because it was so close to my apartment and, yet, I felt two thousand miles away from everything. I'd go up there and look out at the skyline. It was a quiet escape from the chaos waiting below if I went up there at the right time. The day before I left Dallas to move here, Vincent was up there—just staring out into the abyss. We talked about how my dad had just died and how he considered naming his dog Murph. We talked about the last words my dad said to me. We talked about never seeing each other again. He asked me if I believed in fate and I told him no, but now we are here and I'm with you and it would be impossible to believe that there wasn't some intervention to bring us together."

"I can't believe you met him."

Murph considered bringing up how she told Vincent he wasn't actually in love with his boyfriend but there wasn't a good reason to.

"He was very kind."

"He was."

"And didn't realize his potential at all."

"That's true."

"Why didn't you tell me?" Murph asked.

"I don't know." It was the most honest answer Evan could give. There was no logical reason for why he refused to bring up Vincent's death with anyone. The grief just didn't allow him to understand why.

"Did you talk to anyone about this?"

"No."

"Oh, Evan. Grief is a nasty, nasty process. You can't walk through it alone."

"I know that."

"You should read the letter. Do you want it back?"

"No."

"Why not?"

"Because I'm afraid of what it says. I don't know when he wrote it or why he even did. I . . . I don't need to feel any more guilt than I already do."

"Why do you feel guilty?" Murph asked.

"Because I left," Evan whispered.

"Don't say that. What happened isn't your fault or anyone else's."

"Of course you'd say that, Murph. That's what people always say! It's never anyone's fault. But maybe—just maybe—if I didn't move to Denver, things would be different."

"Y'all would have still broken up."

"What?"

"The few times you have talked about Vincent have led me to believe that your relationship was never going to last with him. Evan, if you didn't leave for Denver, Vincent would have still gotten in that car."

"I'm tired of him controlling my life. I don't want the letter back. Please don't ask me about it again."

"Okay."

They both laid back down and didn't speak to each other for a while. Murph pulled out her phone and was likely responding to a text from Elliot. Evan doubted either of them would make it to the bar.

"Paradise by the Dashboard Light" kept repeating in his head. The idea of professing false love to have sex with someone was certainly not something Evan had experienced before, but he did recognize that not all love is created equal. Sometimes it can be ugly and one-sided and lead to conflict, anger, divorce, black eyes, scandals, and so on. But it could also be beautiful and healthy and balanced and nuanced and last a lifetime. There was no equation for it.

Evan's love for Vincent was . . . confusing. It wasn't bad, but it wasn't exactly fulfilling either. It was a lot of things Evan had trouble deciphering for himself.

He stared back up at the dead pixels that were hiding until his eyes started to get heavy. Evan began to drift off—

"Hey," Murph said and stirred him back awake.

"Yeah?"

"Are you okay?"

"I'm fine."

"Yeah, that's everyone's go-to answer."

"Well, it's true."

"Would you go to a medium with me?" Murph asked and looked over at Evan.

His eyes widened and then narrowed. "Why?"

"Because I have some questions for my dad. And maybe you have some for Vincent."

"Oh c'mon Murph. You don't actually believe in that stuff, do you?"

"No, I don't. I think it's a bunch of shit, but I'm willing to do anything at this point to help myself get to that final stage of acceptance with my dad's death. And, honestly, I think you could get something out of it too."

"I have nothing to ask Vincent."

"There's other people you know who are dead. You were close with your grandmother, right? Maybe she has something to share with you."

"I don't know."

"Listen: I get that you don't want to talk about Vincent or anyone or anything that makes you feel uncomfortable, but it is real fucking tiring to be friends with you sometimes."

"I just spoke at length about Vincent. What are you talking about?"

"It took you seven months, Evan. You almost fucking died because your feelings bubbled over and caused you to do something stupid. And I'm sorry. I don't want to put you on blast for cutting yourself, but I feel like we could have helped if you talked to us."

"It was the last time. I'm better now."

"Yeah, I hope so."

Silence spread between them until Murph spoke again.

"Please be more open with me in the future. I'm here for you. I always have been. And please come with me to the medium because I already bought two tickets and Elliot can't go, so I'm counting on you."

"Of course I'll go."

"Thanks Evan."

"Are you ready to head back?"

"Yeah, we probably should before they start putting our faces on milk cartons."

"Is that even a thing anymore?"

"Doubtful. People don't drink milk anymore. I read an article about it on Buzzfeed."

"Mhmm. And that is such a reputable source for news."

"They have stepped their shit up over the past few years," Murph said. "They did an expose on how mass shootings are the cause of death to innocent people. Really groundbreaking stuff."

"Okay, okay. I concede."

They stood up, rediscovered their sense of direction, and headed north out of the park. Fifteen minutes later, they were back at Skyhouse.

"Evan," Murph said after stepping out of the elevator. "I love you very much. I hope you know that."

Evan stuck his hand out to stop the elevator from closing. It flinched and returned to the open position. "I know. I love you too. Thanks for everything. The performance was great. We need to properly celebrate our fourth-place victory."

"I'm sorry about Vincent. I truly am."

"Thanks Murph."

"It'll get easier. At least I hope so."

The elevator let out an obnoxious beep and Murph's face disappeared as the doors closed.

fifty-six

CHRISTMAS IN JULY

It wasn't until 9:30 a.m. that Evan began to get worried.

On the days he and Murph didn't walk to work together, she would still roll in shortly after he did, usually her detour included a stop at a donut shop. (Murph had a weakness for sweets and other unhealthy food items. The weakness was compounded whenever she was high. So to recap: High Murph became a vacuum for carbs and sugar. Drunk Murph stuttered uncontrollably after eight drinks. Every person had their quirks.)

After getting his second cup of coffee, Evan texted Murph. Her response was almost immediate: she was taking a personal day to finish some things she had been neglecting for a while. Evan tried to pry for more details, but she didn't respond back.

At least she isn't dead, which was always the first thought that ran through his head when something was out of place. One time back in college, Evan waited with dinner ready for two hours. Wednesday was the only weeknight where he and Kieran didn't have some separate activity going on, so they designated it as a stay-in date night. They followed this tradition for a year, but as their relationship began to deteriorate, Kieran would come home later each week. On that particular evening when he was two hours late, Evan had made some fried rice for them to devour. The carbs would put them into a coma until the next morning. Evan called and texted receiving no response. He sat there and waited because he was passive, because he didn't want to break the tradition. He pushed away the unsettling thoughts of the harrowing situations Kieran could be in as he tried to focus on the logical. Kieran was only stuck in traffic or Kieran stayed late at work to help a friend. It's not like Kieran was fucking some stranger in the back of his car or having another psychotic break that he was trying to hide from Evan or that he was straight up dead. No, no. It had to be much simpler than that. Evan sat in his own spiral until the door opened and Izzie scurried to see who it was even though it could have only been one person. Evan didn't bother to ask where Kieran was since he was broken from their relationship by that point.

That was then. Memories like that would continue to drift deeper into the past. Evan would pluck them out in moments of solitude, but they'd become fuzzier with the edges blurring into smoke.

In Evan's present time, he spent the day pretending to be interested in his HR responsibilities. He answered emails and scoured LinkedIn for talent that wasn't there. Finding applicants who were interested in the marijuana industry was harder than you'd think considering the massive culture of smoking pot.

He scrolled through Facebook and read the posts that came in from strangers. They wished him well without sounding sincere.

Evan's mom called sometime after lunch and they spoke just long enough for his blood pressure to start rising. Sensing her own inability to have a cohesive conversation with her son, Evan's mom ended the call quickly and with the false promise that she'd "come see the sights of Denver" before the year was out.

Evan left work earlier than normal because why the fuck not? Nobody said anything to him, which was pretty standard.

Skyhouse was vacant in the lobby and the elevators area. He took the nonstop to the eighth floor. Directly across the elevator was a massive sign declaring it was Evan's birthday.

"What the fuck?" he said to no one.

Evan followed the trail of streamers and balloons to his door, which was covered in more paraphernalia.

A note was hanging from it.

Hope you didn't think we forgot!
Happy Birthday to the coolest Evan we know!

Love,
Murph, Elliot, & Franco

P.S. Be downstairs at 7 for . . . well, that would ruin the surprise

Evan obeyed the instruction and was loitering down in the lobby at 7. He always valued being on time for events.

"Happy birthday!" Franco said as he walked into the lobby.

"Thanks. Where are the others?"

"We are meeting them there."

"Am I dressed appropriately for the occasion?" Evan asked.

Franco scanned over Evan several times. "Yeah, yeah. You look fine. It's a casual place."

"What's that you got?" Evan pointed down to the box in Franco's hand.

"You're a smart guy. I'm sure you can guess."

"You didn't have to get me anything."

"What? This isn't a gift for you!"

"Oh—that's awkward."

"My other friend's birthday is today as well, oddly enough. Even stranger, his name is also Evan. The weirdest part is that he is turning twenty-six too!"

"You're annoying," Evan said.

"I'll hang onto it until dinner. If you don't mind."

"Not at all. Are you leading the way?"

"Yes, sir. Follow me," Franco said.

Franco went two blocks up the road and took a right. Evan wasn't familiar with this portion of the city even with the close proximity to the apartment complex.

"What kind of restaurant are we going to?" Evan asked.

"It's . . . more of a . . . concept," Franco struggled to say.

"I don't understand."

"That was the intention. It's right up here . . . keep going . . . keep going. There!" Franco said. He pointed to the next building up the block.

Franco pulled ahead and grabbed the door for Evan. They stepped inside to the . . . bookstore? Evan looked around in confusion. The front portion of the store was dimly lit except for a strand of lights that ran down the center aisle to the back. Indistinct music played and he could see the flicker of candles bouncing light off the walls.

"So romantic," Evan said.

"Something different. Keep going," Franco urged.

Evan moved down the aisle in no hurry. He stopped halfway and glanced at the rows of books that seemed to soar above the ceiling. Evan had found excuses for years about why he no longer read, but it repeatedly looped back to one: he was busy. What an awful word. Everyone was busy. Everyone had commitments to their job or family or themselves, so using the excuse of being busy was a tired cliché that should be left for the uninspired. The reason Evan didn't read anymore was because he never put in the effort of finding a book to captivate him. He didn't need to be whisked away to some exotic land; he wanted something different, but what exactly he couldn't say.

Evan left the books behind and emerged out of the aisle. Murph stood there triumphantly with a huge grin and her arms spread wide.

"Happy birthday Evan!"

She ran over and hugged him. Elliot snuck around the corner and hugged him from beyond.

"This is really cute. I don't really know what to say."

"Just take a seat," Elliot said. "You like red wine, correct?"

"I do."

Evan sat down at the table with Murph and Franco while Elliot walked around pouring out the wine.

"Who is the fifth seat for?" Evan asked.

"Good question! It seemed rude to use his bookstore and not invite him to dinner. Brett was just looking at some inventory in the back. He'll be out in a second."

"I see. This must be where you met him then."

"Yes, it is," Franco said, answering for Murph. "She gave us the detailed story earlier today. I'm sure she will enlighten you with it at a later time."

"Earlier today?" Evan asked. "How long have y'all been setting this up."

"I had to take a personal day for a reason," Murph said.

Evan looked around and noticed all the paper snowflakes cut out and placed around. Gingerbread houses, fake show, candy canes, a Nativity set, and a mid-sized Christmas tree decked out with ornaments were scattered throughout the space.

"I went for a Christmas in July birthday theme," Murph continued. "Seemed like it would be something you never got before. Thankfully, Brett keeps all of his Christmas decorations accessible year-round."

"This is incredible. I've never gotten anything close to this," Evan said to himself.

Murph pulled out her phone and restarted the music through the speakers. "We can listen to a few Christmas songs before switching over to something more . . . topical."

"Brett, welcome back," Elliot called out.

"Can we get you some wine?" Franco asked.

"Yes, that would be lovely. You must be Evan, then? Welcome. We met informally at the lip-sync competition."

They shook hands. "It's nice to meet you," Evan said. "Thanks for lending out your store. This is very unnecessary. A regular restaurant would have been just fine."

"You're right. We had an elaborate meal planned out until Elliot reminded us that this is a bookstore not a fine-dining establishment . . ." Murph said.

"Okay. What are you getting at?" Evan said, scanning the table and looking confused.

"Our meal for the evening will be a delicious spread of the most gourmet pizza you will ever have."

Laughter burst out from the table.

"That is perfect," Evan said.

Murph walked over to the side table and grabbed the four boxes of pizza. She opened each one to show off what kind it was. The audience clapped at each unveiling. They had been quiet for weeks.

They ate and talked for the next hour. The details of the conversation weren't important. We have read through dozens of their chats by this point and this one followed in a similar vein.

"Time for cake!" Murph announced once the pizza had been plowed through.

It was a marble cake that had a crude drawing of Evan with Izzie on top. Twenty-six candles jutted out in various directions.

Murph snapped her fingers and all of them lit up.

"H-how'd you do that?" Evan asked.

"I'm a wizard, Evan," Murph said with a straight face.

"Okay then. With that out of the way, let's sing happy birthday before the candles drip wax all over the cake," Franco suggested.

They sang a rousing rendition of Happy Birthday where any attempt to describe the harmonies and execution of it would be a complete disservice.

Sated by the pizza and now cake, the five people at the table sat back and allowed for the food coma to kick in. It was a short-lived affair as Elliot asked if anyone else noticed the presents under the tree.

"Why yes, yes I do! I wonder how those got there," Murph wondered.

Evan walked over and scooped up the gifts. The first box had a new pair of running shoes with Elliot declaring that Evan's current pair was "quite raggedy." The second box was much smaller. Evan opened it with care and removed all the unnecessary wrapping. Inside was the fattest blunt he had ever seen.

"Do you expect me to smoke this by myself?" Evan asked.

"Of course not!" Murph said. "I crafted that myself with the intention of getting in on the action."

"What a thoughtful gift. You tell me when and we can all enjoy this."

"My turn," Brett said.

"You didn't have to get me anything," Evan said.

"The lucky thing about owning a bookstore is that I don't have to go far to get anyone gifts when there's short notice. Why don't you pick out one . . . or five? I don't mind."

"I haven't read in a while. I don't even know what I'm interested in anymore."

"Fiction or nonfiction?"

"Fiction," Evan said.

"Follow me." Brett walked to the lit aisle and said, "We can probably find you something in this area. Just walk around and see what grabs your interest."

Evan scanned the rows of books more closely than before. He noticed the names of classics he never had the chance to read, but they didn't interest him. Evan looked up at the highest shelf and reached for the bright orange spine.

Evan flipped it over in his hands several times.

"What's that one?" Brett asked.

"It's called *Infinite Scroll*. Have you heard of it before?"

"No, I haven't. It's by . . . Trenton Dire. Who the fuck is that?" Brett said, confused by his lack of book knowledge and merchandise in his own store.

"I haven't heard of him either."

Evan flipped the book over and read the back cover. "The destruction of the universe was caused by one man: Venice Bounty. If you want to find out how, why don't you start reading this? Maybe you'll fall into the infinite scroll too."

"I don't understand if I should be impressed or annoyed by that," Brett said.

"I'll take it," Evan said.

"Great! Any others you want to pick out?"

"No, this should be okay for now. Thank you so much."

Evan showed off the book he chose, and everyone was equally confused and intrigued by the vague premise.

"One last gift," Franco said and slid over his box.

Evan tore into it and looked back up at Franco. "Are you kidding me?"

"You mentioned that you were getting back into photography, so I figured you could use a better lens."

"These cost a fortune."

"Really. Don't worry about that. You better take amazing pictures now," Franco said with a smile.

The Leica lens that Evan held in his hand was ridiculously expensive. He knew because he'd looked plenty of times to find an affordable one, but never had any luck.

It wasn't a gift you got for a regular friend. The thought rotated around in Evan's head until he tossed it aside to free up storage.

"Thank you so much, Franco."

"Way to one-up the rest of us, dickhead," Murph said. "All I got him was a stupid blunt." This last part was said more to herself. (A few weeks later, the gang would enjoy that stupid blunt and all agree it was a worthy birthday gift.)

Evan watched as Murph and Franco went back and forth in a playful argument. Evan didn't feel like he deserved any of this. The decorations, the pizza, the friends, the caring nature of the entire evening, but maybe that was the point: all of this was meant to be a reminder that he should be happy, that the life he started to build in Denver was a good one. Evan didn't need to constantly look for excuses as to why he wasn't deserving. Sometimes people did nice things without being prompted. Every moment didn't need to be commandeered with sad thoughts and regrets of what could be different.

Evan returned to the present and celebrated the last hours of his birthday.

fifty-seven

MEDIUM LITTLE LIES

Miles Millie Nare was born with a ten-carat diamond spoon in his mouth. The son of a real estate mogul and stay-at-home dad, Miles enjoyed a privileged upbringing where money was the object of affection. He was a content child due to the army of maids, chefs, stylists, masseuses, politicians, astronauts, CEOs, CFOs, and UFOs he interacted with. His parents were grounded enough to understand that Miles needed to do normal child things like playing with the poor kids, so they signed him up for the Boy Scouts. Miles enjoyed the weekly meetings with kids that didn't go to his fancy private school or attend the lavish parties his parents held. Earning the badges was a sense of pride that went unmatched to other aspects of his young life. Miles believed that he'd become an Eagle Scout one day and carry on the lessons to the next generation.

He never made it that far and quit unexpectedly after two years. When his parents questioned why he stopped, Miles said he had grown out of it. They pressed him further and got nothing. He didn't think the truth was worth sharing or the potential retaliation that could stem from it.

It was the first time Miles realized how good he could be at lying. He would refine it heavily throughout the years, but that was the basis. Miles understood that any good lie is based on some semblance of the truth.

At the age of twelve, Miles convinced a group of friends at the lunch table that he had a clairvoyant experience. The group heckled him in the obnoxious manner that middle-schoolers do, but Miles persisted. He turned to Layton and said that his dead mother wished he would start washing his hands after using the bathroom. The color drained from Layton's face. He packed up the rest of his lunch and fled from the table. A surge of dopamine rushed through Miles. Lying was so much fun, especially in such an outrageous manner as that.

Miles skimmed through Layton's Facebook and saw photos he had posted of his mom from a few years before the car accident. It was good material, but he needed more, so he observed Layton for a few weeks before he noticed the trend of his unsanitary bathroom usage.

After Miles clued Layton into his lie a week later, they started spending more time together and became inseparable once they got to high school.

It was amazing how quickly teenagers could repair (or start) a friendship compared to adults.

At the age of fourteen, Miles and Layton had developed a reputation throughout the school. Once a week, Miles would set aside his lunch period to practice his psychic abilities. Layton would compile a list of students that wanted to talk with Miles. At the peak of popularity, the waiting list was twenty-seven students long. Layton would scour social media weeks in advance of when Miles would have his session. It was plenty of time to glimpse into the lives students so willingly put online.

See:

The tactic that Miles and Layton adopted is called hot reading. This is when you stalk your clients prior to meeting them in order to gleam an understanding about their life—to find the traumas that they want resolved.

By the time Miles barely graduated high school, he was renowned within the community. His parents talked with him about making this a business opportunity. Miles had no interest in college or learning a trade, so it was either live off his parents' money or scam unsuspecting people. Miles elected for the latter since he had decided long ago that people were monsters and most deserved no respect.

Using the wealth and influence his family had, Miles secured a reality television show on Netflix that ran for three seasons before being abruptly canceled. That was okay though. He had amassed a huge fanbase across social media platforms that believed every lie he spewed. Miles had outgrown the repetitive nature of filming and decided that live audience engagement was a natural progression for him.

Denver happened to be the last spot on his tour.

○ ○ ○

Evan and Murph were in the tenth row of the moderately sized venue. The seats were filling up fast with the predominant demographic being individuals over the age of fifty.

"Is this event sold out?" Evan asked.

"Oh, absolutely. People have been talking about this for weeks," Murph said.

"People? What people have you been asking about this?"

"I'm an extremely social person. I do have friends outside of you in Denver."

"Wait, really?" Evan said, contorting his face in confusion.

"Why are you surprised to hear that?"

"I . . . I don't know. I don't have friends outside of y'all, so I assumed you were in the same situation."

"Give it time. You will meet people, especially if you. *Start. Going. On. Dates!*" Murph said, punching him lightly after each word.

"I have been on a few already. I'm just waiting to compile a shit list long enough to share with y'all."

"Excuse me. Are you saving this seat?"

Murph turned and looked at the woman who was steadying herself with a cane. "It's all yours."

The woman sat down and rested her hands across the purse to protect it from any dastardly robbers.

"Is this your first time seeing Miles? He's a real peach," the woman asked.

"Yes. We just had to see Miles," Evan said with feigned excitement.

"I've seen him before and each time he performs miracles. He just . . . knows how to connect people to the ones they love."

"An admirable talent for sure."

The conversation didn't go much further as the lights dimmed and the screens played a sharply produced video of Miles Millie Nare and the highlights of his illustrious career.

If there was ever an audience that incapsulated the essence of the times one had been following our beloved characters around, this would be it. They were worse than the audience at a taping of Oprah's show. They cheered wildly at Miles's proudest moments as highlighted in the video and continued to clap furiously when he came out on stage.

"Thank you. Thank you. It is great to be here tonight," Miles said. "I love Denver and so thrilled that *this* is the last stop of the worldwide tour." The audience clapped until their hands went numb.

Miles continued. "It has been absolutely incredible getting to meet so many wonderful people and hearing their stories. I believe we have so much to offer one another, but sometimes we need a little help and some encouragement from the other side. So, tonight, I am here for you. I want you to experience the power that I have. I want you to become free from the regrets of those we have lost. I want you to get better."

"Oh, for fuck sake," Evan muttered. Murph stared over at Evan and punched him in the shoulder.

"Keep it to yourself, please," Murph said.

Miles was wearing a pair of jeans and a navy-blue t-shirt—his attempt to look like the average American, not some multi-hundred millionaire. He paced around the stage and kept a hand to his ear.

331

"I'm getting an image of . . . of . . . of a yellow blanket. Does that mean something to anyone?" A dozen hands shot up. "The blanket looks like it would be for a child." Miles pressed a hand to his head and strained for the next vision. "A girl. It's for a little girl. Or it *was* for a little girl."

Miles scanned the audience and saw that one person continued to have their hand raised. "Ma'am, did you have a yellow blanket growing up?"

"Yes," she said.

"Why don't you come down here?"

The woman next to Murph stood up and began to walk through the aisle with her cane.

"I have a better idea: why don't I come to you?" Miles said. He ran up the stairs and loitered at the tenth row.

The audience cheered for his chivalry.

"Tell me more about the blanket," Miles asked.

"My mother gave it to me before I could remember, but she would tell me how much I used to cling to that as a child. We lived right beside some train tracks in the middle of nowhere Oklahoma and the trains were so loud. They scared me as a kid, so I would hold onto that blanket until they passed by."

"What happened to the blanket?"

"I gave it to my daughter."

"Yes, yes. I am sensing a little girl with . . . light blonde hair pulled back in a ponytail."

"That was her," the woman said, clutching at her chest.

"She is telling me that it's not your fault. There was . . . some sort of . . . accident?"

"My daughter killed herself when she was eighteen." The audience gasped.

"I'm so sorry. So, so sorry," Miles said. "She's telling me her name is . . . B-B—"

"Nora," the woman said.

"Yes. Nora. Thank you. Everything is coming in fuzzy right now. Is there anything you want to ask or tell her?"

"Please ask her why. Please, I need to know."

Miles moved through the aisle and stood right in front of the woman. Evan noticed the perfect hair and teeth. He had the lightest touch of makeup on to hide the imperfections that weren't there. Miles Millie Nare was a product of money.

"I can ask, but I'm not sure she will want to answer. In my experience, they tend to be—"

"Ashamed?" the woman asked.

"Unfortunately."

"Is she . . . is she happy?"

Miles grabbed the woman's hands. "Yes. She is happy and at peace."

"Thank god," the woman said with a shaky voice. "Tell her I miss her every day."

"Nora is shaking her head. I think she knows," Miles said with a warm smile.

"Oh, thank god. Thank god," the woman repeated.

"She is telling me one last thing . . . she is saying Dad is with her and they can't wait to see you someday."

The woman pulled her hands away and covered her face. Murph reached out and gave her a hug.

"Thank you so much, Miles. That means everything to me," the woman said.

Miles gave one last smile and returned to the stage. "I have a great feeling about tonight! We are going to learn so much about each other."

Give me a fucking break, Evan thought to himself.

For the next two hours, Miles continued to perform his miracles and enlightened many people within the crowd. Miles spoke of tractor trailers, the city of Des Moines, a pink elephant named Hippo, and many other items of meaning. Each time, hands shot up across the audience as the confirmation bias set in that Miles *must* be speaking directly to them. The elderly woman next to Murph stayed catatonic for the rest of the evening. Murph was enraptured by the entire event, while Evan fought to stay awake. In between the audacious displays of clairvoyance, Miles promoted his upcoming book and gave several gentle reminders that seasons one through three of his Netflix show, *Miles Above*, were streaming on the platform. He also reminded the audience that they could purchase a multitude of merchandise in the lobby with all the proceeds going to a local charity that didn't exist.

When Miles finally exited the stage to a standing ovation, Murph looked over at Evan and said, "I feel like I am finally able to breathe. What about you?"

"Same. He really knows how to play off an audience."

"What a convincing lie that was," Murph said with an exaggerated eye roll that could have disrupted ocean tides.

"Believe what you want."

"The email said we should go to Section 126 and wait there. Are you ready?"

"Following you."

They watched as the crowd filtered out the venue. Evan and Murph stood near the concessions area of Section 126 for several minutes before a tall woman in taller heels sauntered over.

"Are you the VIPs?"

"Yeah."

"Just you two?"

Murph looked around. "I guess so. Nobody else has come by."

"More time with Miles for each of you then. This way," the woman said. She took them around the perimeter of the venue until they hit backstage. She badged through several doors, which brought them outside. People were gathering up the equipment and stuffing it onto the trucks. Three workers were rolling up a huge sheet that had Miles's face plastered with the tagline "Let's make you _MILES_ better than you were before!"

"Hmmm. I've seen worse," Murph said when she noticed the sheet.

"Okay. Okay. Who wants to go first?" the woman asked.

Evan looked at Murph. "I think she does."

"Great. Follow me. You"—she pointed to Evan—"can hang out here. I'll have someone come by to grab you when Miles is ready."

"Yeah, sure."

Murph was pointed in the direction of a trailer. Ya know, the ones that the famous celebrities have when they are on the set of their next big flop. Murph disappeared from view soon after and Evan was out to fend for himself.

She was gone for a long time. Objectively speaking, it was only twenty minutes, but when you're standing around and looking completely out of place, time ticks a tad slower.

This would be the part of the movie where Evan does something clumsy like tripping over an invisible wire or goes off and ventures into an area he's not supposed to, but nay, this is not that tale. Evan is a boring man and boring men do as their told, so Evan loitered in a five-foot diameter from where the woman left him.

When the door to the trailer swung open, Murph emerged. It wasn't until she got closer that Evan saw her expression of—

"Good luck." An odd choice of words from Murph. She walked right past Evan before he could inquire at all.

Nobody came to escort him so he decided not to be passive for once.

Evan felt the pull of the trailer as he slowly marched toward the door. He didn't believe in this shit, but there was a chance . . .

"Hi," Miles said as Evan stepped inside. "You must be Evan."

"I am. Nice to meet you." They shook hands.

"Can I get you something to drink?"

"No, I'm fine."

"Are you sure? Your friend downed two . . . whiskey sours? I think? I don't know. I generally don't have to make drinks for myself."

"Lucky you."

"So, what made you get the VIP pass?"

"I was expecting to be showered in glam, but I just stood around out there for a half hour so not off to a great start. To answer your question though, I didn't buy the pass, Murph did."

"Murph? I could have sworn her name was Mary," Miles said with his fullest smile.

"No."

"It was a joke. I have to be good with names—it comes with the occupation."

"How does this work?" Evan asked.

"You're not much of a believer in this, are you?"

"No, I'm not."

"Then why are you here?"

"To support Murph and get the VIP treatment I don't seem to be getting."

"I offered you a drink. How much more gracious can I be?" Miles asked.

Evan stared back at Miles.

"Okay," Miles continued. "I'm going to start off by asking you some basic questions. Then, I'm going to call on the spirits and see what they return to me. Does that sound okay with you?"

"Yeah."

"Wonderful. What is your name?"

"Evan Eaton."

"Middle name?"

"Ethan."

"How old are you?"

"Twenty-six."

"Younger than most of my fan base," Miles noted.

"We are the same age, dude."

"Where were you born?"

"Florida."

"Where did you go to college?"

"Why is that relevant?" Evan asked.

"You're right. It isn't. Have you ever lost somebody?"

"Yes."

"I've never had anyone tell me no," Miles pointed out.

"Everybody lost somebody. The best perk about living."

"Who was it?"

"Isn't that your job?"

"Sometimes I need to know what I'm looking for. The spirits aren't always so forward. I need to pluck them out sometimes." Miles made a gesture of picking a grape off a stem.

"I'm sure you'll do just fine."

Miles closed his eyes. "Put out your hands," he asked. Evan did. "Now close your eyes." Evan did.

Miles reached out and grabbed hold of Evan's hands. He shuttered briefly when they touched. "A lot of energy flowing through you . . . Be patient . . . I am seeing . . . a journal. Does that mean anything to you?"

"Maybe."

"It's bright . . . it's red but faded. It's old, worn, used extensively."

"My grandmother's notebook," Evan said.

"Yes. Yes. I am seeing an older woman now. Full of life. She is vibrant. She is pointing down at the journal. It's . . . it's flipped to an earmarked page. I can't make out the wording. It is in beautiful cursive handwriting though. So elegant."

Evan pulled away. "What are you doing?"

Miles opened his eyes and stared at Evan. Miles put a hand to his ear as if he was muffling the sound from an explosion. "What's wrong?"

"I haven't thought about that journal in years."

"This is why you're here. Let's try it again."

Evan put out his hands again and closed his eyes.

"It may take me a minute to find her again. Hold still," Miles said. Evan heard the faintest buzzing from somewhere within the trailer, but he couldn't place it. "Okay, I found her again. She says that you're full of more adventure than she ever was. You just need to act upon it. You're meant to be great . . . and you already are, but there's more for you out there."

"Okay."

Miles pulled a hand away and muffled his ear again.

Evan opened his eyes and caught the movement. "Got a problem?"

"I have terrible hearing."

"Uh huh. Is that why you wear an earpiece?"

"What are you talking about?" Miles asked.

"I noticed it when I walked it. Yeah, it's small, but not unnoticeable. Who is feeding you the information?"

"No one."

"Bullshit. Do you think I'm some fucking idiot? I do my research. I read up on all the techniques people like you use. Maybe there are legitimate people out there, but you certainly aren't one of them. You were hot reading me. You have someone talking in your ear who is giving you information based on the questions I answered earlier. Does that sound about right?"

"I think this session is over."

"Nah, I don't think it is. I am trying to get the VIP treatment after all. It's interesting because you had me for a second with the journal, but it was too . . . perfect. Too convenient. My dead grandmother—who I have never met—magically pops up in the spirit realm at your summoning. I'm not an eighty-year-old with thoughts of regrets and what life after this holds. I'm not some cheap prey."

"Murphy was," Miles cut in.

Evan ignored the jab. "And then I remembered that my younger self used to love posting pictures of that journal on Instagram with lengthy quotes about the powerful things my grandmother wrote. That earmarked page you talked about is the one I always went back to. She described a painting she made that was destroyed in a fire. I wished I could have seen it but reading about it was the only consolation I had—"

"Do you think you're the first?"

"No. No, I doubt that. I'm not an idiot, remember? I imagine you'll smother me with vague threats of lawyers or suffocate me with money. Two things that aren't going to persuade me."

"Then what do you want?"

"For you to answer my questions."

Miles sat back in the chair and tossed the earpiece onto the table. "Why?" he asked.

"Because you're as fucked up as the rest of us and I want to know why. Knowledge is just as powerful as money. So, tell me, what person or object were you going to bring up next?"

"I don't know. Layton was going to tell me what to ask you about next."

"I can tell you something: you would have never found out anything else because I don't flock to social media to spread my grief. You wouldn't have been able to exploit me further."

"I don't exploit people," Miles said.

"You are unhinged if you don't actually think that. Miles, you just told me that Murph was cheap prey. I have read all about you and the egregious pile of money your family sits on. You don't need to be doing any of this. Why are you?"

"I am good at lying and enjoy doing it."

"I don't believe you. I can't imagine having as much money as you do and still feeling the need to slum it with the rest of us. Something happened to you."

"Nothing happened to me," Miles said as convincingly as he could.

"Fine. I was giving you a chance to unburden yourself."

"And why the fuck would I do that with some complete stranger? Get the fuck out of here. I'm done with you," Miles yelled.

"You'll need to eventually. Believe me, everyone does."

Evan stood up and left the trailer without saying anything else.

fifty-eight

CLOSURE

"How'd it go?" Murph asked as she was reunited with Evan.

"I want to hear about how your time went," Evan deflected.

Murph gave a wave and Evan turned back to see Miles standing out in front of the trailer. He stood with the earpiece clutched tight in his left hand.

"I think the parking garage is this way," Evan said and redirected Murph's attention.

"He was cute. I got a total gay vibe off him. What did you think?"

"I didn't notice."

"Shame. Maybe you could have gotten his number and went on his private jet or something."

Murph continued to fantasize about the lavish dates Evan could have had with Miles *assuming* he was gay and even interested in Evan. It was a pipe dream that would never come to fruition.

Evan realigned Murph back to his original ask when they reached her car. "Did you get something out of talking to him?" Evan asked.

Murph dropped her head against the steering wheel and cried. "H-he told me that my father thinks I made the right decision about moving to Denver. I was so scared leaving my family behind so soon after his death, but to know that he forgives me means so much. I feel . . . resolved if that's even the right word to use."

Evan placed a hand on her shoulder. There would never be an appropriate time to tell Murph about Miles's fake behavior.

For Murph, this was the last step. The words of a stranger masquerading as her father was enough to propel her forward. The sleepless nights would start to decrease. The distant stares off into oblivion would stop. Her compulsion to send flowers to her father's grave each week would fade to only a few times a year. Murph could finally start planning the wedding — the total blowout she always dreamed of.

Some people don't forget about those they have lost; they just find out how to keep moving forward without them.

fifty-nine

EVERYBODY HAS A STORY

The remainder of summer passed by like a child riding a bike for the first time—slow and confused, but ultimately with a purpose.

Evan's summer was dominated by dates. He allowed himself to say yes to more than he ever had previously, and the result was . . . not favorable. Each seemed to provide him a unique experience he felt compelled to share, but most never led to a second date.

Murph, Elliot, and Evan were perched up at It and waiting for Franco to drop by with their drinks.

"Evan, I gotta ask: Why aren't you telling us about the dates you have been on?" Elliot said.

"I planned to at some point once I amassed a good enough story to share. Most of the dates have been unique on their own but talking about them together would likely make everything seem more absurd."

"I thrive on absurdity," Murph said. "Let's hear it."

"From the beginning?"

"From the beginning." Elliot and Murph said.

"Okay. I need to consult my phone. I took notes . . . okay, here it is. Starting from the top . . ."

A SERIES OF UNFORTUNATE FIRST DATES: THE EVAN EATON STORY

This tale of woe will be broken out into five sections, not including this wonderful introduction and an ending passage to congregate the findings of these affairs. A word of advisement to all of our readers: do not despair. The experiences of one man does not predicate how life shall unfold for the masses. Allow for this man to soak up the mistakes (of others and his own) in order for you to learn from them. For any questions, please contact your state representative. They are obligated by law to give relationship advice when requested.

DATE I – A MAN IN UNIFORM (TINDER)
Long before the name Arcade Fire was taken by the indie rock band, it was the go-to place in the Denver area for shenanigans such as bowling, stupid arcade games, copious drinking, and the legendary laser tag arena. After many long, failed appeals, Arcade Fire in Denver was forced to change their name to something more obscure, so they landed on G.U.T.T.E.R. Only a select number of individuals have been informed of what the acronym means but considering the bond that's been established thus far, we will share it with you.

G.U.T.T.E.R. stands for Gwen Understood That The Emus Retired.

Now, you likely have many questions. *Who is Gwen? Emus, really? Where did the emus retire to?*

None of these questions can be answered due to the fear of what the truth will cause. We apologize for the convenience of not having to tell you.

To make the lives easier for Denverites and to minimize questions, G.U.T.T.E.R. is now referred to as Rock 'n' Bowl. The massive sign out front was painted over to remove any trace of G.U.T.T.E.R., but the legend continues on.

Evan met Jared Alleghany at Rock 'n' Bowl. Their conversation on Tinder had chugged along at a steady rate for two weeks and since Evan wasn't one to waste time, he suggested and organized the meeting.

"Tell me what it has been like in the military," Evan asked after their first game of bowling. Things had been going well so far. Jared seemed genuinely interested in what Evan had to say and didn't seemed bothered by Evan's complete lack of bowling skill.

"It gave me all those things you'd expect—structure, stability, a desire to be a part of something more. I had a tough upbringing so there were pockets of emotion I needed ironed out and the army will certainly do that."

"I can't remember if you are still active or not."

"I was discharged."

"Oh really? Why?" Evan asked.

"An injury. Fucked up my leg beyond recognition. I didn't walk for months."

"How long has it been?"

"I've been discharged for a year now," Jared said. "Do you want to play another game?"

"Sure."

Jared clicked some buttons and their previous scores blinked off the screen. "You're up."

Evan's first frame was a gutter ball and then a disastrous two pin hit. Off to a fantastic start.

"I'm going to keep asking you questions since my bowling skills are way worse than I remembered."

"Go for it," Jared said as he casually bowled his first strike.

"What are you doing now?"

"A work for a non-profit in a management position. They must have really liked my military background because I wasn't qualified in any other capacity."

"Is that a long-term career for you?"

"Hard to say. I thought the military was going to be my life, but that didn't pan out."

Evan got a spare on his next frame. It would be his only one.

"Were you out in the military?"

"I was," Jared said.

"Oh wow. How was that?"

"Honestly, pretty uneventful. Everyone had jokes, but that's the type of environment it always is. People had other things to worry about than my sexuality."

"Do you think that's the same experience for other people?"

"No, I'd imagine it isn't. I'm a big guy, so I can hold my own. I figure that contributed to people not bothering me about it."

"Did you consider not telling anyone?"

"There was a time where the expectation what that you couldn't tell anyone. I would have needed to suppress that side of me while being active. My partner wouldn't have received healthcare or other benefits like I do. Thankfully, things have changed. Of course, I thought about keeping it a secret, but it felt like a disservice to myself. I knew I was a more complex individual than just being gay, so I felt confident that people could see past it."

Evan looked beyond Jared. Evan never thought highly of the military. It was the reason for all his moves as a kid and the dishevelment in his home life.

"Did you serve overseas?" Evan asked.

They were on frame five and the separation in scores between Evan and Jared was continuing to grow.

"Yeah, I did a couple tours."

"Did you ever kill anyone?"

"That's . . . uh . . . that's not something you should really be asking me."

"Why not?"

"Because I didn't ask you about that scar on your arm," Jared said. "It's not always smart to pry into someone's personal business, especially on a first date."

"Considering that I'm the only one who has asked questions this entire time, I'd actually like for you to pry into my business."

Jared glanced back at Evan before dumping his ball into the gutter. He was two strikes away from a perfect game, but neither seemed to notice.

"Here's a question for you," Jared said. "Do you think we will go on a second date?"

"At this point, no, I doubt it."

"I agree."

"This date has really taken a turn, huh?" Evan said.

"It sure has."

The rest of their night is not worth recapping.

DATE II – VIDEO KILLED THE RADIO PSTAR (HINGE)

When Psycho Sal moved to Denver in September of 1988, he had nothing more than his cheap car and the multi-million-dollar lottery ticket he had cashed out on a week earlier. Psycho Sal always wanted to own a burger bar in downtown Denver (allegedly, his first words were *burger*, *Denver*, and *bar*) and with the expanse of money he won, Psycho Sal did just that. Over the next thirty years, Psycho Sal strong-armed every competitor that attempted to infringe upon his territory. They were swiftly destroyed through means of intimidation, embarrassment, and health code violations. Psycho Sal reigned supreme in the burger bar business. This success brought him more money and the eternal happiness of spending it all on his odd hobby of amassing the world's largest collection of Post-It notes. (It wasn't a difficult record to hold since none of the eight billion people on the planet had any interest in Post-It notes quite like Psycho Sal. In another reality, deemed by CRaC as the "most eccentric collection of specimens created in a wicker basket," the inhabitants bred Post-It notes. The world had a massive celebration when the first magenta Post-It note was born. They named it Yellow. That reality was also color blind.)

The burger bar was called Psycho Psalads, which made complete sense considering salads were not a food option.

It was worth sharing because everyone likes a good origin story and Psycho Sal demanded to be included in this book for publicity purposes.

Moving onto more things you likely don't care about, Evan met Derrick

Susquehanna at Psycho Psalads sometime after the failure at Rock 'n' Bowl. As you might imagine, they ate beer and drank burgers. It was a thrilling time.

"First time here?" Evan asked as they settled into the booth.

"Yeah."

"Do you go on dates often?"

"Yeah."

"Do you normally sit on your phone during dates?"

Derrick looked up. "Yeah. Did I tell you what I do for money?"

"When you say it like that, I'm assuming you're a stripper, which is an honest profession I fully support," Evan said, throwing his hands up in surrender.

Derrick ignored the comment. "I'm a vlogger."

"A vlogger?"

"Are you—do you not know what that is?"

"Apparently not," Evan said.

"A video blogger."

"And you are able to sustain yourself doing that?"

"Yes, I have half a million followers on YouTube, and it is growing by the day. People love to hear what I have to say."

"That's cool."

"A massive understatement. I know in a year I'll be getting sponsorships and attending all the hottest conventions with the other vloggers and influencers."

"How exciting."

"What do you do?" Derrick asked.

"I work in HR."

"Oh my god, that is *so* boring. I would *literally* cut my wrists if I had to do that every day. Like, ew." Derrick shivered at the thought.

"It's a stable career."

"I bet you don't get to talk as much as I do."

"Weird flex, but likely not true," Evan said. "My entire job is contingent on talking to the employees around me."

"Yeah, okay. Where is the waiter? Excuse me, excuse *me*! Yeah, hi. I am ready to order."

Evan tried to telepathically tell the waiter to strap into the rollercoaster they were all about to ride.

"What would you like, psycho?" the waiter asked.

"Psycho? Are you kidding me? Are you actually addressing me like that?"

Derrick said.

"It's our policy, psycho."

"STOP calling me that." Derrick thrusted up his hand to show off his annoyance.

"My apologies. What would you like?" the waiter continued.

"I'd like a Cobb salad."

"We don't sell salads at Psycho Psalads."

"That makes no sense."

"It's our policy. Psycho Psalads prides itself on being the top burger bar in the Denver area." The waiter sounded like he was reading half-heartedly off a teleprompter.

"I don't want a greasy burger. Bring me a salad."

"Psy—sir, we don't have the ingredients to make a salad."

"Then go find me the ingredients. I'll make it myself."

The waiter looked down at Derrick one last time and took two steps back. He pressed the button on the wall, and it let out a long, dull siren. "Everyone. EVERYONE! Listen up. We have our first psycho of the year! Please help me in congratulating this truly unique specimen." Derrick began to clap obnoxiously and the patrons around the restaurant joined in. Evan sank further into his seat to hide from the shame.

A man the size of Andre the Giant shuffled out of the backroom. His thunderous applause triumphed over everyone. He ducked under the light fixtures until he reached the table.

"Is this the psycho?" the man asked.

The waiter nodded with a toothy grin.

"Well, it's nice to meet another psycho. We don't get too many in here since everyone seems to be more domesticated these days. Of course, the mass shooters, political extremists, brain-dead politicians, and just plain dead kids from those awful, awful, awful, awful shootings are totally psycho, but none of them ever wander into my restaurant. I'm Psycho Sal. Nice to meet you."

Psycho Derrick shook his hand.

"Get this psycho whatever he wants," Psycho Sal said.

"I want a salad," Psycho Derrick said.

"Anything but that!" Psycho Sal roared with laughter.

"Do you understand that I am livestreaming this right now? I have thousands of viewers who are watching and commenting on this. They will review bomb this terrible, terrible place."

"Oh, I highly doubt that."

"Wanna bet?"

"I don't bet with psychos. It never goes in my favor and I hate to lose."

"JUST GIVE ME A FUCKING SALAD!"

Psycho Sal turned to the waiter. "Give him one of the triple burgers. What about for you?" he said, pointing to Evan.

"I, uh . . . I'll just have a cheeseburger."

"Fantastic choice. Best option we have outside of the Cobb salad."

"WHAT?" Psycho Derrick yelled. "You just told me—"

Psycho Sal walked away with the waiter and left Evan behind to deal with the fallout.

"So, what's your story besides the whole vlogging thing and just being labeled a psycho?" Evan asked after several minutes of silence.

Psycho Derrick didn't respond and spent the rest of the date staring at his phone.

○ ○ ○

Over the next week, Psycho Derrick released five vlogs onto his channel.

1.) Worst Date EVER???
2.) Am I actually a PSYCHO??!?
3.) I Called Justin Bieber and he ANSWERED!! (NOT CLICKBAIT!)
4.) Guys, I'm NOT actually a Psycho (LONG RANT)
5.) i'm taking a break from youtube :(

Nobody was particularly sad or surprised when Psycho Derrick Susquehanna deleted his YouTube channel and picked up shifts as a waiter at Psycho Psalads.

The eternal audience sighed with relief and Evan moved on to someone new, hoping the next one wouldn't be as fantastical and fictional.

DATE III – PRAY THE GAY AWAY (GRINDR)

The date was August 27, 1982.

It was a humid day across the streets of Rome and Igor Nolodomo found himself lost. Igor spent his entire life navigating the waters of Venice, so this much time on solid ground was beginning to make him sick. He stumbled into a building and sat down to rest. A hole in the nearby wall grabbed his attention. Curiosity coursed through Igor as he began to pick away at the hole. The plaster fell away with ease and Igor soon found a box. Inside of it was an unpublished work from Leonardo da Vinci.

Translated from Italian, the title was *Living Ghosts*. It is believed to be the earliest documented account of the term ghosting. Leonardo da Vinci chronicled his experience with a man (though it is intentionally vague) who sailed off to England and never responded to any of his letters. The heartbreak was profound and proved that humans have always had the propensity to disappoint each other. There are hints within the writing to suggest that da Vinci used several physical traits of this mysterious figure as inspiration for his depiction of Jesus within the Sistine Chapel.

On days where you get sad, try to remember that even a badass like Leonardo da Vinci got ghosted and cast aside for no logical reason.

In a more present time, Evan Eaton was ghosted by Leonard Schuylkill after their first date, which was shocking. They had sat at the coffee shop for hours and discussed a multitude of topics from Evan's thoughts on whether ChapStick was a healthy snack to Leonard's particular distaste toward the caps lock option on a keyboard.

Evan believed he learned a great deal about Leonard during that time, but he failed to recognize that none of it was significant.

Leonard was still struggling with the side effects of being forced to endure conversion therapy for most of his young adult life. His inner voice told him that going on a date with a guy was wrong and that the devil would be awaiting his arrival.

Of course, the church group, his parents, and the councilors didn't refer to it as conversion therapy.

The realignment camp was in the backwoods of the Ozarks. Leonard traveled there on the weekends during all four years of high school. He had no friends. He didn't participate in extracurricular activities. He went straight home each day and completed his homework in silence while his parents shamed him for the impure thoughts.

At the camp, they studied the Bible extensively and sat in rooms with the councilors discussing their feelings. Leonard spoke about how he always had funny thoughts whenever he saw an attractive man and those funny thoughts grew and festered. He told his parents about the funny thoughts because he was scared and didn't always think they were funny. They beat the shit out of him hoping that would do the trick. It didn't work based on Leonard's confession. They tried to pray the gay away. It didn't work. They locked him in the attic as the summer heat tore through their town. It didn't work.

The electroshock therapy didn't work.

The constant threat of going to hell didn't work.

Being strapped down to the bed for entire nights didn't work.

Leonard tried to push away the funny thoughts, but they lingered. The most bizarre thing about the entire situation was that no one else knew what he was going through. He'd spend the weekend in the Ozarks and come back in time for first period on Monday. His nonexistent friends didn't notice any changes and the teachers never questioned his frequent detachment from classroom activities.

He became a ghost.

On a random Sunday back from the Ozarks, his father turned his attention away from the road to yell once more at Leonard for being a faggot. He lost control of the car. They smashed into the guardrail traveling ten miles over the speed limit. Leonard's mother died on impact from decapitation. Her head rolled twenty feet down the ravine and came to rest in some loose shrubbery until a pack of wolves began to pick apart her face. Leonard's father burst through the windshield and broke his back. The blood trickled from his nose as his dead eyes looked skyward to find the sanctuary of heaven he'd never make it to.

Leonard staggered out of the car, collapsed in the road, and stared at the sky. He had a much better chance of making it up there. Leonard fell in and out of consciousness and regained his surroundings two days later in the hospital.

A nurse sat beside him and explained how his parents were dead. Leonard turned away and looked at the IV bag next to the bed.

Drip, drip, drip.

It was steady—somewhat melodic. It mimicked his heartbeat.

There was no sadness or remorse.

He sold the house, went to college, and found himself in Denver. An opportunity for him to slowly move away from his past life.

The funny thoughts amplified since no one told him otherwise except for the voice in his head. Sometimes it was his mother with her high-pitched squeal; other times it was his priest who would say in a flat tone how Leonard was a child of god that deserved to be realigned as he unzipped his pants.

Leonard found relief in the tiny pills he was introduced to by a Grindr hook up. By the time he met Evan, he was an addict. Leonard hid it well, but his mind was fried. He suffered from severe paranoia, hallucinations, and extreme PTSD. Evan would never know any of this.

Leonard ghosted every date he went on once it became clear that they wanted more than a quick hook up and wouldn't be down to help score him drugs.

One day, after Leonard took too many pills, his body started convulsing. He was tired of living and made no attempt to save himself. The police found him three days later with his eyes staring up toward the sky likely wondering what waited for him.

There was no funeral. There was no grief. Leonard Schuylkill was forgotten as quickly as the rest.

DATE IV – FAME, FORTUNE, & FUN (VARIOUS)

After Dawn Delaware gave birth to five girls, her husband Russell consigned to the belief that he would never have a son. He couldn't complain though. Being an only child was a lonely experience he didn't want his family to have, so he had done his job there.

As if the house wasn't full enough already, Dawn told Russell that she was pregnant again.

"Do you think it'll be a boy?" he asked.

"It feels different this time," she said with a smile.

She was right. Julius Delaware was born, and, to Russell, it finally felt like the foundation had settled.

Then Bryce was born.

And with definitive assurance that *this* was the last one, Devon was born.

Their family was complete, but the honeymoon never lasts. Each of Russell's sons came to the realization that they were gay around the same age. When Julius told the family about his sexuality, Russell was supportive because he knew there were two more sons to pass along the legacy. When Bryce sat down the family for a similar conversation, Russell was disheartened. When Devon continued the cycle, Russell cried. There would be no one to pass along the Delaware name. Russell loved his children no matter what, but that twinge of sadness carried with him until the Alzheimer's took away the memories of the family that sat at his bedside.

As the Delaware family got older, the kids began to spread out. Their locations were as scattered as if someone blindfolded was throwing darts at a map. Suzanne ended up in the northeast and became a renowned architect. Katerina settled in Prague with her husband and enjoyed a peaceful life until the bombs dropped. Molly discovered the cash cow of sustainability down in Texas and wasn't heard from too often. Ziggy became stardust. And Jac moved to the pacific northwest where she became Creative Director at a major gaming studio.

The boys weren't as blessed. Each of them wanted something but struggled to achieve it.

Julius wanted fame. Whether it was brief notoriety or extended recognition, he just wanted to feel that adrenaline at becoming something greater.

Bryce wanted fortune. He was tired of seeing the bills stacked up at his parent's house and the notion that they'd never dig themselves out. It was the least he could do since they put up with his bullshit for so many years.

Devon wanted fun. As the youngest of eight, he slipped through the cracks so often that his morality meter was fractured. Devon had no ambitions and was entirely content with living a life of mediocrity. His mom had given up on trying to make him better.

The Delaware boys settled in Denver because this wouldn't be much of a story if they didn't. They determined that while their wants were varied, the means to achieve their goals could be done the same way: manipulate the people around them.

Julius, Bryce, and Devon created separate profiles on every dating app they could find. Each of them stumbled upon Evan.

Bryce was the first to score a date with Evan. They went painting and drank wine. Bryce knew it was a complete bust when Evan suggested that they split the cost because "it was the easiest way to do things." If Bryce had to pay for things now, how was he ever going to amass his fortune? Bryce didn't respond to any of Evan's messages after that night. He discovered that older gentlemen never asked for him to pay as long as he took their dick on the rare occasion they mustered up an erection long enough to fuck. Bryce would pull together his fortune, but the money didn't matter much once he realized that happiness didn't come along with it or the cure for the cancer that ransacked his bones.

Julius coerced Evan next. Their date was benign once Julius asked enough questions to gleam how Evan's living as an HM . . . RH . . . HR person was less exciting than listening to grandpa rant about how America was back in his day. Julius's interest piqued slightly at the mention of Evan's rediscovered love for photography, but the notion that Julius could get famous by extension of Evan's notoriety was foolish. If anything, Julius learned to ask more questions beforehand to snuff out whether his potential date could help his fame. It took him longer than expected to realize that Denver wasn't the bustling center of prominence and that's when he decided to ditch his brothers and move to Los Angeles. Julius tried his hand at acting, being a pretty face on social media, and applying to be Chris Brown's next domestic abuse problem, but none of them panned out. Instead, he gained his stardom as being the first house member voted out of the twenty-seventh season of *Big Brother*. The five mentions on Twitter and twenty Instagram likes were enough to catapult him to internal greatness. His family grew tired of hearing the same story repeated at this holiday gathering, but his excitement was endearing and better than leveling with him that his nanosecond of fame was pathetic.

With the two others out of the way, Devon had his shot with Evan. He put in the least amount of effort, which made sense considering his ultimate goal was NSA fun.

Devon's date with Evan was simple enough. Devon had the most charm out of the three Delaware men, and managed to weasel his way back to Evan's apartment.

"When's the last time you were with someone?" Evan asked.

"I got out of a relationship a month ago and have been taking some time for myself," Devon said. It was a boring lie. Devon didn't believe in monogamy.

Evan nodded and didn't necessarily believe the answer, but the margaritas fogged his brain just enough that he didn't care. Evan hadn't cuddled with someone since . . . Vincent and he desperately needed the attention.

Devon scooted closer on the couch and wrapped his arm around Evan. From an outsider's perspective, it was nauseating to watch how suave Devon thought he looked. Evan continued to fall for it though.

"You are really cute. And an interesting person," Devon said.

"Thanks, so are you."

Devon took a deep inhale. "I'm going to level with you: I just want to get laid. I suffered through the conversation at dinner because I enjoy a challenge, but I don't care to know you. You have a nice ass, but if you aren't down to fuck, I'm gonna head out."

Evan stared over at him. "What?"

"Are you trying to fuck or not?"

"No."

Devon got up from the couch. "That's a real shame. My dick is ten inches long. I would have fucked you real good. Wanna see?"

"Get the fuck out," Evan said.

"Whatever, you bitch. Good luck with your boring ass life."

Devon left the apartment, pulled out his phone, and went looking for the next opportunity.

And with that, the Delaware boys went an astounding 0 for 3 with Evan

351

Eaton, which was the same success rate Donald Trump had with marriage.

DATE V – [CENSORED]
The last date was SO bad, SO shocking, SO disturbing that we can only give you the scantest details from it.

It involved two men: Alec Lehigh and Roger Youghiogheny.

There was an elephant and three rolls of toilet paper.

The phrase *The blights of man are smoother than a ride in a catamaran* was uttered fifty-nine times in the span of an hour.

If you are interested in learning more about this delicious date, please purchase the add-on for this book at the tempting price of $27.

Also, subscribe to the mailing list to be the FIRST to hear about all of the upcoming content.

IN SUMMATION
There are three inevitabilities in this boring reality:

1.) [The first is a big portion of this book so it doesn't need to be rehashed.]
2.) Everyone gets kicked in the pants and has to find a way to recover. It's much easier to do when you have people by your side.
3.) Everybody has a story

The sad part of the last absolute is that sometimes those stories never get shared. You should know this by now though.

Evan heard some stories during his winding trail of dates, but he didn't pay much attention to them. Maybe if he had, he would have avoided the situations he wound up in. Amidst the failures though, Evan kept gravitating back to what Vincent spoke about.

The thing before the thing.

The words continued to rattle around in his head like a rock bouncing down the street. For a while, *the thing* carried about as much meaning as Murph's wild chase of the phrase *Follow it*. In an unknown time and place, it finally clicked.

The thing was in front of him the whole time.

sixty

EMBRACE THE HAPPY

Summer was a distant memory as the vibrant green color of the city burst into sharp shades of reds, oranges, and yellows.

On an uneventful October morning, Evan noticed the change during his typical run through the nearby park. He finished several 5K runs throughout the summer with the intention of bringing down his average mile time to better position himself in a half marathon. Of course, he could keep his current average of seven minutes and twenty seconds, but he reveled at the thought of dipping that number below the seven-minute mark.

After walking home from the park, he finished up his routine before work by letting Izzie out and taking several pictures with the camera and the ridiculously expensive lens that Franco got him. Evan was building up quite the collection of photographs from his random travels around downtown and forays to hiking spots on the fringes of Denver.

Life was good.

Several breakthroughs with Dr. Knox gave Evan a sense of relief with his father and the death of Vincent. If his father was to call today, Evan would answer.

Things with his mom were in a lull state. They talked every few weeks and that was enough for each of them.

Obviously, Evan's dating life was subpar, but he dedicated such a minuscule portion of his time to dating that he wasn't overly concerned. The *thing* would work itself out soon enough.

Work was the same hum-drum routine as usual. Evan would have lost his sanity months ago if Murph wasn't always in his orbit and keeping him upbeat.

On that uneventful October morning, Evan sat at his desk and mimed doing work. He was in the breakroom for his second, uninterrupted cup of coffee when his manager crept in. (Birch was fired a month earlier for "gross negligence" so Evan didn't need to worry about his scattered harassments. It was a win-win for everyone involved, especially you because that plotline wasn't really panning out.)

"Can I see you in my office?" she asked.

"Yeah. Yeah, of course." Evan grabbed his coffee and followed her down the hall.

"Close the door," she said.

Evan did and took a seat on the other side of the desk. "Is everything alright?" It was the first time Evan was directly interacting with his boss in months.

"Just a few things I wanted to review."

Twenty minutes later, Evan emerged from the office and went back to his cubicle clutching the piece of paper under the coffee cup.

"Welcome back, Mr. Sir! The cubicle has missed you," Murph announced. She had been working on a dainty lady accent? Possibly, but it was difficult to tell since she bounced all over the place with it. Evan didn't bother to ask why.

"Happy to be back."

"What do you have there?"

"My coffee cup."

"No, you dunce. The piece of paper."

"It's a piece of paper."

"Don't play me for a fool," Murph said, dropping the accent. "I saw you in our fearless leader's office. I swear if you got fired, I will burn this *fucking* place to the ground."

"Murph, I didn't get fired."

"Good because I don't really believe in arson."

"I got promoted."

Murph broke into a theatric display of wild arm movements and convulsions of her entire body. After she calmed down, she said, "We need to celebrate! Dinner, drinks . . . hookers . . . a trip to Mars. We are going to do it all!"

"It's really not a big deal."

"Of course it is! Now, you have to stay here for the rest of your career. That's the unwritten rule when you get promoted within a year."

"No, it isn't," he said with a laugh.

"Just wait. You're still gonna be sitting next to my annoying ass three years from now and I'll remind you of this conversation."

"I'll hold you to that. And, really, it isn't a big deal," Evan repeated.

"Evan, if we don't celebrate achievements like this, what's the point in living? Embrace the happy moments."

So he did.

Evan had trouble deciphering why he was promoted, which was the same conundrum Vincent had way back in another lifetime. Evan didn't dwell on it though.

That night, the four of them went out and celebrated Evan's happy moment. They toasted in his name and Murph told the table about how lucky they were to have Evan in their lives for the past year. Franco and Elliot agreed. Murph hoped that their circumstances would never change.

They would. Circumstances always changed.

But right then, life was good.

sixty-one

FEAR OF THE UNKNOWN

Besides the conversations with Dr. Knox, Evan hadn't thought much about Vincent since the end of June. There were brief moments where his face would flash through Evan's mind, but it was getting fuzzier each time.

It was okay though. Evan had lived six grueling months with the regret of Vincent's death hanging over him. Evan deserved the peace of moving on.

That stupid fucking letter though. The curiosity around what Vincent had written to him occasionally grazed through Evan's mind whenever his fuzzy face showed up.

The means to retrieve the letter was one floor away, but he was afraid that a dark truth was hiding in there. Even worse, Evan could have questions about it and there was no one left in the universe who would have the answers.

Vincent's words had to be left behind. It was the only outcome that made sense.

Evan continued to stick by that belief for years, but circumstances would change.

sixty-two

READING MATERIAL

Evan was reading *The Devil in the White City* when his phone pinged once on the couch. He opened up the automated text message and read that he had a package downstairs.

It was probably one of his endless orders from Amazon, so he ignored it until he let Izzie out several hours later. He was halfway into the elevator to head back up when he remembered the package and scurried out before the doors closed.

The complex had fancy storage containers for all the packages that were delivered. Evan inputted the six-digit code from the text message and a locker across the room opened with a satisfying *pop*.

Evan grabbed the mid-sized box from inside and flipped it over several times. The Amazon arrow was missing from the package. Whatever was in there tumbled back and forth each time he turned it over.

The elevator was zipping past the fifth floor when Evan noticed the return address in the top corner. His heart sank. He couldn't imagine what was in there and a large part of him didn't want to find out.

Once he was in the apartment, Evan tore into the package. The only alternative was to throw it off the balcony and that seemed extreme.

The tape and cardboard pulled away with ease. Evan looked inside the box and found a note. Of course there was a note.

He opened it.

Evan,
 I hope I can go two-for-two and that this package makes it to you. I could have called, but I don't know what I'd say. Somehow, it's easier to take the time to write these notes rather than speak to you directly.
 So much time has passed, and I imagine you have moved on with your life, so I apologize for the randomness of this. I hope it doesn't stir up any negative emotions.
 I'll jump right into it: Vinny wrote two books and I believe the second one is about you. He is honest about what happened during your time together and the thoughts that cropped up throughout.
 Like the letter, it won't be an easy read. The truth never is. Vinny struggled immensely with finding peace in himself. I try not to think too deeply about the content of the books and, instead, look at the holistic

accomplishment. Sometimes I wonder if he would have made a career out of it and wrote about a topic less personal.

I want to share the books with Vinny's dad and other family members, but I'm worried no one else will understand quite like you and me. I don't want anyone else to remember him differently than the loving individual he was.

I wish I had been better for him. I wish I understood him more and knew the questions to ask.

This is likely the last time you'll hear from me. I have a suspicion that my life is going to get chaotic and I'm not sure where it will take me. Anyways, keeping up a one-way correspondence with someone I only met twice feels strange. I don't want to keep dragging you into the past. You are too young to be bogged down by grief.

Inside the package are the two books in an unaltered state from how I found them on Vinny's laptop. You'll read repeatedly how he stressed that no one would (or should) ever read the books. Don't be fooled. It was just a ploy to mask his own insecurities about the writing. He *wanted* someone to find the books. He *wanted* someone to read them and understand his story. He *wanted* to get better.

With more time, I know he would have.

With love,
Ann Besser

Evan folded up the note and placed it on the table. He'd reread it a dozen times. He always felt a connection to Ann as if they were two passengers on a sinking ship. They went through something together that everyone had witnessed but few completely understood.

Beneath the thick layer of bubble wrap, Evan found the two books. They were laid out neatly like clothes set aside for a child's first day of school. He ran his hand across them before picking up each one. They had heft. Evan never realized Vincent had that much to say (which seemed like an odd juxtaposition to the incessant ramblings he could lapse into).

Evan had no intention of reading them, but he didn't feel an urge to rip them up or give them to Izzie for a nice Sunday dinner. Instead, Evan placed them on the same shelf the letter resided on during its stay and next to *Infinite Scroll*—the best book he ever read. Potentially altering how he viewed Vincent was not something Evan was quite ready to do.

He needed to leave the apartment before the thoughts overwhelmed him. Evan checked Grindr and saw the location. It was as he suspected.

After grabbing a jacket and several other items, Evan left. Once again leaving another piece of Vincent behind.

sixty-three

BE HONEST

He wanted to get better. He wanted to get better.

The phrase kept repeating on an infinite loop. What did Ann mean by that? Evan tried to push it away during his walk, but it lingered. Everything about Vincent seemed to linger for longer than it needed to.

If Evan hadn't been there a thousand times before, he would have assumed that the bar was closed. Franco always insisted on being conservative with the lighting as if that was the big money pit. The gang stressed to Franco multiple times that he had to light up the building like a Christmas tree to attract the customers. Like moths to a flame. Franco didn't seem to take their advice.

Evan stepped inside It and went over to the bar. Seated at the far end was the only other patron. It was a younger guy who was intensely typing away on a laptop. Maybe he was writing America's next great novel or maybe he was trying to get better; it seemed like the hip thing to do these days.

"Hey Evan. Just you tonight?" Denver walked over and asked. Ever since Franco pointed out that there was indeed another bartender, it seemed like Denver was there whenever the dim lights were on.

"Just me. Needed to get out of the apartment for an hour. Is Franco around?"

Denver seemed somewhat hurt by the question. "Yeah, he is in the back."

"Thanks." Evan moved through the door marked PRIVATE. Murph, Elliot, and Evan had been to the bar so frequently that they considered themselves part owners, so Franco didn't mind them intruding into the underbelly.

Evan found Franco hunched over a desk and scribbling out some numbers. The room was the size of a broom closet and may have been one before the building was transformed into a bar. The walls were empty with the exception of two small pictures that were tacked up behind Franco's chair. Stacks of paper cluttered his desk, which was unusual considering how orderly Franco kept the bar.

"Hey," Evan said.

Franco looked up. "Hey Evan. I'd say it's a surprise to see you, but you're here often enough that I just expect it at this point. How'd you know I was here?"

"Grindr."

"Huh?"

"Whenever you are at work and using Grindr, you're always 4,072 feet away from Skyhouse so I checked earlier and saw that you were here."

"I'm flattered and slightly concerned," he said with a smile.

"Do you have a minute?"

"I always have time for idle chit chat. What's up?" Franco asked, tossing aside the pen.

"It's been a few months since my birthday—"

"Yeah."

"And I wanted to give you an update on the gift you got me."

"An update?"

"Probably more like an evaluation of my progress."

"Evan, what are you getting at?" Franco laughed.

Evan set down the scrapbook on the desk and pushed it over to Franco. "This is something I have been working on."

Franco opened the scrapbook and flipped through the pages. "Did you take all of these?"

"Yeah."

"This is amazing. They feel so genuine."

Most of them were. Evan lurked around the city capturing moments of solitude or quiet beauty. Something was lost in a photo when the smiles were forced, and the poses were critiqued until perfection.

"There's a lot of blank pages here," Franco noted.

"It's going to be a work in progress for a long time. I took enough photos to fill up three scrapbooks, but I was being picky about the ones I wanted to include."

"Why are you showing me this? You know I wouldn't be able to *evaluate your progress* as you so elegantly put it. I have no artistic ability."

"Because I want you to have it. When it's done someday."

"That's sweet of you to offer, but I think I'm missing the point," Franco said.

"You're not missing anything. I think I have been oblivious. This year has been challenging and I have been running from . . . everything. I'm getting tired of it—"

"Is everything okay?"

"Yeah, yeah. It will be."

"Okay. Good." Franco flipped back through the pages.

Evan knew what he wanted to say next and decided to be like the Nike slogan and just fucking do it.

"Franco, I've liked you for a while. Circumstance has kept me from accepting that. I hated the notion that the first gay guy I met in Denver would be the one I fell for. So I left you at a distance. I waited for your flaws to emerge, so I could prove to myself that you weren't worth it. I haven't gotten it right enough times that I have been afraid of falling into the same spiral again. But you've been great for the year I've known you and the night we went to the gay bars was our first date whether we wanted to admit it or not. Would you want to go on a proper second date sometime?" Evan asked with a shrug.

Without hesitation, Franco said, "I don't know."

"Hmm. I didn't prepare myself for that answer. Maybe I misread the situation," Evan said with a nervous laugh.

"You didn't. There are so many things to admire about you and, quite frankly, I've probably told all of them to Murph when I should have been telling you. This year has been an adventure for me as well. Opening up the bar has been challenging and not successful."

"Murph told me yesterday. I'm sorry."

"Yeah, well, I am just going to fall snuggly into that statistic of a failed business owner. I guess I'd still be qualified to become president, which is comforting. I told myself going into it that there was a high likelihood that this would fail, but it hurts to face that. I'm convinced that you, Murph, and Elliot kept It open for two more months than it should have been.

"I guess I don't want to drag you through whatever happens next because I'm not sure what anything looks like moving forward."

"Franco, for once, I'm ready to step into the unknown."

"Really?"

"Yeah."

"I have a proposal, but it isn't fancy. There is a fully stocked bar right outside that door which will soon be gone. How about we diminish that supply a bit and talk? Maybe our third date will be more exciting."

"I'd like that," Evan said.

Hours later, when Denver rang the bell for last call, Franco looked at Evan and asked the first question that came to mind.

"What now?"

interlude

3-1

ALLEN'S LETTER

Allen,
When I first decided to write my batch of letters, I knew the exercise would be cathartic and a vanity project. I'd be able to type out my thoughts to any person I chose without the fear of them ever reading it. I was satisfied with the idea. It was flawless.

Until I remembered you.

See, you were the one that started a fair amount of my downward spiral or at least made me recognize I was in one. You were the catalyst for me to discover that maybe writing wasn't a complete waste of my time. You were the person that made me realize that my entire life down in Dallas was a total fucking scam and I was holding all the counterfeit bills with no one else to blame but myself. You were the villain.

To a certain degree, you still are.

Listen:

It's not entirely your fault since the bad chemicals have always outweighed the good ones in my head, but I think about you quite constantly. Not in a creepy, I-have-three-shrines-dedicated-to-you type of way, more so about how you're doing. It's a simple question that we get asked frequently. I imagined asking you this a thousand times except your response wouldn't be the canned answer we always receive about how everything is fine or going well. No, you would tell me the truth. You'd tell me that you were fucked up, that you made mistakes that are still rattling around inside of you. Something about guilt or whatever you'd like to call it. You'd profess an elaborate apology and I'd be beaming from ear to ear with the smug satisfaction that I finally heard you tell the truth.

See, I'd be the hero and you'd be the dastardly villain I would conquer. Of course, I'd forgive you and we would yada, yada, yada . . .

It's all bullshit and I'm a pathetic bastard for creating a false reality (even though I started to get really good at it sometimes in my books).

For a while, I told myself you didn't deserve to have a letter written to you as if I was some dignitary whose words actually carried significance. You wouldn't have ever lost a wink of sleep regardless of my choice, so once I realized that factoid I resigned to my fate and decided you should be included in the "stack" of letters. (I put that in quotes because all of my writing is done on my laptop. I'd never take the time to write out everything on paper. My hand would have cramped by the second sentence and no one is worth that kind of trouble.)

With Step One complete, I engaged the next phase, which was to decide on the contents of the letter.

I had this grand vision of putting **FUCK YOU AND KISS MY BALLS** as the only words in the letter, but that felt a tad petty even though writing that just now made my butthole tickle with excitement.

So, here we are.

Where do we go now? What do I actually write to you?

There are moments when I'm lying awake in bed and all the thoughts I've ever had come rushing in and one idea continually stands out: what if people are able to see the stats of their life? It would be an app to download on your phone that would sit amongst the ninety-nine cent games, the manufactured sadness of social media and the 24-hour news cycle, and all the other useless apps we don't bother to use. We'd get super useful information like the total number of steps walked or the amount of times you were in the proximity of your own death or how good of a person you are based on this elaborate algorithm some supercomputer in Switzerland figured out. We'd also get super useless facts like the biggest dump you've ever taken or how many times you didn't wash your hands after using the bathroom or how many white lies you've told or the number of times you stepped on a crack and broke your mother's back or how many times you smoked actual crack. Honestly though, if you told me you smoked crack during the time we talked, things would make much more sense and I would have had an easier time forgiving you for your silly behavior. Anyways, the one stat that I'd be most interested in is reading about the number of people I've liked compared to the number that have liked me. You see where I'm going with this, right? Buckle up bitch.

Listen:

I'd want to see what the overlap was and dig into the details. I'd want to expand the simple number and read the names of each person. It is extremely vain of me, but I like to believe there is at least one person out there who thought I was gorgeous without my knowledge. The funny thing is that I know you wouldn't be on the list.

I adored you. It's slightly unexplainable as to why, but I did. You did a convincing job when you told me all about how I intimidated you and blah, blah, blah.

You were good. Pretty, pretty good.

The charade is up though.

I'm over you. I'd rather decay into nothing then continue to worry about the health and well-being of someone like you.

And guess what? That's exactly what is going to happen to me!

I'd never wish harm on you even though I probably should seeing how petty and outrageous this whole letter as been. But I shall not!

Instead, I'll ask you one last question:

How are you doing?

For a while I would have listened intently to your answer, but now, I don't fucking care.

I tried to leave you behind at the end of the first book. I failed. I told myself (and my imaginary readers) that you were lifted to the void by the end of book two. I lied.

But here, right now, I leave behind the life of Allen Emery to forever be confined to the crappiness of this letter.

You deserve nothing more.

And most of all, you never deserved me.

Good riddance,
Vincent

3-2

THE FORGOTTEN
(Some times)

The cabin was dilapidated to a certain extent. There was a minimal amount of hot water and the lights seemed to flicker incessantly, but it would be a place for them to sleep.

For the time being, they were outside, gathered around a campfire and bundled under blankets. It was unreasonably chilly for that particular October night in Asheville. They all refused to go back inside though. It was their one opportunity to see the stars, to unwind from the pressures that awaited them back in the city.

Allen leaned back in his chair and tilted his head skyward. He didn't know how to find a single constellation up there, but he enjoyed the view regardless. The stars seemed endless. He didn't realize how they were all dead.

"Michelle?"

"Yeah," she called out from the other side of the fire.

"I like Cameron. I've been thinking about it for a while and can't understand why we have never tried being more than friends. I think it is worth pursuing. He is—"

"Yeah, yeah. It's been obvious for a while, and I know he feels the same way."

This dull conversation continued on for a while as Allen unfolded himself to his best friend. She eventually asked about Vincent (referred to him as "that guy in Austin? No, Dallas?"). Allen looked up at the dead sky briefly again for inspiration and gave Michelle a canned answer about how he never really liked him in the first place and was someone to pass the time with.

Every word was true.

They quickly changed the subject when Cameron returned from the cabin with several dogs trotting alongside him.

"What did I miss?" he asked as he took a seat next to Allen.

"Just talking about how Allen thinks you two should go on a date," Michelle said casually.

"Oh fuc—" Allen started.

"I'd like that," Cameron said.

Reflex told him to do it, so Allen reached into his pocket and looked at his phone. Several messages from Vincent were on the screen. He opened them and skimmed through the increasing panic. It was pathetic. Vincent couldn't find friends or a boyfriend in his own city, so he traveled and got attached to strangers. At first, Allen didn't mind it. Vincent was someone to pass the time with through texts and the occasional FaceTime, but Allen could still go out and have his fun since Vincent lived so far away. It became painfully obvious that Vincent caught feelings in the slew of drunken texts he sent when he was back home for that wedding. When Allen read the text that said how Vincent loved him, he wanted to delete his number right there, but he couldn't bring himself to do it.

That was then though. Well, only a month ago.

Now, Allen was reformed. Allen was enamored with the short, stubby man that sat beside them. Their years of friendship meant they already had a jumpstart to a relationship if that's what happened after a few dates. He was excited. He believed everything would go right for him.

With his elated mindset, he decided that Vincent was excess.

He navigated to his contact information and blocked his number right there.

With his phone returned to his pocket, Allen gazed up one last time and was finally satisfied about who he was sharing death with.

○ ○ ○

Two months later, Allen watched as Vincent's rental pulled out from in front of his apartment and made a sharp left toward the exit.

"What the fuck just happened?" he wondered aloud.

He had been in his room talking with Cameron and in all of his glorious stupidity, he spilled water on his shirt. As he came out to get some paper towels, he saw that Vincent was nearly out the door with his luggage. None of it made sense and Vincent's non-answers to his questions made the whole thing even more confusing.

Allen thought he had done a masterful job of dodging Vincent's questions from earlier in the day. He knew when he agreed to let Vincent stay the night that he would be hit with a cataclysmic barrage of questions Vincent had been compiling since the Asheville event.

Listen:

Allen felt sorry for Vincent. That was the only reason he allowed him to stay. The dreadful texts he sent where it was clear he wanted to profess his eternal love for him were enough to make Allen cringe. In his mind, this was the final obligation he owed Vincent.

And his stunt of leaving in the middle of the night made it a whole lot easier for Allen to never talk to him again.

Of course, he broke that rule once, months later, when he texted Vincent some random question about how Southwest operated, but to Allen it meant nothing. As we know, for Vincent, that shit fucked him up sideways.

So, we return to Allen standing outside and watching the last remnants of the car pull away. He shrugged his shoulders, returned inside, and called Cameron back to fill him in on the weird crap that just went down.

○ ○ ○

Allen never found out that Vincent died. Considering how connected the world is, it seemed strange to believe that someone known to you could die and that you wouldn't have any idea, but Allen and Vincent were no longer connected. They had no mutual friends. They did not have each other on social media. And maybe the most important fact: Vincent was only one person in billions, which meant he wasn't very important at all. Vincent was a secondary character in Allen's life. That is being too generous. Vincent was a background actor, a nobody, a dot.

Cameron and Allen didn't last. There was a fundamental difference in how they operated, and Cameron seemed to have an inherit jealousy toward Allen's success. Allen ascended the Nashville social ladder quickly and became a sought-after employee. Complexes in the downtown area were constantly wanting him for new management positions. He'd learn to never settle on the first choice because there tended to be something better (with more money!) out there.

At some point, he went and got his real estate license which is how he met his future husband. We don't really care about any of those details except for the high level, so here it is: Allen finally found an equal, someone who laughed at his sarcasm, and understood his passion for work.

The wedding was nice.

At some point, they bought a house and turned it into paradise. From the outside, they seemed perfect. From the inside, they were perfect. Their jobs were great, their love was fierce, and their worries were minimal.

At some point, they decided to adopt.

At some point, they had a new house with three kids.

At some point, Allen realized it wasn't enough. It never would be. The bad chemicals in his head laid dormant for long enough. They burst through and took over.

At some point, Allen walked up to his son's room and sat on the edge of the bed. He looked out the window and up to the cloudless sky. Death was there, but it was hiding for it was only the middle of the day. He thought back to a simpler time, possibly even a happier time, but he couldn't remember when that was anymore. Without much hesitation, he placed the end of the gun snuggly against his temple and blew his fucking brains out. They smeared the walls and covered the toys. His body made a mild thud as it collapsed onto the floor and emptied more contents onto the carpet. The first police officer on the scene quipped about how the blood seemed to match well with the curtains, but not as much with the carpet.

Listen:

Allen had everything he could have wanted, but it wasn't enough. There was an itch that he couldn't reach. No one saw it. No one recognized it. He hid it extremely well and, in the end, he never found a way to overcome it.

To a certain extent, he wasn't even sure what it was that he needed, which is what scared him the most.

People cried at the funeral because they were sad. Kind words were said. They wondered what they could have done differently. They agonized over not seeing the signs as if Allen was supposed to erect a billboard to let everyone know.

What they never understood is that Allen didn't want to be saved. Allen wanted to die and to not accept that truth was more harmful than not ever seeing the nonexistent signs.

Allen lived thirteen more years than Vincent and would be forgotten like all the rest.

PART IV

EVERYTHING NOW

three years later

sixty-four

THE NEXT STAGE

Rigby was asleep at the foot of the bed. The curtains were pulled tight to avoid any sunlight from creeping in and starting the day any earlier than it needed to. The alarm that used to wake them up at that ungodly hour was no longer on the nightstand.

As soon as the stirring happened, Rigby perked up along with the two other dogs. Jim pushed himself up and quickly reassembled the bed. The Jim from a few years ago wouldn't have done such a thing. Not out of malice, but knowledge that someone else would. If he didn't do it now, he wouldn't bother with it for the rest of the day. He staggered over to the bathroom and parted through the vicious mob of dogs that demanded his attention. They sat patiently at the door and waited for Jim to run through his brief routine. He emerged and moved downstairs where his bones cracked and creaked more than the floor beneath him.

"Couldn't sleep again?" he asked as he walked into the kitchen.

"No."

"I'm surprised the dogs stayed upstairs with me. That never happens."

"Yeah."

The Christmas tree lights were still on and the one strand continued its annual trend of blinking at a haphazard rate.

"Can I get you anything?"

"No."

Jim didn't pursue anymore conversation and moved to make himself coffee. He opened up three empty cabinets before realizing all the mugs must have moved into one of the boxes. The dining room was stacked with cardboard boxes of various sizes labeled with things like DISHES, SILVERWARE, and MISCELLANEOUS.

It turned out that working your entire life and carrying medical insurance didn't mean shit when the bills started pouring in for cancer treatment. At least they were able to stay there through New Year's.

"What do you have planned today?" Jim asked.

"I need to do some more wrapping and continue packing up the house, but my mom has a doctor's appointment today," Ann said with intense weariness. She sat up on the couch with the beanie falling further down her head. She was a loose version of what she used to be.

"I can take care of the wrapping."

"Thanks," she said.

The air was stale between them. The last four years had been the hardest of their lives.

○ ○ ○

Ann picked up Doris from the retirement community. She was already waiting outside and leaning against the walker that essentially became an extension of her body. Doris was bundled up in a large variety of coats.

"Mom, why are you waiting outside? It's freezing," Ann said.

"I hate being cooped up in that place for too long!"

Doris slowly wheeled over to the trunk where she passed off the walker for Ann to stuff into the car. It was a bulky object but fit in with plenty of room to spare.

"How are you feeling?" Ann asked when they were both in the car.

"Oh, I'm fine. I'm more concerned about how you're doing."

"I'm okay. Just wondering when we are finally going to catch a break."

"You'll get past it. Try and enjoy the upcoming holiday."

"How is Walter doing?" Ann asked.

Doris rolled her eyes. "He is good. Feeling his age like the rest of us and continuing to annoy everyone with his terrible jokes."

Ann went down a list and asked about several more people. The majority were her own siblings, which she hadn't heard from during the duration of her cancer treatment. She didn't need their support anyways and only asked her mom about them out of courtesy.

They drove across town to Dr. Vonegat's office. He seemed to be as old as Ann's mom, but still continued to operate his practice.

Ann occupied herself with a germy magazine in the waiting room until a nurse came out asking for Doris. Ann followed them back.

The nurse went through a series of questions that Ann didn't pay much attention to. She stared out the window at the white landscape that opened up beyond.

It took another ten minutes before Dr. Vonegat came into the room.

"Hi Doris and . . . Ann. My goodness, how are you?"

"I'm good."

"Are you cancer free?" he asked.

"The doctors like to call it complete remission."

"You look good," he said.

It was kind of him to say, but the cancer wasn't kind to her as anyone would have expected. Besides the weight loss and the hair that was taking its sweet ole' time to grow back, she looked the same as before except the eternal tired look that commandeered her body. Her limbs hung loose as if her muscles were permanently erased; the divots under her eyes sometimes sunk deeper than a capsized ship; the scars were so faint, but she saw all the times she was prodded for blood. Ann was her worst critic and failed to give herself a pass on what she'd gone through. Ann would wear the beanie everywhere until her hair became long enough to do something with. Internally, the doctors had radiated her lungs with so much chemotherapy that walking up a flight of stairs sometimes proved difficult. During the darkest days of her battle, she wanted it to be over. The pain, the vomiting, the constant fatigue. Combined with the lingering grief, it bogged her down to an incredibly low level. Ann accepted her fate and understood that the cancer was punishment for ravishing her body as long as she did. The 27% chance of survival seemed more minimal than that when she—

There was a reason why we skipped ahead three years. Ann didn't want to remember every detail.

She woke up every day knowing she shouldn't have survived. So many others didn't with stage 3 lung cancer. Why was she special?

An answer she'd never get.

"Thank you. I'm very lucky," Ann said.

"You are. Enjoy your second chance with life. Do everything while you still can." Dr. Vonegat turned his attention to Doris. "What brings you in today?"

"Coming in for a check-up."

"Anything in particular you have going on?"

"Well . . ." Doris rattled off a list of problems she seemed to be having. None of them sounded significant to Ann, but when you combined them all, she could understand the concern her mother had.

Dr. Vonegat listened and nodded as Doris moved through her list. When she was finished, he said, "Doris, listen. You are ninety. You have lived a blessed life and continue to find herself in a healthy state for your age. Be thankful for that. But you are on the downward trend of your life. These issues will continue to stack up. While it's important for you to share with me and others these problems, please consider not stressing about them. Enjoy the time you have left."

There were bright parts over the past three years and Ann's mom continuing to stay in good health was one of them. That loss would have been devastating, but with each passing year, it is becoming more inevitable. A thought for another time . . .

"I understand," Doris said. She would continue to worry no matter what Dr. Vonegat said.

He ran through his routine of checking her heart and lungs and tapping against different joints.

"You are in great shape," he determined. "I don't need to see you for another six months unless something comes up."

"Great," Ann said.

"Good seeing you both," Dr. Vonegat said and left the room.

Once they were back in the car, Doris asked if Ann was ready for Christmas.

"Yeah. Most of the shopping is done."

"Are you still planning on going down there?"

"Just for a few days. I leave the day after tomorrow."

"By yourself?"

"Jim doesn't like to fly."

"Are you even allowed to fly?"

"Yes," Ann said. Some things didn't change. Her own mother hounded her with questions just like Ann would do with Vincent and Leigh.

"Please be careful."

"Of course."

"Can you put on some Christmas music? This song is too depressing for the holiday season," Doris said dismissively.

Doris didn't like Red's cover of "Like a River Runs" but it seemed like everyone else did. It had been skirting near the top of the charts for weeks. Sometimes people connected over sadness and loss, even the manufactured variety.

Ann switched the station and they basked in the upbeat glow of Christmas music all the way back to the retirement community.

<u>sixty-five</u>

LUV WHAT YOU DO

Evan's drive to work was either twenty minutes or twenty-four minutes depending on the traffic. The times where the traffic was light and he slipped in around that twenty-minute mark were bound to be good days where he found solid leads on LinkedIn and all the desirable candidates accepted their offers without too much prodding. The twenty-four-minute commute days were rare and not ones he liked to think about.

Evan maneuvered through the familiar parking lot and found a spot in the third row. He hurried from his car to the door. It was chilly outside and after a long summer of dreadful heat, it was enough to make you shiver.

He walked down the hallway lined with the merchandise and photos recognizing the achievements of former employees. Sometimes he took for granted the celebrated history of the company he worked for.

Evan continued on until he came to the overhead sign that said PEOPLE. He made a sharp left and entered into an area with rows of cubicles. He walked to the fourth row and noticed the balloons drifting lazily above his desk. He should have known they were going to do something; they had been hinting at it all week.

As he moved closer, Evan saw his desk was covered in balloons, streamers, and signs like the one below:

> **HAPPY 1ST ANNIVERSARY EVAN!!**

Evan quietly sunk into his cubicle and attempted to hide from any of the impending celebrations. He hated the attention, but respected that his co-workers remembered. It's just what they did at Southwest Airlines.

"Happy One Year Evan! It goes by so quick!"

"One year closer to being fully vested!"

"We need to go out and celebrate!"

The kind words flowed in a steady stream throughout the day. He didn't get much work done, but no one seemed to mind.

Around noon, he got a Slack message asking if he was ready. Evan had forgotten about the lunch plans that were set up weeks earlier. He responded back saying he could pick them up across the street in ten minutes.

Evan returned to the chilly parking lot and heard a plane land at Love Field. Vincent had talked about what it felt like being so close to the airport and how it never got old seeing them land. Evan couldn't have agreed more.

Evan pulled up in front of the technology building across the street and watched three bundled up forms shuffle out. Athena, Jag, and Lan hopped into the Jeep.

"Happy One Year!" they each said.

After Evan started at Southwest Airlines, he quickly linked back up with Athena and Jag. It took time for Evan to develop a friendship without the help of Vincent. He had been the glue for any Southwest employees Evan met while they were dating, but he managed to figure it out. Now, Athena and Jag were his closest friends in the city. They had been engaged for the past year and were furiously planning the wedding. Mainly it was Athena planning and Jag just cautioning to keep the costs somewhat low. Ann would never know, but their continued relationship was another one of the good, unexpected things that happened over the past three years.

They decided on a local Tex-Mex place that Evan enjoyed. The conversation in the car dove into technology topics he wasn't familiar with, but he listened intently as they talked about the challenges of the cloud.

At the restaurant, Jag was the first to bring up whether it was appropriate to get a round of margaritas.

"Not at all," Evan said, "but I'd consider it if there weren't twenty other Southwest employees at the restaurant."

"Fine," Jag said with a hint of defeat.

"We can drink this weekend," Athena suggested.

"It's just not the same. There is something about drinking when you be working that feels—"

"Rebellious?"

"No."

"Flowery?"

"No."

"Spicy?"

"No."

"Then what?" Evan asked.

"It feels cool," Jag said with a shrug.

"Anyways," Evan said, "Lan, you are celebrating your anniversary soon, right? We will have to do this again."

"I am! Two years already. It's crazy. I never thought I'd be back in Dallas, but the Southwest boomerang effect is a real thing. Instead of a lunch, we need to recreate the magic of New Orleans," Lan said, pointing at Jag.

(After the failed presidential campaign from Jeff Bezos, the drawn-out labor disputes, and the shocking court decision that Amazon had become a monopoly, Lan recognized Amazon was not the company to be at anymore. The grind that she so desired after leaving Southwest was achieved in her 70-hour work weeks, but she found that management position still elusive. Instead of having lots of money and no happiness, she decided to come back to the place where she'd have a moderate amount of money matched nicely with a good slice of happiness and friends she desperately missed.)

"That trip was so much fun. We need to get more beignets from Café du Monde," Jag said.

Evan knew about the fabled trip since it was brought up casually all the time. Sometimes when conversation strayed into territory that involved Vincent, the group would get quiet as if they wanted to observe a moment of silence for Evan's loss like he was some grieving widow not just an ex-boyfriend. Everybody lost Vincent though. But that was years ago, and almost everyone had moved on, especially Evan.

"Let's go sometime," Evan suggested. "I have never been to New Orleans."

"Me either," Athena said.

"Perfect. Add it to the list of places we need to go to in 2023," Lan said.

The waitress came over and dropped off their orders. Evan and Lan got enchiladas. Athena got quesadillas and went to work on mixing all the sauces to create a new concoction. Jag ordered flautas and Evan tried to determine what the difference was between them and taquitos.

Their conversation became more sporadic as everyone focused on the meal. It gave Evan time to think.

How did he get here?

It was simple. Vincent had always indoctrinated him with the idea that Southwest would be a better fit for his talents than the manufacturing plant he was at during his first tour through Dallas. Evan fought the idea. The Southwest culture was too loose, too friendly. Did they actually get any work done? After the promotion at his Denver job, things seemed to change. The laid-back mindset became more regimented as new leadership came in and was hellbent on profit and taking the company public. Evan ignored the changes until they trudged over to HR and demanded that higher quality candidates be brought into the company as if people were advertising on LinkedIn that their dream job was to work at a marijuana joint.

He began the same cycle that caused him to leave Dallas and Michigan and South Carolina. Evan scoured for jobs with a proclivity toward Southwest.

This would be it though. No more moves. No more running. The next chapter of his life was in Dallas, Texas.

"Whenever you are ready," the waitress said as she dropped off the check. Athena, Jag, and Lan each grabbed for it.

"I got this one."

"No, no. You paid last time."

"Who cares? Are you keeping a balance sheet or something?"

"Just let me do it. Please," Lan pleaded. Athena and Jag relented and sat back in their chairs.

"Anyways," Lan continued, "I need the points on my card, but I really should be saving for a house at this point." Confusion passed through Lan.

"Take it from me: home ownership is not as desirable as I once thought," Evan said. "I wouldn't rush into it just to say you have one."

"Jag has been looking but everything is so expensive inside the city," Athena said. Officially, they weren't living together yet, but Athena spent enough time at Jag's apartment that neighbors probably thought she moved in. They had resolved most of the cultural differences between their families, but Jag wanted to respect his parents' wish to live separately until marriage.

"We need to do what Evan did and look outside Dallas," Lan suggested.

"Yeah, maybe Daniel can get you a good deal up in Carrollton," Jag said.

"Why?" Evan asked.

"He is the mayor."

"Are you fucking kidding me?"

Jag looked around the table. "Did you really not know? He left Southwest around the time you started. He was suspiciously vague, but I think he was tired of being a manager. It is a lot of pressure to be constantly delivering initiatives."

"He just decided to get into politics, then?"

"I don't know all the specifics, but his uncle was the mayor up there and people loved him. I guess Daniel was capitalizing on the goodwill."

"This is so bizarre," Evan said. "What about Danielle? What is she doing? Do they have a first lady position for a mayor?"

"No first lady position," Lan said. "She opened up her own bookstore and runs that now."

"And still no kids I'm assuming."

"Correct."

"How do you know all of this?" Evan asked.

"I have my methods. As much as I'd love to delay our return to work, I really have a meeting I need to get back for," Lan said and flashed the credit card. She pushed the check and card to the edge of the table.

The waitress came by and snatched it without saying a word.

"Any luck finding top talent for the technology department?" Athena asked Evan.

"We are making good progress. I can't say any more than that though."

"Always so mysterious."

"Everything is confidential."

"Do you know our salaries?"

"I could look if I wanted."

"Do you have all of our performance reviews?"

"I have access to them."

"Are you the most powerful person in the company?"

"Hardly," Evan said, laughing. "I can only see stuff for the department, not the entire company."

"Even past employees?"

"Yes."

"Did you ever look . . .?" Athena asked.

"No, I never have."

"He was pretty boring anyways. I doubt there'd be much in there," Athena said with a smile.

The waitress came back with the receipt. Lan scribbled some numbers on there and motioned for the door.

"Thanks for coming to lunch and celebrating this," Evan said as they got to the door. "It means a lot."

"They say that great coworkers are the only thing to keep people sane at work, so we are just trying to do our part!"

They squeezed into the Jeep and made their way back to headquarters. Evan listened to the rumble of another plane landing at the airport.

It would never get old.

sixty-six

MILES ABOVE

"Are you over thirteen years old?"

"What?"

"Ma'am, I need verbal confirmation that you are over thirteen years old in order to sit in the emergency row."

Ann looked around the plane. Was anyone else listening to this conversation? "Yes, I am over thirteen."

"Okay great!" The flight attendant leaned forward and pressed her weight into the seat. "Is Dallas your final destination?"

"I am visiting for a few days."

"Oh wonderful. What will you be doing?"

"I'm not entirely sure. Normally, I would be bothered by that." Ann pulled down the sides of the beanie like a nervous tick.

"If you need suggestions, let me know. Born and raised in Dallas," the flight attendant said with pride. It made sense since her accent was thicker than barbeque sauce.

"My son used to work for Southwest, and I visited him many times down in Dallas. He always complained that there was nothing to do."

"Baloney!"

"What would you recommend?" Ann asked.

The flight attendant tugged at her lanyard and rattled off a list of activities. Ann had seen or done all of them during one of her previous trips. Ann nodded and thanked the flight attendant for the suggestions.

"My pleasure, darling. Always happy to spread some Texas love." She turned toward the front of the plane. "What is this lady doing?" The flight attendant hurried up several rows to help the woman hoist her bag into the overhead compartment.

Sensing that their conversation wouldn't continue, Ann put in her headphones. It was a wonderful year for music, but Ann didn't listen to any of it. She couldn't stand the mumbled sadness of many artists or the constant declarations of unending love or the dozens of generic pop, rap, and alternative rock songs that repeated over and over on the radio. Red's first album had come out to quiet acclaim but failed to make it mainstream except for the notoriety of "Like a River Runs." Bleachers had yet to release their third album, which was a shame because Ann wanted to predict what song titles Vincent would have used next in his future writing. Troye Sivan has abandoned music all together and ventured into a life of solitude. His reasons for the seismic shift were unknown. Oddly, people were craving more December Sun. The band (and Arturo) had disappeared for several years and fans demanded to know if there were any new wicked passions to be concerned about. What were the odds that Vincent would know two moderately successful musicians? About as high as his accident being just that.

Three hours later, when the plane deboarded, the flight attendant spotted Ann and gave her one final place to go in Dallas.

"If you go over to NorthPark, there is a tiny store in the corner by the water fountains. Tell one of the workers that *the celery sticks are on ice*. I think you'll like what happens," she said with a wink.

Ann tugged at the beanie. "Thanks. I'll look into that."

Love Field looked the same as when Ann visited three years ago except for the vast array of digital signage flashing and pointing customers to their gate. Ann ignored the distractions and weaved her way through the idling crowds content with blocking every walking lane.

Some things don't change.

○ ○ ○

"Welcome to the DoubleTree in Dallas. Do you have a room with us for the evening?"

"Two nights actually."

"Even better! Last name please."

"Besser."

"What a beautiful name. You know, I'm a bit of an etymologist. Unofficially, of course," the concierge said with a dry chuckle.

"I don't know what that means."

"It's discovering the origin of words!"

"Oh."

"Let's see . . . Besser . . . Besser . . . Is it—"

"My husband never told me the origin of the name, so I wouldn't be able to tell you," Ann said.

"Oh really? How bizarre. Would you like to know?"

"Not particularly."

"It means *bombardment* in French."

"No it doesn't," Ann said incredulously.

The concierge pointed at the computer screen. "I have it right here."

"I know that my husband isn't French."

"That doesn't mean his last name isn't," the concierge challenged.

"Anyways, isn't it cheating if you look it up?"

"How else would I have known?" he questioned. "I'm only an *amateur* etymologist. I always dreamed of going to school and studying etymology, but life has taken me on . . ."

Ann looked around the lobby to remove herself briefly from the conversation as he continued on. An elderly couple were taking a nap on the couch. They were perfectly posed as if they were ready for their Christmas portrait. Beyond them, an idling wave of people were outside the conference room.

Ann interjected. "What's going on over there?"

The concierge prepared Ann's keycards and bent underneath the counter to grab a stale cookie. He popped back up and said, "It's the annual gathering."

"Sounds ominous."

"The DoubleTree is a proud sponsor of the Survivor Campaign and this is their annual stop in Dallas."

"Survivors of what? Like the television show?"

"Not the TV show. People gather together there who have suffered through a traumatic ordeal and celebrate moving past it."

"Isn't everybody a survivor of something?"

"Well, sure. Anyone is able to join in. Very inclusive," he said with a nod. "Ann, you'll be in 846. Need any help with your bags?"

"No, I'm okay."

"Thanks for staying at the DoubleTree!" The concierge passed over her room keys and cookie.

Ann stepped back from the counter and decided on her next move. She was meeting with the mayor of Carrollton in a few hours for dinner, so there was time to kill. She crept past the sleeping couple and over to the entrance of the conference room. The idling crowd had moved back inside. The muffled sounds of someone speaking into a microphone were pulsing out from the closed door.

She opened it and stepped inside.

". . . twenty years since it happened, and I'll never forget." A wave of applause broke out.

Every seat was full. Some individuals were slouched over and seemingly bored by the anecdotes; others were fully attentive and taking notes for their own personal growth. Based on the back of people's heads, Ann determined the audience was diverse. Trauma spared no one.

The guy next to Ann leaned in and said, "No seats anywhere. I already checked." Ann would have recognized him immediately if she kept up with an iota of pop culture over the past four years.

"Yeah, I noticed."

"First time here?"

"Yes."

"This is my second time. I love the Dallas location. People are refreshingly honest here. It must be that southern hospitality or something."

"Apparently."

"Are you from around here?"

"Just visiting."

He extended a hand. "I'm Miles."

"I'm Ann. Nice to meet you."

"What have you survived?" he asked.

Ann went with the second answer that came to mind. "Cancer."

"Oh, I'm so sorry," Miles said with sincerity. He had likely heard about a multitude of traumas that day, but Ann liked to believe he cared even slightly to hear about hers.

Ann pulled the beanie further down her forehead. "It's only worth being sorry if it killed me and if it did, I wouldn't be around to hear any of the condolences or kind words."

"I can't argue with that logic. What kind of cancer? If you don't mind me asking."

"Stage 3 lung cancer."

"That's some serious shit."

"Yeah. It looked a bit dicey for a while. I figured with all the radiation they hit me with that I'd just fall apart."

The crowd cheered again. Ann didn't hear a single word of what the woman spoke about.

"But you made it out the other side . . . and unharmed," Miles said, looking her up and down. Ann was dressed in jeans and a loose fitted shirt with an even looser jacket over top. Nothing fit her anymore and she lacked the desire to buy new clothes.

"I wouldn't say unharmed. Do you know the worst part about having cancer?"

"No, but I'd like if you told me." Miles pushed himself off the wall and turned toward Ann. He was slightly overweight with the compensation being the bright, white teeth and the dusty blonde hair anybody would have swooned over. He looked younger than what Vincent would have been if he were still alive.

"It's seeing your family suffer. You learn very quickly that the pain will be continuous and that you will deteriorate. You come to terms with it because you have no other choice. But how do you deal with a husband that lost his job and has a wife in and out of the hospital? How do you console your aging mother who is potentially watching her own child die? What do you say to your daughter to make her understand how much it means for her to be there? What about the neighbors who bombard you with food and well wishes? You'll never be able to repay them even though that's not what they'd want. I discovered several years back that suffering is a part of life and how much I absolutely fucking hate it."

"Fuck cancer," Miles said quietly.

Ann wiped the tears from her face. "Enough about me. Why are you here? Why do you keep coming back?"

He stared up at the ceiling briefly as if a balloon was hanging from the rafters. "I was sexually assaulted—raped actually—when I was a kid. Multiple times. It changed me forever. Then, I spiraled into this world of deception where I took advantage of others to ease my own pain. A classic story, huh?" Miles said with a half-smile.

"Everybody has a story and there are always subtle differences. I'm sorry for what you went through." Ann flexed her legs one at a time. Things seized up if she stood for too long. "Are you still deceiving people?"

"No. Thankfully I gave that up."

"You got better."

"Not yet, but maybe someday. To answer your other question though: I keep coming back because people seem to gravitate toward my story. That sounds weird, right? It's not that I particularly enjoy rehashing it, but I see how it impacts others and they always open up after I unburden myself and tell them the truth."

"Why do you have that effect?"

Miles knew why but held back. "I don't know."

"Regardless of the reason, helping others is a noble thing."

"It's the least I can do to make up for my past."

Another round of applause from the crowd. The MC announced the last speaker.

"I think I'm going to head out before the crowd disperses," Ann said.

"Okay."

"Before I go, how familiar are you with Dallas?"

"I know enough."

"Could you tell me how to get here?" Ann showed Miles a picture on her phone. She zoomed in on the exit sign that was off centered in the background.

"I, uh, yeah . . . yeah, I think I know where that is."

Ann nodded. "Great."

"Why there though? It's an off ramp from the highway if I'm not mistaken."

Ann examined Miles once more. He was definitely younger than Vincent and had a long life ahead of him from what she could tell. "It's where my son died and if I don't go see it now, I never will, and I'll regret it for as long as I have left in this boring place."

"Oh."

"Could you go with me?" Ann asked. "I'm not sure how I'll be when I get there."

Miles blinked several times. Ann assumed he was formulating an excuse until he said, "Of course. Whatever I can do to help."

"I'll drive," said Ann. "I rented quite the relic and the color is horrendous. You have to see it."

sixty-seven

NOTHING BUT A MASQUERADE

NorthPark mall was thriving more than ever. With the downfall of Amazon and no company to fill the void, consumers flocked in droves to do their Christmas shopping at the local mall.

Evan circled the parking lot a dozen times.

"How about over there?"

"Babe, I was just down that aisle. This is hopeless," Evan said and slammed his palm against the steering wheel several times.

"We can come back another time."

"We are flying out tomorrow. I need to get this done now."

"Or you could just do the shopping out there. You have five days until Christmas. Lord knows I won't be starting my shopping for another three days or so."

Evan looked over at Franco and rolled his eyes. "Your procrastination kills me. Why don't we get the stuff you need while we are here?"

"Nah. Let me suffer. I need to learn my lesson and grow from the experience."

"If you insist."

"Anyways, you know how much I enjoy leaving you alone with my parents. They adore having their *second son* in the house," Franco said in a flamboyant manner. "There! THERE!" he called out.

"Where?"

"THERE!"

"THAT'S NOT HELPING!"

"THERE! THERE! FOLLOW THAT OLD WOMAN!" Franco shouted.

Five cars up, Evan spotted her. She was hobbling along that an excruciatingly slow pace. Evan inched the car forward like he was following Macaulay Culkin home from the grocery store. The woman reached her car and eventually moved inside.

"Thank god," Franco said.

"Never again. This is the last time I ever shop here around Christmas."

"Yeah, yeah. I've heard you say that before." Franco squeezed Evan's leg and extended his widest smile.

Once parked, they began their long journey across the macadam wasteland.

"Holy crap. Do you see this car right here?" Franco said halfway into their walk.

"What about it?"

"It's a Ford Masquerade. They are legendary!"

Evan looked at the box shape of the car and the hideous lime-green color. "It's the ugliest car I have ever seen."

"Exactly!"

"I'm missing the point then."

"The car was so damn ugly that they only made 50 of them before the workers at the plant threatened to go on strike. Naturally, they were all fired and replaced by robots, but once the robots refused to make anymore, Ford discontinued them."

"Can you take my picture with it?" Franco asked.

"It would be my honor."

Franco tossed his phone over and jogged to the car. He leaned against it and pointed at the MASQUERADE name etched onto the trunk. Evan snapped five photos since Franco wouldn't like the first four.

"Thanks, Ev." Franco flipped through the pictures. "Ugh. Gross. No. Lame. Oh, that one's nice! The last one is always the best."

They continued into the mall. They dipped in and out of a dozen stores before Evan was satisfied with his haul.

"You want to grab something from the food court?" Franco suggested as they came within view of the semicircle of restaurants.

"I'd love nothing more than something from the food court."

They settled on salads from Lettuce Eat Salads (And Other Assorted Yummies For Your Tummies) or LESAOAYFYT for short. While the name was a complete abomination, the food was only a mild dumpster fire.

Evan and Franco found an open table next to a woman with a dark red beanie pulled tight against are head and a lanky guy with a charming overbite.

sixty-eight

DEFINE THE THESIS STATEMENT

Dylan Starr resurfaced in Dallas two months ago like a message in a bottle washing ashore. The past three years of his life were spent on the move with his ex-fiancé turned recent husband. Using the money from Alex's family, the two spent time in Mexico, Bali, Dubai, France, Austria, Japan, New Zealand, Canada, Iceland, and Argentina. He discovered a lust for life and a wide range of drugs that opened his mind to the possibilities of the world. Dylan didn't care about going to school for some useless degree and a dead-end office job. Instead, he focused on helping others through non-profit efforts, which paid him enough to support the vagabond lifestyle. It was fulfilling work that wouldn't put him in the Best Of section of any history book, but it helped to ease his mind on those nights where it raced and stopped him from getting any sleep. Things with Alex became dismantled as they always did, but they were two train wrecks destined for one another. The arguments and cheating allegations followed them throughout their travels until they flew down to the Caribbean to get married. Dylan knew he'd never spend his life with anyone else; the gravitational pull that Alex had was too immense, so instead of fighting it, he decided to settle into the domesticated life that he craved after their extensive travels. Some people never find their true worth in the eyes of others.

When Dylan finally reengaged with society, he realized no one waited around for him. Friends from high school and his brief stint in college had moved on. They grew tired of sending text messages that failed to deliver and emails that were never responded to.

His family forgot about his birthday, which was fair considering he forgot about each of theirs. They greeted him coldly and showed disdain toward his selfish decision to abandon everything he ever had there. What they couldn't understand was that there was more to gain outside Dallas than inside of it, but their fears of failure stopped them from ever taking the risk he did.

There was one person though that continued to send him emails long after he stopped responding. When Dylan returned to Dallas, he scrolled through his email mindlessly and contemplated deleting the account entirely. Better to start anew rather than sift through the years of garbage. Every month though, Dylan found a thread continued. It was like reading a book. Ann Besser laid out her battle with cancer and the other happenings within her life. At a certain point, she realized that Dylan would never respond or see the emails, but she continued to do it because it became the only outlet that gave her peace.

Dylan recognized how they were tethered to each other through the tragedy of her son and while it would have been easier to ignore, there was no one else he felt close to anymore. Dylan responded to her emails and they kick started a proper correspondence again. There was too much to tell her through text, so they decided to rendezvous in Dallas.

"Is everything alright?" Dylan asked Ann. They had been seated in the food court for ten minutes and spent most of their time picking away at the meals in front of them. Dylan couldn't recall the last time he'd eaten an entire meal and it looked like this time would be no different.

She ignored his question. "Why'd you want to meet here? It's awfully crowded."

"Because it makes me anxious."

"You like putting yourself in anxious situations?"

"I'm tired of being a shut in. I find way too much enjoyment just sitting at home rather than going out and exploring."

"Didn't you travel around half the world? You must have explored a lot then?"

"No, I didn't. Anytime we got to a new city, we'd shack up in the hotel and only expand out in a two-block radius. Alex always hated the idea of me going out on my own to see the cities and I was too afraid of getting lost. I never saw the Eiffel Tower in Paris or went to the beach alone in Bali or explored Reykjavík or made it to the top of Burj Khalifa."

"Regardless of what you did or didn't do, you still got to travel more than most people do in three lifetimes. Hopefully you can find solace in that," Ann said. She pulled down the beanie. Dylan noticed how often she was doing it and decided to keep track. That was number seven.

"What does solace mean?"

"To find comfort in something."

"Oh. Sorry, I don't read much."

"Don't apologize." Ann looked around the food court and saw the constant shifting of people amongst the tables. The stress of the holidays was distinguishable on many faces. "Tell me about the past three years. You have been vague in our texts back and forth. However much detail you want to share."

"There's nothing exciting that happened."

"Bullshit."

Dylan smiled. It disappeared as quickly as it formed. He hated his smile and his imperfect set of teeth. The superficial nature of Dallas made you have acute awareness to your flaws. Outside of Dallas, he didn't think about things like that nearly as much.

He told her everything he could remember. The drugs fogged his memory somewhat and other details seemed insignificant. Ann nodded and asked questions when needed. Dylan's recap stretched long after Evan and Franco seated themselves five feet away and began to devour LESAOAYFYT.

The universe tried its hardest to provide the necessary synchronicities for Ann and Evan to see each other once more, but most times, the universe doesn't even get it right. What would they have said to each other? *Oh, I'm so sorry for your loss. How's your life been?* Their time together had passed; their paths were never meant to cross, and they were only brought together briefly through a third party, a letter, and a couple of books.

The most disappointing part about Evan and Ann not meeting again was that Franco never found out who the proud (rental) owner of the Ford Masquerade was.

Evan and Franco departed from the table and Ann turned her head to watch them leave. A flicker of recognition passed through her, but she returned her attention to Dylan.

"Why'd you even come back to Dallas?" Ann asked after he finished chronicling his travels. She had reserved judgement as best she could, especially when Dylan decided to delve into the details of his drug excursions.

"Alex made me. He was tired of traveling and wanted to be closer to his family. Actually, they threatened to cut him off if he didn't come back home. I mentioned about the non-profit work I did and that supported me somewhat, but his credit card was the main source of income."

"Does that bother you?"

"I look like a trophy husband, don't I? It doesn't mean I have the intelligence of one. Yes, it bothers me that he relies so heavily on his family's wealth and that I have been sucked into the vortex. I need to find my purpose."

"That's not an easy thing to do."

"What's the point of all this?" Dylan said, holding up several fries and waving them around.

"There have been periods of time in my life where I would have had an answer to that but circumstances have changed."

"Like, you've had cancer. What's the purpose of that?"

"Bad things happen all the time. It's just the way it is."

"But why? No one can answer that for me. What am I supposed to do for the rest of my life to not feel like a complete waste? I've traveled and met beautiful people all over the world and yet I feel so empty and unfulfilled most times. It's exhausting."

"What do you love?"

"Well, I love my family an— "

"Not *who* you love. *What* do you love?" Ann asked again.

Without hesitation, Dylan said, "Helping people."

"In what way?"

"Anyway I possibly can."

"That sounds like a purpose to me. I don't see lines of people waiting around to help others. You can be that person though. You can make this world better than what I grew up in and how it'll be when I'm gone. That's a meaningful life to me."

"How do I do it?" he said in a whisper that almost was lost amongst the chaos of the food court.

"That's not for me to tell you. You'll know."

Dylan shook his head.

In another life, Ann would have scoffed at anyone who came to her and complained about having no direction in life at the age of twenty-six or their proposed direction to be solely helping others. She was married with a house and well on her way to having her first kid at his age. That was then. In the more present, boring reality she occupied, Ann recognized that being young didn't always allow for such things. Dylan was older than Vincent would ever be and seemed to be lost to the ebbs and flows of life. It wasn't her place to fix him, but he could use a guide, he could discover what she knew.

"Vinny wrote about you," she said.

"Me? Why?"

"Because he believed in you."

"That's dumb. Why would he do that?"

"I wish we could ask him." She had to go further. "He really cared about you. Vinny understood that you two were both damaged people when you met. Given different circumstances, you two may have had something more significant." A path not taken.

"I don't—I don't think that's true."

"Maybe not, but it's a pleasant thought. Did you get the letter I sent you that Vinny wrote?"

"No. When did you send it?"

"I can't be sure anymore. So much has happened." Ann grabbed at the beanie. Seventeen.

"My parents supposedly kept all my mail, but I never went through it. I didn't think anything important would be in there, so I threw it all out."

"Oh."

"What did the letter say?" Dylan asked.

"It wasn't meant for me, so I didn't read it."

"Oh."

"I'd like to read it sometime if you could send it again."

"Sure." It was a tiny lie. Ann destroyed the laptop during a particularly rough day several years back. She didn't make any more copies of the letters prior to the destruction.

Their conversation drifted toward lighter topics that gave Ann the impression that Dylan would turn out fine. He told her about his desire to go to school again, what Christmas presents he got for Alex, why the square root of twenty-seven isn't three, and other oddities about his travels around the world. He was a sharp guy who needed to realign his rationale. At one point, Ann asked if Dylan knew who Ochi was in relation to Vincent and he had no idea. It was a thread that needed to be revisited another time.

They parted ways sometime later (of course, the total beanie tug count was twenty-seven) with well wishes for the upcoming holidays and the promise to see each other again.

It was a small lie.

Ann would stop sending the emails and discontinue the effort to get ahold of Dylan. He began to blitz through life and forgot about the things that were left behind. He didn't need to be burdened by it any longer.

It was just a matter of circumstance.

sixty-nine

FINDING WHAT IS NEEDED

Evan was always told that relationships were hard. Not exactly told as the notion was constantly shoved in his face via podcasts, television commercials, books, social media, and the context clues he picked up from watching friends and family struggle in various ways.

Who hadn't been told the same thing?

Until he began dating Franco, Evan believed what *everyone* said. Kieran was an absolute mess and it bubbled over into Evan's life. Vincent wasn't ready for a relationship and then died, so not exactly a desirable outcome you'd want for an ex unless they were particularly awful. Franco, though, just didn't give much of a fuck. Evan couldn't think of another way to describe it. Yeah, Franco cared when he lost the business and attempted to find the next thing for himself, but it never bled into their relationship. They never argued about Evan supporting him for a few months and when the career change to Southwest became evident, Franco was supportive the entire time. The fucks he didn't give materialized in the constant attention he gave Evan and the daily assurances that Evan was everything he needed.

Franco was the *thing* and would always be. Evan was sure of that much.

He pulled himself back to the car turning off the California highway. They were somewhere east of San Francisco, heading out toward Yosemite National Park, but with their destination in-between. Evan challenged himself to remember the town Franco grew up in, but he came back with nothing.

"What town do your parents live in?" Evan decided to ask. It would have slowly eaten away at him if he didn't.

"Corn Cob City."

"Oh, c'mon. I would have recalled a stupid name like that."

"It's true!" Franco said defensively.

"Where'd the name come from?"

"Fuck if I know. I never took that much of an interest."

They passed by a sign that read **WELCOME TO CORN COB CITY**.

"I stand corrected," Evan said with a long sigh. "That name is almost as bad as Blue Ball, Pennsylvania."

"Makes sense. I never had any luck in that state."

Evan let the joke pass without a response.

"Do you want to stop anywhere before we get there?" Franco asked.

"I have everything I need."

"Okay great. We should be there in five minutes." A moment passed. "They are really excited to see you."

"They must be if they invited me back for Christmas again. I guess getting wine drunk with your mom had a lasting impact." It would be Evan's second Christmas with Franco's family. While Franco was an only child, his extended family was massive, so there was no shortage of entertainment and names for Evan to fight hard to remember. He was accepted into the fold with relative ease by everyone he had met except for the little cousin named Aristotle who cried incessantly whenever Evan tried to have conversation with him. Maybe a year of reflection and maturity will have changed Aristotle's stance toward Evan.

There was guilt that he no longer intended to spend holidays with his own family. His mom produced just enough tears the year prior to make Evan think she was actually upset. Their fractured relationship was one that he came to accept with no harsh feelings. As for his father . . . Evan tried not to think about it much. A year and a half earlier, the elder Evan Eaton had been walking on the sidewalk of a major thoroughfare in his town and was struck by a drunk driver. He died instantly. The irony was not lost on Evan that his father had been killed by the demon that plagued him most. Not everyone got such a poetic, storybook ending. Sadness crept into the fringes of Evan's life, but the tidal wave of grief never stuck him. His father was gone, but it wasn't much of a loss.

There isn't much else worth mentioning on the matter.

Franco's parents lived in the middle of the cul-de-sac in an upper-class neighborhood. Franco didn't discuss the wealth he had growing up, but it became apparent when Evan stepped inside the house for the first time. They were flanked by the Muntazar's on the left and the Belinsky's on the right. The cul-de-sac (and general radius of the neighborhood) saw a very low turnover rate, which meant everyone knew one another. Lots of block parties occurred and someone was always devising an excuse to get a large group together.

They pulled into the driveway. Franco let out a long stretch from the driver's seat. "You ready?"

"Of course. I can see your mom standing in the window. She seems excited," Evan pointed out.

Franco reached out, found Evan's hand, and squeezed it tightly. "She is always happy to have her family together."

Evan smiled back, unsure of what to say. His life had been dominated by broken family moments of abuse and unhappiness. Those times kept receding further into the past, but could they ever be completely forgotten? To find something so pure and meaningful seemed entirely foreign to him—even the thought that he was undeserving of it crossed his mind. It would take several days for him to settle down and accept the continued doting from Franco's mom or his dad's insistence on talking about their rapidly expanding gaming channel on YouTube. (Franco's parents enjoyed a semi-retired lifestyle until they discovered that people seemed to love watching an older couple get progressively better at competitive multiplayer games. Over the course of three months, their subscriber count increased by a thousand percent after another major gaming channel plugged how they had stumbled upon the Old Dogs, New Tricks YouTube channel and was fascinated by the content.)

"I love you so much," Evan said.

Franco leaned over to kiss Evan. "I love you too. I'm so lucky to have you."

They stepped out of the car and moved toward the house. Franco's mom ran out yelling and waving her arms wildly.

It's not about luck, Evan thought. *It's about finding what you need when you need it.*

Evan watched as Franco gave his mom a long hug. They rocked back and forth for several seconds like a metronome.

"Your turn!" she said and walked over to Evan. He smiled and gave her a gentler hug.

It was good to be home with family.

seventy

PASSED ALONG

A white Christmas.

The town of Easton, Pennsylvania hadn't experienced one in decades. The storm of 1995 was devastating and halted any travel for three days. The Besser clan was relegated to an isolated Christmas with the occasional invitation to a neighbor's house to break the insanity. Ann remembered how often her and Jim went out to shovel just for the plow truck to come by again and toss up more snow onto the driveway to clean out. Leigh tried to help with her tiny shovel, but she got no further than an inconsequential patch at the top of the driveway. Vincent—only two at the time—was virtually useless and just wandered around kicking the drifts of show and laughed hysterically every time he fell backward into the growing piles.

Now, times were slightly different. They always seemed to be. No longer was their hideous artificial tree crammed to capacity with presents or ornaments hanging from each branch. No longer were there miscellaneous Christmas themed knick-knacks scattered throughout the house with the hopes of spreading good cheer and full hearts for the holiday. No longer was the outside of the house decorated with lights that rivaled a Griswold family Christmas.

Many things were no longer the same. It was a matter of circumstance and what tended to happen when half your life was packed into boxes.

Ann went downstairs and peered out a window. The snow was falling at a rhythmic, steady pace. It was supposed to let up soon. Only enough to cover up the dirty snow from the last storm a week ago.

She moved down the hallway and into the kitchen.

"Merry Christmas," Jim said. He always looked sad. Losing the job, losing the house, losing a son, nearly losing your wife. It all weighed heavily on him. Would he ever be able to find himself in a happier place?

Would she?

"Merry Christmas," Ann said and bent down to kiss him. She pushed aside any of the existential thoughts for another day.

"What time are they coming over today?"

"They are supposed to be here at ten, but I'm not sure because . . ." she trailed off. Ann grabbed her phone and read the text. "Leigh said they are still coming up."

"Okay great. Want to start cooking breakfast?"

"Sure."

Jim rummaged through the cabinets and pulled out various pans and bowls—the ones left that weren't packed away. Their mission was simple: make more food than any of them could possibly consume in one meal. The leftovers would be packaged up and sit in the fridge until they turned a suspicious shade of green. Breakfast was undoubtedly the only meal where reheating leftovers was never worth the effort. Pancakes tasted like tar, the bacon looked rubbery, the muffins could be chucked and cause as much damage as a rock. Nonetheless, Ann and Jim danced around the kitchen working to create their abundance of food. The Christmas music chimed quietly in the background and the dogs each fell into an early morning nap.

Ann yearned so much for what was. It was sickening. Did she ever take it for granted? No, no, she didn't think so. But Ann sure as hell wished she had taken more pictures.

The doorbell rang an hour later, and the dogs raced down the hallway to take stock of the intruders. Their barks morphed into whines as soon as they recognized the visitors.

The door opened.

"Rigby, chill out."

"Marshall, stop jumping."

"Lorenzo, can you grab Phillip?"

"Where's Emilia?"

Ann turned the corner and saw Leigh struggling to gain control of the situation. "Need me to grab something?"

Leigh looked up and pointed to Emilia. "Grab her."

Emilia was busy playing bongos on Rigby's butt and didn't notice Ann until she was scooped up in her arms. "Grandma!"

"Hi, Emilia. Merry Christmas!"

"Merry Christmas." It came out in a jumble of syllables that loosely resembled the phrase.

"Let's go see Grandpa." Ann walked into the living room and handed off Emilia. She told Jim about the presents she got for Christmas in a series of misconnected words.

Ann went back into the hallway and helped Lorenzo with the bags he was juggling while trying to hold Phillip who was very vocal about not wanting to be held.

Twins, Ann thought. *I'm glad I didn't have those. One at a time was hard enough.*

Phillip and Emilia came during the height of Ann's chemotherapy. She was barely involved in Leigh's pregnancy, which was probably for the best. Given their different philosophies, Ann kept her distance and only stepped in when Leigh reached out directly with questions. Their relationship had been lukewarm for years, but it was better than the alternative. Once the twins were born, Ann tried not to meddle, but she found that Leigh started coming to her and asking for advice. Being a first-time mom could be frightening, so Leigh sought shelter with the people who were familiar with the process. Now, Ann and Leigh spoke multiple times a week. Leigh likely recognized the stress of their current situation and felt the weight of potentially having to support her parents if things didn't work out.

But still, things only felt lukewarm. They'd never have the quintessential mother-daughter relationship that was highly coveted. Leigh didn't possess that empathetic trait even with two kids; she would always remain standoffish and fearful of displaying emotion. Ann spent enough time wondering where she'd gone wrong to conclude that she hadn't done anything to induce the behavior. It was just the way Leigh was. And that would need to be good enough.

"Come here Phillip," Ann said with her arms outstretched. Lorenzo passed him over and Phillip began to ask questions about the hat Ann was wearing. She told him it made her strong and protected her.

Phillip laughed and buried his head into her shoulder.

"How's it been this morning?" Ann asked Lorenzo.

He gave a long sigh. "It's been a struggle, but we are here now," he said with a weary smile.

"It's only going to get more exciting," she said and gave him a hug. "You'll think twice about having anymore."

"Leigh is already talking about trying again. Let's just hope we don't have twins again."

"I doubt that will happen. I have never heard of families having multiple sets of twins."

(Three years down the road, when the technician was doing an ultrasound and confirmed that Leigh was having another set of twins, Lorenzo fainted in the examination room. "He does this all the time," Leigh noted.)

The family settled into the dining room and observed the feast laid out in front of them. Phillip grabbed at the pancakes. Emilia tried to scoop up the eggs, but the attempt was halted when she couldn't pick up the spoon.

Rigby sat eagerly underneath and waited for the inevitable scraps.

Joy.

Ann felt unfiltered joy by having her grandchildren over on Christmas and hoping to continue the tradition her and Jim had started so many years ago. Ann watched as the table broke into conversations about meaningless topics that didn't matter. It was the idle chit-chat that dominated most family dinners. No one would remember the details, but the feeling of togetherness would always be apparent.

Ann didn't eat much breakfast and began to clean once it was clear that everyone else was done eating too.

She didn't get far before Lorenzo came out. "Go in and sit. I can take it from here," he said. Ann understood what went unsaid. *Go spend time with your family.*

Ann sat back at the table and felt peace. A sudden longing crept in without notice.

"Leigh?"

"Yeah?"

"I have something for you," Ann said.

"Right now?"

"Yeah."

Ann got up from the table and Leigh followed. They went upstairs to the end of the hallway. Vincent's room. It was empty except for a nightstand in the corner. Divots in the floor showed where the furniture had been. Marks on the walls gave hints as to where picture frames once hanged.

"It . . . it feels even smaller without the furniture. You'd expect it to be the opposite," Leigh said.

"Yeah. We cleaned it out last week. I wanted to leave it for last, but it just . . ." Ann trailed off.

"Is everything okay?"

"Yes, yes. It will be." Ann walked to the nightstand and grabbed the gift. A tiny bow sat on top of the small box. She handed it to Leigh.

"I thought we said no presents this year."

"We did. Just open it," Ann said softly. She took two steps back and watched as Leigh gently undid the wrapping paper with multi-colored balloons on it. Ann hadn't bothered to get Christmas wrapping paper. Leigh let the paper fall to the ground. Rigby sat in the doorway, tempted to snatch the paper and run.

Leigh pulled off the top half of the box and peered down into it.

"Do you remember this?" Ann asked.

Barely above a whisper, Leigh said, "Of course. Vinny wore this and got it from Grandpa." Leigh pulled out the polished gold chain and let it dangle. It swayed slightly and eventually came to a stop.

"I want Phillip to have it."

"Why? You wore this every day."

"It's time to move on. I know that you and Lorenzo aren't religious—neither was Vinny—so I think the significance is different than that. I just needed to know that someone else would get this after I was gone. Phillip is too young to wear it now, but when he's ready—"

"Mom, you're not going anywhere. You're healthy for the first time in a while. You have a lot of years left."

Ann tugged absentmindedly at the beanie. It sank further down her head. "I should have died. I deserved to. All those cigarettes. Years and years of abuse and somehow I managed to survive. But Vinny didn't. Why? Why?"

Leigh stepped closer and grabbed her mom's arm. "Please don't think like that."

"You would too. You have kids now and finally understand how your love for them is practically limitless. It's . . . it's almost undefinable."

"I know."

"Four years next week. Four fucking years. I'm not sure it gets any easier. I thought grief was a downward trend, but I've been stuck at this plateau for a long time. I don't want to forget him, but I don't want to keep crying over him because it won't change anything. I need to focus on you and Lorenzo and your father and Grandma and Phillip and Emilia and . . . all the things I can impact."

"You need to focus on yourself."

"I did, Leigh. I did. All those days I was lying in bed, staring up at the ceiling, and wishing I was anywhere else but there. Believe me, I was focused on myself. I was selfish, but I think I had to be. Cancer does that to you. The self-preservation mode is triggered. I don't deserve to be here now, but I'm grateful I am."

Leigh hugged her mom. Once they broke apart, Leigh put the chain around her neck. It would stay there for years until Phillip was ready. When she did give it to him, Leigh told a story about the uncle he never got to meet.

"I love you," Ann said.

"I love you too."

"More than you could ever understand."

"Mom," Leigh said, reaching out a hand, "I finally understand . . . having kids of my own now . . ."

Ann nodded. Whatever smug satisfaction she may have felt was buried incredibly deep.

"Let's go back downstairs," Leigh suggested.

"Okay," Ann said and wiped the tears away. "Leigh?"

"Yeah."

"I just want to be happy again."

"You will be. Give it more time."

Time.

Of course. The one thing Ann hadn't run out of yet.

seventy-one

REUNION TOWER

Evan looked up.

The balloons were cradled within a large net that expanded across the dance floor. They swayed just enough for him to catch their movements. If the balloons had feelings, Evan guessed that they were tired of being confined up there. His ears rang from the heavy bass that was reverberating from the speakers. He didn't recognize the song—just another bop of the week.

"Do you want to dance or just stand here?"

No response.

"Hello?"

A tap on the shoulder shook Evan loose from his trance. Evan turned and looked at the guy. He was slightly taller than Evan with a lean build that made him feel guilty for not going to the gym since before Christmas. "Yeah?" Evan asked.

"Do you want to dance?" the guy repeated, stressing each syllable as if Evan was an expert at lip reading. Little did this guy know, but Evan was a pro at lip-*syncing*.

"No, I'm good."

"Whatever man. It's New Year's Eve and you're standing out here alone like a loser." The Dallas gays never change. Many believed they had the money of an LA resident and the looks of a New York model when in reality their wealth and attractiveness measured up to that guy who peaked in high school and thought smoking bowls in his parent's basement until twenty-five was the pinnacle of existence. Was everyone that way? Of course not, but Evan enjoyed the idea of generalizing for once. He always appreciated that most of the time during his two stints in Dallas were of him in a relationship.

"My boyfriend is at the bar getting us drinks. Chill out."

The guy gave Evan one final look before melting back into the crowd. He'd find a stranger to make out with and possibly take home, but he'd wake up the next day with the same pangs of regret that followed everyone. What a wonderful way to ring in the new year.

Evan craned his neck back toward the ceiling and began counting the balloons. The music continued to pulse around him. He felt the bubble of space between him and everyone else widen.

Twenty-three, twenty-four, twenty-five, twenty-six, twen—

A hand pressed into his back. Evan turned and was met by Franco with a wide smile and an outstretched arm holding a beer. "Here you go. Sorry about that. The line was long."

"It's okay."

The screen past Franco's head started a countdown. One hour until midnight.

"I was thinking we could ditch this place after we finish these. What do you think?"

Evan leaned in closer. "I would love that. Where do you want to go?"

"I have an idea, but it is reliant o—" Franco paused and reached into his pocket to pull out his phone. His eyes skimmed over the screen briefly before putting it away. "Confirmation."

"Of what?" Evan asked.

"Of where we are going after this drink."

"Are we getting too old to come out anymore?"

"No. Well, I don't know. Try not to worry about that right now." Franco took a long sip of the beer. Evan followed his lead. "I just want to enjoy this night with you, which is easy because you are an enjoyable person."

"That probably sounded more romantic in your head, huh?"

"It certainly did," Franco said with a shrug.

Evan's heart was so full with Franco. He didn't know what their long-term future looked like, but he knew there would be one.

They danced halfheartedly to a couple of songs before the beers were empty. Franco grabbed Evan's hand and led him off the dance floor. The guy from earlier was standing alone on the edge and staring up at all the balloons tucked away. Those damn balloons were as powerful as the deadlights from *It*.

Their new destination was two doors down from where they were. Street's Fine Chicken was moderately busy with half the tables full. Most of the patrons seemed to be holding themselves together for the next half hour until midnight.

"We are watching the ball drop at a chicken place?" Evan asked as they stepped inside.

"Yeah! Haven't you been here before?"

"I don't think so."

"Oh wow. You are about to unlock the next level of life after eating here.

They say the chicken is fine, but I say the chicken is *amazing*."

Evan shook his head and laughed. "That is a pity laugh because it wasn't very funny."

"And yet you still laughed. That's a win for me."

The hostess came by and showed them to their table. Evan sat in the booth and looked up at the television. They were showing images of the nonexistent crowd in Times Square. People no longer flooded the streets of New York City for New Year's Eve, instead, anyone who wanted the experience went to a VR party, which allowed people to simulate they were in Times Square without the need to stand outside for twelve hours wearing a diaper and watching a fucking disco ball drop.

Times were different. Of course, it was just a matter of circumstance.

The television abruptly switched over to a local channel. The blonde bombshell to attract in viewers looked strung out from a long night of delivering fake news. The screen cut to an image of Reunion Tower. Evan turned his attention back to Franco.

"Are you ordering food?"

"Food and drink—the deadly combination."

"What would you recommend?"

Franco dove into a long-winded explanation of the menu. Evan tried to keep up but realized there wasn't much need to. Everything on the menu was labeled as artificial chicken.

"Hi."

Expecting it to be the waiter, Evan looked over and readied his drink order. "I'll have a—what the fuck?"

"Hi," Murph and Elliot repeated in unison.

"You're here! How? Why?"

They pointed at Franco. "It took some persuading, but I got them to stay in Dallas for a couple extra days. We haven't seen them since the wedding, which is unacceptable.

Evan stood up and gave them each a hug. They were responsible for some of the best moments of his life and he missed them intensely. Leaving them behind had been the hardest part about moving back to Dallas. Murph and Elliot entertained the idea of venturing back as well, but their lives hadn't pushed them in that direction yet.

They looked the same. You always expect some monumental change when you see someone for the first time in a while, but that rarely happens. People are creatures of habit—one might even say that people don't change.

"This was my favorite spot when I lived in the complex over there, so I couldn't pass up the opportunity," Murph said.

"Nothing better than chicken on New Year's Eve!" Elliot said.

Murph sat next to Evan; Elliot next to Franco. They immediately peppered each other with questions. Evan knew enough about Murph and Elliot's lives through social media, but the devil was in the details and he intended to find out. Following their wedding and their lovely honeymoon across Europe, Murph and Elliot settled back into a rhythm in Denver. With their two closest friends from the city gone, they had to venture out in different ways. Elliot made a larger effort to network within his company and slowly begin plotting out his next move. The baseball business was rather elite, so he needed to have his head inserted far up people's asses to be recognizable. As for Murph, she expanded her list of activities to helping out with local non-profits. Denver, like any other city, had its share of problems. Murph focused on helping the Denver youth that found themselves in an abnormal (or normal, depending on how you look at it) family situation such as a single parent household, living with distant relatives, in the foster care system, or moving on from the loss of a parent.

The waitress came by and asked for any drink orders. Elliot, Evan, and Franco all decided on a beer; Murph was the only one to abstain.

"Are you pregnant or something?" Franco quipped.

Murph looked over at Elliot and back to Franco. "I might be."

"You're joking!"

"We have sex like once a year, so I had to make the most of it," Elliot said. Murph reached across the table and tried to punch his arm. "Hey, hey. Sorry. I meant two times a year. Arbor Day and Flag Day. It can get—"

"You're too much," Murph cut in.

"Really though. Are you two trying?" Evan asked.

Again, Murph looked over at Elliot. Her face lit up. "Yeah, we are. We've talked about it for years, but of course we wanted to be in a more stable place. Our careers are solid now. At least, his is. I may be in for a change soon. We don't think Denver is our forever home, but that's not the biggest concern right now. I'm scared though. The world isn't exactly thriving at the moment. And what if we suck as parents?"

"Y'all will be incredible!" Franco said.

"That's what everyone tells us and what every new parent believes. They always think they'll do it better than how they were raised, but how can anyone be that confident?"

Evan understood Murph's concern. Becoming a parent didn't grant you the eternal wisdom to raise a child properly (as if there was a way to do that). Sometimes you got a loving family with two involved parents that were a part of their child's life the entire way; other times you got an abusive alcoholic who really did nothing for you besides cause extreme stress and then died in a quiet implosion. Forgotten like all the rest.

So it goes.

"It's okay to be scared. We are always here to help. Your gay uncles," Franco said.

"Thanks. I expect Evan will read up on everything I need to know." Evan probably would so no sense in denying it. "Are you two ever going to get married?" Murph asked.

"Honestly, I don't know the etiquette on who is supposed to propose to who. Like, does the bottom ask the top or does the most masculine of the two have the right to ask?" Franco said with only slight seriousness.

"Or," Elliot said, "one of you can take the lead and just do it. Only if you guys are ready for that next step, of course. I'd like to see you top what I did for our engagement."

"Oh, I'm sure you'd love to top," Franco said. Elliot's face flushed at the comment. They hadn't discussed his bisexuality in years, mainly because nobody gave a fuck. Not in a mean way, but more so in a let-the-man-live-his-life-in-peace-because-he-isn't-hurting-anyone type of way. Ya dig?

Evan was ready for the next step. He had been since they successfully moved to Dallas. If you can live with someone and survive a move, that is a great indication y'all can handle other life shit that's bound to be flung around. Evan believed Franco was ready too, but you can never be too sure. It was a conversation they needed to have when the time was right.

Satisfied with their non-answer, Murph pivoted her questions to Dallas and how Evan and Franco were liking their jobs. The conversation spun and twisted in many directions, most of each we aren't concerned with.

What we are concerned about is their complete disregard for midnight. It passed by without the faintest mention from anyone at the table. Midnight carried such a significance to people like Vincent, but you'd find that most others don't care. It's more about the company you're with than counting down the seconds until you can hit the reset button on your life.

For them, midnight wasn't the only time they ever took note of.

They left Street's Fine Chicken right before the waitress warned them for the third time that they were trying to close up for the night. They loitered outside the building, trying to delay their departures.

Eventually, Evan and Franco's Lyft pulled up.

"This is it," Franco said. "I'm glad we got to see y'all. Please let us know when we can come visit. We need to cause havoc again and I'm also curious what has become of the old bar."

"A Starbucks," Elliot said.

"Ah, of course." Franco walked over and gave them each a hug. "I'll meet you at the car," he said to Evan.

Evan hugged Elliot and moved toward Murph. "I miss you so much. Please don't be a stranger."

"I won't. We will be back in Dallas at some point." Evan understood that she didn't mean for just a visit. "The question is if you guys will still be here."

"I'm done moving. I've found my home."

"If you ever have any doubts, be sure to follow *it*," Murph said with a smile. "That idea hasn't led me astray so far."

"I will. Love you."

"Love you too." They hugged one last time and Evan moved slowly to the car.

"Everything good?" Franco asked.

"Yes."

For all the promises and desires throughout the years for Evan to stay in touch with someone, he knew this would be the one time he followed through with *it*.

seventy-two

ONE SIDED CONVERSATION

Ann didn't make it to midnight. She was catching flies by 10 p.m.
   Jim fell asleep even earlier. He had work in the morning, so he didn't see the need to stay up and watch an empty Times Square celebrate a giant ball dropped down until it lit up the midnight sky. After the lumber company closed down, Jim decided to find a job closer to home. Of course, at that time, he didn't foresee their eventual move from Easton, but having the gift of sight was not a luxury he was ever afforded. He wore glasses since the age of eight. Thankfully for him, his twenty-five years at the lumber company came with at least one benefit: they threw oodles of money his way. Sure, he had earned the sixty-thousand dollars of PTO that he never took advantage of, but the additional money was meant to buffer the stress of having to find a new job and minimize the stress of his cancer ridden wife. (Jim wasn't foolish. He understood that he would have rather had that time with his family instead of the sixty-thousand dollars. He used to think his work was the catalyst for change within his family, but in the boring reality he occupied, it was the constant force that kept anything from ever changing.) Closing in on sixty-five, Jim had the opportunity to retire and collect Social Security, but he decided to stick it out until seventy where he would collect an additional thousand dollars a month. What a fucking joke. Would he even make it to seventy? He still had a couple years until then. All that work for the possibility that he'd be around long enough to see the culmination of his twelve-hour workdays. The American Dream is thriving! Still, it wasn't bad for a man who came from a broken home and carried only a high school diploma. Finding a new job wasn't as difficult as he imagined, but his working style clashed with the newer, gentler approach exhibited by many employers. The work ethic wasn't the same anymore and he had no patience for it, but he did what he had to because he loved his wife. *Just a few more years*, he continually told himself. What would he do when he was retired? His friends were limited, and his hobbies didn't surpass more than a handful. A question and answer for another time. Now, their lives had taken another turn when it became evident that the house was no longer viable. The medical bills crushed them. Another part of the American Dream that people fail to consider—you carry medical insurance

your entire life and the one time you actually need the support, it never arrives. And yeah, the house was paid off, but the maintenance never stopped. He could go on, but he paused the spiral for the night and let sleep take over.

Ann never made it upstairs and spent the night on the couch. The television continued to hum when she woke up. The dogs formed a barrier on the floor in front of her and each perked up once they sensed movement. Ann wanted to lay on the couch the entire day, but it was the one day where she needed to summon the energy to visit him.

She got off the couch and moved into the kitchen. She noticed the torn-out page on the counter the third time walking by it.

> I'll be thinking about him all day today.
> Call me if you need anything.
>
> -Jim

The note was brief, but more than enough. She grabbed it and tossed it into the garbage. Ann didn't need another reason to cry; there would be enough of that later on.

An hour later, Ann paced around the first floor of the house. She had showered and put on the most minimal amount of makeup to save her from looking like a ghost. She had grown tired of trying to impress strangers, so her layers of daily makeup had receded in the past few years.

"I'm gonna go. See you in a bit," she announced to the dogs, but it was more for her own encouragement. The dogs just stared back at her; Rigby gave a modest tail wag with the meaning behind it left for interpretation.

Ann took the long way to her destination. She drove past Chubby's, the place where she had that fateful cigarette several years earlier. It was an abandoned lot now. Ann had read in the local paper (yes, they still had one!) that the township was in a stalemate with what to do. A large contingent floated the idea of turning the space into a community garden. The idea was mocked ruthlessly by the vocal minority of traditional citizens who believed small businesses were still the best move in 2023. The void left behind by Amazon created an uptick in small business revenue until JEC stepped in and gobbled up Amazon's assets. Small businesses were now indentured to another conglomerate. A smaller group of residents were lobbying for the world's largest planetarium to be built in the lot. Ever since the confirmation of extra-terrestrial life during the Area 51 raid in late 2019, people have been itching to learn more about the universe. You'd think more people would have cared about the discovery of extra-terrestrial life, but people don't give much of a shit about anything outside of their tunnel vision. A third squadron of residents, and by far the smallest, argued that the lot should remain abandoned to symbolize how Earth was dying due to the cruel, destructive nature of human beings. The decay of the building over the next twenty years would serve as a reminder to all those who live in ignorant bliss. While a noteworthy art project, Easton was not home to a thriving tourist market and a majority of the residents didn't believe the eye sore would be worth the minimal gain. What the residents didn't know is that the individuals who wanted the building to stand were actually using it four nights a week to summon some nasty shit via the Necronomicon Ex-Mortis. It would explain the weird occurrences that had been going on in the area.

Regardless of what happened to the space, Ann was happy that Chubby's was out of business. She sat in that parking lot for many hours after her diagnosis, contemplating what the fuck she was supposed to do with her life.

She still didn't have that answer, so, instead, she focused on driving. It seems like most of our characters don't have answers to much, which you wouldn't expect in a fictional book such as this one.

The parking lot was scarce besides an old pickup truck stretched across three spaces. Ann settled on a spot in the middle. She walked from the car and over the guardrail separating the parking lot from the expansive field that lay beyond. A small trickle of melted snow flowed down the edge of the curb to the nearby sewer grate. *The only warm day we are going to have for a while*, Ann thought. She tugged on the red beanie just to make sure it wasn't going anywhere.

The snow that was left crunched beneath her feet as she moved down several rows. Ann took an abrupt left and walked another twenty paces before coming to a stop.

Every grave looked the same when they were covered in snow, so you had to know where you were going. Ann had visited enough times that she could have done it blindfolded.

She wiped away the snow that sat atop Vincent's gravestone. It still looked fresh—like it hadn't been four years since he died.

"Are you still there?" she asked. A silly question due to its ridiculous answer. Of course he was still down there—at least whatever was left of him. There was the potential that the casket had caved in from the weight of the dirt on top. Once the fad of the tassel and whistle caskets died out, people found that they were cheaply made. If the top had collapsed, oh boy, Vincent was certainly being chewed on by all the crawly things that live in the soil. His eyes would definitely be gone, along with his nose, lips, ears, and essentially anything else that didn't have bone. Ann tried not to envision that possibility. She preferred the notion that Vincent's body was still perfectly preserved as if he was taking the longest nap ever. Ann could dig down there, rip open that casket, and find the son she buried long ago. Regardless of what fantasy she wanted to believe in, it would be just that.

Vincent was gone forever. Happily ever after. The end.

So it goes.

Ann waited for a response, but all she was given was the sound of metal slapping against a headstone. She had no luck locating the source of the noise. It continued each time the wind picked up.

Disregarding the infrequent slapping sound, Ann spoke again for much longer and in wide arcs that covered everything on her mind.

"Four years today. The worst kind of anniversary I could ask for. Is it weird to draw attention to the day you died? Whenever I do, I think about the seconds leading up to the crash. What were you thinking? God, I hope you weren't scared. I hope it was quick. I hope . . . Whenever I come here, I think about what you would be up to. By now, you'd have definitely moved away from Dallas and someplace closer to home. I honestly believe you would have done that regardless of how many times you said you'd move further west. You always cared about your family too much to do something like that. For the first two years, that's what helped me get by: the made up life I created for you. You would settle down with someone who'd understand your humor and cater to your more sensitive side. You'd find the job you could ease into where it would take up forty hours of the week but never feel like a chore. You'd do better than your dad and I ever could have, and we would take a large amount of credit because I think we raised you and Leigh pretty well . . . Still though, was I a good mother? *Am* I a good mother? For all the times I think I was, I could rattle off a list much longer where I failed you. I shouldn't have pushed you to stay involved with baseball as long as I did or make you go to the school dances when you didn't want to. I should have trusted you more with your grades. I shouldn't have written those emails to you. My god, those fucking emails. I was beside myself when you came out and was convinced for months that it was just a phase. What a weight to carry. Nobody tells you about the potential regret you live with as a parent. And nobody warned me for all those years growing up that you'd die before me. Maybe if I'd known, I would have planned—no, what a terrible thought. Do you believe in destiny? Do you think your path was set in stone from the day you were born? I can't help but think that God has a plan for everyone, but if that's the case, why would he be so cruel? The fake reality I built for you in my head began to slip away when I remembered you were sick. Four years. You'd be nothing, huh? A sliver of what you once were. That disease was going to waste you away without remorse. You knew at Christmas. I wish you had told us. Maybe you would have stayed an extra day and wouldn't have been in Dallas that night. I can't fault you though for not telling us. I have never been able to settle on what's worse: watching your son decay over time or losing him in an instant. I wish it had been me in that car. I wish it had been me that was diagnosed with the disease. I always wanted to take your pain away and that time I failed . . . Sometimes I still think about the books you wrote. Maybe they should have had a larger impact, but at the time, I was so broken that most of the words never sank in. Did you actually believe some of the things you said? You portrayed me as some monster and the relationship you described with your father—I hope you didn't actually feel that way. I can never pick those books up again. I'm sorry, but I don't want to relive any of that . . . Four years . . . What am I going to do when it's eight years that your gone? Or twenty? Will it ever get easier? I'm so tired of not knowing what's next. *What now? What now?* rattles around in my head constantly. I should have the answer. I'm getting close to sixty for goodness sake. Life shouldn't be this hard . . . I went to the guardrail that you crashed into with a kind man named Miles I met. He had demons of his own but took time to help me sort out mine. The guardrail was pristine, as was the ditch on the other side. It was hard to imagine that any trauma happened there, but I know it did. I was so close to where you died. I felt you so strongly in that moment as if you rested your hand on my shoulder and told me it was okay. It wasn't okay. It won't ever be okay . . . I tried to deliver all your letters. I did pretty well I think. You helped because of all the addresses you had saved in your phone, which I thought was strange, but then I figured you had planned all this out. You wanted people to read the letters; you needed people to read the books. Ochi though. Who is he? Everyone I have asked had no clue who he was. I've read through your letter for him enough times, but I still can't define what your relationship was with him. It consumed me for a while to figure it out, but I have come to terms with the idea that not every mystery about a person's life can be resolved. Your life wasn't some novel with characters that behaved the way you'd expect them to . . . I wish you'd answer me or give me some sort of sign.

Vinny, I'm sorry for not being good enough. I should have been better. I've had a lot of time to think because of the cancer and yet that stupid question still rolls around in my empty head. What now? I suppose the answer is everything. Why limit yourself? Maybe I'll start with something small and work my way up . . . You know, I hate this fucking beanie. It smells no matter how many times I wash it. You probably would have told me to ditch it months ago and that I looked great without the hair. That's what I love about you—always so caring and pretty good at lying to make someone else feel better . . . One in a billion. You were one in a billion and I get to say that because you're my son and I love you more than you'd ever know . . ."

Ann continued to talk and caught Vincent up on what happened over the holidays and how the packing up of the house was going.

The only acknowledgement to Ann's talking was the slapping of the metal as if the audience was giving her a round of applause.

Sometime later, Ann stepped over the guardrail one more time and returned to her car. She sat there for a while and cried because doing anything besides that on the anniversary of her son's death seemed sacrilegious.

Everything now, she thought while she drove away. *Yes, I can do that.*

seventy-three

ABOVE IT ALL

The typical cruising altitude for a Boeing 737 is thirty-five thousand feet, which is six thousand feet higher than Mount Everest (or twenty-seven hundred feet above Dalatila Crest). Interestingly, NASA defines outer space as anything fifty miles higher than sea level. So while you may think that flying in an airplane is scary enough, imagine what it must feel like for those individuals aboard the International Space Station. They get to look down at all of the human life that's ever existed. The daily inconveniences of life must feel so trivial. The spilt milk, so to speak, is as meaningless as the milk that wasn't spilt. It was all about perspective. There will be a point in time where human life travels beyond Earth and to the far reaches of the solar system. Will we destroy it? Is Earth the anomaly or are human beings capable of ruining everything they touch? The ideological disagreements that pit one group against another certainly wouldn't matter anymore when life expands beyond Earth. With the confirmation of other intelligent life out there several years back, you'd have expected there to be a seismic shift in thinking and rationale, but no dice.

The sad, boring reality was that **people don't change**.

Evan didn't know any of the facts just laid out (or the opinions expressed), but he did wonder about perspective. He was currently thirty-two thousand feet in the air and descending at a steady pace. Unlike Vincent, Evan preferred the middle seat during a flight. Unwritten rules stated that he was obligated to both arm rests and he was skinny enough to fit between most people without issue. On the rare occasion he did have issues, it was due to a smelly or rude person. With Southwest's new Bathe Before You Fly policy, the smelly people were like getting a holographic Charizard in a deck of Pokémon cards—the stuff of legends.

He spent the weekend in some city with some people from work. Do the details actually matter anymore? We are so close to the end that wasting anymore of your time feels cruel.

The point is this:

Evan understood that his life had never been ideal, but the reflection time he had on most flights helped him to realign to the belief that his past was not indicative of his future. It wasn't easy to toss aside what had been, but he was trudging through toward something better. That perspective was what he needed to constantly remind himself.

Once the wheels touched down in Dallas, Evan turned Airplane Mode off and sent a text to Franco saying that he landed and how much he loved him.

After all, what was the point in loving someone if you didn't tell them whenever you could?

seventy-four

ONE LAST LOOK

"Everything is in the truck. Ready when you are," Jim said. He leaned against the hood and knew Ann would need some time.

"I'm going to walk through one more time. Is that okay?"

He nodded and moved to sit in the car. The winter weather had relented enough that the piles of snow began to melt, but there was a biting wind freezing anything that wasn't covered up.

Ann entered the house through the garage and felt the emptiness surround her. What was once a thriving area of family and dogs was reduced to four walls. That emptiness was always there but kept at bay for nearly thirty years with the evolving furniture, wall art, and paint colors. She knew the moment they moved into the house that there would be a day where they'd say goodbye, but with each passing year, the inevitability became more distant, more foreign.

How could she feel sadness toward an inanimate object? Contrary to the litany of horror novels that tried to convince otherwise, houses don't have emotions or feelings or the ability to murder their inhabitants. It was shelter. In many cases, it was the culmination of hard work and achieving the dead idea of what the American Dream was. But it was still a house. The people inside of it created the memories, not the structure itself.

Ann moved into the kitchen. Her only regret. If she had more time (and money), she would have remodeled the kitchen for a second time and made the cabinets bigger, the backsplash brighter, and the granite less gaudy than it was. *What-ifs* danced through her mind.

Ann repeated the process for each room in the house, recalling distinct memories from each. The parties they had or the sleepovers her kids insisted on having or the quiet moments around the fire where the whole family would camp out and sleep on the floor with the dogs. Those moments seemed infinite because they were. It seemed that the good rarely outweighed the bad anymore, but for Ann, there was nothing bad about the house on Cornwallis Drive. She and Jim raised two kids there. Two fiercely headstrong, independent kids that found their way in an increasingly complicated world. She watched them struggle to take their first steps. She watched them race through the house with the dogs chasing them step for step. She watched them dress for Halloween each year and disappear into the neighborhood to return several hours later with their haul of candy. She watched them struggle with homework and spend too much time staring into the abyss of their phones. She watched when Vinny would sit at the table for a half hour after everyone else had gotten up because he didn't want to eat the broccoli on his plate. She watched (and tried to console) during the times when Leigh had broken up with insignificant boyfriends, but the loss seemed insurmountable to her. She watched as they celebrated achievements like Jim's 60th birthday or Vinny's college graduation or Leigh's wedding or her mom's 90th birthday. She watched herself decay and become bedridden during the worst moments of the cancer. The vomiting and aches were constant stakes holding her down and stopping her from getting better. But she did. She watched herself tell Jim that she was in remission. She watched herself as the medical bills came in and she wondered why the easy part had been beating the cancer.

All of it should have been enough, but it wasn't.

Those thirty years would be reduced with time. The moments of clarity would become faded and eventually vanish. All that time would become emotion, a feeling of what was.

That would have to be enough because if it wasn't, what was the point?

Ann stood outside Vincent's room. They'd never know. The new owners of the house would never know about him. His smile or his willingness to help others. They'd never know how many nights Ann woke up and walked down the hall to check on her kids to make sure they were in their beds and still breathing. It was manic, but she believed every parent did the same. That striking fear that something could happen with the rationalization that it could never happen to *my* child. No, no. *My* child would never get gunned down in a mass shooting. *My* child would never commit suicide. *My* child would never get into a fatal car accident.

She closed the door to his room and returned downstairs.

Ann stepped out onto the deck and felt the stillness. The trees swayed and partially uncovered the view of the Blue Mountains in the distance. The shrubs were all dead for another couple months until their miraculous spring awakening.

Would the same thing happen to her? It was a pleasant thought. Ann had a second lease on life and needed to take advantage.

She had a new house to decorate. She had to find another job. She had grandchildren to fawn over.

There were new places to discover and old ones to revisit.

One last look, she told herself. *It's okay to be sad. This meant something to you.*

She dropped the keys on the counter and left the house.

The rest of her life was waiting, and she was ready.

seventy-five

better now

It snowed in Dallas.
 Okay fine, it was only a quarter inch, but it did snow! And it was enough to cause highways to be backed up for hours and people filing out the doors of Southwest to rush home before the worst part of the nonexistent storm hit. It fit the mantra that any sort of precipitation in Dallas was the cause of a massive drop in everyone's driving IQ.
 Evan sat in traffic for a considerable amount of time that afternoon and felt his mood sour with each inch he crawled forward. Was this what his life had become? The daily hassle of driving to work, looking occupied for eight hours, and then returning home to prep for the cycle to repeat itself. At least he had Franco. But would it last? Evan wasn't able to make his previous relationships last, so it's likely that this could fall into the same trap. *This time is different though*, he told himself. Franco possessed all the intangible qualities Evan desired in someone else. He was supportive and—
 Evan slammed on the brakes and looked up at the red light. "Pay attention," he scolded himself.
 He abandoned those destructive thoughts. It wasn't easy though. A simple sentence doesn't take away from the fact that Evan struggled to push them aside. The doubts lingered. They always would because he was flawed—just like everyone else but he had trouble finding solace in that.
 When the light turned green, Evan surged ahead without any more disruptions for the rest of his drive.
 Franco was stretched out on the couch when Evan walked into the apartment. "Tough ride home?" Franco asked.
 "How'd you know?"
 "You're a creature of habit and you look very tense."
 "I miss how people in Denver knew how to drive in the snow."
 "We can move back if you want," Franco offered.
 "No thanks. I don't miss it that much."
 "Now I'm offended!" Franco said in a mocking tone. "If you never moved there, you wouldn't have met the love of your life."
 "Oh stop it. You know I didn't mean it like that." Evan kicked off his shoes and threw one of his socks at Franco. "Chew on that for a while." Izzie

hopped onto the couch and tried to wrestle the sock away from Franco. With one lone tooth remaining, Izzie didn't have any tugging power left, so Franco conceded and let her run off to the corner with the sock.

"You know, they are calling for more snow tomorrow. Like an inch, but it's a good excuse to pull out the winter jackets. We need to prepare for the fallout of the century's biggest storm. Didn't we bring all that stuff with us from Denver?"

"I don't remember. They would be buried in the closet somewhere if we did. It's only an apartment, so they shouldn't be hard to find. I'll go check." Evan went to the spare bedroom. It didn't get much use, but it was convenient on those nights when they had visitors. He opened up the closet and peeked inside. Evan was never highly rated in the looking-for-things department, so he forced himself to do more than just an ocular pat down of the area.

Two of the older scrapbooks chronicling Evan's photos of random things and the numerous adventures he and Franco went on sat on the highest shelf. The first scrapbook took the longest to fill out—a year—with each one after taking a quarter of that.

A few articles of clothing hung on the rod stretched across the closet. None of them were jackets. Evan bent down and pulled out one of the boxes. No luck. He tried again with two more boxes with the same result.

"Babe, I don't think they are in here," Evan called out.

"Keep looking. I swear we brought them. If not, we can buy new ones."

"What a waste of money," Evan said to himself. "I'll find them."

Determined now, Evan focused his efforts and stepped back into the closet. *I just need to trick myself into thinking that I'm not looking for the jackets and then they will show up.* What was lost could always be found when you actually stopped looking for it.

Evan opened the third box labeled **MISCELLANEOUS** and dug through it. At the bottom, he found two jackets.

Jackpot.

He unfolded the first one to get a better look at it when he noticed the paper fall to the floor.

Evan picked it up. Another note. Of course it was another *fucking* note.

He opened it and a smaller piece of paper slid out. Evan read that one first.

> Hey, hi.
> Don't be mad. I'm not sure when you'll read this or if it'll get lost in some blackhole, but please don't be mad. I know you said

you never wanted to read the letter, but I had such a strong feeling you didn't actually mean that. I had to *follow it* after all. You wanted to know what it said; you have just been scared, which I can relate to.

You need closure and I hope you find it here.

Love,
Murph

P.S. I only broke into your apartment once to plant this note before you left for Dallas, so please don't call the cops or anything. I guess you wouldn't have known if I didn't just admit to the crime. Okay, I'm going to stop now before I admit to breaking anymore laws.

Evan wanted to run from it. He didn't have to read the letter. Evan didn't owe Vincent anything and he'd been dead for four years now.

But still.

There was an unseen force that moved him toward the letter. He picked it up. The first line from all those years ago were still etched into his mind. Evan stared at the paper; the words were fuzzy. He blinked several times.

"Any luck in there?" Franco asked from the other room.

"Y-yeah. Still looking."

Evan sat down on the bed. He was tired of running away. God, he was tired of the excuses and the moves and blaming his family for how he turned out. He needed to finally put a checkmark next to something in his life.

Vincent couldn't linger forever. It wasn't fair.

Evan steadied himself and read the note.

Evan,

You are long gone. I said my last goodbye to you. I am excited for your new adventures and the joys you'll find in Denver. I don't want to burden you with melancholy thoughts and hopeless gestures, but this will help me to become unburdened.

When you met me, I was broken. I had no interest in going to the bar that night to meet you. It was likely going to be more of the same, and if it was different, it would just fizzle out before anything of value started. We both know the story about us. It wasn't a fairy tale by any means. We jockeyed for understanding between us. We thought the other person was flawed without realizing the cause of it. We struggled to grasp that differences don't need to cause separation. In the end, you followed what you thought was best and I'll never fault you for that. I still experience the wanderlust that life could be better elsewhere.

For much of my time in Dallas, I was plagued with self-destructive behavior and meaningless interactions. They caused me to bend and eventually snap. I felt as if I was irredeemable during the first month of our relationship, but you showed me how much another person could care for me. Selflessly and full of love. You started to piece me back together.

With that success comes the realization that I could have done more. Now, I think about the times I should have reached out to hug you, but I was too scared. Or the moments when I should have told you how important you were to me but was too nervous. Or the fact that I didn't fight for you enough when you talked about leaving.

I have to live with those things. With that weight, I am unable to send you this letter. I'm fearful of the rejection, of the notion you'll receive it and never read it. I'm ashamed I don't have more trust in you, but my brain likes to sabotage me.

And now, I have this disease ravaging my body. I never told you. I wanted to, but it just felt . . . surreal. All those years of saying—practically preaching—that I'd live a short life and now my wish is fulfilled. There is always hope, but I will leave that to others. I don't mean to tell you this to stir up guilt. I just needed you to know that clarity often shows itself in the darkest times.

I'm sorry I don't have the courage to send this.

This is the last letter I'm writing. Most of them came easy. I actually had kind words for people that I never expressed to them before and for others, I had harsher words, so I hope they would understand the reasoning behind them.

Your letter has been far from easy. I have struggled with what to tell you because my mind has been racing around and unable to focus.

I'm writing this on New Year's Eve—my least favorite day of the year—which may be a good enough excuse as to why my thoughts are scattered. I just want to get past all the fireworks and false commitments and hugs and other useless gestures. Everything will be fine after midnight. I want to return to my boring reality and the clarity I have from writing this letter.

Remember when I talked about how I wrote a book? I wrote another one and it's only about you. About how you came into my life and undid years of misery. I'm sorry that you'll never get the chance to read it, but I don't want you to view me any differently even with all the parts I made up.

I think I would have been good at telling stories that weren't my own. As I write this, I can picture you finding what you need. It may not be in Denver, but you will find it. The sense of purpose, the desire to live somewhere without the fear of missing out on something more exciting elsewhere. You'll be surrounded by the people you care for and Izzie will live to be a hundred! You never needed much to live, but you have needed an immense amount to live happily. Don't be afraid like I was. Well, still am. It's okay to stumble and question and wonder, but don't remove yourself from the people and events that truly matter. You know how much I enjoy to ramble, so I'll stop myself here.

I'm sorry that I didn't tell you I loved you more. I'm sorry for a thousand other particles of time you likely don't remember but have etched themselves into my mind forever.

In a time where I am wasting away, I've had an unsettling amount of time to think because nothing else seems quite as important as finally understanding myself.

I lost my way after you left because I was scared of being alone and never finding satisfaction with my life, but the answer has been with me for a while.

I find myself going to the top of my parking garage to think. The city skyline expands out in the distance and returns a calm feeling. The soft glow of the lights promises something I won't ever find—you can't ask a rock for blood after all (or however the saying goes). I seem to get into an endless loop of running through all the things I have ever done with an intense fixation on the negative. I'm tired of living that way. I'm tired of holding myself to an impossible standard and expecting to operate at a top tier every moment. I'm tired of feeling sorry for myself and thinking about whether my story was worth writing about. It's okay. My story was never my own to begin with.

I'm tired of thinking that I had to fix everyone else before I could fix myself. I was never good at being a savior anyways.

I'm fortunate to have a loving family that has tried to console me without ever understanding the nature of my problems. I'm lucky to have met numerous people in Dallas and other travels of my life that have shown me what trivial friendships can look like. For the tiny minority that have ventured past the walls I have built up, I'm happy they took the time to.

But here's the thing:

I will never be happy. I will never be satisfied with my life or the person I turned out to be. Discontentment stalks me like a wild animal in the woods. The shadow continues to move closer and I don't have a way to stop it. It will devour me one day and then I'll wish for the moments of clarity like this. We think so much and forget most of it later as if none of it mattered in the first place. What a shame.

I deserve this disease and the punishment that comes along with it. I don't know if I'll live along enough to see it through until the end, but I hope you aren't there to see the pathetic version of myself that I become.

Evan, you couldn't fix me, no matter how hard you tried. I've said it before, but I'm a defect from the factory. A discounted model that sat on store shelves until the dust became thick and smelly.

People don't change, Evan. You know it whether you choose to be blind to it or not. I'm no different from the rest of the flawed creations that sit beside us. Maybe we are all defects.

There was a time when I wanted to get better. I really did. I can promise you that I tried so much. Whatever the rest of my life looks like is not your burden or anyone else's.

What would "getting better" have even looked like anyways? What kind of "changes" could I have gone through? It was an immature exercise with a false ending nestled within.

If you can believe it, there is a good side to all this.

I'm finally at peace with who I am. No more long-winded declarations of change or daydreaming about getting better.

I know I'm not a bad person, but I'm not convinced of how good I have been. Is it possible to exist in a neutral state your entire life?

Regardless, I'm the best version of myself I'll ever be, and I hope that's good enough.

Take care,
Vin

Evan looked up from the note and stared at the wall. A giant smudge mark stared back and went in a parabola similar to how he pictured shooting stars to zip across the sky. He never noticed it before and would forget about it once he left the room.

You need to feel something about that note, he thought to himself. Evan focused on the smudge until it began to contract and expand as his eyes became hypnotized by it. He eventually blinked several times and the smudge returned to its normal size.

"I never tried to fix you. I knew there wasn't any point in trying," he said out loud. The smudge listened intently, and the audience let out an audible gasp. They had been waiting for the climax to Evan and Vincent's story, and much like life itself, it seems to have ended with a dull thud rather than a thunderous clap.

Evan folded up the letter and placed it in the bottom of the box. He'd never read it again but throwing it away (like he had done with the unread books years earlier) seemed unnecessary.

(Just imagine how different things would have been in regard to Vincent if Evan read the books. He probably wouldn't have made it past the supposed cheating, but who's to say that wasn't another of Vincent's lies? It would have been an odd choice on his part though. Consider the whole situation surrounding the books as another path not taken. But try not to get bogged down by the potentials and hypotheticals at this point. We are nearly done here.)

People changed. He knew they did. They had to. What was the point of living if people couldn't evolve and become greater versions of themselves?

You haven't changed. The box. It's around here somewhere.

It's true. The box of razor blades that was wrapped tightly around a plastic bag was hidden within the apartment. The small threat of Franco finding them was there, but Evan was confident he never would.

Just in case, he had told himself.

If things went awry with Franco.

If he had a string of bad days at work.

If the relationship with his mom descended further into sour territory.

If the nightmares started again.

If the pain ever became too much.

If . . .

If . . .

If . . .

The scenarios were endless. The dull throb and subtle push that sat beneath the surface always tried to break its way through like a parasite exiting its host.

Sure, Evan was changed. Just as much as Vincent was when he died. Just as much as his dad was when he took his last breath. Just as much as you when you sit here and try to deny the boring reality.

He looked up at the ceiling and fought back the tears. There was no reason to cry anymore. This chapter of his life was finally closed. Vincent had no more power over him. It was up to Evan now to continue down his own path. Maybe he could break the cycle.

"Did you get lost in here?" Franco asked from the bedroom door.

"Quite the opposite actually." Evan held up one of the jackets. "You have a good memory."

"One of my best qualities if I may say so."

Evan fixed up the closet, turned off the light, and closed the door.

"What now?" Franco asked.

"Dinner and a movie sound nice. Unless you think we need to prepare for the snowpocalypse that's incoming."

Franco walked into the bedroom and kissed Evan. "A movie with some Chinese takeout is exactly what I could use right now."

Evan kissed him one more time. "You can order it though. You love talking to strangers on the phone."

"You're right. My stint with the sex hotline was very enlightening."

"You have the strangest sense of humor," Evan said.

"I own it. Another one of my amazing qualities. You *better* appreciate it because these jokes don't just write themselves."

Better.

What an unfunny word that carried more meaning than Evan would have thought.

Who cares about that now?

It took a while, but Evan finally had everything he wanted. More importantly, what he *needed*. He found the thing.

And for now, it's more than good enough.

seventy-six

moving on

Ann woke up before the sun peeked over the rocks.

It was a good start. She wanted to beat the crowds and get back to Phoenix for an afternoon flight.

The hotel lobby had a mediocre breakfast. Ann settled on soggy eggs and a crusty muffin she didn't necessarily trust but decided to eat it anyways. She needed the energy for what was next.

Her rental was modest enough. Ann splurged for an upgrade to make sure there wouldn't be any worries for the rough terrain she may encounter. If memory served her correctly, not all the roads were paved once you ventured away from downtown.

Two miles away from the hotel, she pulled into the parking lot of a convenience store.

"Good morning, sunshine. Beautiful day out there. What can I do for you?" the cashier asked when Ann walked in.

"Do you sell parking passes for the hiking trails around here?"

"We sure do. Just a day pass?"

"Yes."

"Visiting?"

"Yes."

"From where?"

"Pennsylvania."

"No kidding! I grew up out there. Which part?"

"Easton. It's right on the border of New Jersey." A simple lie. Ann hated how she wasn't living in Easton anymore.

"I'm familiar. I was a western girl though. Out near Pittsburgh."

"I never traveled out that way."

"You aren't missing much. Lots of industry and bridges. Even though I suppose most of the industry is dying off considering the . . ."

The cashier continued on to rehash politics to Ann. She didn't pay much attention and cut in the first chance she had.

"How much do I owe you?" Ann asked.

"It'll be nine dollars for the pass."

Ann handed her the credit card. "Oh, I'm sorry. We can't take that unless you spend more than ten dollars. The damn transaction fee keeps going up, up, up."

"That's fine." Ann began to sift through the purse and pushed aside all the loose change. There was an abundance of it.

". . . arettes?"

Ann looked up. "I'm sorry. I missed what you said."

The cashier rubbed at the small wart on her chin. "I asked if you'd like anything else, so you didn't have to dig through to find the cash."

"No, no. It's okay. I have cash in here."

"Booze?"

"No."

"Cigarettes?"

An almost unnoticeable hesitation. "No."

"Okay then. Everyone else seems to smoke around here, which isn't a problem. It's not like they can burn down the rocks!"

Ann let a sympathy laugh squeak out and handed over the discovered cash.

"Nine dollars even." The cashier punched more buttons than expected on the register and stuck the money inside. "Need your receipt?"

"No thanks."

"Here you are then. Enjoy!"

"Thank you."

Ann placed the parking pass on the dashboard and drove the remaining seven miles to the trailhead.

One other car sat in the parking lot. Ann walked by it and saw there wasn't a parking pass on the dashboard. Tsk, Tsk.

The Cathedral Rock trailhead was as she remembered. Slightly wooded and relatively flat. Ann recalled the exact place where she broke her foot, but to avoid the same pitfall she kicked away any rocks in front of her.

After a short foray up the slight incline, Ann reached the portion where she'd need to shimmy between the two rocks. She gathered herself for a moment. Last time she was at Cathedral Rock, she protested with Vincent about going up there and as she watched her son make his way up, an incredible wave of shame and shouts of her pathetic nature stalked around in her head. She hated the feeling so much that she overcame the initial fear. It turned out to be relatively easy.

That was then.

Ann felt less pressure this time around. No one else was on the trail, at least from the portion she completed so far. Being seven years older and still reeling from the cancer, Ann took her time. She approached the two rocks and stepped in-between them. She leaned forward until her weight was focused on her hands. *Go with the left leg first.* She did. *Okay, now bring up the right.* She did. *Perfect. Repeat that all the way up. It's not a race. If it was, you'd surely get last, but participation trophies are still a thing, right?* She kept going up, up, up at a steady pace.

Ann pulled herself over the edge of the rock and stood atop to gather herself. Her pulse was thumping rapidly in her neck; her wrists ached from the added pressure.

Keep moving forward like a—

She did.

After the shimmying, the remainder of the hike was uneventful. Ann bounded up and over all the rocks, hoping her pants wouldn't rip in the process.

The morning was quiet. It would be a cloudless day by the look of things. Almost reminiscent to last time.

As Ann reached the top, she whispered, "I found it."

The view was as incredible as she remembered. The vibrant greens of spring popped out in the distance beyond the red rocks. Mountains of staggering heights doted the horizon. Phoenix was out there in the distance, but well beneath the curvature of the flat earth. Ann spotted a hawk swooping up and down with little understanding of where its destination may be.

This was what she needed. It was perfect.

Ann moved past the sign and sat down on the edge. She didn't look down. No, that was what she would have done years ago. Instead, Ann looked straight ahead and continued to take in the view that expanded out in front of her. It was limitless.

"Whoa there. You aren't thinking of dropping off the side, are you?"

Ann turned around and saw the woman with the blue hat standing with her hands pressed firmly against her hips. Ann remembered large swatches of time that day in Sedona and the subsequent trip back to Phoenix, but her recollection of the Blue Hat Woman was lost.

"Sorry, I didn't realize anyone else was up here."

"I was the first car in the lot. Always am . . . You didn't answer my question." Blue Hat Woman stepped closer.

"No. Jesus, no. I am not—no."

"I trust ya. When you come up here often enough, you're bound to catch someone trying to do something silly."

"Yeah, I bet."

The woman kept going: "There was one time where a couple was up here jostling around with each other. Innocent stuff I think, but still, ya dingbats, you're on the side of a cliff. Anyways, I yell over to them 'Hey! This is Cathedral Rock, not Fuckaround Rock.' They immediately stopped. I may have saved a life that day."

Yeah and I bet the audience cheered afterward, Ann thought. (Actually, for the Blue Hat Woman, her audience stopped following her around nearly a decade ago due to her "strict adherence to a horrendously dull schedule.")

"How often do you come up here?" Ann started to scoot her butt away from the edge and tried to stand up. Let's hope the hip doesn't give out.

"Every day," BHW said. "Except for Sundays and major holidays because I know the Lord doesn't expect me to exert myself on those days."

"If you don't mind me asking, how old are you?" The hip didn't give out. Ann stood up and wiped away the red dust from her pants.

"Old enough to collect Social Security. How about that?"

"You're in great shape."

"I am and it makes me annoyed when pussies half my age can't make it up here."

Ann's face flushed. She'd been one of the complainers, but she was hardly half the age of the feisty woman.

"How long before it gets crowded up here?"

"Another half hour."

"Do you mind if I take a couple minutes for myself?" Ann asked as if she needed permission from the teacher.

"The world is your oyster." BHW stepped away from Ann, moved toward the other end of the landing area, and loitered around until Ann would be ready to engage in conversation again.

"I found it," Ann repeated to herself. "Just like you wanted me to."

So much had happened in Ann's life over the past four years. The filing cabinet in her mind tried to pull the most significant things, but it crapped out before it could even get halfway through. Vincent's death, her rocky relationship with Leigh, the cancer, the—

Who cares though?

The words were harsh, but true.

That was then.

The world expanded out beyond her. Ann needed less time up at the top of Cathedral Rock than she anticipated. The answer was clear.

She walked over to BHW. The woman turned and said, "That was quick. I figured you'd need more time. I've seen lots of people spend hours alone up here."

"What now?" Ann asked.

"I suppose we head back down and go our separate ways. Don't worry though, I'll go slow so you can match my pace," the woman said with a sharp smile.

Ann's question wasn't meant in as literal of a sense, but she accepted it regardless. What was now?

Well, everything, of course.

"You look better without the hat," the woman noted. "I find them burdensome and always getting in the way." She missed the irony.

Ann opened her palm and looked down at the red beanie. It seemed insignificant and half the size she remembered it being when she put it on a few hours earlier. She didn't even realize she had taken it off. Ann finally felt the sun against her head. Subtle, like an uneven drop from a leaky faucet. God, she'd missed the feeling.

"Thanks," Ann said. "I don't like the hat as much as I once did."

"You ready?" the woman asked.

"Yes. Lead the way."

Blue Hat Woman quickened her pace and began her descent down the rocks. Ann turned one last time toward the landscape out beyond the edge. Her eyes focused on the sign.

END OF TRAIL

The words were beginning to crumble away. Ann wondered briefly if it was the weather that ruined the sign or just time.

"I don't believe that," Ann said, turning away from the decaying sign and stuffing the beanie into her pocket. "This isn't the end—just another beginning."

A better one.

Made in the USA
Middletown, DE
09 August 2021